BLAZED

BLAZED

JASON MYERS

Simon Pulse
New York | London | Toronto | Sydney | New Delhi

SIMON PULSE
An imprint of Simon & Schuster Children's Publishing Division
1230 Avenue of the Americas, New York, NY 10020
This Simon Pulse edition June 2014
Text copyright © 2014 by Jason Myers
Cover photograph copyright © 2014 by Getty Images
Also available in a Simon Pulse hardcover edition.
All rights reserved, including the right of reproduction
in whole or in part in any form.
SIMON PULSE and colophon are registered trademarks
of Simon & Schuster, Inc.
For information about special discounts for bulk purchases,
please contact Simon & Schuster Special Sales at 1-866-506-1949
or business@simonandschuster.com.
The Simon & Schuster Speakers Bureau can bring authors
to your live event. For more information or to book an event contact
the Simon & Schuster Speakers Bureau at 1-866-248-3049
or visit our website at www.simonspeakers.com.
Designed by Jessica Handelman
The text of this book was set in Tyfa ITC.
Manufactured in the United States of America
10 9 8 7 6 5 4 3 2 1
This book has been cataloged with the Library of Congress.
ISBN 978-1-4424-8722-2 (hc)
ISBN 978-1-4424-8721-5 (pbk)
ISBN 978-1-4424-8723-9 (eBook)

For my beautiful family. Thank you so much for your endless support as I've pursued this writing dream. Thank you for putting up with my terrible behavior over the years (and there was so much of it). These books wouldn't exist without each of you and your encouragement.

For Nayla, and all of the times you've talked me down from the ledge after two in the morning (especially during the last draft of this book). Thank you for answering your phone whenever I call. Your friendship means everything to me.

For Sydney Erin Fleishman. They broke the fucking mold when they made you. I am so proud of you and everything you've defeated and accomplished. The first time I met you, people were raging tough in my apartment while you sat in the kitchen till two in the morning, cribbing a paper for school. I thought you were a weirdo and kinda crazy (both turned out to be true), which also meant I knew we'd end up being the best of friends ("Well, you weigh 160 pounds and I weigh fucking 90, man."). You are an amazing fucking soul.

For Annette Pollert, my editor for the last three years. You've been so great to work with. Thank you for bringing out the best in these stories and characters.

For Youth Lagoon (Trevor Powers). Thank you for making the wonderful, beautiful, haunting, and nostalgic music you do. This story was born out of an image that flashed through my head while I was listening to your song "Montana" for the first time. And as that image evolved and grew into this book, Year of Hibernation became the soundtrack that guided the main character, Jaime, throughout his complex and very difficult journey. Your music is where these characters sought out so much of their refuge and safety, and it was where I went time and time again for inspiration and comfort.

And finally, for all of my fucking fans! I've always said I have the best fans in the world. You all mean the world to me. There wouldn't be The Mission, Dead End, Run the Game, or Blazed if it wasn't for your tremendous support of Exit Here. My success has been strictly word of mouth all these years. Your loyalty continues to inspire me. And this fucking book is for all of you! I love every one of you! Stay rad, kiddos. Stay rad forever!

There's smoke in my iris,
but I painted a sunny day on the insides of my eyelids.

—Aesop Rock, "Battery"

1.

"WHY ARE YOU SO ANGRY?" SHE ASKED ME.

We were sitting on a green park bench, and she looked so anxious and so pretty. I'd known her for three weeks.

"That guy is so fake," I said. "He's a phony. How can you like that? He looks so generic and he's not cool and he never will be. He'll never like good music or good books. Who cares if he has a fucking car? He's not real. He doesn't have a soul."

"I wasn't just talking about right now, Jaime," she said. "I was asking why you're so angry all the time?"

"I'm not."

She threw her arms into the air. "Oh my god! Yes, you are! You are an amazing boy. You're cute and so talented and so fucking sweet. But you're also the angriest boy I've ever met."

"Fuck you," I said. "Why don't you go climb back into his car and listen to that bullshit music and listen to him lie to you? I thought you were better than that."

"And I thought you were better than this," she said, before standing up and walking away.

I never saw her again.

And I've thought about her every day since that afternoon.

I'M FOURTEEN YEARS OLD NOW. AND I SET AN
Oxycontin 30 in the middle of a sheet of aluminum foil the
size of my hand. I've had the Beach House album *Teen Dream*
playing on my computer for at least twenty minutes, and I
hold the lighter underneath the foil. When the pill starts to
smoke, I chase it back and forth and back and forth with the
hollowed-out Bic pen in my mouth.

I close my eyes as the smoke slowly releases from my
mouth and nostrils.

Everything is very different now.

I feel like fog.

It's so perfect.

When I open my eyes again, the world is glass and it's
beautiful and I'm happy.

I'm so fucking happy here.

In my castle.

All alone.

This glass castle.

I set the foil on my bed and stand up and grab a blue-
and-gold-striped tank top off my floor and slide it on.

Stare at myself in the mirror that hangs on the back of
my door.

I flex both my arms for a second and then wipe the sweat off my face with the bottom of my shirt. Then I sit down at my computer and open my notebook up to the page my pen is sitting on.

I read over the poem a couple of times and decide it's ready, so I turn the music off and turn my webcam on and adjust the screen, making it just perfect.

I look fucking great.

I'm ready now too.

So I start recording.

I go, *"I dreamed that I was made out of wood and glass one night, it was on the same day I chartered a tugboat to find this island of rare parrots and elk . . . when I woke up with her arms around me, she asked me what my biggest fear was and I told her that I didn't have one until I realized that wasn't true . . . there was mystery to everything we did, from the puzzles we built with the teeth of sharks and the* Twin Peaks *VHS tapes that I carried in my backpack for a decade . . . on the radio, the commercials ended and Nirvana played four songs, my mind was full of pictures of shredded jeans and cardigans and the lyrics to "About a Girl" . . . One time she asked me when she would ever get all of me and I told her that it wasn't so complicated, that I'm a simple boy and that a smile and the perfume she wore and that baby-blue sundress she was wearing on that afternoon behind the ice cream store she was spray painting was just that . . . well, kind of, it was all I needed . . . the time moved so fast and I began to distrust the numbers on the clock and the snooze button one of us would hit . . . I never liked time, it kills those afternoons on the couch watching*

Chinatown *and daydreaming about Cuban beaches . . . she refused to answer the same question she'd asked of me, and that was okay because we were already answering it . . . we each had all of each other, it was just that we thought it meant something else . . . six years later I was at a Mobb Deep show on a big boat and I bumped into her, I asked her about the dress and she blushed and smiled as I told her I'd never seen someone wear something so good . . . Back on the land, I got a hotel card in the mail one afternoon . . . I stared at it for hours until I realized I didn't have to go, I didn't need to go . . . I wanted to keep the memory of that day in my head, it was perfect, and how on earth can a person live with themselves when they go out and they destroy the lasting image, shred the gorgeous memory and make it irrelevant, because talking about work and your basic cable package is how it all ends up . . . it was then that I sought out the beach, every girl there was something but none of them wore a dress like she did . . . It's been ten years now, and if I ever run into her again, I'll ask her to meet me at the drive-in and I'll buy the tickets for* Point Break *and the popcorn and the cherry Coke, and then I'll ask her to never wear that dress again, and then, just maybe then, I'll finally be able to tell her my biggest fear . . . someday forgetting exactly how she looked on that day, during that moment, and how I forgot what her name was and how she never asked me mine. . . ."*

The end.

I turn the webcam off and save the video. Then I grab Tao Lin's book *Shoplifting from American Apparel* and read a few pages before the alarm goes off on my phone.

It's five.

I grab the tinfoil and smoke the rest of the Oxy.

I've found that being really high on this shit makes playing the piano for three hours in front of my mother much
more fucking bearable.

"JAIME, JAIME, JAIME . . . PLEASE WAKE UP, BABY.
I need your help."

The voice on the phone is my mother's. It's her wasted and high voice.

It's one in the morning and she's been drinking all day. I saw blue powder on her nose twice while I was playing piano for her. Both times were after she excused herself, glass of red wine in her hand, to use the bathroom.

I sit up in my bed.

"What's going on, Mom? Where are you?"

"I'm at the place where the monsters come to get me, Jaime. I need you. Please come save me."

"Where are you?"

"Hell."

"Mom! What bar are you at?"

"The Checker Board, sweetie. Oh, please come and save me. Please, my boy."

"Okay. I'm leaving right now."

I jump out of bed and throw on a T-shirt and a pair of black jeans. This hurts. I'm so pissed at her. I grab the switchblade from the desk drawer and put my earphones in

and put that Kendrick Lamar song, "HiiiPoWeR," on repeat
to get me pumped.

Like a minute later, I'm on my bike.

And I wonder if it's a good idea I didn't get high before
I left.

THERE'S MY MOTHER AND SHE'S GOT THIS GUY ALL
over her and they're pushed up against the side of the bar
in the parking lot.

I jump off my bike and yell at them. My mother, she
starts to push the guy off of her.

"Stop it, you jerk," she hisses at him.

He laughs and rips her arms off of him and then slams
her back against the cruel brick.

"Leave me alone!" she screams this time.

But he doesn't stop. He puts his mouth on her neck and
jams his hand over her crotch and tells her to calm down.

My skin is red.

Blood is boiling.

I rush over to them and I grab the guy and try pulling
him off of her.

He turns around and looks shocked to see me, this fucking kid, trying to break this up.

"What the fuck?" he snaps, and then whips an arm
around my head.

I knee him in the thigh and he gets pissed off now,
which is what I want.

We struggle.

He's trying to get his other arm around me, but I've got him off balance and he can't do it and then my mother swings her purse right into his ugly face and demands that he get his hands off me.

This is when he fucks up.

He pulls his arm loose from me and charges at my mother.

"You cunt bitch!" he yells. "What is this?"

"Leave us alone," she says, then swings her purse again. This time he bats it away, and then he grabs her shoulders and shakes her.

"Get the fuck off of her!" I'm yelling. "Don't touch her!"

Dude spins around and smacks the side of my face. "Scram, bitch!" he growls. "This is none of your business."

When he turns back to my mother, though, I grab a rock the size of my fist and lunge at him and smash the rock into the side of his head.

He yells out and then tries to duck away.

When he does this, I hook my foot around one of his and yank it back and he trips and falls down.

"Jaime," my mother cries out.

The guy looks up at me. He's so fucking nasty and gross. I can't believe my mother.

My beautiful, sophisticated mother, who was once a ballet star in New York before she had me, would even talk to a piece of shit like this, let alone kiss his lips.

I'm so furious as the man sizes me up.

Then he laughs and goes, "Now you're gonna get it too, boy."

But right when he starts to get to his feet, I take my switchblade out.

He stops.

"What?" I go. "What?"

"Are you fucking crazy?" he snorts.

"Is this what you do with your pathetic life? Stalk the drunkest woman in the bar and force yourself on her?"

"Fuck you." He laughs.

"What?" I go, and then grab his hair and yank it as hard as I can.

He screams in pain and I say, "You will never touch her again."

"That cunt doesn't deserve to be touched by me."

I pull his hair even harder and then start ripping the blade through it.

It's tough.

It's stubborn at first.

And it sounds like sandpaper rubbing against gravel.

But finally, a huge chunk of it comes off in my hand.

"You bastard," my mother shouts. "You miserable, pathetic bastard."

She spits on him and then the door opens and this guy walks out and tells us he's calling the cops.

My mother grabs my arm now and goes, "Let's go, Jaime. Now."

I drop this dude's shitty hair and then I knee him in the face before me and my mother take off running for her car.

"Give me the keys," I tell her.

She hands them to me and we both get in and then I start the car and peel out.

BAM!

The car bounces up and down and there's this horrible crunching noise.

"What the hell was that?" my mother goes.

"My bike," I tell her, pressing the gas pedal even harder. "I just ran over my new bike."

"Oh."

Me, I don't say anything at all after this. I just drive us back to the house as fast as I can.

5

MY MOTHER WALKS OUT OF THE DOWNSTAIRS bathroom wearing a white nightgown. Her beautiful auburn hair hangs straight down her back. There are traces of blue powder below her nostrils. Dark circles dominate her face. She looks so exhausted.

She opens the liquor cabinet in the dining room and pours a glass of whiskey.

Her eyes, they're so empty and lost.

Her eyes can be so beautiful too when she's not wasted and high, which ain't very often anymore.

She downs the drink and pours another.

She looks over at me finally. "What?"

"This has to stop," I say.

She looks irritated and rolls her eyes.

"Mom."

"What?" she screams. "Goddamn it! I do everything for you. I gave up my career as an artist for you. I've made you so talented and smart. And now you come after me? You come after me!"

"I'm not coming after you."

"Yes, you are."

"I'm not. This is the fourth time in the last month you've

pulled this shit, and you never remember anything the next day. One of us is going to get hurt real bad."

"I was having fun, Jaime."

"I sliced off a chunk of a guy's hair. Are you for real? I had a knife pulled on some drunk stranger you were kissing. I'm gonna get killed one of these times."

My mother, she looks away and doesn't say anything.

"I can't do this anymore. I don't know why you're trying to destroy yourself so hard right now. It's like you're trying to get away from me, this world, and it's scary and it's sick. You don't care that I'm gonna get fucked up real bad one of these times. You just don't even care, and that's the worst part."

I'm glaring at her and she's shaking and her cheeks are getting red. And just like that, she whips her glass across the room and it shatters against the wall.

I jump back.

"What are you doing?"

She turns toward me, scowls at me. She looks like she hates me, but I haven't done anything except help her. I've done everything she wanted me to—practice piano, guitar, drawing, learn about philosophy and literature. And she still resents me because of what I represent to her. She hates looking at me because of how much I look like my father.

My father I've never met.

I watch her grab the bottle of whiskey and pour some down her throat. Then I walk toward her and I go, "I can't watch you do this."

She makes another face. "And what are you going to do, huh? Where are you going to go?"

The fact that she's being so fucking evil to me right now is really making me resent her.

I don't say anything.

And she says, "I'm all you have, Jaime."

Stopping a few feet in front of her, I say, "Oh yeah? What about my father?"

The way her face contorts, well, I wouldn't wish this image on my worst enemy.

My breath leaves my lungs.

My face turns white like snow.

My mouth goes dry.

"How dare you?" she rips. "After what he did to me, the way he ruined my life. You have the fucking nerve to stand there and say that to me."

"I don't know anything about him except from the things you've told me. I bet if I went to live with him in San Francisco, he wouldn't put me through this kind of shit."

My mother's reaction sends chills down my body.

I've never seen anything this wild.

"Excuse me," my mother whispers.

I double down.

No way I'm backing off.

I say, "All you do is demand things from me. Perfect piano playing. Perfect guitar playing. Demanding I debate Sartre for hours. And I've never complained. I always do what you want."

"You don't have any friends."

"I don't have *time* for friends."

"Why are you saying all these mean things to me?" she cries.

"Because I do everything you tell me to. Every fucking thing. And the only thing I'm asking of you is that you stop this madness before one of us gets hurt or dies."

"Just shut up!" she yells. "You're not making any sense."

I look away from her and bury my face in my hands.

"I can't stop," she barks. "I need this. It's the only way I can deal with this horrible life."

Shaking my head slowly, I go, "Then maybe it's time for me to go to San Francisco."

This bloodcurdling scream just unleashes from the pit of my mother's gut and she runs at me, grabbing my shoulders and pushing me into the wall.

My head slams so hard that chunks of plaster rain down.

"Stop it," I tell her. "Why are you doing this?"

"Take it back," she says.

"What?"

"Your father did this to me," she barks. "He did *this*!"

Then—

POW!

Her right fist slams into my left eye. The rings on her fingers gouge flesh on my cheek.

My ears ring.

Then—

WHAM!

The same knuckles pound against my temple.

This time, though, I grab ahold of her arms and beg for her to stop while she furiously tries to shake herself loose.

My grip tightens.

And she starts crying.

"Just stop it," I beg again. "Leave me alone."

Her whole body goes limp. She looks so worn.

She stops fighting, and I let go of her, and she falls down, curling up into a fetal position.

"I'm so sorry," she sobs, over and over and over. "I'm so sorry for bringing you into this hell."

Blood's running down my face.

I grab a paper towel from the kitchen and hold it against the cut.

I wanna vomit.

I don't recognize this lady right now.

The greatest woman that ever lived.

At least she used to be. Until a minute ago.

The only things I'm thinking are how pathetic she's acting and how skinny she's gotten.

How beautiful her skin and hair still are, and how fucking thrilled I am knowing she won't remember any of this tomorrow.

She'll never know what she did.

I'll never tell her.

My mother, she deserves way better than that.

She deserves my silence.

6.

IT'S FOUR A.M. WHEN THE MORRISSEY RECORDS
stop spinning downstairs. I can hear stairs creak next. Every
time one does, I wince and my body shakes.

I hold my breath until her bedroom door finally shuts.

A couple minutes later, I smell the dope she's smoking.

I'm sitting at my computer. Three lines of Oxy remain
on the cover of the book *Our Band Could Be Your Life*.

I've read it twice since someone recommended it in this
Sonic Youth chat room I was in a few months back.

I lean down and go.

There's only two lines now.

That Youth Lagoon song "Montana" is playing on my
computer. This is the third straight time I've listened to it.

Their first record changed me.

"July" was the first song I heard from it.

The music ripped a hole in me. It struck an emotional
nerve so deep, I felt debilitated by the time the song was over.
Never in my life has music pierced me so hard I felt like my
life had been stolen from me once the music stopped.

I cried when I listened to it the second time.

And when I played the entire record in order, the spell

of nostalgia that was cast over me was so potent and heavy, it was like I was still clinging to a beautiful dream when the final track had concluded.

The music is mesmerizing.

It's not sad, but it makes you yearn for those afternoons or mornings or nights when you felt so damn alive and attached to the moment. Those times when you were really experiencing life instead of thinking about how you wished you were experiencing it.

The feeling is gorgeous.

Its beauty lies somewhere in the sentimentality of the past. It doesn't matter if the memory was of a great moment or an awful moment. It was an important moment.

And the nostalgia gives you all the comfort you need in the present.

Everyone needs the comfort of nostalgia.

This is the genius of the first Youth Lagoon record.

When the song ends again, I grab my acoustic guitar and continue writing this new song of mine called "Black Vulture." It's pretty good right now, but it can be so much better.

It's sorta hard to concentrate, though, as my face keeps swelling from the vicious hits of my mother's angry fist.

She has to be passed out right now.

Images of her losing her mind two hours ago and attacking me smash through my head.

I set the guitar down and stand in front of the mirror on my door.

My left eye is turning more blue.

It's so ugly.

I put my finger against it and wince.

I hope my mother is lost in some kind of gorgeous dream of her own right now. Somewhere far, far away from all her demons and monsters.

I hope she's standing in the middle of a thousand meadows filled with beautiful flowers.

I hope she's writing her name in the wet sand of a gorgeous beach.

Barefoot.

Humming.

All her horror kept at bay.

Back at my desk, I lean down and go again.

One line remains.

I scroll through my iTunes and play the Future Islands song "Balance."

After that, I upload the video of me reading my new poem to my Tumblr page and my YouTube channel and write an entry about it.

Twelve hours ago, I couldn't wait to get home from school and play my mother the new tracks Washed Out posted on their Bandcamp page.

I was so fucking excited to hang out with her.

It just goes to show how quickly things can turn against you.

In a matter of seconds, your life can get turned upside down without your consent.

My mother will never know what she did to me tonight.

This is exactly how silence becomes deafening.

7.

THAT LCD SOUNDSYSTEM DOCUMENTARY *SHUT UP* *and Play the Hits* is playing on the laptop in the kitchen. My mother is still sleeping, and I'm cooking us breakfast: bacon, omelets, fruit cups, and coffee.

Even though I cook for the two of us all the time in the morning, it's rare she ever sleeps in this late, no matter how smashed up she got the night before.

But it is nice to have the kitchen all to myself.

I've watched this documentary eight times, and I take something new from it every time. The idea of bringing your band to a halt at the height of its success in order to go out on your own terms is one of the most intriguing concepts I've ever heard. But then to go through with it while the cameras are actually rolling, like, that's brutal. It's brave. And most of all, it's real, which is hard to find in music anymore.

And I value that.

I fucking love it so much.

I was seven the first time I heard them. I woke up really late one night when my mother came home with some friends. They were listening to the *Sound of Silver* record, and I crept downstairs to hear it better.

It took me thirty seconds to fall in love with their music.

For the next six months, I tried to learn their songs on the piano and the guitar. It didn't go very well. But I became so much better at both instruments. By the time I was ten, I could play every song off of *This Is Happening*.

And although I don't know shit about my father, I do know that he's a huge LCD Soundsystem fan. I know this because my mother walked right out of this piano lesson of mine once after I cut into the song "All My Friends."

I stopped playing. I was stunned and totally pissed off because I was doing so well at that moment. My instructor, he told me not to take it personally.

"How could I not?"

"It's the song you're playing."

"She loves this band."

"She found out that your father and his new wife flew to New York for their last show and hung out with James Murphy afterward."

"What?"

"Yeah."

"So she can't listen to the music anymore?"

"Jaime," he said. "You know your mother."

"Right. I do. At least she's consistent," I said.

He shook his head and grinned. "Your insight into other people's emotions. It's so impressive."

"I don't know what you mean."

"You're one of the brightest and most talented kids I've ever taught, Jaime."

"I don't believe you."

"You don't have to."

"I can't believe my father kicked it with James Murphy. Like how?"

"What do you know about your father?"

"Nothing."

"Google him," he said.

"No. I would never do that to my mother," I told him. "Never."

Back to breakfast now.

After I flip both omelets and turn the bacon, I get a new message in Google chat.

It's from this girl Cheyanne, who lives in Chicago and goes to DePaul University. She's a freshman majoring in journalism. She's been a huge fan of my video blogs and my writing on Tumblr and WordPress for almost a year.

Loved the new video, Jaime. So gorgeous. The mood, that nostalgia in each line, it was so suffocating. But so liberating, too.

Thank you, I type back.

I'm going to work on getting you published in a cool lit mag.

That would be incredible.

I can't believe you're only fourteen.

It's just a number. I'm a fucking geezer if you're going by experiences.

LOL. Right. So what are you doing right now?

Cooking breakfast for me and my mom. I Googled my father, too.

You don't know him???

No.

What'd you find out?

That he's way successful. He lives in San Francisco, but I already knew that.

I love SF. I went out there last summer to see some family and fell for the city. What does he do?

He runs some big-time hedge fund, owns two art galleries. That's about it. He's got a stepdaughter, too. She's seventeen and looks like Ivanka Trump. It's scary how much they look alike.

Scary? Why?

Cos I always thought that if there was a God, he'd be one cruel bitch to only make that kind of beauty once.

OMG, dude. You're too much.

You love it.

Of course I do. And I gotta go. Later, duder.

Word. Have a great day.

I close out of Google and walk back to the stove to begin plating the food while LCD Soundsystem sings about losing their edge.

8.

I'M ALREADY EATING WHEN MY MOTHER FINALLY emerges from her slumber.

It's hard for me to look her in the eyes at first.

Even though she gave birth to me and has raised me and gives me a hundred dollars each week just to buy records and books with, she punched me.

Twice.

My goddamn eye is black and blue.

It feels like a fucking amp got dropped on my head from twenty feet.

My mother, she walks slowly through the kitchen. She's holding her right hand.

"Hey," she says.

I can tell she doesn't remember anything, so it's gonna be easier to carry her through this.

"Are you hungry?" I ask.

She shakes her head. "My hand." She lets it go and holds it up.

I'm five feet from her and I can see how swollen her knuckles are. They're big and bruised and so sore.

"I don't know what happened," she says.

This is when she really notices my face. Whatever sort of life is in her just drains immediately. Tears begin running from her eyes.

"Jaime," she gasps. "No. No." She peels her eyes from my face to her hand. "No."

I stand up and go, "You didn't do this to me, Mom."

She looks horrified and sick.

This is the first time in my life that I've seen every single trace of beauty and class completely vanish from her face.

Her body starts shaking violently.

"Mom," I say. "It's okay. I'm fine."

"No," she goes again. "Jaime . . . what is this? What happened?"

"I got into a fight."

She covers her face with the hand that's not busted and says, "What did I do? I don't remember."

"You didn't do anything. When I was picking you up from the bar, there was this man. He was attacking you. When I was trying to pull him off of you, he punched me. And that's when you punched him. That's why your hand is messed up."

"What?" she shouts. "Where was this?"

"Outside the Checker Board. You called me and asked me to pick you up. I did and there was a fight."

I try to wrap my arms around my mother now, but she turns away and leans on the kitchen counter. When her hand touches the surface, she screams out in pain and throws her arms around her waist. "I'm so sorry."

"It's okay."

"I'm a monster," she says.

"Mom," I say. "It's over. Everything is fine now."

"No," she sighs, shaking her head wildly. "No, it's not. None of this is fine."

"But it's over, okay? It's over and there's nothing we can do about it. You should see a doctor about your hand."

"I'm such a monster," she says again.

"No, you're not. You're the furthest thing from a monster. Look at this gorgeous house, and look at all the nice things we have. You've done all of this for me," I say. "Nobody else has this."

"Bullshit. Goddamn it! This is no good."

Reaching toward her now, I slide a hand over her arm. "It's over, Mom. I have to go to school now. We have to leave in five minutes."

"Shit," she says. "I can't drive you."

"It's too late for me to take the bus."

She squeezes her forehead and goes, "I'll call a cab."

A good chunk of my anxiety falls away when she says this.

That car ride would've been so miserable.

And I go, "Okay. I'm gonna go grab my bags."

"All right."

After I'm done jamming my backpack full of notebooks and novels—*The Human War* by Noah Cicero; *I Steal Hearts and Knives*, a short story collection by James Morgan; *Black*

Spring by Henry Miller—and this Sony camcorder I carry most places with me, I crush an Oxy on my desk and just snort the whole pile.

There's no time for lines right now.

Then I grab my iPhone and earphones and hurry back downstairs.

My mother is standing at the front door.

"You look so handsome," she tells me.

"I guess I look tougher now too," I tell her back.

Her teeth grind, and she forces a smile.

"You're going to pick me up from school, though, right? I've got a piano lesson."

She nods her head. "Yeah," she whispers.

Then she looks back down at her hand.

She looks disgusted by it.

When she looks back up at me, she says, "You wouldn't lie to me about what happened, would you?"

"No," I say. "Never. Why?"

She leans toward me and touches the side of my face that's all fucked up. "No reason."

"Are you sure?"

She shakes her head. "No. I'm just hoping you wouldn't lie to me."

"Mom . . . ," I say.

She bites down on her bottom lip. "Yeah."

"I'll be fine," I tell her. "And so will you."

"I hope so."

"What does that mean?"

"I don't know," she says, as the cab pulls into our driveway. "Just have a great day at school for me."

"All right," I say.

She hands me forty dollars and goes, "There's no way I would've attacked you, ya know."

My face turns red. "Yeah," I sigh. "There's no way."

Her eyes tear up. "Good," she whispers. "And don't worry about me. I'll be fine."

Pause.

"I really will, Jaime."

9

I ATTEND THE MOST PRESTIGIOUS AND EXPENSIVE private school in Joliet, Illinois. It's also one of the most expensive and prestigious private schools in the entire state.

And I hate it.

I've been going to private schools my whole life. I don't have any friends here. Which is fine, actually, because none of the kids who go here have good taste in music or books or movies.

None of them listen to Beach House or Deerhunter or Grimes or the Fresh & Onlys.

None of them have ever even looked inside a Sartre book, let alone read a page. And they've never touched *House of Leaves* or even know about Joan Didion's *Play It As It Lays*.

The girls in my grade, it's like they're mad at me because I don't stare at them in class. I don't ever try and talk to them. I never give them any attention during the day.

Like, why would I?

Not a single one of them is even close to the girl I used to have. She listened to Purity Ring and the Growlers. Her favorite movie was *Black Swan*, and her favorite author was David Foster Wallace.

And then she turned out to be really evil.

So these girls I go to school with, I already know that none of them are real.

School uniforms are mandatory here.

Dudes: brown khakis, white button-up shirt, a solid black tie, and a navy-blue blazer.

Chicks: Gray skirts, black leggings, white button-up shirt, a solid black tie, and a navy-blue blazer.

The rule is enforced rigorously. On me, at least.

Just this year I've been given detention four times and a two-day in-school suspension for making "modifications" to my uniform.

I made my khakis into shorts.

I turned my blazer inside out and spray-painted the Wu-Tang logo on the back of it.

I took a knife to my shirt.

And I took white paint to my black tie to make it look like a bandanna and hung it out of my back pocket. That day I also wore the pair of brand-new, hot-pink Chuck Taylors I bought with the money my mother gave me for grading out higher than any of the 140 other piano players, ages twelve through twenty-two, at this statewide recital at DePaul University a week earlier.

So far this year, I've been suspended three times. For the uniform bullshit, and then for punching this junior asshole, Timothy Beck.

He was whipping this fat kid, Miles Worthy, with a wet

towel in the locker room. Miles was crying, but Timothy kept doing it.

It was so wrong and so evil and the teacher wasn't even doing anything to stop it.

Timothy Beck is the starting quarterback and the starting point guard.

So I just walked up to him, and he went, "What the fuck do you want, faggot?"

And I smirked and I said, "Your girlfriend's a fucking gnar pig and her haircut sucks."

And then I punched him in the nose. As he stumbled backward, falling on his ass, I ripped the towel away from him and whipped him right in the nuts with it. He started crying, and I got in trouble.

The third time I got suspended was for correcting my English teacher about something he said about Steinbeck as fact. It wasn't true, and when I said so, he dismissed it and double downed his assertion. I couldn't let it go. I know for a fact that *Grapes of Wrath* was never translated and published in Japanese under the title *The Angry Raisins*.

What a fucking idiot.

It turned into an argument, and I called him a few names, and he kicked me out of class. But before I left, I looked at all my classmates and told them that for a hundred bucks, I'd write their three-page paper on "Of Mice and Men" that'd been assigned to us earlier in the period.

That suspension was for two days, and even though

I'd made this proposition in front of my teacher, four kids reached out to me to write their papers.

I jacked up the price to $150, and they all paid.

They all got As.

Me, I got a C+.

It was a joke.

I understood what my teacher was doing by giving me that grade, but he wasn't being honest with himself. He was being such a fake by giving me that phony grade.

And I can't stand fake or fucking phony.

This school year is over in a week, and I've got a 3.9 because of that grade instead of the 4.0 I've gotten every semester since sixth grade.

Whatever and shit.

I've still got the best overall grades of anyone in my class over the past three years.

MY BLACK EYE IS DRAWING SOME SERIOUS ATTENTION.
As if rolling up in a taxi, like, ten minutes late for school wasn't intriguing enough for these boring souls, a shiner befitting an amateur boxer is just too much for these kids.

They keep glancing at me during class. I hear them whisper to each other. Some of them point and most of them laugh. Even two of my teachers do the same as I'm grabbing books from my locker in between classes.

It's all so miserable and pointless. And it comes to a head in the locker room when this turd burglar, William Cross, starts talking shit about my face.

"Hey, faggot," he says. "Did you fight your piano?"

I roll my eyes.

"Queer Miles," he rips. "Did you fight your imaginary friend?"

I say nothing and run the video for that Future Islands song "Little Dreamer" through my head.

William throws a towel at me.

These people just can't stand to be ignored.

And he goes, "Did your crazy momma beat your face up, little boy? Did she get drunk and beat up her loser kid?"

He wanted my attention and now he gets it.

"What's your fucking problem, asshole?"

"I hate queers," he says. "Especially queers who let their momma smack them around. Drunk bitch."

I don't even hesitate.

I run right at him and slam him into the wall.

This pussy doesn't even know what to do.

I punch him. And I punch him again. And then I grab his neck and slam his head against the wall before the gym teacher pulls me off.

A few minutes later, I'm in the principal's office. Again. I don't feel bad or sorry. I feel nothing except worry for my mother. All alone at the house. Full of questions. With a busted hand. Probably drinking to numb out all the guilt and hate that's overwhelming her and making her panic, because she hates to feel anything other than pity and sorrow.

One of the secretaries comes into the office and sets my backpack on the desk.

Before she leaves, she glares at me and shakes her head all disapprovingly.

"Yeah?" I snort. "What?"

"It's a shame to see such a bright kid behaving like this."

"Right. Sticking up for myself, and sticking up for my mother. Putting asshole bullies in their place. It's awful."

"Such a filthy mouth."

"Then stop talking to me," I go. "Leave me alone."

She leaves the room, and while I wait for the principal, I dig into my backpack for *The Human War*.

I'm reading it for the third time this month.

I love Noah Cicero's writing. It's brutally honest and funny, and a lot of it is weird. His style, too, especially in this book, is incredible, and the pacing is brilliant.

Pacing is everything to me when I'm reading a book or a poem.

It has to flow and move and reflect the nature of the characters the author invented.

This book does all of that.

Of all the authors in the forefront of the Alt Lit community, he's my favorite. Tao Lin is probably my second favorite.

The principal finally walks in. Dude's a jerkoff.

Fucking pilgrim scum jerk.

He's bald in the center of his head, with thick brown hair wrapping from side to side.

I think he's nailing the secretary that was just in here. I saw his hand on her ass in the parking lot one day while I was waiting for my mother to pick me up. She was an hour late and showed up in her bathrobe and a pair of sunglasses with a thermos full of wine and a cigarette between her lips, blasting the Talking Heads. I drove us home. I've been driving for two years now.

Plus, he's always creeping and lurking on the girls who attend this school. He stares at their asses when they walk by him in the hallway. And he puts his arms around them when he's talking to them to stare down their unbuttoned blouses. They're supposed to be buttoned all the way to the neck, but I've never heard about any of them getting detention for that particular uniform "modification."

Also, he sucks up to the jocks.

Those assholes never get into trouble, even though they terrorize kids.

And they openly cheat on tests.

And they never turn in their homework on time.

And they're super bastards to most of these girls.

It's so rude and annoying.

And they never get shit from this prick.

Every day I see him bro-ing down with them. Cracking jokes with them. High-fiving them and calling them by their last names to address them.

This place is so bullshit.

Leaning back in his chair and crossing his legs, he says, "What would you do if you were me?"

"Really?"

"Yes, Mr. Miles."

"I'd shave the hair I got left, man. Have some respect for yourself."

His face gets red. He scowls. But it's such a joke. I don't get intimidated. He should know better. I'd fight him if he wanted to fight me.

"Kids like you, privileged, smart-ass rich kids like you . . ."

"What about it?" Pause. "Sir," I say, smirking.

"You're just pests. I've seen so many bastard kids like you come through this school and never amount to anything."

"Good story, bro," I say.

"You'll leave this school one day. You will. And then you'll drop out of college and live off your trust fund until you've blown through all of it and you and your drunk mother have to move into some shitty apartment. You'll never see the world, Mr. Miles. You'll never have a good life, and that's a shame because you are one of the brightest kids I've seen walk through these prestigious doors."

Images of me jumping over his overpriced desk and landing a haymaker on this jerk before putting him in a Boston crab smash through my head.

He's gonna pay for bringing my mother into this.

"I've heard all of this before," I tell him. "Mostly from you."

"I know you have. But obviously, none of it's gotten through to you. It's pathetic. I've seen your path play out before with other students. It's not pretty. It's a path that leads to nowhere."

The fact that he can't rattle me infuriates him. He's seething. Men like this, who spent their childhood and teenage years, all the way through college, desperately trying to be liked and accepted by the popular kids but never were, never even got a fucking sniff from those assholes, they use any kind of power they acquire later in life to try and right all the slights and the wrongs they've carried around for so long.

It's why he coddles those jocks.

It's why he gets close to the pretty girls who walk down these "prestigious" hallways.

And it's why he hates me.

Because I'm handsome enough to have any of these girls.

Because I'm gifted enough.

I could have friends in every single social circle in this school if I wanted them, because me and my mother are very well off.

Coming from money in a place like this gives you automatic popularity and acceptance if you care about those kinds of things, but I don't.

It's phony.

Nothing genuine can ever be cultivated under those circumstances, and I'm fine with this.

I've fucking chosen this route.

I'll never compromise a thing I love in order to be liked by anyone else.

Shrugging now, I snort. "And what you do in life . . ."

"What about it, Mr. Miles?"

"It's nothing. You're a principal. You've never done a thing to influence culture. Nobody knows who you are outside of Joliet, so spare me your crystal-ball reading, man. You're old and you've never seen the world."

Slamming his fist against the desk, he yells, "I'm done with you!"

"Great."

"No wonder your mother is a drunk. I'd drink like that too if I had to deal with you every day."

I stay calm. As much as I wanna destroy this man's ugly face and piss on his cheap Sears suit, I take a deep breath and look him dead in the eyes. "All the girls who go to school here make fun of you. How do you like that?"

"I don't care."

"How does it feel to know that the second you turn your back, these rich girls and these rich boys are pointing at you and laughing and calling you names?"

"Enough!"

He presses a button on his phone and orders that same secretary back into the room.

"My mother was more successful by the age of twenty than you've been your entire life," I tell him. "You know nothing about her. My mother is better than you."

The principal looks over my shoulder and at the secretary. "Any word?"

"No."

His eyes jump back to me. "Your mother isn't answering her phone, either."

"I've left five voice mails," the secretary says.

The principal smirks again. "Not even she wants to deal with you, Mr. Miles. That leaves nobody. You have no one."

My hands ball into fists.

"Please escort this violent student to detention."

The tension releases from my hands. "Cool."

"That will be your classroom for the remaining seven days of school. You'll check in with me upon your arrival to the building every morning, and I'll bring you all of your reading assignments and homework for the day."

"Works for me."

"When your mother does come to pick you up at the end of classes today, I'll explain everything to her and we'll begin to explore other schooling options for you next year, because this isn't going to work."

"Whatever."

"The path you've chosen, Mr. Miles, is a very poor one, and often ends on an assembly line somewhere or behind the cash register at a hardware store."

I stand up.

"Is that all?" I ask. Another pause. "Sir."

"I feel sorry for you."

"Yeah," I say. "I was about to say the same thing to you, dude."

11.

INSTEAD OF WORKING ON THE THREE-HUNDRED-WORD essay about the Trail of Tears the principal demanded I write before the end of the day, I read two of the short stories—"She Kills Love" and "The Whore"—from James Morgan's book *Where the Mean Girls Are*, then I slam some words into my writing notebook.

I just want this day to end.

About a half an hour before the final bell, I crib the assignment. I write five hundred words instead of three. And then I get excused to go to the bathroom. While I'm in there, I crush an Oxy on the back of a toilet and snort it up with a ten-dollar bill that was left over from the cab ride to school this morning.

There's this line at the end of "She Kills Love" that is stuck in my head. It's a line that Morgan uses in a lot of his stories.

This is the game that moves as you play . . .

And me, I've got this incredibly intense feeling that everything in my world is about to begin moving quickly and violently and there ain't nothing I can do to stop it or even slow it down.

I'm not exactly sure why I've got this feeling, but I think it has something to do with my mother.

12

MY MOTHER DOESN'T PICK ME UP. SHE DOESN'T answer her phone when I call, either. This is strange. My mother has never been late picking me up on a day I have a music lesson, no matter how bombed she is. On lesson days, she's there. Sometimes she's even early.

Dread runs through me as I sit on the school steps and wait. This sinking is just leveling me.

I'm trying to hold on to the thought that maybe she's sleeping. Maybe she was so hung over, so sick and sore, she took a couple of Xanax and a Vicodin and washed them down with whiskey, because the pain and the memory loss were finally too gnarly for her to deal with.

It's tough to believe, though.

She's just too darn committed to me and music and art.

Finally, after an hour, I walk home.

It's probably a thirty-minute walk. I put my earphones in and crank some RZA. I should be halfway through my piano lesson right now. Instead, like ten minutes into my walk, I take my backpack off and pull my camcorder out. There's this piece I've been thinking out for weeks, and I'm pretty sure I've got it down now.

Holding the camera above me, I hit the record button and go for it. . . .

"*Her name was Emma and her hair was black like the night and she rode a sick yellow bike with a wood basket and two Nirvana stickers on it . . . It snowed for a month straight and with nothing to do, she dug an old photo book out of her closet . . . she started crying before she'd even opened it . . . there was a time when she had everything she'd ever dreamed of, yet she never stopped to enjoy a single moment of it, she never even thought to think this is it, this is my dream come true . . . the photos tortured her and broke her heart all over again . . . She vowed to never look at them again, but when she tried to close the book, she couldn't and the pain stung like a million bees because there she was, the failure she'd come to accept . . . That spring I saw her running down this dirt road in a blue dress . . . Her hair blew in the wind and her body had all grown up . . . The year before I'd asked her for a slow dance at the community center's annual Halloween party . . . I was dressed as the Karate Kid and she was dressed like Snow White . . . The song I asked her to dance to was "Skinny Love" by Bon Iver . . . I'll love that song long after the day I die . . . She declined because she already had a man . . . He wasn't there that night, though . . . He'd been gone for a while, though, even if she didn't care to count the days as I had . . . Someday, we'll all be a thousand years older than we are now and I'm not sure we'll be any wiser when it comes to the heart and when it comes to love . . . This is the story that never changes . . . You mark my words on that . . . A week ago I played a pickup game of basketball and scored twenty-three points . . . Afterward, I jacked off in the park's bathroom and I wrote her name on the stall with my come . . . It's not often that you think about one person so kindly for so long, it's not often that*

*you don't take the memories for granted the way you had the person . . .
I once dreamt of driving through El Paso and becoming a drug dealer, it
wasn't so bad . . . I need New York like I need a blow job . . . I need San
Francisco like I need Oxy . . . the dress she wore that day when she ran
down the road was handmade by her mother . . . her mother made all her
clothes because they couldn't afford to go shopping for anything new, in
fact the last new thing she'd bought was an MC5 T-shirt because they
were her favorite and she'd dreamt about being in their band every night
for three weeks straight . . . In the end, Emma is just this girl, she's a crush
that won't go away . . . And in the end, I'm just a boy, a boy who wishes
he could've shoveled that snow for her . . . One day I'll have someone to
cook pancakes and sausage for, one day I'll get my slow dance . . . Next
spring I'm going to Taipei cos Tao Lin wrote about going there in one
of his books . . . Next winter I'm gonna head to the Marshall Islands
and go scuba diving through the remains of all those World War Two
battleships . . . Tomorrow I'll eat ice cream for breakfast, then go back
to bed; the next day, I'll Gmail chat with a stranger I met on Facebook
and make her a shirt, buy her a poster, maybe send her some music . . .
It's been a long time since I've seen a bluebird fly . . . The next time I see
Emma running, I don't think I'll chase her, I think it's better if Emma
just gets away. . . ."*

After I put my camera away, I throw my headphones
back in and play the M83 album *Hurry Up, We're Dreaming*.
If I could play one album on a twenty-four-hour loop from
some invisible speakers in the sky, it would be this one.

There was this one afternoon where me and that girl,
that bitch, sat next to each other on a swing set and ate ice
cream cones.

She told me that she wished her parents had named her Emma, and I asked her why.

"It's so beautiful," she told me. "When you hear that name, all you can think of is how lovely and pretty that girl must be, and I don't feel very pretty even though everyone says I am. I never have, Jaime. So I've always wanted the prettiest name in the world. That way, when boys and girls heard it, they'd get an image of this girl with a pretty face and an amazing smile."

"Maybe you should ask your parents to change it."

She smiled and licked her ice cream. "I don't want to ask."

"Why not?"

"Cos I'll never be Emma," she said. "And that's fine. Just daydreaming about it is wonderful. And I'd never want to ruin those daydreams by having them become real. When you lose your daydreams, you lose the only place you have where life can actually be perfect."

What she said that day, it still makes more sense to me than almost anything else I've ever heard anyone say.

I told her she was pretty right after we were done with our ice cream.

She blushed and told me I was cute, then she put one earphone in my ear and one in hers and she played that National song "Slow Show" and grabbed my hand.

That was the first time we held hands, and my palm was sweating so badly.

13

THE HOUSE IS STILL AND SILENT. IT'S UNNERVING.
Everything is the same as when I left it this morning, except
in the kitchen. On one of the counters are four bottles of
pills—Oxy, Vicodin, Xanax, and Valium—and at least forty
of them are scattered together in a big pile.

I call for my mother over and over and over, but she
never answers.

The way the natural light is pouring in through the
windows would be one of the most beautiful things I've
ever seen if not for the unsettling feeling looming over the
house.

I set my backpack down.

I look over the pills and I pick out an Oxy. Then I turn
on the sink faucet, fill my cupped hand with water, and
wash the pill down.

I walk upstairs.

It's much darker up here.

The steps creak and moan.

I call her name again.

Wish the Oxy would just hit right now.

I want it so fucking bad. It makes you feel so happy.

I could be on a chain gang picking up trash in 120-degree weather, and if I was riding a wave of baby blue, I'd be so fucking happy stabbing pieces of garbage with a poker.

I could be hanging out with some dumb girl who's drunk on Fuzzy Navel wine coolers and playing me the worst songs ever. Songs from bands like Kings of Leon or that awful Gotye shit or Macklemore tunes. But if I've entered the glass castle, if I've dropped a blue dream down my throat, I'd have a big, fat, fucking smile on my face. I wouldn't cut her down the way she deserves to be cut down. The way anyone who gets into that bullshit deserves to be shredded and bled.

A cool draft blows through the silent hallway.

I call for my mother one more time.

Still nothing.

I turn the handle on her bedroom door and push it open.

I fall back a couple of steps. My body shakes.

Sprawled in the middle of the bed is my mother. My beautiful fucking mother.

And she's covered in vomit and blood.

Her eyes are closed.

There's a frown on her face.

Her face is white like the snow, and her hair is spread out underneath her. It looks so perfect too, the way she's lying, she looks like a wrecked angel.

She looks better than a wrecked angel.

She's wearing her ballet dress. The one she wore during her final run in New York when she was considered to be one of the finest talents.

I run to her.

I'm not even sure I feel anything.

I'm just moving.

I wrap my arms around her waist and pull her to me.

I'm cradling my mother like a baby. She's still warm. The blood and vomit are wet and gooey and stick to my skin. They smell like iron and whiskey and hate.

I shake her. "Just wake up!" I scream again and again and again.

Look around the room, there's pills everywhere. Three empty bottles of red wine and a half-empty bottle of vodka lie on the floor and the nightstand beside the bed.

"Mom!" I yell. "Please, wake up! Please."

But there's nothing.

Tears slide down my face. I lay her back down and put my fingers against her neck.

Finally, I find a pulse.

It's light and weak but it's real.

I whip out my cell phone and call 911 and beg them to hurry.

"I can't lose her," I tell the operator. "She's all I have. She's my best friend. We listen to records all the time together."

The phone drops from my hand.

I'm so fucking confused and angry.

And then I see it. It's a note. It's lying on top of a pillow.

Reaching over my mother, I grab it and read.

I hate what I've become, Jaime. I'm so sorry for what I did to you last night. I hurt you so bad and then stood there as you lied to protect me. And I let you do it. I can't face you again after that. You were right. I think it's time you met your father. I love you so much. Don't ever forget that. I'm in a better place now. A place where I can't hurt you anymore. My baby boy, my life. I tried my best. I really did. But I'm not good for you. Please keep being amazing. I love you so much, and I know you'll take the world by storm. It's better that this ends now. I can't live with myself knowing I hurt the only reason I have to live. God, you are so much better than I'll ever be. Take care, my beautiful boy. I'll see you in the good place a long time from now. I'll be watching you always. . . .

Part of me thinks that this is one of the most beautiful things I've ever read. The other part of me thinks it's the most pathetic thing I've ever read.

Either way, no one can ever see this letter. This was an accident. That's all. She just partied too much. I'll never let anyone find out she tried to kill herself, because if they do, they'll take me away from her, and I won't let that happen.

I rip the note into pieces, then run into the bathroom and flush them down the toilet.

After that, I sit down next to my mother. The first wave of baby blue crashes over me as I take out my iPhone and play New Order, which is my mother's favorite band of all time, while we wait for the ambulance to show up.

14.

MY MOTHER DOESN'T DIE. HER STOMACH GETS pumped. She wakes up. She gets questioned. She gets sedated. Now she's resting peacefully in a room that I'm not allowed to enter.

So I sit in the waiting room and read Rimbaud's *A Season in Hell* (I grabbed it from my room while the paramedics were putting my mother on the stretcher) and listen to *The Year of Hibernation* on my headphones.

This album continues to help me and give me comfort.

And I've always felt this almost, like, spiritual connection to Rimbaud since the first time I read him.

I've read *A Season in Hell* at least eight times. The first time was when my mother was sleeping with this twenty-one-year-old girl named Simone.

Simone was majoring in English at the University of Saint Francis. The two of them, they'd do cocaine a lot. They smoked lots of pot, too. And drank tons of wine while they listened to records in the living room. My mother has always slept with women here as far back as I can remember, but I've never seen her as happy as she was with Simone.

I walked in on them once.

That was the last time I'd seen my mother in that same ballet dress.

Simone had my mother bent over the grand piano in our music study at our house. My mother's dress was hiked up to her waist while Simone fucked her.

They never saw me that day. My dick got hard. I hid behind the couch in the living room and slid my hand down my jeans.

Less than five seconds later, I came.

Guilt and embarrassment and shame immediately followed.

I ran out of the house and washed my hands off with a hose in our neighbor's yard. After that, I climbed a tree in a nearby park and sat there till it got dark. I don't remember what I thought about while I was up there, I just remember how calm and quiet it was there.

When I finally did go home, my mother was smoking a joint in her bathrobe and listening to the Magnetic Fields on vinyl. She didn't say much to me, but I knew she was happy.

I made a sandwich and ate it in my room.

Later that night, while my mother was asleep, I went downstairs and played two Sonic Youth records, *Daydream Nation* and *Washing Machine*, to practice guitar.

This is when I saw the book. It was sitting on the piano. The cover sucked me in. A black-and-white figure had its arms raised in the air, as if it was asking to be saved.

I opened it and began reading. I fell in love on the spot. And for the next two days, Rimbaud saved me from everything normal and boring I had to live through.

15.

SO HERE'S THE DEAL, AND IT'S A TERRIBLE ONE, IT'S absolute bullshit. The doctor who takes care of my mother in the ER tells me I won't be able to talk to my mother or see her at all tonight.

There's also a child welfare service representative and a cop standing on each side of him.

He says she's under way too much duress. And that she's confused and scared. And that she's too emotionally unstable right now, and that seeing me might push her back over the edge.

"You really think you pulled her back from it?" I ask.

"She's more stable now," the doctor answers.

"What does that really mean?" I snap.

"She's still alive," he says.

"But that's all," I say. "Ya know. *That's* all."

He stares awkwardly at me for a few seconds. And then moves on with the plan that all these other people, these adults who have never met me before today, came up with.

It turns out my mother won't be coming home anytime soon. After tomorrow, they're going to put her in the psychiatric ward for an eight-day evaluation.

Me and my mother, we don't have any living blood relatives in Joliet or the entire state of Illinois. My mother was an only child. Her parents died in a car accident when I was three, and me and her lived in Chicago at the time. She got everything in the will (they were really well off), so we moved into the house she grew up in about a month after their funerals.

She always wanted to be back in Joliet, but she couldn't handle the embarrassment and the stress of the ridicule she would've gotten from her mother if we'd moved back.

"She hated me for having you." My mother told me this one morning when I was, like, four and woke up to find her watching a recording of her first lead performance in a ballet right after she moved to New York.

Right before she met my father and fell madly, insanely in love with him.

"The night I told her I was pregnant with you, she walked out of the restaurant where we were dining. Then she called me an idiot. She told me I'd never dance again."

My mother paused. She looked over at me. Her eyes were filled with tears. And then she shook her head and looked at the floor. "She was right," she whispered. "She was right about everything."

Back to the waiting room now.

The doctor says, "Your father is coming here, Jaime. He'll be here in the morning to take you back to San Francisco while your mother is being evaluated."

I'm pretty sure I'm fucking speechless for the first time ever in my life. My head gets all fuzzy. It feels like Mike Tyson just slammed a fist into my head.

I'm dizzy.

My chest tightens and my hands shake.

The child services rep steps in now.

And she says, "We know about that night in New York, Jaime. We know your father struck your mother across the face and pushed her down. And we know about the restraining order against him. But she never pressed any charges. Instead, your father agreed to fast-track the divorce and pay the amount of child support she wanted. It's been thirteen years, and without any other guardian, your father has legal rights to step in, given your mother's current state."

"Jaime," the doctor says. "Do you understand this?"

My mouth is dry. It feels like chalk.

"Jaime," the doctor presses.

"No," I say.

"No what?" he asks.

"No," I say again. "I don't understand any of *this*. You're sending me to stay with the man who betrayed my mother. He ruined her fucking life and made her crazy for all these years, and I have to go live with him now."

"Just until the evaluation is over," the doctor says.

"What happens if she doesn't get better?"

The doctor looks back at the child services rep.

"Don't look at her," I snap. "I asked you a question. Look at me, dude."

He sighs. "We'll cross the bridge if we come to it."

"Great," I snort. "That's real, fucking great. And what about school? Final exams are next week."

"You'll be allowed to take them after this gets resolved," the woman says. "You don't have anyone else to care for you here. You don't have any other family besides your father."

A scowl cuts across my face. "He's not my family," I rip. "That bastard is the reason why my mother is here right now. So let's just be clear about that. He's *not* my family."

"Well, there's nobody else," she says. "You don't have anyone else."

"I know," I snap. "I know I'm alone. So please just stop saying it. I understand *that*."

16.

WHERE I'M SPENDING THE NIGHT IS AT THE APARTMENT of my mother's first-ever dance instructor. This seventy-one-year-old woman named Ida who taught my mother until she was sixteen and moved to Chicago for dance school.

Ida doesn't like me too much, though. Just like my grandmother, she condemned my mother for deciding to have me. Unlike my grandmother, though, the two of them made amends not long after my mother came back to Joliet with me.

Ida's apartment smells like old. I've never been able to describe that smell, but it's definitely a thing. And it's rough on the nostrils.

It's eight on Thursday night, and Ida tells me that on Thursday nights she likes to stay up an extra hour to watch *Law & Order*, which means she'll be going to bed at ten.

Normally, I wouldn't give a shit, but there are a couple of things I need to do before I leave for San Francisco, so it's nice to have this information.

Not once since Ida picked me up have we talked about what happened, which is a stinking relief. Cos I can't do that. I don't wanna do that. There's nothing to talk about anyway. Everyone—the doctor, the cop, the child welfare lady, the paramedics, fucking Ida—they all think she was partying too hard. None of them know the truth.

I told them she'd been kinda sad lately and was on a bender.

I told them she hadn't slept in two days.

I told them she's an alcoholic and a prescription pill abuser.

Hearing those things come out of my mouth, it made me sick. I felt like I was betraying her. I'd promised her a long time ago, promised myself, that I would never do that. That I'd never ruin her in the eyes of other people. I promised her that I'd never leave her.

But it had to be done. I had to tell people the truth about my mother's depression and addictions in order to preserve the lie about what really happened this afternoon.

I wait Ida out from the kitchen. I put my headphones on and listen to the Neutral Milk Hotel record "In the Aeroplane Over the Sea." I read about it on Pitchfork's website when I was ten. The way the music made me feel that first listen, so good, even though it is this kaleidoscope of emotions just the like the Pitchfork review said.

For me, it's an album I can put on no matter what my mood is, no matter how good or shitty things are in my life.

I think that's what most people want.

Not always, but most of the time.

When I write music and poetry, that standard is always

in my head. I aspire to that for every note or lyric or sentence I create.

I give it a half an hour after Ida goes to bed before I sneak out. I call a cab and it drops me off at my house.

It feels the same as it always does when I walk in. It's like the house doesn't remember I flushed my mother's suicide note down the toilet.

I'm strong. I know this about myself. I don't break. That's one thing I've really learned about myself since my mother's drug-and-booze-induced spiral started a couple of years ago, right after her boyfriend was killed in a car accident. She was in the car with him, and they were wasted. They jumped a median and crashed into the side of a car wash. He was driving. It ripped another deep, deep hole in her. Poor fucking thing.

In the kitchen, I take a beer from the fridge. Then I go upstairs and sit down at my computer. Ripping a piece of aluminum foil from the roll next to my desk, I drop a baby blue on it.

I smoke the entire pill in less than twenty minutes while I listen to the Growlers album *Hot Tropics*.

But memories of the girl who wished her name was Emma come storming back to me and it's too much right now, so I stop playing music and float, like the fog I am now, into the bathroom.

I finally take off my school uniform and strip down to my underwear.

I flex the muscles in my stomach.

Tomorrow morning I'm going to do a hundred push-ups and two hundred crunches.

I plug in my razor and touch up the two lines I keep shaved into the left side of my strawberry-blond hair.

When I'm done, I step back and just stare at myself in the mirror. I'm so cute and in awesome shape, and my black eye doesn't even bother me.

I don't get why that girl didn't want me anymore. That guy she went to, he was total garbage. He had these stupid black plugs in his ears, and his bottom lip was pierced, and he was always wearing these dumb leather wristbands. His hair was dyed black too, and it was always styled messy. It looked like he bought all his clothes at Hot Topic.

Fuck that, actually. Dude looked like he stepped out of a Hot Topic catalog.

He was so gross.

The first time I saw him he was wearing a black AFI T-shirt that looked two sizes too small on him. I was embarrassed for him, and part of me is embarrassed for myself because I was with a girl who wanted that.

She was so pretty, though. And she was reading a James Morgan book the day I met her.

She bought a root beer float the first time we, like, really kicked it together. She asked me to split it with her. Later that day, she played the Murder City Devils song "Boom Swagger Boom" on her iPhone. We were at the playground near her house and she did this awesome dance to it just for me.

It was really sweet. I smiled a lot that day.

I thought it was really cool that she wanted to use the same straw for the root beer float.

Back in my room now.

I snap a blue in half and drop one of them on a new sheet of foil.

When I'm finished smoking that, I put the Growlers back on and slam the rest of that beer while I pack my backpack.

Like, fuck it.

There's no way I'm gonna let a fucking girl ruin an entire album for me. I love this band too much.

Plus, I totally listened to them before she ever did.

17.

I'M ON MY SKATEBOARD, FLYING DOWN THE STREET with an address written on a small slip of paper. Besides grabbing my laptop from the house, this is the other thing I need to do before I leave tomorrow morning.

It takes me about ten minutes to get there. Right away, I see his car. It's parked in the driveway, next to a really nice white house, even though I was prepared to break into the garage.

I dump my skateboard in some bushes about half a block away and open my backpack. I take out two cans of spray paint, one red, one black, and then I slide the black bandanna that's tied around my neck over my face and shake the cans for a couple seconds.

I wait for this dumb truck to drive by and clear the intersection up ahead before I go back and survey my new canvas.

I go ahead and spray the words: *Shave the rest of your hair, dick,* on my principal's white Mercedes-Benz.

I write: *Quit talking shit.*

I paint: *Your secretary's a whore.*

I tag: *I'm better than you, bitch. And so is my mother.*

When I'm through, I sprint back to my board, pull on my backpack, and skate away listening to that Cage song "Agent Orange."

I'm laughing, too.

I'm stoked.

And like, fuck that guy.

No one says shit about my mother in front of me.

That dude's a piece of shit.

Like six blocks later, I stop skating for a second and drop a baby blue down my throat.

Now I'm ready to leave Joliet, I guess.

My business is finished here, I'm thinking as the chorus begins. . . .

"People said his brain was infected by devils . . ."

18.

MY MOTHER'S RIGHT PINKIE FINGER IS IN A SPLINT. IT shattered when she hit my face. They did surgery on it, which I wasn't aware of at all yesterday. To me, it just shows you how tough my mother can be. Like, she spent all morning and most of the afternoon with a shattered finger.

According to the doctor, she'd ingested the majority of the booze and drugs about an hour before I found her. That's some tough living right there. And it makes me super happy, as fucked up as that may seem.

I stand in the corner of her hospital room, underneath the TV that's hanging from the ceiling, with my arms crossed.

"There he is," my mother says slowly. "There's my boy, my big hero, my Jaime."

She looks terrible. Her face seems sunken, and the bags under her eyes are so dark and big.

"Jaime," she whispers. "Come here. Let me touch you."

"Why?"

"So I know that this is real."

My eyes well up. I'm so pissed at her. Goddamn it, she tried to kill herself, and she's handed me right over to the one person she's tried to keep away my whole life.

"Please," she whispers again. "Please, Jaime. I'm your mom."

And she's right.

She is, even if I barely recognize her right now. Even if I've barely recognized her over the last year or so.

She's still the woman who raised me all by herself, and sacrificed everything that was sacred to her so I could even fucking be here right now.

She's still the most amazing soul that ever existed.

She's still the beautiful lady with the best taste in music and books.

So I go to her, because that's what you're supposed to do. You're supposed to go to your mother when she needs you the most.

She lifts her left hand, and I take it in mine and squeeze it. She smiles so big and pretty.

"That's nice," she says. "It's so nice to see you again, Jaime."

"You too," I say back.

Then she frowns and pulls her hand away and sits up.

"What's wrong?" I ask her.

"Your face," she says. "What happened to your face?"

As hurtful and sad as it is for me to hear that question spill from her lips, it's exactly what I wanna hear from her. It's perfect. She really doesn't remember anything about what happened the other day. So I figure that at some point yesterday, she put two and two together. Her busted right hand and my black left eye.

This had to have been what triggered her suicide attempt. But she drank too much, and she took too many pills, and now she can't even remember why she tried to take her life.

It's disgusting.

It's also the best scenario that can come from this total disaster.

I sigh and shake out my shoulders. "I got into a fight at school yesterday," I tell her. "That's what happened to my face."

"Oh, Jaime," she says. "Why? Why did you get into another fight?"

I shrug. "It just happened."

She groans. "Great. What did the principal say?"

"Not much. I just had to spend the rest of the day in detention."

"Damn it," she says. "Do you know how much I pay for you to go to that school?"

"Does it even matter right now?" I ask. "They're sending me to San Francisco with my father."

This incredible look of shock and anguish washes over her face now, and she slides her left hand slowly down it.

"Oh my god," she whispers.

I make a face. "You didn't know?"

She doesn't say anything.

"Mom, you didn't know this was happening?"

"I did," she finally says. "I did. I just . . ." She stops and closes her eyes.

With all the rad drugs my mother is being pumped with right now, I bet she's in heaven.

I bet she feels so fucking good.

Opening her eyes, she goes, "I just forgot. Oh, fuck."

"Yeah, Mom."

"That bastard is here, isn't he?"

I nod.

When I arrived at the hospital with Ida (she was rather curious how I had a skateboard and why I wasn't in my school uniform still), the doctor informed me that my father was in the cafeteria having breakfast.

I rolled my eyes. Like I fucking care what he's doing.

"Fuck him," my mother shouts. "Just fuck him!"

"Hey," I say, and grab her hand again. "Just relax. It's only for eight days. I'll be back here next Monday."

My mother, she begins to cry. "No," she sobs. "No, no, no. He can't have you. He doesn't deserve you. He ruined my life."

I bite my tongue.

And she goes, "He's a monster, Jaime. Don't trust him. You can't trust him. He's the worst man in the world."

Swinging my eyes back to her, I say, "I know."

"I'm so sorry. I didn't want any of this to happen."

Again, I say, "I know."

I say, "I'm not scared. It'll be over before you know it."

Her lips press tightly together and she forces a smile.

"It will be," I say.

"I'm sorry," she says again.

"You're gonna be just fine," I tell her. "You'll get out of here, and you'll be sober, and everything will be better than it was. Better than it's ever been."

She looks away.

This whole thing is brutal and ugly.

Turning back to me now, my mother goes, "Be strong, Jaime."

"I will."

"And don't like him. Okay, my boy? Don't trust your father, and don't like him."

"Right."

"He's a monster."

"I know."

"Don't let him ruin your life too."

"I won't."

19.

MY FATHER LOOKS EXACTLY LIKE ALL THE PHOTOS I saw of him when I Googled him the other night. I guess he's about six feet tall, maybe even an inch bigger, and he's got strawberry-blond hair too. It's parted very neatly from the left to right and shaved down about an inch shorter on the sides and in the back.

His eyes are brown. His face is very defined. And he seems very fit and toned. His skin looks healthy. He just looks healthy and looks successful and happy despite how awkward he gets when I appear in the lobby and stare at him.

The man who hit my mother and pushed her down.

The man who's never spoken to his son or even fought for the chance to speak to his only son.

His name is Justin, by the way, and he's wearing a pair of tight black dress pants that look expensive. A charcoal-colored button-up shirt is tucked into those slacks, and a black leather belt wraps around his waist.

His shoes are also black. They're leather and they're shiny and he's also wearing a gold Rolex on his right wrist.

Maybe I'd be more nervous if I was meeting him before

I saw my mother laid up in that stuffy room, but I'm not. And I don't feel anything in particular at all right now except for anger and a hint of hate.

He smiles at me. Sweat gleams from his forehead.

"Jaime," he says.

"Sure. What?" I snort back.

"Oh my god," he goes. "My son. It's so good to see you again."

He steps forward, his arms spread like he thinks he's gonna be able to hug me or some bullshit. I step to the side; he ends up holding out his hand.

Instead of shaking it, I make a fist and tap it. "Yo," I say.

His cheeks turn mildly red. "Hi."

"Cool."

"It's just . . ." He stops and shakes his head. "I mean, here you are. You've grown so much. I can't believe it."

I roll my eyes. "It's what happens, dude. The last time you saw me, I was one and you were hurting my mother."

"Hey," he starts.

But I cut him off. "I'm fourteen. People fucking grow a lot in thirteen years."

The doctor, my father, and the child welfare lady all look horribly uncomfortable after I say this. And they should.

They should feel more than uncomfortable. They should feel shame and guilt for what they're doing to me right now, and what they're doing to my mother.

My father sighs. "You're right. Kids grow up. It's so

much different, though, when it's your own family. Your own son."

"I'm not your fucking family."

"Jaime," the doctor snaps. "Let's keep this civil."

Me and my father, we lock eyes and stare at each other. We look so much alike, too.

"I'm really happy to see you, Jaime. I know this has to be incredibly hard for you right now, but I want you to understand that we're excited for you to spend a week with us. I think you'll really enjoy it. San Francisco is a great place for you to get your mind off of what's happened."

"You think I'm gonna start hanging out, and stop thinking about finding my mother lying in that shitty bed?"

"That's not what I meant."

"You think I'm going to enjoy myself while my mother sits in a mental hospital?"

"Oh, come on," my father snaps. "You're my son too. I'm your father."

"You're a fucking sperm donor, dude. I don't have a father."

"That's not fair."

"Right," I sigh. "Right . . ."

Pause.

"Please go on, man. I'd love to know what you think is fair."

He doesn't say anything.

"I'm betting my mom would love to hear it too."

"Okay," the doctor says. "That's enough. You two have a plane to catch. I'd suggest you accept that, Jaime, and make this as easy on yourself as you can."

"Piss off," I go. "I'll be outside when you're done signing all the paperwork, Justin."

20.

THE MOST IMPORTANT THING I'M TAKING TO SAN Francisco besides my laptop and notebooks and camcorder are thirty baby blues. I take them from a safe under my mother's bed, along with five thousand dollars (she has more than a thousand Oxys and twenty thousand in cash in this thing).

My father stays in the car. He said he had to make some important phone calls.

"Great for you," I said back. Then, "I bet it must be neat being you and stuff," before going into the house.

I dump the Oxys into a Tylenol bottle, and then take the last three from my own stash and put them in the tiny pocket of my jeans.

After I'm done stuffing my backpack, I grab a fairly large black suitcase from a closet in the hallway and pack it full of cut-off jean shorts, tank tops, tight black jeans, flannels, slip-on shoes, and a green parka.

Holding a piece of aluminum foil in my left hand, I chase the dragon. I don't smoke it all, but I smoke enough.

Not even my stupid fucking father sucks enough to leave a stain in the lovely glass castle I've just built.

In the kitchen, I slam a beer.

I'm numb.

I look around the house and it means nothing at the moment.

This is what really matters. Feeling nothing.

I put my headphones on and play that Angus and Julia Stone song "Big Jet Plane."

It seems kinda fitting, even though I'm not taking some gorgeous girl I'm in love with on a trip.

I walk outside. My father is leaning against the car, smoking a joint. I laugh.

He quickly puts it out. He says something, and I take my headphones off.

"What was that?" I ask him.

"I said, it's just something I do from time to time. Not a lot. Just when I'm stressed. But I don't do it all the time."

"It's just pot," I say.

"What do you mean?" he asks.

"I mean that it's just pot, dude. Who cares? Most of the kids in my class do the same thing during lunch."

"Really?"

I make a face. "Yeah, man. Really. You get stoned. So what? There's a ton of shit you've done that you need to answer for, but smoking joints ain't one of them."

21.

WE FLY FIRST CLASS. IT'S A DIRECT FLIGHT FROM O'Hare to San Francisco. The two of us, we both pull out our laptops the second we get in the air.

I've rejected all my father's attempts at conversation so far. He looks stressed out anyway. And not just because of me and my sudden reappearance in his life.

Right before takeoff, he bit a Xanax bar in half and washed it down with a glass of white wine. He's on his fourth glass now.

He pounds the keyboard with his fingers. He shakes his head and rolls his eyes and rubs his face in obvious frustration.

Finally, I take my headphones off and go, "What's got you so creased?"

He looks almost shocked that I've addressed him. "Excuse me?"

"What's got you so creased?" I repeat.

"Nothing," he says.

"Doesn't look like nothing."

"I had a number of meetings that I couldn't push back, and I'm trying to decipher exactly what happened in my absence."

"Sucks."

"It's not ideal."

I make a face. "I'm really sorry if my situation is fucking up yours, man. This is the last place I wanna be."

"Your language."

"What about it?"

He sighs.

And I say, "I'm sure you know where it came from."

A smile cuts across his face, and he laughs. "Yes, I do." He laughs again and leans his head back against his seat. "I've never heard anyone cuss that much. Never."

"Rappers don't even cuss as much as my mother."

"I used to give her so much shit for it, and how she—"

"Never knew she was doing it," we both say at the same time.

We laugh. It's the first time me and my father have ever laughed together, and it comes at the expense of my mother.

My father goes pack to pounding his keyboard, and I turn and look out the window.

"So how'd you get your black eye, Jaime?" my father asks, just like that, without even looking at me.

"I got hit. How do you think?"

"Who hit you?"

His questions irritate me. I scowl. "This kid at school yesterday."

"Why'd he hit you?"

"Because I decked him for talking shit."

My father finally looks up from his computer. "You get into a lot of fights, don't you?"

Shrugging, I go, "Not a lot. Some. But not a lot. How would you know anyway?"

"Your mother told me."

"When? You didn't see her at the hospital."

"Last week, I think. Maybe the week before. It came up in our conversation. She's said it before too, that you get into fights frequently."

I get nauseous.

My cheeks begin to burn.

"I didn't know you two talked."

"We talk a couple times a week, Jaime."

"Excuse me?"

My father looks confused now too. "Your mother and I talk frequently. You didn't know that?"

"No."

"She always tells me you don't want to talk to me when I call. She tells me that she can't force you to talk, and that's the end of it. You didn't know?"

It feels like my heart's sitting in the pit of my stomach. I didn't know. She says that my father calls maybe once a year, if that. And when he does, she says he never wants to talk to me.

This is so gross.

I need to be away from him.

I walk into the bathroom and lock the door. Then I

grind an Oxy and snort the whole pile with a one-hundred-dollar bill.

Splash cold water on my face repeatedly.

My mother warned me about my father. She's always said he's manipulative and a liar. It's how he got her to go along with their plan after they found out she was pregnant. She was going to take a year off from dancing after she had me, then he was supposed to quit his job in the financial world and go back to freelance carpentry so she could focus on getting back into shape to join the ballet again.

It never happened, though.

She said he never intended to leave his posh job and was lying to her the whole time. That's when she said she knew she'd married a monster, and he couldn't be trusted.

"He'll lie to get what he wants," she's told me so many times. "He's selfish like that, Jaime. Never believe anything he tells you."

"I won't," I always said. "I'll never meet him."

"I'll make sure you never have to."

"I know, Mom."

"He's a bastard, Jaime. He doesn't even ask about you when we talk. He's never wanted anything to do with you or me."

I dry my face off with a couple pieces of toilet paper.

Like fuck that guy out there thinking he can just say whatever and I'll believe it.

Just fuck him.

I won't listen anymore.

When I sit back down, my father starts to say something else, but I turn to the window and put my headphones on.

I play the Lamborghini Dreams album *Mulatto*.

I don't talk to my father the rest of the flight.

The only time I speak is when the stewardess asks me if I need anything.

And I don't.

I've got my baby blues and my music and my notebooks.

What more could anyone ever need anyway?

22

IT'S ALMOST FOUR IN THE AFTERNOON WHEN WE land in San Francisco. I take a photo of the sunny runway surrounded by this perfect blue water and tweet it, tagging my school, and writing, *What you seen today, you bald, creepy fuck?*

By the time I'm walking off the plane, it's been retweeted thirty-seven times.

Sixty-one people have favorited it.

I smile cos I'm proud of that, but fuck all the kids who liked it and passed it along.

Just fuck all of them.

Those fakes.

Those goddamn phonies.

My father spends every second at the bag claim on his phone. He's going on and on about some amazing artist chick painter named Savannah.

It's annoying.

And it's interesting.

And he keeps barking at whoever is on the other end of the call to make sure she's got everything she needs to work this week and be comfortable.

"She gets whatever she wants," I hear him say. "Anything Savannah needs, she fucking gets."

A black town car with tinted windows picks us up.

The driver tries to take my bag to put in the trunk, but I refuse to let him do this and put it in myself.

"It's his job, Jaime," my father says.

"It's my bag," I say back. "Plus, it's not hard."

"What?"

"I can put my own bag away. Nobody needs to do that for me."

"But it's his job," he says again.

"Not with my stuff it isn't."

The car speeds down the highway. My father is wearing sunglasses. He taps his fingers nervously against his legs.

"Who's Savannah?" I finally ask as the car begins to merge into traffic and the cityscape appears in front of us.

My father looks over at me and pushes his shades to the top of his head. "Savannah is an extraordinary artist. She's so immensely gifted," he says.

"What kind of art does she make?"

"She paints," he says slowly. "Her work is stunning, Jaime. It's on the verge of brilliant. She's only twenty-one years old, too. How goddamn phenomenal. The quality of her work at that age, it's just incredible. And she's just arrived in the city, too."

"From where?"

"Charleston, South Carolina."

"Why is she here?" I ask. "What does she have to do with you?"

"I flew her here. One of my galleries is hosting the opening of her new exhibit next Friday night. She'll be staying in the apartment above my gallery in the Lower Haight to work on the final piece of the collection."

"Wow," I say. "Sounds important."

The car takes an exit and we move into the actual city.

My palms begin to sweat. My heart beats faster. This is it. This is fucking San Francisco, and I'm here and I'm excited and I'm scared and I'm nervous and I'm enamored.

My father lowers his shades back over his eyes and goes, "It is important, son. I believe she's a once-in-a-lifetime talent. Potentially *the* most important painter of her generation. The fact that she's debuting her new pieces at my gallery, it's a very big deal. It's one of the most important things I've ever done."

I turn away from my father. So much makes sense to me right now. My mother always said my father was a wannabe artist. She told me he painted all the time but wasn't any good and nobody liked his work.

"But he knew a lot about art. He was a fixture at gallery openings. He was at all the after parties. It's how we met. But he couldn't cut it as an artist. I don't think he ever sold a piece. That must be really hard on someone. To love something so much, yet not to be very good at it. It's cruel," my mother would always say. "He wanted to be an artist so bad. He probably wanted it more than most artists do. He just had no talent."

Now he owns the places that show artists' work to the rest of the world.

It makes perfect sense to me.

If you can't join them, own them.

23

ME AND HER, WE SAT ON THE ROOF OF HER GARAGE
one afternoon when her parents were at the grocery store.

She asked me what was wrong.

"Nothing," I told her.

"You look out of it," she said. "You've been really quiet since we got here."

I told her I was fine. That I was thinking about this dream I'd had the night before. I couldn't shake it or ignore it.

"What was the dream?" she asked.

"I don't wanna say," I told her.

"Was it about me?"

I nodded.

"Come on," she went. "Tell me."

"It's fucked up. It was so fucked up and gross."

"That just makes me wanna hear it even more."

She was wearing these dark-blue jeans that buttoned right under her belly button. She had a loose black tank top on and a black bandanna tied backward around her forehead.

She was smoking a joint.

I didn't smoke any weed that afternoon.

"Please tell me," she said. "You have to now. It'll be good for you. It will."

This made me cringe. I went, "How the fuck do you know what's good for me? *How?*"

She looked away, and I admired the way the sun looked on the pale skin of her shoulder, highlighting her tiny freckles.

A few seconds later, she stood up. "Fuck you," she said.

"That's fair," I said back.

"What was your dream about?"

I ran a hand down my face and told her.

By the time I was finished, she was standing on the other side of the roof from me.

And she looked sick.

Later, when it was time for me to leave, she grabbed me and she threw her arms around me and told me that someday, she'd let me do anything I wanted to her.

"That's not what I'm expecting," I told her.

"Well, I wasn't expecting to hear about your dream."

We never talked about dreams again.

That fucking slut.

24.

MY FATHER'S HOUSE IN ASHBURY HEIGHTS IS THE nicest house I've ever seen this close up. These two older Hispanic ladies emerge from the front door as the town car stops in the driveway.

My father and I get out of the car.

The ladies rush toward the trunk as the driver grabs my suitcase from it. I take it from him, and my father hands his bag to one of the ladies.

The other lady tries to take mine.

"Stop it," I say. "I can carry my own bag."

The lady looks at my father, and my father shrugs. *Está bien. Gracias aunque.*

My father hands the driver a fifty-dollar bill.

"So this is it," he says. "What do you think?"

"It's nice."

"I like to think so."

"I bet you do," I say.

He shakes his head and tells me to follow him.

25

HERE'S THE WAY THIS HOUSE GOES: FIRST OF ALL, it's on Ashbury and Clifford. It's two stories, and light gray on the outside with a white border.

Natural sunlight fills the first floor of the house. It's so pretty and calm.

Straight ahead is the living room. A white couch sits in front of a huge bay window. A blue-and-white rug covers the hardwood floor, and a nice wood-and-glass coffee table sits on the rug. The wall across from the couch is white, and a huge, sixty-inch flat-screen TV is on it. There's a white leather reclining chair in the corner of the room and a white leather love seat against the far wall. Paintings hang everywhere. So do plants.

To the right of the front door is the dining room. A chandelier hovers over a huge oak table.

The dining room spills into the kitchen. It's a big room.

And it spills into a stairwell that leads to the basement, which my father's stepdaughter, my stepsister, Kristen, occupies.

Right next to the stairwell is a door that takes you to the backyard. There's a hot tub on the deck out there.

On the other side of it is a set of stairs that takes you upstairs.

I'm impressed with all of this.

I'm also disgusted.

It's not like me and my mother have been living in a dump or anything like that.

Cos we don't.

Our house is pretty okay.

But we certainly have never lived like this.

We've never come close to even thinking about living how my father has been all these years.

26.

LESLIE WALKS INTO THE ROOM. SHE IS VERY PRETTY, which I expected.

She's like two, three inches shorter than me, and very tan. Her hair is short and blond and she's got a toned, curvy body, which normally I ain't into, but she's making it work really well.

She's wearing a blue sundress and she's barefoot.

Her eyes are big and blue.

My father introduces us, and she gives me a hug.

She smells really good. Like she's just bathed in a tub full of juices squeezed from fresh fruit.

She kisses my cheek.

I feel a small rise in the crotch of my pants.

"Wow," she says. "You look so much like your father did when he was your age from the pictures I've seen of him."

"Oh yeah?" I snort.

She nods.

"I wouldn't know. I've never seen a picture of him before."

Her and my father glance at each other.

I say, "If you guys don't mind, I'd like to take a shower and get my things put away."

"Not at all," my father says, then asks one of the maids to show me to my room.

"You can just tell me where it's at," I snap.

"She'll show you," he says.

"I'll show him," Leslie says. "I'm going upstairs anyway."

So I follow Leslie up the stairs and down a long hallway, where more art hangs from the walls.

She leads me to the last door on the right and goes, "Here it is."

Obviously, the room's big. Way more than I need. Way more than anyone needs.

A king-size bed is directly to the left of the doorway, with four massive pillows on it and blankets sitting at the foot of it.

There're two walk-in closets.

A bay window directly across from the door lets in more natural light.

There's an oak desk to the right of the doorway with a computer and printer on it, and a really nice dresser on the same side of the room as the desk.

"This is a really nice place," I say as I walk to the middle of the room and set my things down.

"I'm glad you think so," she says. "We've lived here for five years and just love it."

"What's not to love?"

"Exactly."

An awkward moment of silence follows.

And then Leslie, she says, "I'm sorry we're meeting under these circumstances, Jaime. It's not the way anyone wanted."

"Right."

Pause.

"You're implying that anyone ever wanted this meeting to happen, though."

"Well, yeah, I am. Of course we did, Jaime."

"I didn't."

"Okay," she goes. "I understand."

"No, you don't. And that's not your fault, Leslie. But you don't understand any of this."

"Right," she says. "I'll just let you get settled then."

"Thanks."

Leslie leaves and closes the door behind her.

Me, I lock it and then I dig the small sheet of foil from my suitcase and drop a blue on it.

A minute later I'm coasting through the castle while the Fresh & Onlys song "Waterfall" echoes from the chamber.

27

MY FATHER WANTS TO GO HIS GALLERY IN THE LOWER
Haight to meet with Savannah, and he wants me to go with him.

Leslie says she'll have dinner ready for us when we get back, even though I tell her I'm not hungry and won't be anytime soon.

The blue dragon takes care of everything I need.

I'm wearing tight black jeans and a blue-and-purple-striped tank top. I put on my parka and dangle a black bandanna out of my right back pocket.

My father drives his black Mercedes-Benz.

Duran Duran plays from the speakers.

We make a right on Haight and Ashbury. It's totally unimpressive. Most of the people I see are a bunch of nasty-ass, strung-out-looking white kids with dreads and their dogs polluting the four corners of the intersection.

It's pretty gross.

A couple of them are playing bongo drums, and I laugh because it's so lame.

Like, way to go, losers.

All that 1967, "Summer of Love" bullshit is dead, and that's a good thing.

Fucking hippies.

White kids with dreads are the worst.

"This is going to be a really busy week," my father tells me. "I don't know how much I'm going to be around."

I shrug. "That's fine. I know this isn't ideal for anyone. I don't care if we hardly see each other."

My father seems irritated with my comments. He scowls and I smile. It's perfect.

And he goes, "What I was getting at is that you're going to have a lot of free time, and I encourage you to explore the city. That said, avoid those fucking dirtbags hanging out on the corner."

"Oh, I will, just for the sake of my nose. It looked like their skin was growing dirt."

My father laughs. Then goes, "A couple of those street-kid assholes followed Kristen for a couple of blocks one night and tried to rob her."

"Jesus."

"She maced them, though, and got away from them."

"Nice."

"She's a tough girl. But you have to be careful, Jaime. Have eyes in the back of your head. Those losers will try something if they think you're not paying attention."

"Got it."

"Good."

My father parallel parks in front of this bar called Molotov's.

That Misfits song "Hybrid Moments" blares from it.

"This is the Lower Haight," my father says after we both get out of the car. "And that's my gallery."

He points across the street at this two-story building on the corner.

The word TRANSMISSION is spelled out in shiny, lowercase black letters above the door.

"Why that name?"

"Joy Division," he says, grinning.

I can't help but grin back. "Nice, man."

"Come on," he goes, and we jog across the street and go inside.

The Talking Heads are playing on a record player that sits on a stack of crates behind this glass counter.

There are maybe ten other people here too.

This gallery is pretty sick.

Clean white walls. Beautiful hardwood floor. An information desk at the back.

There's a small, finely crafted bar on the right side of the room. And a winding stairwell next to the glass counter that ascends.

Regardless of how big an asshole my father is, dude's got some good cultural taste.

This middle-aged black lady with glasses appears, holding a clipboard and a manila envelope packed with papers.

Her hair is pulled back tightly, and she's wearing a white dress, a black cardigan, and black heels.

She's pretty.

My father and her immediately engage in a very intense and important-seeming conversation.

I already feel like a third wheel.

Maybe if I would've ogled over his house and his wife and the maids earlier, he wouldn't have dragged me down here in his ninety-thousand-dollar ride (I looked it up on my iPhone) to show off some more.

I wonder where Savannah is.

I don't see her anywhere.

I Googled her in the car too.

Her picture left me breathless and clumsy.

Savannah is beautiful in the way that Van Gogh's *Starry Night* is beautiful.

In the way that Françoise Hardy's voice is beautiful.

In the way that Kim Novak looks during every second her face appears on film in *Vertigo*.

My father finishes his conversation, then waves me over to introduce me to the lady.

Her name is Jackie, and she's the publicist for both my father's galleries.

She gives me a hug and says it's such a privilege to meet me. "You look just like your daddy. Welcome to San Francisco, Jaime. Welcome to the Transmission Gallery."

I thank her and follow my father up to where Savannah will be staying and working all week.

Savannah opens the door. The look on my father's

face as he meets her in person for the first time, well, it's something else. Something I've never seen before.

Eager.

Intense.

Engrossed.

Her dark-brown hair is pulled back into a bun. Her lips are thin and her cheekbones are raised and so defined. She's wearing this baby-blue and soft-pink plaid shirt that's buttoned up just past her decent-size tits, leaving her cleavage exposed. She's also got on a pair of cutoff shorts that are practically covered by the shirt. And she's barefoot. And she's wearing this large silver chain with a locket that hangs down to the middle of her stomach.

As they begin to chitchat, my eyes drift to the studio space.

Like, holy shit!

In the center of the room is a black Bechstein Model B grand piano.

Now I'm salivating.

"Damn," I say, walking toward it. "This is amazing. I've never played one of these before."

"You play?" Savannah goes. "So do I."

"Have you tried it yet?" I ask.

"I have."

"And?"

"It sounds beautiful. It's tuned perfectly."

I glance back at the two of them, and my father looks creased because I've butted in.

"May I?" I ask.

"Ummmm, sure, Jaime," my father goes. "Savannah, why don't you come downstairs with me. I want to run over some things with you and Jackie now that I'm back."

"Sure," she says.

"Great."

"Jaime, have fun," she says.

The two of them leave, but they don't shut the door behind them.

Me, I take my seat on the bench and strip off my parka and stretch my arms and fingers. My knuckles crack. I have no idea what I'm going to play, so I warm up to get going. I've always done this one hand at a time. I gently set my right fingers down and go up two octaves. I go through the two octaves, like, ten times with each hand.

After that, I go through all twelve scales and play them in tenths. Then I increase the speed. I do this for about ten minutes and it feels great. All the other shit from the past two days, it feels irrelevant at the moment. Right now, it's just me and this piano. Me making my life art the way I do with the poems and the videos.

Once I'm done warming up, I think for a moment, before deciding to play that Youth Lagoon song "Montana."

I learned it right after I heard it first. I even played it once for that whore I was with. It was really cool when it happened. We were all alone together this one Saturday afternoon, and she was wearing a blue skirt with black socks pulled to her knees and a red cardigan buttoned up with a white collar shirt underneath it. She hopped onto the piano at my house and lay across it, resting her head on her hand, and asked if I'd play her something amazing.

Without hesitating, I went straight into "Montana."

She didn't know the song, but she really liked it when I played it for her.

She really did.

She smiled all the way through as I sang, and when I was done, she leaned down and lifted my chin and pulled my face right up to hers and we French-kissed.

It was the boss.

She was the best once.

Now she's just a stupid whore.

I count off and begin. Hearing my own fingers making this gorgeous sound gives me goose bumps.

I start singing. . . .

"Your honesty was killing me, the monsters in the room were all dancing to the music all around us . . ."

Right as I'm about to slip into the haunting chorus, another voice cuts in.

I stop playing. I'm totally put off. I turn around.

Standing in the doorway is this extremely pretty black chick who looks a little older than me.

She's probably my height, like five-seven. She's got this black hair that falls to her shoulders. The right side of it is shaved down and the four Black Flag bars are cut into it. Her eyes are intense. Her body looks pretty tight.

It's lean and fit and she's got a nice pair of tits.

A large earring hangs far from each ear, and they're different. A large gold loop with the Wu-Tang logo dangles from her left ear, and this silver-and-white feather hangs from her right. Around her neck is a large black necklace with some kind of imitation animal tooth tied to it.

She's wearing a white T-shirt with the sleeves rolled to her shoulders. SALEM is written in black Sharpie across the front. She's also got on these tiny black shorts and a pair of black socks that are pulled past her knees. Bright-red Keds with black shoelaces cover her feet.

And her septum is pierced. It's hot. I like everything I'm seeing a lot. But I'm still fucking irritated about what she did. And I tell her this.

I go, "That's really fucking rude, ya know."

"Excuse me?"

"What you just did. This wasn't a duet."

She makes a face. "Whatever. I was going to make what you were doing better."

"Is that right?"

"It is."

Now she smiles at me. And me, I smile back.

I love her attitude. It seems genuine, and I can usually tell if someone's a phony except for that one slut.

Swinging my legs over the bench, I go, "Salem, huh?"

She walks toward me. "Love that band."

"Me too. You make that shirt?"

"I did."

"Beautiful."

"So is your playing."

"Thank you," I tell her. "That's super nice of you to say."

Pause.

"Do you make a habit of interrupting like that, though?"

"Not usually. Close the damn door if you wanna be left alone next time. Fucking attitude."

"It's rude," I say.

She rolls her eyes. "Whatever, man. I heard it from downstairs. The scales you were playing. You're trained. I could tell by how you were warming up."

Even though I'm agitated by how she butted in, in reality, this is like the most perfect and rad and unbelievable moment ever. A real teen dream, just like that Beach House record. I'm skeptical, though. Like, maybe none of this is real. Maybe I slipped into an Oxy coma two weeks ago and none of this has really happened and I'm gonna wake up, with my bed drenched in sweat, and obsess about this dream, missing it, even the cruel parts, and I'll wonder what it all means, what it was really about. Then slowly, I'll forget the details, but the nostalgia will keep me yearning for that dream again, but nothing will ever be that good.

Wiping my forehead, I go, "How long have you been watching me?"

She shrugs. "Maybe since the seventh scale. I ain't really sure, though."

"What's your name?" I finally ask.

"Dominique."

"Nice name. I'm Jaime."

"I know," she says.

"How?"

"Jackie's my mother. She works for your father. You look just like him."

I rub my face and go, "Don't say that, please."

"You do, though."

"Just stop," I snap.

"Okay," she says.

Another pause.

"Can I sit with you?"

"Why?"

"Because I want to."

"There's other places to sit."

"Jaime," she says. "There's plenty of room on that bench too."

"You really want to?"

She nods.

"Fine." I swing my legs back over the bench and slide over to make more room for her.

As she sits down, she puts her hand on my shoulder. Her skin is so soft and her palm is sweating. Immediately, I think of that Postal Service line from their song "The District Sleeps Alone Tonight":

"Smeared black ink, your palms are sweaty, and I'm barely listening..."

Also, she smells really good. She's wearing Chanel. I know it because it's what my mother wears.

"Thanks for the seat, Jaime." She winks.

"You're welcome."

Dominique cracks her knuckles and starts playing that Knife song "Heartbeats," then cuts to that Shins song, "Caring Is Creepy," before rolling into "Dramamine" by Modest Mouse.

I'm super impressed. She's pretty good.

When she stops, she says, "I can't play like you, but I got some chops."

I roll my eyes.

She folds her arms. "What? Are you that surprised, man?"

"Kinda. I'm surprised when pretty much anyone outside of the kids who take lessons where I do can sit down and play like that. It's fucking rad. Do you take lessons?"

She shakes her head. "Nah. I taught myself."

"Seriously?"

"It's the truth. My older brother Jamal, he got this Casio keyboard for Christmas when he was twelve cos he wanted to be some kinda music producer, but then he never touched the thing. So I started messing with it and I couldn't stop."

"How old were you?"

"Ten."

"Fuck yeah."

"I was obsessed with it, and I'd spend hours after school learning how to play other people's songs. After a couple of months, I started making up my own and writing lyrics for them. I can also drum a little, and play some guitar, but my main thing is the keyboard synth."

"No shit."

"Swear on my grandmommy's grave. You play anything besides the piano?"

"Guitar, ukulele, synth, bass, and I drum a little too."

"You're like a prodigy, huh?"

"Something like that. My mother pushed it on me. Art comes first. Music comes first. They're the meaning of life in my house. They're the only things that matter."

"That sounds intense."

"It is."

"Your mother sounds really cool."

I look away from Dominique and nod. "Yeah, she is. She's a cool lady. She's my whole life, ya know."

"Your father's an awesome guy too."

I make a face. "Can we not talk about him, please?" My hands are shaking.

"Okay," she goes. "But he's a great guy."

"Just stop!" I snap. "Stop it. You don't know anything, all right? My mother's a great person. My father's a piece of shit."

"Hey," she goes. "Don't yell at me like that."

I bury my face in my hands. I can feel the Oxy leaving me.

It's a miserable thing. I get really short with people. I get pissed off way easier than I normally would.

"I'm sorry," I finally say. "I'm just tired. It's been a long couple of days. I should go find my father."

"Right."

Pause.

"But hey," Dominique says, as I stand and slide on my parka. "Can I have your number?"

"Why?"

She makes this exasperated face. "Are you always this wound tight? All I was thinking was that it might be nice to see you again before you leave."

"Even though I'm an asshole."

"Especially cos you're an asshole."

I laugh. "Sure," I say. "You ready?"

"Of course."

I give Dominique my number and she saves it and then texts me hers, and I leave the room as she resumes playing.

I think Dominique might be the coolest chick in the world.

A total babe.

Which means nothing in reality.

All the monsters I've met in my life have come gift wrapped in gold or killer band shirts.

28.

"I'M GOING TO TELL YOU THIS RIGHT NOW, JAIME. AND it's the absolute truth. Okay? If there's one thing about life that I really want you to understand, it's this."

I watched my mother take a drink of red wine and light another cigarette.

"Women will try to ruin you. They will sink their claws into you and rip you to fucking pieces. They'll destroy you, and they won't think twice about it."

She yawned and slid her hand under her sunglasses, rubbing her eyes.

"There's no such thing as a nice girl, Jaime. We're all fucking insane and we're all fucking evil. We will betray you. We will. And then we'll laugh behind your back afterward. We'll lie to your face like it's nothing. We'll make you believe that we love you, but it's not true. It'll never be true. All we want is to fucking tear you down and shred you to pieces because we can. Because it's so damn easy."

She poured another glass of wine and smiled.

"If it has a cunt, it is a cunt, Jaime. And there's no exception. Every woman you'll ever meet is a cunt. You understand me?"

I nodded and watched my mother drop a pill down her throat.

"So keep that in mind when you want to have a girl-friend. It doesn't matter how old that girl is, if she's got a pussy, she'll try her hardest to destroy you. She will ruin you, and she'll enjoy it."

I didn't say anything.

And she went, "Nod if you understand."

I understood.

"Good," she said. "Because it's important. I fucking ruined your father before he ruined me. That's why he got so violent in the end. He couldn't stand the fact that I could make him feel as small as a dead dandelion. That fucking prick."

She yawned again and twisted her cigarette out.

I was ten years old.

29.

I'VE NEVER BEEN THIS ALONE BEFORE. I'VE NEVER really belonged anywhere, belonged to anything, but I was never all alone. She's always been there. It doesn't matter what state she was there in, she was always there. It was something at least. It mattered. It was better than nothing.

And now she's gone.

I'm totally fucking alone.

I wanna hurt someone so bad. I do. I'd love to take a knife and cut somebody.

Watch them bleed.

Watch them hurt.

Watch them live through pain like I've felt all these years.

I'd shoot my father if I had a gun right now. I would. I'd shoot him in the face and laugh as pieces of his skull flew through the air. That fake. That materialistic prick. And then I'd steal a fucking airplane, and fly toward the sun as far as it can go. Then it's done. It's over. It crashes into the ocean, and the waves will swallow me, and no one will hear a thing.

I'll just be gone.

And who the fuck cares that they're alone when they're just gone.

30

DOMINIQUE TEXTS ME AN HOUR LATER. IT'S A PICTURE of a Casio keyboard synthesizer and she's written, *I make fucking magic with this.*

I text back, *It looks dope.*

Her response reads, *You're really cute.*

I roll my eyes. *Why tell me that?*

Cos it's true.

You barely saw me.

Whatever. You need to relax.

You don't know anything about me.

I'd like to start knowing.

Why?

Cos I just do. Why are you so fucking resistant, man? I'm hot.

This makes me smile, and I write, *I know you are.*

So what's your problem?

I don't trust you.

You don't know me yet.

No, I write back. *I don't trust you in general. I don't trust girls. I've never met one who wasn't evil.*

Dominique texts back a sad face, and I shut my phone off when I start thinking about how nice she's being to me.

31.

THE REST OF THE NIGHT: IT SUCKS. I MISS MY MOTHER.
I won't be able to talk to her for three more days. Dinner was weak. I said, like, three words and took two bites of the BLT that Leslie made. I also found out that Leslie teaches art history at the Academy of Art University. Also that neither her nor my father have talked to Kristen since last night. And that my father is "super bummed" and "totally frustrated" that his yearlong suspension from all Academy of Art property in the city was upheld after an appeal.

"It's so ridiculous," he fumed at the table. "The professor I punched doesn't even work there anymore. They fired him at the end of the semester. I mean, the jerk was being such an asshole to everyone that night. He was so smashed. His shirt was untucked, and his gut was showing. And he's the one who got all crazy after I laughed at him for bragging about being backstage at some Jack Johnson show in Hawaii. He totally lost his cool. Not me. *He* poked me in the chest and asked me if I had a problem with Jack Johnson. He started it. I mean, *he* was bragging about Jack Johnson. I wasn't the only one who was laughing either. And when he poked me again, like sorry, like all bets are off at that point. I never thought I'd break his nose. Hell, that grundle pig outweighs me by a hundred and fifty pounds. Who knew he'd drop like that? So fuck him and fuck the ruling," my father snarled. "And fuck Jack Johnson, too."

I excused myself before Leslie or my father had a chance to see me smile because of that story, and laugh because of that story.

Back in my room, I spent two hours chatting on Gmail with some kids who follow my Tumblr. Then I uploaded the poem from my walk home from school yesterday. After that, I smoked half an Oxy and read some poems by Frank O'Hara.

Around eleven, I tried to jack off but I never came. Three times, I worked myself up to the verge of ejaculation only to stop because the scenes in my head weren't the scenes I wanted to come to.

The image of my mother's stained body just won't leave. It comes in flashes, and I can still feel her sweat on my skin, and smell her vomit. Smell the iron in the puddles of her blood.

After I viewed all the comments my poem had already received, I deleted them. That's when I heard my father and Leslie go into their bedroom down the hall. The smell of dope then filled the air. I could hear them laughing and coughing and coughing some more. They listened to Pulp, the Violent Femmes, and Mazzy Star.

And then the house got still.

I left my room with a piece of foil, a whole baby blue, and my notebook.

Down in the kitchen now, I write the first page of a screenplay about a boy who robs a liquor store to buy a crate full of rare Smiths B sides and signed LCD Soundsystem records and the entire Nirvana catalog signed as well. Then he buys a one-way ticket to Baltimore to see a Future Islands show and ends up living on the floor of the apartment of one of the members of Beach House for a week.

I immediately throw the page away after I've written the last word on it. Then I grab this bottle of red wine from the kitchen counter and a wine opener from a drawer, and go downstairs because I haven't been down here yet.

It's so fucking nice. A huge part of me wants to smash everything down here. To break everything, throw it in the middle of the floor, and piss all over it. This chick isn't even my father's biological kid and her space is nicer than the house me and my mother have been living in for most of my life.

It's so wrong to me, but it's not her fault. Besides, I don't want anything from that bastard. My mother told me once that sometimes he'd ask her to dress up like a super-young girl, a young teen, and let him pretend that he was raping her.

When I asked her why she told me this, her face got white and she looked like she was going to be sick.

When I pressed her about it, she fumed, "Because you

need to understand how evil this man is. I'm not going be around forever, Jaime. If something happens, he will try and swoop in for you. He'll try and fuck your girlfriend, and she'll probably let him."

There are two black leather couches down here and two black leather reclining chairs. There's a record player and four stand-up speakers. Just like in the living room, a large flat-screen television hangs from a wall. I see an Xbox 360 and a Wii. Crates of records are stacked against another wall. There's a refrigerator down here.

But the most interesting thing are the six racks of clothes and shoes, each one at least fifteen feet long, that occupy the back half of the basement. Two of the racks are full of tops. One rack is full of bottoms. One rack is full of dresses, all kinds of sweet, pretty dresses.

My eyes are drawn immediately to this peach-colored sundress with these four white squares on the front. There's a certain unflattering innocence about it. The color makes me feel calm, but the dress itself has an aura of shame and guilt, too. Like this is the dress a girl wears on a date with some older boy who finally asked her out after she grew some tits. It's the same dress that girl wears when she loses her virginity in the backseat of some shitty Honda that smells like Newport cigarettes and Boone's Farm wine while a Jewel song plays from the speakers. It's the dress that soaks secretly in a bucket of warm water the next morning to get out all the blood that wasn't there before she got fucked.

I run my hand down it slowly before crunching the hem in my fist. I hold it up to my nose and bite down on it. I imagine the brutality of the girl putting this dress back on a month later for a date with another boy, a nice boy this time, a boy who will call and make plans to see her again, a boy who won't high-five his stupid friends and laugh every time he sees her, a boy who'll have to wait a long time before he gets to push up the bottom of this dress in a dark room because somebody has to be punished; somebody has to pay for a simple girl's disastrous foray into the false, bright spotlight.

I let go of the dress and turn away.

There's a bathroom down here, and Kristen's bedroom is across from it. The door is locked, though.

A picture of Basquiat is taped to it.

Pulling my tank top off, I walk over to the record player, and this is when I spot the acoustic guitar leaning next to a stack of crates.

I pick it up and sit down on the couch. It's a beautiful fucking piece too. A Gibson Hummingbird that's so clean. That looks like it's barely been touched, let alone used. If I had decided to turn this basement upside down and ruin its existence, I would've saved this.

I woulda also saved the stack of first pressing Replacement records and first pressing D'Angelo records that were sitting out.

Other things I woulda saved: This pair of sick fucking boots on one of the racks. This amazing poster of Madonna from the *Bedtime Stories* album. The *Pusher* film collection on DVD that's lying a few feet from me. And I woulda carefully peeled off the Basquiat picture and folded it perfectly and slid it into my wallet.

I pop my notebook open to continue working on my song, "Black Vulture."

I tune the guitar.

While I do, I think about the last forty-eight hours and how fucking insane they've been. My life has totally changed forever. Like, nothing will be the same as it was. That call from my mother in the middle of the night fucking altered my world the way a tornado destroys everything in its path once it touches the earth.

It's like James Morgan said a few months ago in an interview. Most of his books, they all take place over a week or so, but they're all superthick. All of them four hundred pages or more.

He was asked about that in the interview. Why they were so long when other writers can span a year in two hundred pages? And Morgan immediately rolled his eyes, wiped his nose, then laughed, before naming off everything he'd done in the last twenty-four: taking a shower with his chick and balling her in the butt before she moved the rest of her shit out of his apartment, scoring ten handfuls of pills, flying to New York and pissing his pants midflight after falling into a Xanax coma, having drinks with Selena Gomez to discuss a script he was developing for her to star in, him receiving an all-access pass to the M83 show later that night, making plans to go to the show with James Murphy, hanging out at *Vice* headquarters so they could tape him reading his short story "Fisting You on Your Boyfriend's Couch," which is from his short story book, *Where the Mean Girls Are*, buying a new pair of Asics and grabbing a burrito with Zachary German, and then finally getting to the studio where the interview was taking place and changing into the new suit he'd bought the day before, then talking to Chloë Sevigny on the phone for a half hour and text bombing Earl Sweatshirt.

"Point being," he said, grinning ear to ear, "there's a ton of fucking shit that can happen in a day. Important shit. Seminal shit. And I like to think about all of it and crib those details."

Dude's a fucking hero.

Once the guitar is tuned, I drop my blue heaven onto the foil and spend the next thirty seconds chasing the dragon.

When my eyes open, I'm back in the castle.

I open the bottle of wine and take a pull. It's really good too. Like, I've never tasted wine as good as this and I've drunk lots of wine in my short life. I was twelve the first time I got drunk. I puked. At first my mother thought I was puking blood, and freaked out until she realized it was red wine. She grounded me for a week, but then undid the grounding two days later when she got wasted while shopping and needed me to bike to the mall to drive her home.

I count off and begin playing.

First verse:

"Black vulture, black vulture, gliding through the sky, black vulture, black vulture, he's going for a ride . . . remains and death, doom in the air, black vulture gonna smell you, black vulture doesn't care . . . Cos he's a lurker, he sits and waits, to get what he wants, he knows his time is coming, he knows he's gonna shine, black vulture don't care, black vulture's gonna feed, black vulture's flying high, just waiting till you die . . ."

Second verse:

"Moving down the coast, these sunny warm days, the remains of our memories, buried in a grave, I thought I saw her in Texas, I thought I saw her die, I thought I saw her in Portland, I knew I'd made her cry, wings spreading wide, cutting through the wind, black vulture's gonna catch you, gonna swallow all your sins . . ."

Bridge:

"Those sticks and stones, gonna break them lovely bones, feeding on your misery, stealing your ivory throne . . . he breaks into your dreams, he lives in your shadow, laughing at your simple life, he's winning all the battles . . ."

I play what I have three times before setting the guitar down and chasing the dragon some more. I've become better at playing the guitar than the piano, which means I've become really fucking good.

In the last six months, I've self-recorded and produced six songs under the name Tiger Stitches. The first two were called "Cuddling" and "Blood Zebra." I used a drum machine I stole from this place called the Instrument Center. Me and my mother used to go there all the time. My two electric guitars, my bass, and both amps were purchased there. So were my two keyboards and my sampler. I used to love that place. Then the store manager, this fucking crusty loser who wore tie-dye shirts, baggy pants, and shorts and sandals, exposed himself to my mother. He cornered her in his office after she used the restroom while we were there once. He groped her and told her he'd give her a thousand dollars' worth of free gear if she gave him a blow job.

She laughed in his gross, fat face, and he kicked us out of the store.

Two weeks later I jacked the drum machine right from under that dude's double chin. He never got that hummer, but we got that free gear.

Anyway, I named the drum machine Coady after my favorite drummer in the world, Coady Willis (Murder City Devils, Big Business), and over an eight-hour session one night, I recorded the two songs, and then mixed them on my computer using Ableton.

At first I was pretty bummed about the sound quality. You could tell it was recorded in a garage with no soundproofing. Also, the fucking cops showed up three times. Not only did they finally write a ticket for the noise on their last visit, my mother was super wasted and threw an egg at their squad car when they were pulling out of the driveway, which resulted in two additional tickets. One for vandalism. And one for public intoxication (after she threw the egg, she ran after the car and stepped off the property for, like, three seconds).

Whatever.

I didn't think it was funny at the time but right now, sure, it's making me smile pretty big because it reminds me of how much she can care when she wants to.

After, like, a week of debating it with myself, I finally decided to release the songs. I created Bandcamp, SoundCloud, and Facebook accounts and uploaded the tracks. I fucking spread my beautiful filth all over the web, posting links to the pages, like, six times a day on my Tumblr, my regular Facebook, and my Twitter. Then I e-mailed the songs to at least three hundred media outlets. I just fucking pressed that shit onto people, because that's what you have to do. Like, it's insane how accessible your art can be to people now. I could start a band tomorrow and a week from now, we can release a digital mix tape or an EP and have a thousand fucking listeners from all over the world a few days later. That's some beautiful shit right there. A totally built-in advantage that my generation has over any other generation.

Back to the songs now.

It sorta worked for me doing what I did. Kids really dug it. After a month, both songs had over ten thousand listens, and kids were sharing them on social media and writing reviews of Tiger Stitches's music.

So I pushed forward with it. I decided to release a four-song EP.

The songs were:

1. "Hard Palms"
2. "Night Diamond"
3. "Fogman"
4. "She's Pushing Her Luck (She's Still Winning)"

I needed a better place to record this time, though. After thinking about it for a couple of weeks, the only place that made sense was the band room at my school. So I staked out the place for two weeks. I snuck out of my house at night and biked to the school and did surveillance and figured out who came and went after school hours and before school hours. I got the schedules down perfectly. I saw some pretty incredible shit too.

Like the head volleyball coach, saw her and this freshman girl, who made all-conference, pull into the school parking lot together late at night. The passenger-side door opened, and the dome light came on, and the freshman chick got out, but not before kissing the coach on the lips.

Also, I saw two of the English teachers and the head librarian smoking a blunt in the parking lot one night while AC/DC blared from one of their car stereos.

Rad.

The most fucked thing I saw, though, was the blow job that my, like, fifty-year-old, married-with-three-kids science teacher got from a student, Byron Malone. It disgusted me so much. It pissed me off real bad. Dude called me a faggot at least ten times every day. He would swing at the schoolbooks in my hands while I walked down the hallway. Sometimes it worked and my books would go slamming to the ground, which everyone seemed to get a big kick out of. A couple of times, when I wasn't paying attention, that turd burglar pegged me in the back of the head with a basketball. All this pseudo-macho hate talk directed at me and there he was, on his knees, blowing some overweight science teacher with gray hair, glasses, and brown-stained teeth.

Man, what a loser. I mean, to call me a fucking faggot and a queer every day to get some laughs out of the blubber butts who attend that awful school. Then I see him actually being gay with some disgusting older man.

I was so upset.

I also thought it was sort of funny.

How he was the one on his knees with a dick in his mouth. My first reaction was to expose this douche, out both of them, but then I decided not to. Doing something like that woulda made me no better than him. Actually, it woulda put me on a lower level, and that's not something I could've lived with. I'm better than that meathead. I'm better than all those trolls.

Like, I'm sure he hates himself, which is why he was so cruel to me to begin with. Just total deflection. If you call enough people a faggot enough times, I guess everyone else thinks it's impossible for you to be one. So I let *that* sleeping dog lie, although I did extract a little bit of revenge against that terrible dude.

One afternoon I snuck out of the school building after I asked to use the bathroom. I walked out to the parking lot and found his new Beamer and broke into it with a hanger. Then I took my switchblade and cut a small hole in the upholstery on the back of the driver's-side seat, dumped a can of sardines into it, then sealed it back up with superglue. I also slashed his back tires and keyed that nice paint job.

Anyway, on the night of April 13, when the janitor left the school for the night and the coast was totally fucking clear, I climbed to the roof and pulled an amp, a keyboard, and two guitars up to me with the three bedsheets I'd tied together to use like a rope.

Then I popped open this access panel with a crowbar, and I was in.

For the next nine hours, I played my fucking heart out and recorded my four amazing tracks. The acoustics of the room were pretty all right (so much better than my tiny garage). It was so sick. So dope. Then, before I left the building, as the sun slowly rose outside, I took a piece of chalk and wrote this on the blackboard:

Ten best bands of the new millennium:
1. LCD Soundsystem
2. Beach House
3. M83
4. Thee Oh Sees
5. Lamborghini Dreams
6. Youth Lagoon
7. The Fresh & Onlys
8. Tycho
9. Future Islands
10. Deerhunter

Then I wrote, *Run out of school now & go listen & learn, bitches!!*

Then, *Dickpigs! All of you!*

Then, *James Morgan is God!*

And then, *Purity Ring & Salem rule too.*

Also, *The principal is a total d-bag. Fucking Hallway Monster Booger Pussy! Yeah!*

Then I threw away all the stained black pieces of foil, the empty six-pack of Coronas I'd taken from my house, and the half-eaten peanut butter and jelly sandwich I'd made, and fucking bailed back home.

When it was time for me to get up and go to school

just an hour later, I told my mother that I wasn't feeling well, then shoved a finger down my throat when she wasn't looking to make myself throw up (which I did. A couple times actually).

My mother called the school and told them I wasn't going to be there. She left a couple of hours later with her Realtor to go look at buildings for the dance school she's been talking about starting for at least ten years and never will. She just never will do it. She doesn't have the toughness to do *that*. To be responsible for more than just me. I mean, she's struggling just trying to take care of me.

While she was gone, I got to work mixing the tracks. This time I used Pro Tools. She bought me the program after I played her my first two recordings. When she heard the songs, water flooded her eyes.

Then this soft, sweet smile spread across her face. I remember thinking how I hadn't seen her smile in three days when that happened.

"Blood Zebra" ended and there was silence for at least a minute. My heart was beating fast. The thing is, I don't share my art with my mother. She knows I'm great at the piano because she hears me practice and comes to my recitals. But those songs aren't mine. They're somebody else's.

Truth is, before that night, I was terrified to show her my own, original work, because she's a harsh critic. She takes art *that* serious. It's as important as breathing to her. My mother's favorite quote is from Nietzsche: "Art is the highest task and proper metaphysical activity of this life." That quote lives in at least ten different places in our house.

My mother was a pure artist. At one point, she was considered one of the top artists in her medium. That's insane. She was that good.

I've seen tapes of her dancing. She was mesmerizing onstage, under those sharp, hot lights. Me, I know nothing about dancing. Nothing about the ballet. It doesn't interest me. But every time I watched her on those tapes, I was transcended into the story she was telling with her body. Watching her dance was like reading a book. I understood what she was saying and I didn't want it to end.

This is why I was so nervous to play her the songs. When I was recording them, I knew she wasn't paying attention. She was doing drugs and drinking scotch and watching Terrence Malick movies in the living room.

I've heard her scathing opinions about people's work that isn't up to her standards. The things she's said to describe their underachieving, lifeless work, and the cruel, cold delivery and pitch of her words. Hearing something like that from your own mother will wrap your heart in ice and fuck with you for the rest of your life.

It's nasty. And I'm her son. And all she wants me to be in life is a successful, beautiful, popular artist. There's a standard there as high as the heavens, and it would break our relationship if she didn't like it.

My mother, she started clapping. She even stood up like people did for her after she performed.

She loved it. That's when I asked her for the Pro Tools. She delivered that to me, and I delivered my four-song EP, *Peril Alley*, as Tiger Stitches, a week later.

To date, each song has gotten over twenty thousand plays.

To date, Tiger Stitches is the best fucking name ever.

After another gulp of wine, I grab my pen and start cribbing the third verse. Maybe three minutes later, it's done.

And then I play "Black Vulture" for the first time ever all the way through.

32.

I'M WALKING OUT OF THE BASEMENT BATHROOM when I hear a door open upstairs and this girl laughing and high heels thumping against the floor.

I grab my tinfoil and hit the rest of the pill real quick. Then I look around the room, panicked, then spot a garbage can. I throw away the foil as the heels begin descending the stairs to the basement.

Wipe the sweat from my face with my hand and wish I was upstairs in my bedroom.

Then I see Kristen and do not wish that anymore. Not at all.

The girl is so lovely. So pretty. Just absolutely perfect-looking. I mean, she looks nearly identical to Ivanka Trump. I'm totally serious. It's sort of bizarre, actually. Kinda creepy in the way that kinda creepy can be super awesome.

She's got this really healthy blond hair that's parted in the middle and hangs down past her shoulders. She's prolly an inch taller than me. Her body is very lean and her skin is tan. Her lips are thin and her teeth are snow-white and her eyes are bright blue.

Kristen stops at the bottom of the stairs and grins. "Well,

hey there," she goes, then winks. "Another stripper waiting for me when I get home. My mother is so rad."

I don't get it at first until I realize I'm still shirtless and we've never met before.

I'm embarrassed now and I cover my face with my hand.

"She's got the best taste, too," Kristen continues. "You're a total babe."

Swinging my eyes back on her, I say, "I'm Jaime. Your stepbrother. The kid that got made when Justin donated his sperm."

"Ha," she goes, and starts walking toward me. "You refer to your father as a sperm donor. It's nice to know there's someone else in the world who does that too."

Kristen stops just a few inches from me. She smells like Chanel, cigarettes, peaches, and booze.

It ain't bad.

"Hi," she goes.

"Yo."

She sighs, then reaches toward my face with her hand.

"Whoa." I duck away. "What the fuck are you doing?"

"Helping you."

"With what?"

She pulls a black compact from her handbag and flips it open, holding up the small mirror in front of me.

"Fuck," I groan.

"What is that?"

"It's nothing," I say.

"It's not nothing."

"It's nothing important," I say, looking around for a towel.

"I got you." She pulls out a couple of tissues from her bag and a bottle of water which she opens and pours onto the tissue. "Take it," she says.

"Thank you."

I run the wet tissue all over my face a couple of times to rub off the black from the foil I used to smoke.

That shit can get everywhere.

It *does* get everywhere.

When I'm done, Kristen grabs the tissues from my hand and says, "Missed a couple spots, Jaime."

She leans right into my face and carefully cleans off the rest of the black.

She winks again. "I like people who still play in the dirt. Never growing up is so much fun."

I roll my eyes when she turns around. A large bulge has formed in the crotch of my jeans, and I quickly readjust myself as best I can.

"Do you often hang around in strange houses without your shirt on and drink very expensive bottles of wine by yourself?"

"Excuse me?"

"This." She picks up the bottle I've been drinking and turns back to me. "This is a hundred-dollar bottle of pinot noir you've been smashing. I'm surprised this wasn't all over your face too, you messy, messy boy."

"Shit," I say. "I had no idea it was that expensive. It was sitting in a basket. Like a gift basket."

"What's that gotta do with anything?"

I shrug. "It's a gift basket."

"My mother and your father have very rich friends. Every gift in this house is fucking expensive."

"Right."

She puts the bottle to her lips and takes a drink. "Tasty," she goes. "Out of all the wine in this house, you open this one. You've got great taste."

"It was a lucky pick."

"You can't say that here, dude."

"What do you mean?"

"Everything you choose while you're staying here is because you've got great taste. It'll be easier for you that way."

"Why?"

"Just because." She takes another drink. "People expect that."

"I don't give a fuck about anyone's expectations. Like, if not living up to expectations is gonna be a *thing* this week, I'll have a few things to toss around that'll trump my lack of experience in the area of red wine."

"Great," she says, and takes another pull.

I like her a little bit already, which is nice because I wasn't planning to.

"Come on," she goes, waving me over to her. "Come

here." She hands me the bottle of wine and then gently pushes me onto the couch and stands over me with her hands on her hips.

I take a pull and eye her up and down and up and down.

She's wearing these black floral lace stockings and a very large white Tearist T-shirt with the sleeves cut off of it and a V cut down the middle of it. A large silver necklace with a red pendant hangs from her neck. Rings wrap around every finger. And a pair of scuffed-up white heels cover her feet.

"I was listening to *Living 2009-Present*, like, two days ago," I tell her, and take a drink. "They're so good. I love them."

Kristen's smile, like, doubles as I hand her back the bottle, and she goes, "Yes. You. Just yes."

"Excuse me?"

"You're fucking cool. I see the guitar out and the notebook. You jack a pricey bottle of wine and get drunk in the basement by yourself, then reference Tearist within five minutes of me meeting you. I'm stoked." She takes a monster drink, then says, "Yasmine Kittles is prolly one of my top five favorite singers and performers easily. I love that bitch."

"She's good."

"I drove down to L.A. during spring break and saw them play with Chelsea Wolfe."

"Rad," I say. "Did you use Ivanka Trump's ID to get into the show?"

Kristen's face gets super happy-looking. "You're a little fucking hustler. A charmer."

"Nah."

"No," she says. "You are. You're a little Justin Miles, just sweetening up the air in every room you walk into."

"Screw you," I rip, pushing myself off the couch. "Just screw you, Kristen."

"Hey," she goes.

I slide past her and pick up my tank top and notebook off the ground.

She grabs ahold of my arm. "What the hell was that all about?"

Ripping my arm free, I go, "You know nothing about me, okay? Nothing. Yet you've got the nerve to say I'm like that evil bastard. Fuck you. I'm nothing like that prick. You have no idea who I am. How dare you?"

"Jaime."

"That's a cunt thing to do to a boy. Backstabbing girls with dirty mouths say shit like that."

"Hey!" She grabs my arm again. "Don't blow up on me."

"Piss off."

She jams her other hand into my chest. "You don't get to intrude in my life and treat me this way. Now *that's* some real asshole-type shit right there. Just like *my* father. Only little bitch boys with annoying daddy complexes and filthy souls say shit like you did. Is that what you are, man? A little bitch boy?"

I pull my arm free. "Stop it," I say.

"Answer the fucking question."

"I don't have a filthy soul," I snap.

"And I'm not a backstabbing bitch."

"Great," I say.

"It's the best."

I throw my shirt back on and Kristen starts laughing. The tension crumbles straight off my shoulders now and I start laughing too.

It's nice. Laughing with a girl is nice sometimes.

"Drink," she goes, pushing the bottle at my face. "Keep drinking, Jaime Miles."

I take two big gulps. She finishes the bottle.

"What now?" I go.

"Lots of things," she says.

She goes over to the fridge and opens it and comes back over with two bottles of Corona.

"This work for you?" she asks.

"Sure."

"Great."

She pops off both bottle caps with a pink lighter and hands me one.

"Cheers," she says.

"Cheers."

"To strippers paid for by my mother."

"And Ivanka Trump look-alikes."

"Word, dude."

"Yeah, word." We clank our bottles together. "Word, forever," I finish.

33.

ME AND KRISTEN, WE'RE ON THE BACK DECK A FEW minutes later. She's sitting Indian-style with her back against the hot tub, smoking a cigarette, and I'm sitting on a short bench.

That Naked and Famous song "Young Blood" is playing from her phone.

"So, like, how are you holding up, man?" she asks. "Your head must be a blur right now."

Shrugging, I go, "Sort of. But I don't think anything can faze me really. I've been dealing with crazy my whole life, and this is just another thing."

"No way," she goes. "You found your mother dying."

"Blood and vomit don't scare me. Those were the only two things that were new this time."

"Damn," she says. "I'm so sorry for you. But I'm glad you're here."

"I don't get that. How can anyone be happy that I'm here?"

"You're my stepbrother, man. We're family."

"No, we're not, Kristen. My father would have to be family, and he's not. He never will be. Fuck him. I've been alive for fourteen years and this is the first time I've seen my father and talked to him. He's never reached out."

"That's not true, Jaime."

"Yes, it is!" I snap. I take a swig of beer and go, "I bet you're an awesome person, but excuse me when I say, you don't know shit. That prick ruined my mother. He fucking hit her and stalked her after she left. Since I've been able to walk, I've been dealing with those demons and fighting those monsters. And him, he's been living this posh fucking life while me and my mother have been trapped in the world he fucking destroyed. So fuck that. My mother had a bad day, and that's the only reason I'm here. He's more excited about Savannah being here than me."

Kristen nods and says, "Jaime, he's more excited about Savannah than anything in his life right now."

"Whatever," I go. "Point is, just cos you say you're happy I'm here doesn't mean you really are."

"I am," she goes. "So many times I've thought about reaching out to you on Facebook or Twitter."

"But you didn't."

She takes a drag. "No . . . I didn't. But would it have mattered if I had?"

I don't say anything.

"Would you have even responded to me if I had?"

"No."

"Exactly."

I finish my beer and say, "This is all so fucked."

"Let's unfuck it then."

I shrug. "We can't."

Kristen pulls out a cocaine bullet, twists the cap off, and loads a bump.

Me, I only know what a cocaine bullet is because my mother has one.

Actually, she has four. And she has these personalized snooters made out of silver too.

"Love my life," Kristen says, then drops the blast pony into her nose.

She holds the bullet out and offers me some.

"I'm good," I tell her.

"Come on," she goes. "Live a little."

"I've got Oxys with me. That's my jam."

"Really? How many?"

"Enough."

"Which is?"

"A lot," I say. "You want one?"

"Not right now. But yeah, sometime."

I finish my beer and she goes, "I want you to play me the song you were working on."

"All right."

"And we'll drink cold beers all night and talk about everything."

"Why?"

"Cos that's what you do when you're on cocaine. You talk about everything and you pretend you know every band and every song in the world and you make certain it's known that you heard all of it first. It's a perfect kind of awesome just puking up words like they'll last."

I stand up and stretch my arms.

"One more thing," she says.

"What's that?"

"We really can unfuck whatever we want."

I make a face.

"We're kids, Jaime. And we can do whatever we want. We will do whatever we want. If we wanna make something happen, we will. As long as we're passionate, dude. As long as we care. Anything in the world we want to be or do is in our grasp. We just have to care enough and show the fuck up."

"You're so high right now," I tell her.

"I'm so fucking right, too." Then she winks at me as I grab her hands and pull her gently to her feet.

34.

"JUST LOOK AT KANYE, FOR INSTANCE. HE'S A certified motherfucking genius. And all those people hating on him or trying to figure the dude out are doing nothing but feeding the monster they say they despise. They're the ones making him bigger. It's all rooted in jealousy, too. The people sitting around judging Kanye, and talking shit, are just jealous of him and can't stand the fact that he's smarter than them. Kim Kardashian did it right. She did him right. What a rad life she has cos she said yes to *Yeezus*. I'm jealous that she gets to push those beautiful chocolate Kanye babies out. The man is brilliant and beautiful. There's nobody I'd rather fuck on this whole damn planet than him."

Kristen snorts the huge line of cocaine lying across the cover of the Babyshambles record *Down in Albion.*

I'm sitting on the couch again, drinking a Corona. I pull my phone out. It's still shut off, so I turn it back on, as Kristen drinks from this bottle of chilled white wine.

"Tyler gets so fucking jealous when I talk about Kanye," she says. "So now he hates Kanye's music, even though he used to love it more than me. Isn't that crazy? Jealousy made him hate something he used to adore. How insecure is that? It's kind of psycho, ya know. Like, Tyler's a total babe. We've been together for over two years and I love him and I think he's really cool, but he'll never be Kanye. Tyler's a coke dealer from a wealthy family. He's got a decent-size dick and can be totally fashionable at times, but I find it really gross and psychotic that he's so bothered by my admiration of Kanye. It's bizarre and totally unhealthy. He's been dealing coke for six years. It's all he does, Jaime."

"But you love him."

"I do. Even though he can be a prick. I love that boy so much, dude."

She takes a swig. "I love the free blow, too."

Kristen falls onto the couch, next to me. She lies on her back and drapes her legs over my lap.

I can see her crotch. I can see the lace underwear she's wearing and the soft skin of her inner thighs.

"What about you, Jaime?"

"What about me?"

"Is there some lucky girl who gets to call you her boyfriend back in Joliet?"

"Nope." I take a drink.

"Really?"

"It's the truth," I say.

"How come?" she asks. "You're a babe."

"I don't need to have someone in my life who's just going to make it more complicated. Girls want attention.

They don't want love. They don't want anything genuine. The girls I know are phonies to their core."

"Ouch," she goes.

"It's true. The only girl I know who's not a fake is my mother. She's as real as it gets. But she had to play the role of my father, too. And she never backed down from anyone. In sixth grade, football is mandatory at my school. Twice early in the season, she punched out some other kid's loser dad during practice for making fun of me. I've never seen anything like it. My mother defended me, and it was swift, precise, and cold. All the other fathers and their kids were speechless afterward. So were the coaches. My mother reacted like a wild animal that got cornered. It was so fierce, Kristen. My mother's eyes were black and thirsty. Both those guys got dropped to the grass. Their noses were bleeding. I got kicked off the team and both men filed restraining orders against my mother. When you actually think about that, I mean, it doesn't get any more real than that."

Kristen scoots her bottom closer to me, and part of her right leg falls into my lap.

My face turns bright red.

"Well, hey there."

I push her leg away and say, "Come on. That's fucked up."

"I just moved my leg, Jaime." She's smiling.

"Stop."

"Stop what?" she asks, after taking another drink. "There's nothing to be embarrassed about. We're not blood related. It's a fucking boner."

"Right," I say, while running a hand down my face. "Anyway, I don't believe in needing a girlfriend. It's a waste of time. Even when you're giving them all the attention you can possibly give, it's never enough. You all just want more. I've watched dudes attempt to give the world to their girlfriends, only to have it not be enough. They get dismantled instead. And then they get crushed. Like, I have no problem if a girl isn't into it anymore and wants out. Just say something. But most of you don't ever do that. Instead, you torture that guy. It's so sick. While he's saving up money to buy you something nice or he's spending all his free time writing a song for you, you're fucking trashing him to all your evil friends and laughing behind his back. While he's opening himself up, you bitches are out talking to other dudes and flirting with them and exchanging fucking phone numbers, then playing it off like the guy just wants to be your friend. Bullshit."

Kristen looks almost stunned. Appalled even.

And I go, "Trust me. Every guy you've met since you started middle school was only being nice to you because he wants you naked, and your legs spread. Regardless if that ever happens or not doesn't matter. All you sluts want is attention, and more attention. It's so gross. It lets you get close to this new guy and figure out if he's got more money and a nicer car and more popular friends. None of you even care what you're doing to the boy you already have. The one you supposedly like so much. You're all whores, ya know."

"Jesus Christ," she says.

"It's a fact. And this is why I don't need a girlfriend. Just like I don't need a group of friends, just like I don't need anyone else to justify my tastes in music and books and movies. I watch these girls who go to my school, right. And they're so pathetic, some of them. It's like they need to have a boyfriend and when they break up with the guy they just wrecked, they jump right into another relationship. It's twisted. My happiness will never be defined by my inclusion of a girl in my life. A relationship will never make me feel more complete or whole. From what I've seen, they cause more misery than joy. I can't even fathom wasting the amount of time some people do talking about this other person and how much this other person sucks or doesn't make them happy. They spend hours doing it. They spend hours shitting on the person behind their back and saying the meanest things about them. All those hours spent doing something so meaningless and trivial while they could've been using that time to do something significant. Something the world might remember them by."

"I get it now," says Kristen. "I just wanna know who the little cunt is who did this to you."

"What do you mean?"

"Clearly some girl destroyed you, Jaime. That kind of bitterness doesn't come naturally. You have to earn that kind of hate, dude."

"Right."

"Somebody fucking hurt that heart of yours."

I take a drink and shrug. "It was my mistake."

"How's that?"

"I trusted her."

Pause.

"That'll never happen again."

My phones buzzes, like, eight times right after I say this. I take it out of my pocket and am shocked to see, like, six texts from Dominique. The last one saying, *It would be better if you told me to fuck off than ignore me, dude. Grow a pair.*

This feeling of loss and sadness quickly sinks into me. I'm confused. She actually wants to kick it with me. After reading the other texts, it's clear she wants to see me and spend time with me.

I don't get it.

Kristen stands up and walks back over to the Babyshambles record and I go, "Question for ya."

"Ask away," she says. "Whatever you wanna know."

"Do you know some girl named Dominique?"

Kristen immediately looks back over her shoulder and goes, "Totally, bona fide, like hot, like plus-ten black girl Dominique whose mother works for my father's galleries?"

I nod.

"Yes, I know her. I love that girl. She's the coolest bitch I know. Why?"

"I met her today at the Transmission Gallery. She asked me for my number and keeps texting me."

"Whoa," snaps Kristen. "Come again?"

"She asked me for my number and I gave it to her and she keeps texting me to hang out while I'm here."

"And you've said yes, right? You've totally made, like, ten million plans already and are gonna see her every chance you get."

I make a face and watch her lean down and pound another rail. Then I say, "Not exactly. I shut my phone off after she texted me a ton."

"Are you crazy, Jaime?"

"I don't know, actually."

"You know how many guys would fucking kill to have Dominique Taylor texting them to hang out?"

"No," I say. "I don't. And that's why I'm fucking skeptical. Like, why the hell would she be all over me if all these other dudes you know would line up for her? I don't trust it."

"She's a sweetheart, Jaime. I know her. She doesn't have a mean bone in her body."

"I just think it's strange."

Kristen slams another drink of white wine and goes, "What were you doing when you met her?"

"I was playing the piano. She interrupted me. It was rude."

"You're some kind of piano master, right? You're like this amazing pianist."

"I'm good. Sure."

"Well, that's it, man. Dominique is a great musician. Her band is dope."

"What band?"

"Her band, man. Vicious Lips. They're pretty incredible. They've actually got a pretty nice following in SF."

"You've seen them?"

"Duh, man. A bunch of times. I usually design the clothes she wears for the shows."

"Dope."

"So you got nothing to worry about. If she's reaching out like that, it means she wants to kick it with you. She likes dudes who know music and can play it. I'm pretty sure you got both those covered, homie. Don't blow it by being such a dick about girls."

Kristen falls back onto the couch again and I go, "Is that what this all is then?"

"What?"

"The racks full of clothes. It's like a section in a department store. You make all of these?"

"Most of them, yeah. I've got my own clothing company called Ambitious Kids. I've got over ten contracts with boutiques and shops around the city. It's good. I've made over twenty thousand dollars this year so far. There's, like, six dope bands I dress for free. They wear my clothes onstage, and people always ask who made it for them. It's a beautiful thing, Jaime Miles. Now lemme hear this song you wrote."

"Sure."

I pick up my guitar and drop my notebook between my feet and start playing. She seems to like it too. She's smiling and nodding her head up and down at least.

Then I hit the last verse. . . .

"Blood is simple, tissue tough, bones in the desert, sunsets full of lust, the remains of the day left lying in a pile, these birds of prey just swarming in style, we pillaged and we scoured, we gave away our own, we battled and we won, then we died all alone . . . black vulture coming hard, black vulture coming fast, black vulture gonna get ya, black vulture eats you last. . . ."

That's it. I'm done. Leaning the guitar against the couch, I go, "It's good, right."

"It is, Jaime. You're really good. I can't believe you're only fourteen."

"Age doesn't matter once you've been playing long enough. That's a beautiful guitar, too. Whose is it?"

"Your father's."

"He plays?"

"Ha," snaps Kristen. "He can play 'All Along the Watchtower' and maybe 'Tambourine Man.' That's it, though. He hasn't touched it in a year probably."

"Figures," I say. "That fake artist."

"He owns the galleries."

"He doesn't own the art, though. He'll never be *that*."

Kristen jumps off the couch again, and she snorts the last line on the record.

Man, she's a total babe. And she's smart with great fucking taste and totally ambitious.

She's perfect, and I bet she'd be a fucking monster to date.

Kristen grabs her bag and pulls out a Sharpie. "We should get tattoos while you're here."

"I'm fourteen."

"Who cares?" she laughs. "I know a guy. He's got a gun and a basement."

"Sounds like something I'd hate for the rest of my life."

"Maybe," she says. "But say we got words done on us."

"Yeah."

"Write what word you'd get on the place you'd get it done."

She tosses me the Sharpie and takes another drink of wine. I think about it for a few seconds before sliding the cap off and writing *Yeezus* on the inside of my upper left arm.

"Great fucking choice," Kristen goes, taking the Sharpie from me.

Sitting back down beside me, she goes, "I don't know if I can top that."

"Sure you can."

And then she writes a letter on the knuckle of each finger on her left hand.

She turns to me and shows me. The letters spell *cunt*.

I don't say anything, and she goes, "Pretty fitting, right?"

"You shouldn't take what I said personally. I don't even know you."

"You said all of us, meng. All of us."

"Right."

Pause.

"It's just how I see it."

Kristen smiles and says, "I like that you stand by what you say. Even if I think it's totally fucked and wrong, you're honest at least. It's more than I can say about pretty much anyone else I know."

"And it doesn't make you hate me?"

"No," she goes. "It makes me wanna beat up the bitch who did this to you."

"Rad."

"You're rad, Jaime."

She hands me the bottle of wine. I take a swig and then lean back.

"So you really think I should see what's up with Dominique?"

"I do," she answers. "At least give it a shot and see what she wants. They broke the fucking mold when they made her, man. What's the worst that could happen?"

"I don't know."

"Maybe you'll fall in love with her and stay in San Francisco."

"Yeah, right," I go. "No girl is that powerful."

"Oh, you'd be surprised, Jaime Miles. If a girl can make you hate every other girl in the world, why can't another girl make you wanna stay in the city you met her in?"

"My mother would be all alone without me."

"Hopefully your mother would get behind your choice to be happy."

"It's more complicated."

"Complications are just excuses, man."

"Maybe in your world, Kristen."

"Hey," she says, grabbing my arm. "It's your world now too. All of this, everything, it's all yours, and it's a fabulous fucking world if you let it be fabulous to you."

35.

"LISTEN, FIRST OFF, I JUST WANNA APOLOGIZE ABOUT
last night. I shut my phone off and forgot that I did. I didn't
see your texts till really late. So I'm sorry. It was lame. And I
do wanna see you again, Dominique."

This is the voice mail I leave for her before I do two hundred crunches and a hundred push-ups.

When I'm done showering and getting dressed—tight
black Levi's, white V-neck, red-and-navy flannel, white
Keds—I break a blue in half and swallow one half of it, then
smoke the other one while I listen to Nirvana's *Unplugged*.

Before I leave my father's house, I stand in front of the
large mirror on the wall. I hate me and what I look like and
how alone I am even though I'm glad I'm alone right now.

My father wants to have a huge dinner tonight at this
really nice restaurant called the Cigar Bar & Grill. He wants
the whole family there and Savannah, and Kristen's boyfriend, Tyler, and a few others.

It sounds terrifying to me. Leslie is the one who told me
this when I was in the kitchen eating a fruit plate that I made
plus some toast and orange juice.

Anyway, the only thing I wanted to know was where

Amoeba Music was. She told me that, too. She was drinking champagne straight from the bottle, and there was a joint sitting behind her ear.

I wanted to tell her that my mother likes to smoke blunts in the morning and drink whiskey. I wanted to brag about that until I realized how fucking trivial and stupid it was.

Like, just go and buy records, dude.

And by the time dinner comes around, I'll be so high and numb that none of these people will be able to get to me at all. The castle protects me. Not even a cannonball can dent my glass fortress.

36

THE RECORDS I BUY ARE:

1. "New Country," Beachwood Sparks
2. *Matangi*, M.I.A.
3. *Life Is Good*, Nas
4. *Tropic of Scorpio*, Girls Against Boys
5. *Stranger Ballet*, Poison Control Center
6. "Big Black Delta," Big Black Delta

This is easily the best record store I've ever been in. I'm here for three fucking hours that feels like ten minutes. Aisle after aisle after aisle with records I never even knew existed from bands that I fucking love to death. It's awesome. I only wish my mother was here. Cos if there's anyone who would appreciate Amoeba Music more than me, it's her.

See, my mother got me into music right away. Not just playing it but listening to it and reading about it and collecting it and educating myself about it.

We spent so many afternoons at record stores. She played her records constantly and talked about them and what they meant to her life and all the concerts she went to with her friends.

She even talked about how her and my father both had an obsession with music. She told me once that a couple of times their collection got so big that they had to hold sidewalk sales so they could get rid of them and make more room in their tiny apartment.

I remember so clearly the night she told me this. She was in a great fucking mood and we'd just finished eating the dinner I helped her make. We were in the living room, and she was pretty buzzed on wine and dope. I could smell it all over her. I put on the Magnetic Fields record *Distant Plastic Trees*, and this huge smile eclipsed her face and she stood up and started bopping around. While she did this, she said, "There were a few moments, not many, Jaime, when your father was so perfect and wonderful in my eyes. Before you were born, when we first moved into that small and cold apartment on the Lower East Side. We had nothing back then. I was coming up really fast but your dad, he was kind of lost, ya know. He was slowly coming to terms with the reality that he was never going to cut it as an artist and was always going to be on the outside, ya know, just one of those people who hang around, hang on to the creators without having the ability to make something that anyone cares about. But he tried. And it was cute. And he knew what he was talking about at parties and openings and performances, but he never had the talent or the vision or the instincts to grab an audience's attention, and that's what you do as an artist. That's your ultimate job. To arouse people's curiosity, to draw them into this world, this moment you've created, and to give them a reason to care and get lost and forget about everything else while they consume your vision. You elicit an emotional response. You make them think about the very essence of why they're alive, get them questioning everything, and when it's over, after they leave, they're left haunted. They've devoured your vision, and all they want is more. That's the artist's job. But even though he was coming to terms with his reality while I was just beginning to tap into my potential, we'd have these nights at the apartment together, just me and him, drinking and smoking and listening to our records till sunrise. We'd dance, we'd lie on the bed and talk about the first time we listened to the Beatles and the Stones and Television and Bowie and the Violent Femmes and the Talking Heads and Joy Division and the Replacements and it was so wonderful. Us doing that. Laughing and forgetting about everything else and not worrying about the future, not thinking about anything except the music we loved that changed our lives."

She lowered her head, I remember, after she said that last part. She stopped dancing, too. She went into one of her infamous dazes, and when side A was finished, she looked back up, the magic gone from her face, and she said, "Maybe he was just fooling me then too. Maybe he was never really into any of that. I mean, look what he turned into the minute he had me. It was all about him and his business world and all this material shit that he wanted, that he seemed to need.

We never had those nights again after I got pregnant. We barely ever went to any shows or openings. And that's when the monster revealed itself. That's when everything in New York began to die."

She finished her glass of wine, then walked out of the room, and two hours later, I found her passed out on her bed, clutching her ballerina dress, a recording of one of her recitals playing on her TV.

As I'm paying for the vinyl, I ask the girl checking me out where I can get a decent taco. She tells me about this place Zona Rosa just a block down from the store.

I tell her thanks, and then my phone starts ringing. It's Dominique and like that, I've got what feels like a thousand butterflies dancing around my stomach.

"Well, there he is," she starts. "It's so crazy, cos I thought you might've died or something."

"Nah," I go. "You can't kill something like this."

She laughs and says, "I figured if I was annoying enough, you'd at least have to call me to tell me to stop it. But you wanna kick it now, so that's even better."

"Right. I'm sorry about all of that. It just took me by surprise."

"What's that?"

"You wanting to hang out with me."

"Why is that surprising?"

"Cos you're really pretty and you're older, I think, and you know I'm leaving soon."

BLAZED   155

"Maybe that's why it's so perfect."

"Maybe. I was just surprised. It was really nice to talk to you, and then getting those texts . . . It's hard for me to handle that kind of stuff."

"Well, I'm glad you came around."

"Me too," I say, a little shocked to hear these words coming out of my mouth and how good it feels to say them.

"I've got band practice tonight," she says. "But what are you doing tomorrow, like, after three?"

"Seeing you."

"Yeah?"

"Yup."

"Good," she goes. "Well why don't you meet me at my work around three and we'll go from there."

"Sure."

"I work at the Squat and Gobble in the Castro. Just type it into your phone and it'll tell you exactly how to get there from wherever you're at."

"Perfect."

"How you liking San Francisco so far?"

"It's cool. This is my first time out on my own, and I'm holding six amazing records in my hands and about to eat a taco. So pretty all right, I guess. Plus, Kristen is really cool."

"I love your stepsister, man. She's got this city dialed in too, so if you need anything, you should call her. She knows everyone and everyone loves her."

"I got that feeling too."

"She's a good person to know. Her clothes are amazing."

"Indeed," I say.

"So tomorrow at three, Jaime. And don't be late."

"Never. I'm stoked."

"Fuck yeah," Dominique says. "I think you'll like hanging out with me too. We'll have fun."

She hangs up, and I order a carnitas soft taco to go and Coca-Cola in a bottle.

As excited as I feel right now, I also feel guilty just about smiling, with my mother in the condition she's in and me way out here, so far away from her, shopping for records and staying in a fucking mansion and meeting cool kids. It doesn't seem right. But she's the reason this is happening. It doesn't make me feel any better to think this. But it's true. At least I have that on my side.

37

I END UP JUST FOLLOWING HAIGHT ALL THE WAY down. I eat my taco on a stoop right off of Clayton Street, and then I buy a pair of sunglasses and say no, like, eight times to these gnarly street goblins asking if I need buds or if I can spare a buck.

A couple of them even talk some shit to me, but I don't pay it any mind. Like, you smell and you have dreadlocks and you suck at playing music. That's my victory over all of them. Me not being that lame.

I listen to Thee Oh Sees as I walk. They live in San Francisco, and it would be fucking radical to bump into one of them, like Dwyer, and just shake the dude's hand and tell him how awesome his band rips and how much they mean to me.

I walk down this hill. There's babes everywhere. While I'm stopped at this red light, a couple of kids bomb the hill on their skateboards. I need to get a skateboard while I'm here. There's not a better sound in the world than a skateboard grinding on concrete.

I keep moving, and some of this is starting to look familiar from yesterday. I'm in the Lower Haight again, and when

I walk past this hair salon with a bunch of hot chick stylists inside, I look across the street and see Savannah standing in front of my father's gallery, smoking a cigarette.

She's wearing a white sundress, a navy-blue cardigan, and black cowboy boots. Her hair hangs down to her shoulders.

She sees me crossing the street toward her and waves.

I take my earphones out and nod at her. She gives me a hug.

"Jaime," she says. "What are you doing down here?"

"I don't know," I say. "I just kept walking from up there and here I am."

"You got some records."

"Yeah. So how's the painting going?"

"Great," she says. "Well at least the preproduction stuff. Wanna come up and check it out? Maybe play a couple of pieces on the piano?"

"Sure," I say. "I mean, I don't wanna distract you or anything. Keep you from your work."

"You won't be at all. This will be a nice break. Come on."

She grabs my hand and squeezes it and leads me inside without letting it go. Her hand feels nice too. It's warm and soft just like I'm sure the rest of her is.

We ascend the winding staircase into the apartment. Probably a hundred or more Polaroids of Savannah are spread out on the floor next to these two large sketch pads.

Savannah picks up a bottle of Heineken and takes a drink. "So this is my disaster right now."

I set my records down and look over the pictures. Savannah is naked in all of them. She's holding all these different poses with different angles in each picture.

My face turns bright red and I begin sweating. Her body is beautiful. It's sculpted like a statue of some Greek goddess. I notice my fingers slowly bending now as if they're squeezing the milky skin of her body between them.

I look away and step back.

She's standing right next to me now. "What do you think?" she asks.

"It's interesting. I thought you painted, though."

She grins. "I do, Jaime. This is my style. What I'm known for. I have a bunch of photos taken of me in certain situations, a lot of them nude, compromising situations, and then I paint the picture onto canvas with all these unique and intricate backgrounds I design long before the picture's taken."

"Who took these pictures?"

"A friend of mine. Do you like them?"

I don't say anything.

Savannah giggles and goes, "It's okay to say yes, Jaime. You shouldn't be embarrassed because you like nude pictures of me. I want you to like them. I want to think you think I'm attractive."

"Sure then," I finally say. "I do like them. A lot."

Savannah finishes her beer and runs a hand down my face. "Good," she goes. "Do you smoke pot?"

"Ummmm . . ."

"I'm not gonna tell your father if you do, Jaime."

"That's not it at all. I don't give a fuck what he knows about me, and I don't care if he doesn't like what he knows."

"There ya go."

"I just don't smoke that much. Only a couple times in my life, I guess."

"You wanna get high with me?"

I shrug. "Okay. Yeah. Can I get one of those beers, too?"

"Now that's more like it," she says. "Put on one of the records you bought."

"Word."

So I walk to the record player and select the Beachwood Sparks record and put it on while Savannah opens two more beers and lights a joint.

Savannah leans against the wall now and plants her left foot against it, which hikes the bottom of her dress up to her thighs.

Me, I'm sitting on the piano bench sipping on my Heineken, unable to pull my eyes off this lovely, nice creature who seems to be the furthest thing from a whore or a cunt.

She takes a hit off the jay and tilts her head back as the smoke exhales slowly and thickly from her nostrils and mouth. It's almost perfect. I should be taking a picture of her now. With the way the sunlight is draping half her body and the shade claiming the rest of her, this would be the first picture to say a thousand words to me.

"I'm so sorry," she says, looking back at me now. "I've been hogging the weed. I do that sometimes, ya know. I forget to pass it to other people."

"It's fine," I tell her. "It's your dope."

"But you're my visitor," she says, winking.

She pushes herself off the wall and struts over to me, handing me the joint.

I take it from her. When I do, her fingers slide all the way down to my forearm. I look up at her and she's just staring at me.

"What's up?" I go.

"Nothing," she says, then leans down so that our eyes are even. "You are so fucking handsome."

I hit the joint. "Thank you."

"Can I sit down next to you?"

This crap again, I'm thinking.

"Go ahead," is what I'm saying.

And Savannah does while I'm taking my second hit. She sits down and scoots right up next to me and I pass the joint back to her.

Our legs are touching, and I've got another fucking boner.

Savannah takes a hit and says, "Can I confess something to you?"

"Ummmm . . . okay." I take a drink of beer. "Is it crazy?"

"I don't know," she says.

"What is it?"

"I looked you up last night after you and your father left."

My heart skips a beat. My chest tightens. I say, "Why would you do that?"

"When I heard you warming up, how you played the scales and the octaves, it drew me in emotionally. This attachment to something formed immediately. Nostalgia just washed all over me like a fucking wave, Jaime. And I was in a trance for a few seconds. That's when your father told me how good you were and that you are some kind of prodigy. Some sort of musical genius."

"First off," I tell her, "my father doesn't know shit about me, okay? Fuck him for speaking about me in that manner. And second of all, I'm not a genius. I'm good, but I'm not a genius at all."

"I came across Tiger Stitches," she says. "Then I came across your poems and your essays."

Burying my face in my hands now, I go, "You didn't tell anyone, did you? You haven't said a word to my father, right?"

She shakes her head.

"Good," I say. "Thank you."

Savannah takes another hit and passes me the joint. "Your poems," she goes. Then she grabs my hand and holds it again. "Fucking gorgeous, man. Some of them moved me to tears. The way you put words together and formed those images. Emma and her black hair. *Twin Peaks* and shark teeth and Mobb fucking Deep. All of it, dude. Every word. I probably watched those videos ten times each. I was so turned on."

"Wow," I say. Then, "I don't even know what to say, actually."

"I hope this next thing doesn't weird you out at all."

"What do you mean?"

"I watched the videos and I fucked myself with my fingers."

Seriously, I might blow my load just listening to her talk right now.

And she says, "I've never felt so connected to an orgasm before. After I came, I was covered in sweat and I was exhausted. I didn't even know where I was at first when I opened my eyes. That's the kind of reaction an artist dreams about getting, Jaime. You are an incredible fucking artist and I wish you were four years older."

"Why?"

"So we could fuck right now."

"Jesus Christ," I go. "Savannah."

"Shhhhh," she whispers. She puts a finger to my lips. "Don't say anything, Jaime. It's fine. I just thought you should know all of this. I fucking love your work."

We lock eyes. I'd fuck her right now. Screw the age difference. I want my dick inside of her, even though I wouldn't last longer than thirty seconds.

"You're so beautiful," she tells me, and then she leans

toward me and puts a hand on the side of my face. "We can kiss, though, yeah."

I don't say anything. Instead, I put my hand on the back of her neck, and right as our lips are about to touch, her phone starts blowing up.

It's sitting on top of the piano, and I see the name Justin Miles on the screen.

"My father is calling you," I say, backing up.

"Shit," she says. "I have to take it."

"Take it then."

She grabs the phone and stands up and leaves the room.

My head is so fuzzy now. I'm dizzy. In shock almost. I chug the rest of the beer and then swallow an entire blue.

A few minutes later Savannah comes back into the room and goes, "He just wanted to remind me about dinner tonight. Should be fun."

I make a face and shrug. "I doubt it. Food will probably be good, though."

"That's the seventh time he's called me today."

"Really?"

She nods. "He's texted me at least fifteen times too."

"Jesus," I say. "What a weirdo."

"He's a sweetheart," Savannah goes.

I shake my head. "Bullshit. It seems like he's obsessed with you."

"I think he's got a crush, sure."

"Dude's fucking married. That's horseshit."

Savannah grabs two more beers and opens them. When she hands me mine, she goes, "You hate him so much. I can tell."

"I sure do."

"What happened between you two?"

"Nothing," I say. "Nothing's ever happened between us. It's what he did to my mother. How he fucking ruined her and drove her insane. Now you wanna talk about a real artist, that was her. That was my mother. One of the best ballet dancers of her generation before my father went and fucked it all up. Just fucked her over and then crushed her after that."

"How long ago was it?"

"I was one when we left in the middle of the night."

"That was a long time ago, Jaime. People change."

"Maybe," I say. "But you can never change what you've done to another person. You can't take *that* back. And I judge people based on their actions, not their fucking empty words, ya know. And I've been alive for fourteen years and yesterday was the first time I spoke to that pie grinder. That fucking d-bag."

Savannah walks around the piano and leans back down. "Hey," she says. "Maybe you should give him a chance."

"A chance at what?"

"Redemption."

"Why would I do that?" I snort. "My mother's never been given that chance."

"So be bigger than both of them," she says.

"Whatever," I say. "You're rad, but you don't know what you're fucking talking about right now."

"That's true," she goes. "But you're so amazing, Jaime, and it sucks to see you so angry."

"I'm not angry."

"You're the angriest boy I've ever met."

I roll my eyes and go, "Just stop it, please."

"Okay," she whispers, then kisses my cheek. "You're so beautiful. Such a beautiful boy, Jaime Miles."

She kisses my cheek once more, and then her phone rings again.

When she looks at it, her face explodes with joy.

"Yes!" she says. "My boy is here."

"Your boy?"

"A good friend of mine," she goes. "You might've heard of him before."

"What's his name?"

"James Morgan," she says. "He writes books."

Now my face explodes with some goddamn joy. Like, James fucking Morgan. Like, my favorite fucking author ever. And he's here. And I get to meet him.

Savannah says, "From the look on your face, I take it you know about him."

"Dude's one of my heroes. I've read all of his books and short stories. All of his poems. I've seen every fucking interview I can find with him on the Internet. So yeah, totally. I totally know about James Morgan."

"Awesome. I met him a year ago in New York. He was at the opening of an exhibit of mine. We've stayed in touch ever since."

"That's so sick."

"I think he's coming to dinner tonight too. Your father told me to invite whoever I wanted."

"You invited Morgan?"

"I did."

"Jesus," I go. "Yes! Fuck yeah!"

Savannah starts laughing and goes, "Come on. He's downstairs."

I jump to my feet and grab my records and shades and follow Savannah out of the apartment.

"James," Savannah shouts out when we hit the bottom of the stairs. "Oh yes. My fucking boy is here!"

James is standing near the door, looking at one of the photographs hanging in the gallery. He's wearing a pair of dark aviator shades, a black Sleepy Sun T-shirt, a pair of tight white jeans with a black bandanna dangling out the back right pocket of them, and a pair of red cowboy boots, and his hair is combed, parted from the right to left and shaved on the sides.

He turns and looks at us. "Sav," he goes. "Fuck yeah, baby. You look great."

Savannah, like, jumps at him and he catches her. She wraps her legs around him and squeezes him hard. I can see the muscles on her legs flexing.

She kisses the side of his mouth and he sets her down.

Then he turns and points at this other dude I didn't see standing there who looks super familiar.

And James says, "This is Michael from Lamborghini Dreams. I think you two have met before. But maybe not."

Like, *holy shit!*

Like, *Greatest fucking moment ever!*

And Savannah goes, "We definitely have. I met you in Charleston when you guys played there last year."

"Oh cool," says Michael, clearly not remembering. "That's right. Totally. Definitely."

Michael's brown hair is long on the top and short on the sides. A skinny blue bandanna is tied around his forehead. He's got a beard and he's wearing a pair of big sunglasses. He's also wearing a maroon Members Only jacket, a gray Terry Malts T-shirt under that, tight black jeans with both knees totally blown out, and a pair of black-and-white Chuck Taylor All Stars.

Savannah hugs James again before turning to me and going, "And this is Jaime Miles. His father owns this gallery and the gallery where I'm showing my new work next Friday. Jaime just got here too. Yesterday."

"From where?" James asks.

"Joliet, Illinois."

"No shit. I'm from Illinois."

"I know you are, man. I'm a huge fan of your work. I've read everything you've put out."

"Oh wow," he goes. "Why?"

"James," Savannah says.

And James goes, "You must have some kinda fucked-up head, man."

"Maybe I do."

"You have to if you've read all my stuff."

"I haven't even read everything you've written," Michael says. "I stopped after that short story you posted about those two kids, the teenage brother and sister in Kentucky who are fucking each other, then they murder their dad and bury him in a field and run away. Shit was so gross, dude. Especially how detailed the sex was."

"You pussy," says James. "That story was totally hot. Made me wanna fuck my sister."

"Jesus Christ, James," Savannah snorts.

I'm laughing right now.

"What is wrong with you?" she asks.

"Nothing at all, baby." He smacks Savannah's ass. "Even he's laughing."

James is pointing at me.

And I go, "That's pretty funny."

"See," he snaps.

"I'm a big Lamborghini Dreams fan too," I say. "*Always Driving Drunk* is one of my favorite records ever."

"Shit's overrated," says James.

"So are your fucking books, you pilgrim dick."

"Blubber cheek," says James.

"Rim muncher," Michael snorts.

"Jaime makes awesome music under the name Tiger Stitches," says Savannah.

I totally wish she hadn't said this either. Like, these dudes don't fucking care. Such an amateur fucking move by her.

"Tiger Stitches, huh," Michael goes. "That's a dope name, man."

"Yeah, it is," says James.

"Thanks," I go.

"So it's good then," Michael goes. "The music."

I shrug. "I like it just fine. Probably some of the best stuff out right now."

"Well," snaps James, "we should go listen to it."

"What?" I go. "Nah, you don't need to do that."

"So it's not good then," James says.

"No, it's dope. All my songs are dope."

"I wanna hear it then," Michael says. "Let's go to the Whip Pad and get high. Blast some Tiger Stitches."

I've always maintained, always told myself that I'd never give a shit if one of my heroes took an interest in my work at some point. I've always said it wouldn't matter, wouldn't be a big deal. But this is pretty fucking rad. This is actually the coolest thing that's ever happened in my life.

"So you're holding?" Savannah asks James.

James makes a face. "Is that a serious question?" he says.

"It was."

"I was born with a bag of coke in my hand, Sav. Without the blast, this life is bullshit."

38

THE WHIP PAD. FIRST OFF, IT'S RIGHT ACROSS THE street on the other end of the block from my father's gallery. Before we jump in there, we stop at a liquor store across the street. James buys a twelve-pack of Budweiser and a pint of Jameson.

"Warm-up drinking," he says, when he walks back outside.

Savannah seems in awe of him. I wonder if they've fucked before. I wonder if Savannah's fucked Michael. Or if she's fucked both of them at the same time and is going to today.

She's a slut. Like, she wants to fuck me because of some poems she saw me read online. It's nice, I guess. I was hard. But that seems crazy to me.

I wonder if she's gonna blow my father for flying her out here and showing her paintings to a sliver of the world.

We walk down a small set of stairs and inside. I've read about this place before. This kid Kaden, James's cousin, he wrote about James and the Whip Pad in a book called *Dickpig Sux*.

I hadn't even thought about that before now. It didn't even occur to me that the Whip Pad was so close.

We walk down this long, narrow hallway full of graffiti and bikes and posters and into the last room on the right.

"Make yourselves comfortable," says James.

Me and Michael and Savannah sit down at this round table in the center of the room.

James, he grabs a record from a crate next to the door and puts it on.

"Who is this?" Savannah asks.

"Shannon and the Clams," James answers. "From Oakland."

"They're fucking great," Michael goes. "They opened for the Dreams on a small East Coast tour we did last year."

This is insane to me. How I'm sitting in James Morgan's room. Life is such a fuckhead like that. If my mother doesn't go insane, go fucking crazy on me a few nights ago, then I'm never here. I'm never in San Francisco. Never meeting Savannah or Dominique or Kristen. Never in James Morgan's fucking room in the famous Whip Pad listening to a sick garage/psych band.

James grabs a mirror and sits down at the table.

"When did you get back to San Francisco?" Savannah asks.

"This morning."

"How was L.A.?"

"Fucking radical," he says. "We got the funding for the movie. We start shooting next spring."

"What movie?" I ask.

"This screenplay I wrote based on a short story of mine called *The Whore*," says James. "Nobody wanted to touch that shit for a year, man. It's the most honest, perverse, and violent depiction of a two-faced slut you'll ever see. I'm directing it too. One of Michael's old homies, this dude Travis Wayne, stepped in to produce it, so it's going to happen for sure."

"Sick," I say.

James dumps an entire bag of coke onto the mirror and starts cutting it with his ID.

"So what's this dinner you want me to go to tonight?" he asks Savannah.

She looks at me and goes, "Jaime's father wants to get a bunch of people together at the Cigar Bar and have a nice meal. He's invited me and told me to invite whoever, and since I don't know anyone here really besides you, you're my fucking date."

"Sounds boring," says James.

"Hey," Savannah goes.

And I say, "It will be, man. Unless you show up. My father's a dick."

"Jaime," says Savannah.

"You don't know," I say. "He is. He's a fucking asshole."

"You hate your dad?" Michael asks.

"Actually, I just met him yesterday. But from his track record, I'm thinking that he's pretty much an asshole."

James laughs. He rolls up a hundred-dollar bill and snorts a line and then hands the mirror to Savannah.

"So why are you here then?" Michael says.

"My mother OD'd. We don't have any living relatives near Illinois. Now I'm here for the week while she's getting treatment."

Savannah does a line and Michael goes, "And now you're kicking it with us. Worse things have happened, dude."

"Tell that to my mother."

"She's the one who OD'd," says James. "The thing I've figured out with family bullshit, like, total dysfunction is that these people who you start figuring out are really just a bunch of selfish assholes, these people can turn your life upside down in a second and you don't even have a say in it. No choice. It's just done and you're left to navigate through the shitstorm you didn't start. It ain't fair."

"Right," I say.

"But if you're smart about it," James continues, "if you're really fucking smart about it, man, you can turn that shitstorm into a goddamn paradise. Those people can go fuck themselves. They're evil and the quicker you realize that, the quicker you can take your life back. It's your life, man. It's yours. And you can take it back and carve out a path that has nothing to do with them. This is the window, man. This is the space in which you decide to be a legend or a pussy. Be a legend, dude. Use their dysfunction to make yourself better than they'll ever be."

Savannah passes the mirror to me, but I decline and then Michael takes the mirror and does a line.

James is staring at me.

I go, "What?"

And he goes, "I can see the anger in you, man. I can see the hate in your eyes. How old are you?"

"Fourteen," I say.

"Tiger Stitches, huh?"

"Yeah."

"That's dope, man."

"Thanks, dude."

"You don't do coke?" he asks.

"No."

"You should," he says. "It's fun."

"It's the tits," Michael snaps. "Totally righteous and shit."

"Really, guys," Savannah goes. "He's fourteen."

"That's just a silly number," says James. "Anyway, dude, use that hatred, that anger." He lights a cigarette and takes a pull from the Jameson. "Use that to carve yourself out of stone, man. Make yourself better than them. All of them. They've turned your life into chaos."

"Yeah."

"There's nothing better than chaos to prove you're worth a damn, man."

James takes the mirror back and does another line. "The second you start listening to those ancient people, that's the moment you stop living your own life. The life you want for yourself."

Savannah hits another line and passes the mirror to Michael.

"I love cocaine," says James.

"I love good cocaine," Michael says back, then does another line. "That's the shit I love the most."

"Me too," James goes.

39

"SO WHAT DO YOU THINK SO FAR, SON?"

Me and my father, we're in his Benz again driving to the restaurant, just the two of us, while the National plays from the speakers.

And I'm stoked about this. The music, I mean. It's cool my father likes the National. They're one of my favorite bands. I guess my mother, despite despising every ounce of my father, was telling the truth after all about how rad his musical tastes are.

"Your house is nice," I say. "The maids are cool. Rad car." I shrug. "It's okay."

"That's it," he says.

"Yeah," I groan. "What were you expecting me to say? Thanks for picking me up at the airport and listening to Pulp before you went to bed last night."

He laughs. "You heard that."

"Duh, dude."

We stop at a red light. "Okay," he goes. "I'm sure you hate me and don't want to be here, but could you do me one favor?"

I don't say anything. I just look at him and fold my arms.

"Address me as something other than 'dude' or 'man' or whatever else. I know I haven't been a part of your life, Jaime, but I am your father."

I roll my eyes. "Why should I care what you want me to call you?"

"I'm only asking, son."

"Fine," I say. "Deal."

"Really?"

"Yeah. I'll address you differently as long as you address me as something other than son."

I watch his jaw clench. He appears to be agitated, but it's only fair. To me at least.

"We have a deal?" I go.

"Sure," he says. "Deal, son—I mean, Jaime. We have a deal."

"Great, Justin."

My father turns left onto Market Street, which is really busy right now.

He says, "Kristen told me you guys had a nice visit last night."

"She's great," I say. "I like her a lot. She seems to really appreciate all the nice things she has. Must be nice for her."

"Jaime," my father says. "Come on now. Don't start this."

"I'm not starting anything," I tell him.

"I give your mother two thousand dollars a month in child support, and I send you a check for a thousand dollars every birthday and Christmas."

My body goes numb. This ringing in my ears starts now. Like someone's punched me in the gut or the back of my head. I've never seen a thousand-dollar check from my father. I've never even seen a goddamn card from my father. But I don't say anything about that. Instead, I take a deep breath and keep in mind what my mother has told me about him. How he's the world's biggest liar and how he's selfish and such a dick.

I say, "It doesn't matter anyway. It's not like I'm jealous of Kristen. My life is dope back in Joliet."

"That's good," my father tells me. "Your mother is a wonderful person. Despite all of our problems and what happened in the past, Morgan has one of the best souls in the world. When we found out that she was pregnant, to this day, I have never seen someone look so happy. She was beyond thrilled, Jaime. That look on her face was pure joy. She gave me a hug and squeezed my neck and went, 'There's gonna be a little us running around. What a dream. We're going to have the most beautiful child in the world, and he's going to have the best life.'"

Tears form in my father's eyes and he looks to his left, away from me, and wipes them.

"I know it hasn't been the best life, Jaime. God, I wish so many things had happened differently. But I look at you, and you're handsome and healthy and so talented, from what your mother has said, and I couldn't be prouder of anyone."

"Ha," I say. "That's rich. It's been fourteen years since you got that news about me. Fourteen damn years. And now I'm seeing you. Now I know what my father looks like, what his voice sounds like, how he dresses. I don't care how hard you try and revise the past in order to look good in my eyes this week. All that stuff happened. It happened and you can't change what you've done. No amount of money or words can change the way you treated someone else. What you did to someone else. Okay?"

"You've only heard one side, Jaime."

"Shut up," I say. "Just stop. Nothing you say can justify what really happened that night. So don't even try."

My father doesn't say anything. I can actually hear his grip on the steering wheel tighten. See his knuckles turn white.

"Do you understand that?" I go.

"Sure," he whispers.

"Yeah?"

"Yes."

"Awesome," I say. "Thanks for working with me on that . . . dude."

I put my shades back on and stick two fingers into the tiny pocket on the right side of my jeans and touch the two blues inside it.

Everything is better now.

I wish more of life was this way.

40

THE CIGAR BAR & GRILL. IT'S ON THE EDGE OF THE
Financial District. A valet takes the keys from my father
immediately after we pull up, and the two of us, we head
down a steep set of stairs and walk through a heated patio
full of men in expensive suits, smoking cigars and drinking
cocktails.

A hostess takes us to a large room that's been reserved
by my father just for this dinner party.

Also, everyone on the staff we've encountered knows
who my father is. The hostess, this pretty Latina girl with
short hair and big brown eyes, even winks at my father.

She winks twice, actually, and looks back over her
shoulder at him before she leaves the room.

This server hands my father a glass of red wine and tells
him it's a Malbec, then asks me what I'd like to drink. I order
a Coke.

Leslie is here already with two other couples. She's
wearing this purple strapless dress with a slit on the left
side, leaving her thigh and the "stay up" part of her stocking
exposed.

My father introduces me to his friends, including the other founding member of my father's hedge fund and his wife. The other couple work out at Bay Club San Francisco, this super-nice health club in the city.

They ask me all this cheesy question bullshit, like what do I think about the city so far and if I'm excited to be in the city and if I hate my father yet.

That last question is sorta relevant and funny, I guess.

But I spare that man the embarrassment and say, "You can't hate someone you don't know, right?"

It's the most honest way to answer that question without being a total dick about it.

Still, though, a moment of total awkwardness definitely follows this answer and only dissolves when two different servers bring in these two big trays of appetizers, which they set on a small table a few feet from ours.

They're followed by the first server, who hands me my Coke and sets two more bottles of wine—a red and a white—on the table. He opens them both and pours a small sample into two different glasses for my father to breathe and taste.

My father tips the three servers twenty bucks each.

"Help yourself to some food, Jaime," Leslie tells me.

There's a quesadilla platter on one tray and what I'm told are house-made tortilla chips with guacamole and salsa sides on the other.

I grab a plate and place a tiny bit from both trays on it and sit down.

Kristen finally shows up. Thank fucking god for her. I'm pretty sure she's drunk, too, and possibly high with the way she's talking really fast and rubbing her nose. She even checks her nostrils for powder residue with a glance at the back of a spoon.

She's with her boyfriend, that dude Tyler, and he's a real fucking treat too.

Dude's about as tall as my father. He's got thick black hair that's parted cleanly from the left to right, the sides about an inch shorter, with a fucking lightning bolt shaved into the left side of it.

Lame.

He's wearing a Cal-Berkeley letterman's jacket with a charcoal-colored cardigan and a deep black V-neck underneath that. Also tight purple jeans that are rolled past his ankles, a pair of black TOMS, and a large gold chain that hangs past the middle of his chest.

My father is, like, the happiest person ever right now. He practically tackles Tyler and they hug and high-five, and I look up at Kristen. Her jaw is pretty alive right now, and she flashes me a smile and points at my father and Tyler and then makes a gun with her right hand and shoves it in her mouth, squeezing the fake trigger with her thumb.

She's wearing skintight black jeans, a white Nirvana T-shirt that's two sizes too big, and a brown cardigan the same size as her shirt, with darker brown patches over the elbows. A black bandanna hangs from her neck.

My father introduces Tyler to me. I stand up and he extends his hand and goes, "There he is."

"Excuse me?"

"There you are. The kid I've had to hear about all day. I'm Tyler," he snaps.

"What up?" I decide not to shake his hand and shove my hands in my pocket. "Sorry you *had* to hear about me all day, dude. Hope it didn't impede too much on whatever . . . ya know, whatever it is you were doing."

My father jumps in and goes, "Don't be offended by his bluntness."

I make a face and look at Leslie, who says nothing. Just takes a drink of wine and looks at the ground.

"He gets that from his mother."

"Are you fucking serious right now?" I snap.

"Jaime," Kristen says. She turns her hand to the side and moves it back and forth real quick.

Dude's a dick. I can tell.

"Anyway," my father goes. "We've got some hors d'oeuvres and some wine. Help yourself."

I sit back down.

Tyler glares at me.

I glare back.

"Thank you, Mr. Miles," he says. He picks up a bottle of wine and pours a glass.

I'm wondering if anyone besides Kristen knows he's a drug dealer. I'd never say anything, cos narcing is bullshit, but I wonder if they know at all or if Kristen and him lie about it to my father and Leslie and make up some kind of ridiculous story about what he does for work and how hard his days are sometimes and his plans for the future.

But as I'm processing through all the scenarios, I watch my father and his hedge fund partner pull Tyler aside. I see Tyler nod and my father smile, and then I watch the three of them leave the room together without telling anyone.

Kristen sits down across from me.

"Is that what I think it is?" I ask her.

"My boyfriend selling coke to your father and Mark?"

"Yeah."

Her lips squeeze together, and she nods. "It sure is. Justin's been texting Tyler for the last hour to make sure he's coming."

"Jesus," I go. "How does that happen?"

Kristen laughs out loud. She pours herself a glass of wine and says, "Your father was looking for it one night. This was a year ago, probably. Him and my mother were drinking before a David Byrne show in Oakland, and me and Tyler happened to walk into the house right before their car service showed up. Justin just asked if we knew anyone who could get them some cocaine. He said his normal guy moved to New York. I never knew he had a normal guy. Like, I already assumed they did coke. I've seen Baggies laying out upstairs. I've seen both of them walking out of bathrooms together at parties and restaurants just sweating and talking all fast. Like, duh, ya know. When Tyler said he had some, I thought I was going to get sick. I couldn't believe it. But they didn't even bat an eye. They've never said anything to me about it. I guess as long as I've got that 3.8 GPA and kicking ass with my clothes, it doesn't matter that my boyfriend deals coke, which means that I'm probably doing it too. It's crazy. They've been letting me drink since I was fourteen."

"Damn," I go.

"It's kinda like you," she says.

"No, it's not. With me, my mother is too fucked up to know I'm drinking and stealing her Oxy. No way would she ever sanction that shit if she found out."

"Doesn't matter," says Kristen. "It's still the same. Just because you're too fucked up to pay attention doesn't make you any less guilty of being negligent."

Nodding, I say, "That's a great fucking point."

"You want some wine?"

"I can't."

Kristen looks around and laughs. "Sure you can, dude." She pours me a glass.

I lift it and take a drink, and then Leslie says, "It's really good, huh, Jaime?"

"I guess."

"Cheers," she goes.

"As long as you don't make them parent you too hard or

become some kind of big nuisance in their life, you've got the freedom to indulge, Jaime."

"Great."

"Welcome to this life," she says.

"Welcome to *your* life," I say back.

41

FINALLY, LIKE FORTY MINUTES AFTER ME AND MY father arrived, after listening to these people talk about million-dollar trades, shopping for new BMWs, this twenty-thousand-dollar-a-plate fund-raiser for the Democratic National Committee that Barack Obama spoke at that my father and Mark attended, about skyboxes at AT&T Park and Oracle Arena, and after five more bottles of red wine have been ordered and brought to the table, Savannah shows up with James.

"Oh my god," Kristen says. She's still sitting across from me, next to Tyler now. She turns back to me. "That's James Morgan. He's one of my favorite authors."

"I know," I say. "I met him today."

"What?" she snorts. "And you're just telling me. How?"

"I was at the gallery, and he showed up to see Savannah."

"No way," she says. "Did you talk to him?"

I nod. "I went to his place, the Whip Pad, and kicked it for about an hour. He's a cool dude. I thought he'd be a bigger dick than he was. He throws parties now with that rapper dude Omar Getty. I also met Michael, the drummer for Lamborghini Dreams."

"Fuck that band," Tyler snaps.

"Fuck you," I snap back. "Jock."

"Excuse me."

"I can't believe you hung out with Morgan," Kristen continues, just glowing now. "I can't believe he's here."

"Dude's so overrated," Tyler says.

"You don't know shit," I say back.

"I'm so excited," Kristen says. "Ahhhh. Dude's straight up at my family dinner right now. It's the shit."

"Whatever," says Tyler. "Who's the babe?"

"That's Savannah," I go. "She's the artist my father flew to San Francisco."

Tyler slams a drink and rolls his eyes at Kristen, which she doesn't see. I can't believe she fucks this dude. He's like a wannabe fucking hipster. I can smell the fakeness, the phoniness all over him. Like he's the jock, the goddamn meathead, who used to listen to Linkin Park and Incubus and 50 Cent and then he heard "Float On" by Modest Mouse or watched *Garden State* or read his first issue of *Vice* and saw himself and his best friends represented in, like, seven of the "Don'ts" and was totally embarrassed. So his jeans got skinnier. His "nu metal" CDs got tossed (actually, probably sold to Rasputin or some shit like that). His jackets got smaller and his shoes got brighter and his hands carried shopping bags from used clothing stores and he dropped the "bro" and picked up the "brah."

He was prolly fifteen or sixteen when this all happened.

So now he's totally cool. He's had four years to memorize the Wikipedia pages of bands and authors and movies. He's had time to tell the same lies over and over and over, so now they're his truth. And he's not in high school anymore, so his past doesn't mean all that much and he's had time to make a new Facebook and Twitter and Tumblr and re-create himself from scratch with links to videos and songs from dope-ass bands and pictures of himself holding tickets to dope shows and him posting links to rad articles from cool magazines and him dressed all hip and selfies of him with some nerdy-looking indie rock kid with black-framed glasses and a gigantic sweater who doesn't know this guy woulda beat the shit out of him after giving him an atomic wedgie just five years earlier and now he's getting coke from him and they're staying up late talking about Coachella and the Violent Femmes and Two Gallants and Nirvana.

I'm surprised that Kristen's been fooled by him.

Savannah's pulled her hair back and up into a fancy ball, making a part on the left side. Two large brown-and-black feathers hang from each ear. She's wearing tight white jeans, a loose beige tank top, a baby-blue Members Only Windbreaker jacket, and a pair of black leather boots that stretch up to her knees.

Everyone at the table stands up to greet her. Me, I'm thinking about how she wished we could fuck.

"There she is," my father says. I notice he's not smiling, though. He actually looks a little bit put off, which is weird until I realize he's being like that because he didn't know James would be with Savannah. When he told her to invite anyone she wanted, he probably assumed it would be a girl.

James looks nice too. He's wearing a black peacoat, a gray V-neck sweater with a blue collared shirt underneath that, the collars tucked into the shoulders of his sweater, a pair of tight, shiny dress slacks, and white alligator-skin shoes with pointed toes.

My father gives Savannah a hug. A long hug, complete with a couple of small squeezes and a hand rub.

It's embarrassing. Kristen notices it too. How my father is basically drooling over the young, beautiful artist he paid to come here.

I look over at Leslie. She's smiling, but that smile is fucking fake.

"Who's your friend?" my father asks.

"Justin, this is James Morgan. He's pretty much the only person I know in San Francisco."

"James," my father says. "Welcome."

They shake hands.

"What do you do, James?"

He laughs.

So do I.

Then, after a few seconds, he goes, "Is that for real? Like a real, serious question?"

"Yes, it is."

"I write a little bit," he says.

"Great," says my father. "Another San Francisco writer."

"Come again?" says James.

"Isn't that the running joke?" my father goes. "Everyone in San Francisco is a writer."

"Justin," Savannah says, cutting in, "James has written six books, three of them *New York Times* bestsellers, two of them turned into movies, a couple collections of poems and essays, and he's about to direct his first movie next year."

Leslie laughs.

It's so awkward now that my face is turning red.

My mother was so right about him. The wannabe. The fake. Like, if she was right about this, then I know he's been lying about all the other stuff. The phone calls and the money and the cards.

"Well, fuck," my father goes. "That's impressive."

"It's what I do," says James. "Thanks for having me, I guess. Do you try and ridicule every guy you're jealous of?"

"What?" my father says.

"Hey," Savannah goes, turning to James and putting her hands on his shoulders. "It's fine, man. Be cool."

"Nothing," James tells my father. "I just got back into town and haven't slept much. Makes me a little cranky."

"You're fine," my father goes. "Grab a seat and a glass of wine. We're about ready to order."

As Savannah says hi to everyone else, my father grabs her and goes, "Sit up here, please. With us."

He pulls out a chair next to him and across from Leslie.

"Sure," Savannah goes, and sits down.

But when James tries to sit on the other side of her, my father goes, "Excuse me, James. Those seats are for my friends."

Kristen leans across the table and goes, "He's wasted."

"He's an idiot," I say.

"Right," she says.

"It's fine," Savannah tells James. "Just sit by Jaime."

Leslie looks sick. I'm so ashamed of my father.

James walks around the table and pulls out the chair next to me. "What's up, partner?"

We fist bump.

"Is your father always such a douchebag?"

"I don't know," I say.

"That's right," he says.

Pause.

"What a prick, and his wife is right there too," James continues.

"It's bullshit."

"Yeah, it is." James looks at Kristen. "Hi," he says.

Kristen is glowing. Just staring at him. "Hey," she says.

"How are you?" James asks.

"Just fine," she goes. She introduces herself and Tyler to him and then says, "Can I tell you something?"

"It's not gonna be some asshole shit like your father said, is it?"

"Not at all. He's my stepfather, actually."

"Same thing," says James. "What's up?"

"You're probably one of my favorite authors ever, dude. And it's an honor to meet you."

I watch Tyler make a face after she says this.

"Well, thank you," James says. "Thanks for supporting my art."

"Art," Tyler says, not asks.

"Yeah," says James.

"Oh, come on, man," Tyler goes. "It used to be art."

"Tyler," Savannah snaps. "What the fuck is your problem?"

"Nothing," Tyler snorts. "I used to read your books. And then you wrote yourself and your book *PieGrinder* into *The Bottle Cap Gang*, and after that, I was over it, man."

"Why was that such an issue with you, man?"

"The ego you have to have to do that. It's fucking gross, man. Like we all know you wrote *PieGrinder*, but you gotta throw it in another book."

James downs his glass of wine in one gulp and then says, "If only you knew what you were talking about."

"I do. I read it, man."

"Not that I need to ever explain my fucking work to anybody," James starts. "But that was an inside joke for some friends. When *PieGrinder* came out, all these people I knew, some of them vaguely, came out of the woodwork and began telling everyone that the characters in the book were based on them. That the story was about them and their lives. So when I dropped that part in *The Bottle Cap Gang*, with that made-up author saying I was an asshole for having hung out for a week to see all this shit go down and then write about it, that was the joke. And the people it was intended for got it. And that's all it was. It was for those fucking people, man."

Tyler blushes. "Whatever," he says.

"Yeah," James goes. "Whatever, brah. Like, some jock wannabe hipster from the Marina thinks he knows some shit about my books. Fuck that. I see right through you, man. Right through you."

I laugh as this waitress comes up to the table and asks if we're ready to order.

Glancing back at Savannah, my father's sitting, like, six inches from her now with his arm on the back of her chair, while Leslie sits with her arms folded across her chest.

Like, great idea, dude.

Like, some family fucking dinner.

And this is when I realize that I've never had dinner with this many people before.

42

"COME WITH ME," KRISTEN SAYS.

I'm standing up, looking at all the plates on the dining table still filled with food.

Everyone's so high on coke that they couldn't eat.

Only James and I ate the majority of what we ordered.

Bathroom trip after bathroom trip after bathroom trip I watched, and at one point, I thought about screaming, "Just dump the shit out on the table, yo, and ask the waitress for eight straws. Everyone knows you're going to the bathroom to do blast or shit because you did blast."

"Where we going?" I ask Kristen.

"My car," she says.

"I'm in."

She gets the keys from the valet and lights a cigarette immediately after we get out of sight.

"Damn, I needed this," she says, as a cloud of smoke flows from her mouth and nose.

"What a shitshow," I say.

"Right. Worst idea ever," says Kristen. "Although having dinner with James Morgan is pretty fucking cool."

"It's insane," I say. "I can't believe this is happening."

"I told you this life is fabulous if you let it be. Besides all the other crap that's happening."

"I feel bad for your mother," I say.

"Don't," says Kristen. "I've seen her pull that shit on your father so many times."

"That's bullshit," I go.

"It is what it is. They do it because they can."

"That's stupid."

"It happened once, Jaime, ya know. One of them did it first. And once is all you need for the other person to become so jaded and cynical to the point where they decide to do the same thing and perpetuate the situation instead of dissolve it."

"It's so fucking childish."

"It is," says Kristen. "I mean, you think your father and my mother have accepted the role of being adults just because they brought a kid into the world?"

"Obviously not."

"They're friends more than parents. Your father married my mother when I was nine. He's been hands off my whole life, which is fine by me. I've never needed their hands to guide me. I just do what I do cos I love it. I like school. I love to learn. And I love making clothes and selling that shit. I'm easy."

"Me too." I guess.

"I'd hate to see them have to actually parent or give a shit. That's probably a huge reason why I stay so busy. So I don't have to put them through that grind and watch them be miserable by having to truly care. It all works, ya know. This is the dream scenario that any kid would fucking love to be living."

"Sure," I say.

"I'd rather have it like this than watch the two of them fucking fail cos they don't know how to be involved and not be the center of their own universes."

"Do you really think they don't care at all, though?"

"No. I think they've figured out that pretending to give a shit is just easier than giving a shit, and since I've never complained about it, I think they're actually convinced that pretending is the same thing as being."

"It's easier."

"And that's what it's all about, dude."

43

"JUST HOLD THE FOIL UP TO THE END OF THE TOOTER
and chase the smoke when it starts peeling off the pill," I tell
Kristen. "It's easy. You're just chasing the dragon until your
world becomes glass."

Kristen flicks the lighter and it starts. I hold the foil for
her like a gentleman, and she gets high while Youth Lagoon
plays from the speakers.

"Thank you so much," she says slowly, smiling. Her eyes
are iced. "This is so wonderful."

"I know."

"Beautiful," she says.

We end up splitting the pill, and she tells me that I'm
coming with her and Tyler after dinner is over. Some rad all-
girl rap group Toast is playing a free show at RVCA, which
is a store right on the corner of Haight and Ashbury, and it's
gonna be sick and Tyler is gonna do a ton of business there.
I tell her that sounds cool, and then I ask her why she's with
Tyler.

"He's kind of a turd burglar," I say. "I don't get it."

She lights a cigarette and grabs my hand. "We've been
together two years, Jaime."

"That's not a reason."

"Sure it is," she says. "The longer you're with someone the stronger your bond becomes, even if the surface is getting more and more smudged up."

"Does he treat you well?"

"I guess so."

"And that's good enough?"

"I don't know. For right now it seems so, though. Prolly I could find somebody else who would treat me better, but he doesn't treat me bad. He still fucks me all the time and makes me laugh."

"He's got free coke."

"Yeah," she says, laughing. "But that's not all. Like, he can come off like a total asswipe who's in over his head, like at dinner. Two fucking days ago, he was telling me how much he liked James Morgan's books. It's just like with Kanye, though. He's jealous, which I guess is good, ya know. If anything, it means he still cares and gives a shit."

"In the biggest dickhead way ever."

"It's still something, though. Our history is so intense and so long, too. He's really all I've known since my freshman year, and he loves my family and he loves to be around me."

"Do you trust him?"

Kristen starts to say something, then stops. She takes a drag and sighs.

"Kristen," I say.

"Sometimes I do," she says back. "When I'm actually with him I do."

"But not when you're apart?"

"It's not that I don't," she says. "It's just that there's all that coke and all those hot girls who buy from him so late at night. . . ."

Her voice trails off for a second.

Then, "It's just something I think about from time to time. But I don't think he'd ever hurt me like that."

"Never think that way, Kristen."

"What way?"

"That a person who loves you won't hurt you in the worst way possible. They will," I say.

"But why?"

"I think it's easier to hurt the people you love the most because you know they love you and you know their forgiveness is easier to come by than other people."

Kristen throws her cigarette out.

"They have a history with you. All those bonds you've formed, those superstrong bonds, that's what they're counting on to win you back over once they've fucked up and destroyed you. Fuck your history. Looking back and feeling nostalgic about someone who's hurt you is how you make your future miserable. So screw that."

Kristen leans over and wraps her arms around my neck. "Thank you, dude."

"Thank you," I say.

She lets go and says, "James fucking Morgan eating dinner with my family. Insane."

"Awesomest thing ever."

Digging into her purse, Kristen pulls out the coke bullet and loads a hit, then smashes it.

"Want some?" she goes.

"No, thank you."

"Boring, brah."

I start laughing and go, "Drop the bro and pick up the brah."

"What?"

"Nothing," I say.

"You're a weirdo, man."

"Fucking normal compared to the rest of those vultures inside."

44

"SHOW IT TO ME," SHE SAID.

"Show what to you?" I said back.

"You know, it," she said.

We were at her house. Her parents were gone. We were in her bedroom.

"My dick," I said.

"Yes. Your dick," she said back. "I wanna see it."

I was scared and anxious.

She'd been drinking wine coolers all afternoon. She was so drunk and I wasn't.

I went, "Why?"

She laughed. "Are you for real?"

I looked away from her but couldn't think of anything to say.

"Come on," she went. "Just do it. Show it to me."

I was so excited at the same time. So hard. I pulled my jeans and underwear down to my knees and there it was. My hard dick hanging all crooked and to the left.

The smile on her face doubled. She giggled.

"That's it," she said.

"What?"

"Nothing," she said back.

Then she set her wine cooler down and walked up to me.

She ran a hand down the side of my face. She leaned into me, her face just inches from mine. Her hand slid from my face to my neck and down my chest. Her hand stopped moving once it touched my dick.

"Hey," she said.

"Hey," I said back.

She jerked me once and I came. It shot all over my stomach and my leg.

It felt amazing. I felt so good. My eyes were closed. But when I opened them, she was shaking her head.

She said, "Really? That's it?"

"What did you want from me?"

"Never mind," she said. "But that's it?"

I nodded.

She ran her hand through my cum twice. Then she licked the cum off her fingers.

"Tastes okay," she said.

"Yeah?"

"I guess. I can't believe that was it, though."

"Why do you keep saying that?"

"No reason." She shrugged. "Clean yourself up. You should go now."

"Really?"

"Yes, Jaime. Really. Go now."

Spring break, spring break, spring break, forever . . .

That's the only thing I remember thinking while I got dressed and hurried out of her stupid house.

45.

JAMES AND SAVANNAH ARE SITTING AT A TABLE IN the heated patio when I come back in. They're both smoking cigarettes and drinking whiskey on the rocks.

"Jaime," I hear James say as I'm walking past them.

I turn around. "What's up?"

"Sit down," says James. "I wanna talk to you for a minute."

My first thought is to say go fuck yourself until I realize that besides Kristen, him and Savannah have been the only other people to be cool so far tonight.

I pull out a chair and sit.

"Hey," I say.

James laughs and says, "It sucks, huh?"

"What are you talking about?"

"Tonight," he says. "This. Your family doesn't give a shit about you and it's obvious."

"I know, dude. So what?"

"I'm just letting you know that while you're in San Francisco, if you ever get too overwhelmed or feel like you're totally alone, come by the Whip Pad and say what's up."

I can feel my face light the fuck up right now. "Really," I say, not ask.

"Yeah, man. I mean it. And if you knock and I'm not there, tell Savannah and have her get ahold of me. These people suck," he says. "These people only care about themselves."

"Right," I say. "I've figured that out."

"It's obvious," says James. "They don't have your back."

"But you do?"

James twists his smoke out in the ashtray. "I don't know about that. But I'm sure I'm better company than these fucking monsters. Just look at them."

"I don't want to."

"Exactly," he says. "You don't have to. You already know the truth."

46

THE RVCA PARTY IS KILLER. IT FEELS LIKE KRISTEN and Tyler know everyone here. This is my first party too. If you don't count me wandering downstairs in the middle of the night in my underwear right into the heart of one of my mother's epic after-hour parties.

And all those strange faces.

The thick, hovering clouds of dope smoke.

The B-52's and Pretenders records blasting.

And my mother dancing by herself with a bottle in her hand. Or dancing with a much younger guy or younger girl or both.

Every second of it like some blurry dream and me pinching my skin as hard as I could to see if it was real and it always was and everyone was smiling or crying and one time I saw this man with a mustache wearing skinny jeans punch a mirror cos he saw a ghost and he hated ghosts more than anything.

Toast hasn't played yet. Some DJ is spinning records. Tyler disappears with two girls.

I look at Kristen. "Customers," she says. "Not worried."

I grab her arm and go, "You think Dominique might show up here?"

"I don't know. Call her and find out. Don't be a pussy."

"We're kicking it tomorrow," I say.

Kristen stops moving. She puts both her hands on my face and goes, "That's my fucking boy! See what happens when you loosen up, man? The bitches start showing up. The hot bitches come right at ya."

"Ha, ha. I still don't trust it."

"You trust me, don't you?"

"I don't know."

She kisses the side of my mouth. "You're lying so much when you say that. Of course you trust me. You've been opening up to me since the second I caught you stripping in the basement."

When Toast finally takes the stage, Kristen is so hammered. Neither of us have seen Tyler since he bailed with those two "customers." She's acting like she doesn't give a shit, but it's not true. Every time I look at her, she's scanning the store with her eyes. Totally preoccupied with getting a visual of that piegrinder, and it makes me mad because the fun has been sucked out of her. This tension exists. I feel it. She's disconnected from the moment, and it's such a shame. Dude's not worth it. Nobody who makes you spend a fucking second of your life feeling anxious about what they are doing while you're not around them is worth that second, let alone a kiss or a high fucking five.

It's really creasing me.

I'm also bummed at her for even being in this situation.

I ask her if she wants to go to the front of the crowd with me. She says no. I don't wanna stay back with her, though, and watch her not have any fun so I roll up there, swallowing half of a blue on my way.

Kristen was right. Toast is rad. Their raps are fucking dope and hilarious. Nasty as hell too.

Plus, they're really pretty and got good style. Like, the whole crowd is jumping. Arms in the air, talking shit back to the girls cos they're asking for it, everyone smoking weed except me.

Thoughts of all the assholes and bitches I go to school with slam through my head. None of them are doing anything even close to as cool as this. That's one of the things that's always kept me going during all those times they've tried to crush me and embarrass me for no reason whatsoever. How it can't last forever. Those years in that private school and being forced to be around them and interact with them. It does end and then you get out and you go into this gigantic fucking world where nobody knows or even cares that your mother acts really strange and drinks a lot and fucks a lot of people. They don't care that reading a book or watching an amazing movie or just listening to records in the basement all by yourself was more fun than going to some shitty kegger or lame school dance. They don't care that you weren't fucking popular and had no friends. It's not funny to them. They won't try to shove you around and stick notes on your back and wipe their hands on their friends because they accidentally touched you.

None of that bullshit.

All those bands and books those assholes and bitches will eventually get into and love and swear by, well, I was indulging in that while they were finger-banging some drunk, passed-out girl. Or crying because they found out their boyfriend was the bro doing the finger banging and their best friend was the girl who drank too much and passed out in the wrong place.

That's what's kept me going.

Knowing that it does end eventually.

Knowing that when it does, that new, gigantic world that awaits me is full of Beach House and Youth Lagoon and Noah Cicero fans.

I'm looking around the room right now. The killer hip-hop show I'm in the middle of. All the pretty kids in the room who smile at me when I look at them, who won't trip me just to get a few laughs, who shave lines into their hair too, and who know what a bad day really fucking feels like.

Right after Toast finishes their last song, "Burnt," I look over my shoulder and see Kristen and Tyler arguing. She seems really upset, and he's waving a finger in her face.

I push myself through the crowd as quickly as I can. When I finally get to them, I hear her say, "Screw you, Tyler. You disappeared for a fucking hour with those bitches. Screw you."

She turns away from him. He grabs her arm, but she yanks it loose and starts walking away.

"Kristen," he shouts. "Just stop it! You're being a cunt."

He lunges at her and tries to grab her again.

Me, I jump in between them.

"Let her go," I tell him.

Kristen races outside, and Tyler shoves me.

"Mind your own business, dude."

"Fuck you," I snap back. "Leave her alone."

"This doesn't concern you, Jaime. That's my girlfriend."

"Then treat her like one, man."

"Fuck off," he says.

He tries to get around me, but I step in front of him.

"What's your problem?" he says.

"You," I tell him. "Just give her a few minutes."

Tyler looks over my head and makes a face. "Ya know what, fuck both of you," he says. "Look at her."

Kristen is standing outside on the sidewalk, and this dude is lighting a cigarette for her.

"Fuck that," Tyler goes. "That slut."

"Are you serious right now, man? You bailed with two chicks the second we got here."

Tyler rolls his eyes. Shakes his head. He's sweating like a pig, too. It's taking everything I have in me not to punch him in the face.

"You're nobody," he tells me. "Nobody."

"What does that even mean?"

"You're here for a fucking week and that's it, dude. I've known your dad longer than you have. He likes me better."

"Shut up," I say.

"You don't know anything about these people or their lives, man. None of this is your business. None of it."

He looks back over my head.

"Look at her," he goes.

Kristen's talking to two other guys now and laughing.

"Typical," says Tyler.

I don't say anything.

"Seriously though, bro," he goes. "Like, stay the fuck out of my way, okay? You're nobody here. Nobody to those people. You think they want you in San Francisco, man?"

"Shut the fuck up," I say again.

He starts laughing and goes, "The second that bitch needs to get high again, it'll be like none of this even happened."

Tyler flips me off after saying that and stomps off.

My high from the show, from the blues, has disappeared just like that.

Visions of me beating that twat, Tyler, with a baseball bat smash through my head.

Like great, dude. Awesome.

My father likes you better than me.

I'm sure he likes bacon cheeseburgers better than me too.

Fuck that dude and fuck his jacket.

And fuck his TOMS, too.

47

"YOU OKAY?" I ASK KRISTEN.

"That piece of shit," she snorts. "What'd he say to you?"

"Nothing."

"Like, who does he think he is? Just disappearing like that and showing back up smelling like a dumb bitch's perfume."

"That guy sucks," I say. "My father should be ashamed for liking him."

"Your father loves him."

"Cos of the coke?"

She shakes her head. "No. He thinks Tyler's cool or something. He actually wants him to work for his hedge fund so he can bring him into the business."

"You're joking."

"No. That's what fathers do with their sons."

"That phony is not his son."

"Closest thing he's had to one, Jaime."

My shoulders bunch up. "Besides the one he made with my mother and never fucking tried to talk to before she OD'd."

"He's tried," she says. "Jesus Christ, he's tried so hard. Your mother won't let him get near you."

"Bullshit."

"It's not," she says. "God, it's not. I've seen him cry about it, Jaime. I've seen him break down and just lose it. Fucking lose it, man."

Right as I'm about to respond, this street kid pops up right next to her, throwing his arm around her shoulders.

"You're so pretty," he snarls. "Wanna date me?"

Kristen jumps away.

"Come on, sweet thang," he says. "How about a cigarette instead?"

"Get lost," she says.

Dude steps toward her. "Just a cigarette." He reaches for her, but she steps away. "Come on, girl. Give me a fucking cigarette. I saw your pack."

"No," she goes.

"Give me one!" he yells, then steps at her again.

So I shove him and he slams against a newspaper box. "Leave her alone," I snap.

Then, *BAM!*

I get shoved from behind by this other street kid I didn't even see.

BAM!

I get shoved again by a third kid I didn't see.

"What the fuck?" I say.

BAM!

Another shove by the first asshole.

When I turn around, all three of them have me surrounded.

"Not so tough now," the guy that went after Kristen barks. "Not so fucking tough now, are you, bro?"

"Relax," I say.

I try and move past them and around the corner of the building, then—

BAM!

I get shoved again and nail the store window.

"Give me your fucking money!" one of the kids shouts.

"Screw you," I say.

"What's that?" he goes, then pulls out a switchblade.

I'm trapped against the building.

"Give me your wallet," one of them says again.

"Fuck you, you dirty pieces of shit."

"Nope," says the kid with the knife. "Fuck you."

He comes right at me and I close my eyes.

Wait for the blows and the blade.

Take a deep breath.

Just breathe.

Fucking breathe, man.

But they never come. Instead, the two dudes who Kristen was talking to when I was talking to Tyler come jumping in.

One of them pummels the kid holding the knife with a backpack. Just slams it right into that cocksucker's head and he drops hard.

Then the other guy punches the street kid to my right in the back of the head. That kid buckles over and when he does, I pound my right fist into his face and knock him down on his ass.

The other street kid, who's got fucking dreadlocks and baggy jeans, he takes off running across the street, yelling at this huge pack of street kids standing on the corner watching to help out.

"Shit," says the kid with the backpack. "We gotta bail now. Come on."

I step around the corner and grab Kristen's arm. "Let's go," I say.

Before we take off in a dead sprint up Ashbury, Kristen fucking kicks the street kid who pulled the knife on me two times in the face. I spit on him.

"Fucking loser!" she screams.

We start running, but I turn back.

"What are you doing?" she goes.

I kick the dude three times, screaming, "You pussy fuck! Don't touch her again. You fucking pussy piece of trash! You never touch her again. Fucking creep!"

"Jaime," Kristen goes. "Stop."

She grabs me and tries to pull me away.

"Let's go," she says.

I spit on the dude again.

"Now, Jaime. Come on."

I kick him one more time.

"Jaime!" she screams, yanking me backward now.

"Hey," I say, calmly turning toward her. "You okay?"

"I'm fucking fabulous," she goes.

"Great."

I'm smiling.

"Let's go, dude."

She grabs my hand and we run away laughing.

48

THE FOUR OF US FINALLY COME TO A STOP WHEN WE get to my father's house. We catch our breath in the driveway. All the lights are turned off inside.

"Fucking thank you," I say right away to those dudes. "Jesus Christ. I thought I was gonna get cut."

"No problem, dude," the kid with the backpack says. "I'm Eddie."

"Jaime."

"Brandon," the other kid says. "Fuck those dirty-ass street losers. Just fuck them. I hate them."

"Pure garbage," Eddie snorts. "That's what they are."

"Fucking trust fund runaways," Brandon snaps. "They read *Into the Wild* and decided their parents sucked for making a ton of money and giving them nice things and making sure they had all the food they ever needed."

"They probably didn't even read it," says Kristen.

"No shit," Eddie laughs. "They probably watched the movie. Fell in love with Emile Hirsch and took off in the middle of the night with their parents' credit card in their sock."

All of us laugh.

These dudes are rad.

Eddie's got black hair that hangs down to his shoulders. He's a little bit taller than me and skinny. He's wearing tight black jeans, a red hoodie with a white zipper, and a pair of black Nike Cortez.

Brandon's got short blond hair that's all messy. He's my height and he's got black plugs in both ears. He's wearing a blue-and-black flannel shirt, white jeans with both knees ripped out, and a pair of all-black Chucks.

Eddie opens his backpack and pulls out a pint of Wild Turkey whiskey and the remains of a twelve-pack of PBR.

He hands a beer to each of us.

"So you live here?" he asks me and Kristen.

"She does," I say.

"Not you?"

"Nah."

I open the beer and tell them about my situation. When I'm done, both of them cheers me and Brandon goes, "Welcome, my man."

"Thanks for saving my fucking life."

"That dude wouldn't have cut you," Eddie snorts. "Just robbed you."

"Well, it was still awesome what you did."

I take my wallet out and try to give them both a hundred dollars. Kristen is on her phone, not really paying attention, texting someone.

"Fuck that," Brandon says. "Buy the beers the next time we see you."

"I'll probably never see you dudes again," I say.

"Come to the Mission tomorrow," Brandon says.

"I don't know where that's at, man. I just got here last night."

"There's a bus that'll pick you up right on that corner and take you there in five fucking minutes. Maybe less," Eddie goes.

"Well, what's going on there?"

"Our band is playing a show in front of the Twenty-Fourth Street BART station."

"What's your band?"

"Devil Feeder," Eddie answers. "It's the two of us. I play bass and Brandon drums."

"Sweet. What time?"

"We're going on right at four," says Brandon. "You're gonna wanna be there on time, too. I doubt we'll get more than two songs in."

"Why?"

"Cops will shut it down pretty quickly. We don't have a permit to play."

"I don't get it," I say.

"It's fun," says Eddie. "There's nothing to get besides it's fun. We stole a fucking Live 105 banner from one of their booths at Outside Lands last year. Figure, if we hang that up before we play, people will think it's official till at least the second song. Maybe the third. It's gonna be dope regardless. It's gonna be fun, and that's the whole point of being in a band."

"Cool. I'll totally come by."

"With beers," says Brandon.

"Sure. With beers."

"Here," Eddie goes, then hands me the Wild Turkey.

I take a swig. A small one. And hold it in my throat for, like, ten seconds before I finally choke it down.

"Damn," I say, coughing. "Rough."

Kristen puts her phone away. "You guys live in the hood?" she asks.

"Nah," Brandon says. "I live in the Sunset on Taraval and Forty-Sixth."

"I'm in the Excelsior," Eddie goes.

"How deep?"

"A few blocks past the Safeway."

"That's deep," Kristen goes. "How old are you guys?"

"How old do you want us to be?" says Eddie.

Kristen laughs and takes a huge pull from the whiskey and just downs it tough.

"Funny," she says. "But really?"

Eddie's eighteen and Brandon's seventeen.

Kristen takes another whiskey drink and then takes her bullet out.

"You boys do coke?"

"Sure," says Eddie. "I live for the drip."

Kristen hands the bullet to him. As he's taking it from her, he squeezes her hand and winks.

"You're a babe," he says.

"Is that right?" she goes, smiling from ear to ear.

"Yup," says Eddie.

"And what about it?" Kristen goes.

"Nothing," Eddie says. "I'm just musing."

"Lovely."

He lets go of her and does a bump and then passes the coke to Brandon, who does a bump.

This is when Tyler shows up. Of course that's who Kristen was texting.

He's real heated, too.

"What the fuck is this?" he snaps. "Who are these guys?"

"That's Brandon and Eddie," says Kristen. "They saved Jaime's life a few minutes ago."

"Bullshit."

Eddie laughs. "Are you for real?" he goes.

"What are you talking about?" Tyler asks.

"I don't know," Eddie says, waving a hand in the air. "Like the letter jacket and the cardigan."

"Fuck you," Tyler snorts.

"Dude," I go. "Piss off."

"Fuck you too," says Tyler.

He grabs Kristen and tells her about this party in Hayes Valley.

"There's a cab on its way right now," he says.

"Maybe she doesn't wanna go," I say, looking at Kristen.

She looks away from me. Tyler pulls out a Baggie of coke and puts it in her hand.

"Sounds fun," she says.

Tyler shoots me a look. "What'd I tell you."

"You're a dick," says Brandon.

"Mind your own business," Tyler says.

"You dress like a dick too," snaps Eddie.

"Oh really," Tyler snorts.

He starts toward Eddie, but Kristen grabs him. "Just stop it," she says. "Jesus, man. Just stop it."

The cab shows up. Tyler walks over and sticks his head through the passenger-side window and then opens the back door.

"You don't have to go," I tell her. "We're better company anyway."

Kristen comes over and gives me a hug. "I have to," she says. "What a wild fucking night, though."

"Day," I say. "The whole day."

"Right," she goes.

"Morgan."

"Yes," she says. "James motherfucking Morgan."

"So rad."

"Yes, it was. Have fun with Dominique tomorrow, dude."

"Hopefully she's cool."

"She's the best, Jaime."

"Let's go, Kristen," Tyler snorts.

"You know he sucks," I say.

"He's all right," she says back. "You'll see."

"You're better than all right."

"Obviously I'm not," she goes, and lets me go and hops into the cab.

I flip the car off as it pulls away. Pretty sure Tyler flips me back off with both hands.

D-bag.

And the three of us, me, Eddie, and Brandon, we kick it for another hour in the driveway and finish the beer and whiskey and listen to this band I've never heard of, the Shipping News, and they're really good, and then the Murder City Devils, who I love so goddamn much.

49

AFTER I JACK OFF TO THESE IMAGES OF ME FUCKING
Yolandi from Die Antwoord—twice—I get out of bed, smoke
an Oxy, and jot down this idea for a new poem I've been
kicking around my head for the last two days.

Something big, something that spans time [insert random
Buffalo '66 joke anywhere now], *about a girl, lots of images,
something nostalgic*...

This is what I write before chasing the dragon some
more. On my way to the shower, I run into my father in the
hallway. He's walking out of his bedroom, holding a bottle of
champagne, wearing nothing but the towel around his waist.

"Oh, hey there," he goes.

It's pretty much awkward.

No, it's totally awkward really.

"What's up with you?" I ask.

"Nothing," he says. "Just relaxing with Leslie. Sunday
Funday."

"Right," I say.

"What?"

I grin. "Nothing. Just sounds like something sorority
girls make up their freshman year."

"Christ," my father says. "It does, actually."

"Have fun."

I start back up for the bathroom when he goes, "Hold on, Jaime."

I sigh and turn around.

"Yeah. What?"

"Did you have fun last night?"

"Sure. I got to sit next to one of my heroes at dinner. It was awesome."

The smile that appears on my father's face now seems forced. "What about everything else?" he asks.

"Everything else?"

"The party you guys went to. The food. The conversations."

I make the okay sign with my right hand and nod. "Splendid," I say. "All of it. Really splendid."

"Now you're being sarcastic."

Dropping my hand, I go, "Sorry. This is already really weird, though. I don't know you and you're trying to have this conversation with me about last night and you're only wearing a towel."

"Right," he says, looking down. Flipping his eyes back up to me, he goes, "Maybe I can throw on some clothes and me and you can go do something together."

"Like what?"

He bunches his face and squeezes his forehead. "I don't know. Something. What do you want to do?"

"I'm gonna go see someone I met the other day."

"Oh yeah?"

I nod. "So just keep doing your thing. Keep making Sunday a Funday."

My father starts laughing. "All right. Just call me or text me and let me know you're all right if you plan on staying out late. Past dark."

"Sure," I say. "Totally."

"Great."

My father starts back toward the stairs, and I head into the bathroom and get into the shower.

While I'm in there, I think about Selena Gomez now, and start jacking off.

"Spring break, spring break, spring break forever . . ."

50

THE NUMBER 33 BUS PICKS ME UP AND WINDS ITS way through all these hills and then back down. It's on the way down that this big, beautiful portrait scape of the city and the Bay Bridge and the ocean fucking opens up.

My heart starts racing. It's sunny out and the sky is so clear and I can see everything. It devours me.

When the bus makes this awkward, like, 180-degree turn, I glance at all the people riding with me, and none of them are looking at this beautiful painting right in front of them.

Most of their faces are buried in their phones. Some of them are sleeping. None of them are reading. And the rest of them are looking the other way at a huge wall of brick.

It makes me angry. There's nothing like this in Joliet. Nothing. And if there was, I'd never take it for granted because I lived there and passed it every day.

No way.

This is so beautiful, so wonderful, and how the hell can you not choose to embrace something that's both of those things that you didn't even have to make.

It's just there for you.

It's amazing.

I don't get off in the Mission. Instead, I get off when the driver yells to me that we're on Market Street, cos I asked him to when I got on.

I'm so fucking nervous too. My palms are sweating again and my chest is tight and my breaths are short.

I shouldn't be feeling like this. I shouldn't even be in this situation. I don't know this girl. I don't know what she's about or what she wants or needs or what she likes.

I hate this.

I hate being around people I can't trust.

After popping my headphones on and playing Thee Oh Sees, I start moving up the sidewalk toward Squat & Gobble. This is the gay neighborhood of San Francisco. Dudes everywhere holding hands and laughing and minding their own business.

Stopping in front of a storefront window, I check myself out one last time. Make sure I look as good as I should.

I'm wearing a pair of skinny black jeans and this blue Modest Mouse T-shirt I found at a thrift store in downtown Joliet a few months ago when me and my mother went record shopping and thrifting. This is another thing me and her do a lot. We go to thrift stores. We even drive to Chicago to thrift sometimes.

The day I got this shirt, though, it was one of the most fun afternoons I'd had with her in a while. She was in such a great mood. She'd made me breakfast in the morning and was relatively sober. The day even started out with her giving me the *Nirvana Live at the Paramount* DVD.

It was so cool to get that.

She said that she'd overheard me playing a lot of Nirvana songs on guitar and heard me sampling some for these beats I was making and she loved it.

My mother, she's always maintained that they're one of her favorite bands of all time, so she ordered me the DVD after she'd come across a great review of it online.

It's things like that, ya know, that have always helped to offset a lot of the bullshit she pulls. It meant the fucking world to me. Because she only bought it after she'd heard me devouring them for a few weeks and observed how much I loved them.

That really means something, ya know.

Later that night, we watched the DVD together after I played her the Modest Mouse albums *The Lonesome Crowded West* and *This Is a Long Drive for Someone with Nothing to Think About.* She'd never listened to them before. She liked them a lot. It was a blast.

But three hours later I found her sitting on top of the car in the garage, crying hysterically, a bottle of wine in her hand.

When I asked her what was wrong, she looked me dead in the eyes and said, "You."

We didn't talk for the next two days.

I'm also wearing my parka and my Nike Cortez and I've got a bandanna tied around my neck. I've got a backpack stuffed full with six Coronas and a bottle of champagne I snaked from the house.

Basically, I look great, but I'm still so damn nervous and can't figure out why I fucking care so much. But I do.

And here I go.

51

EVERY SINGLE QUESTION I HAD ABOUT WHY I'M doing this right now is annihilated when I see Dominique.

Man, she's so pretty. She's perfect. And she's always smiling. I've never seen anyone do that before. It's strange to me. It's awesome, too.

"Looking good and you're early," she says, when I walk in.

She's standing behind the counter, working the register, and she's wearing a pair of super-short, supertight white cutoff jean shorts with black stockings covering the rest of her legs.

Her hair is the same as it was on Friday except for this wicked fucking pheasant tail feather that's been braided into it.

A large gold earring that says *Fila* dangles from her left ear and a black cross hangs from the right one.

But the best thing, besides her face, tits, and smile, is the dope sweater she's wearing. It's black with the face of a white wolf painted on the front. She also wearing a white collared shirt under the sweater with the collar tucked into it.

"How's your day?" I ask her.

"Pretty good," she says. Man, her smile is contagious.

I can't help a grin as big as hers spreading across my face. "And yours?"

"Better now." I can't believe I said that.

"Good," she goes.

This older but really flamboyant gay dude with a shaved head, a goatee, and a gut comes up behind Dominique and grabs her shoulders.

"Is this him?" he says.

"It is," she goes. "Jaime, Chuck. Chuck, Jaime."

"Oh my," he gasps, both his hands touching his cheeks. "It's such a pleasure to meet you. I've been listening to this princess going on and on and on about you all dang day. And believe me, sweetie, this girl rarely has anything nice to say about boys. Especially since Ricky."

"Chuck," Dominique snaps. For the first time, I see her smile disappear and turn into anger. "No," she goes. "No."

Chuck turns to her and puts a hand over his mouth. "I'm so sorry," he gasps. "I pulled the Band-Aid right off of—"

"Hey," she snaps, cutting him off and shaking her head. "Stop, please."

Chuck tells her he's sorry again and then gives her a hug. She glances at me while he does this. There's hurt in her eyes and anger, too.

I'm curious, but it's none of my business. Clearly. And then Chuck tells Dominique she can leave.

She heads into the kitchen to grab her backpack, and then Chuck turns to me and says, "Don't be weirded out now, Jaime."

"I'm not."

"Good," he goes. "She's an angel and deserves to be treated like one."

"Whoa," I say. "I'm a nice dude, so it's fine, but we're just kicking it for a couple of hours and that's it."

Chuck starts laughing hysterically and says, "Oh please, Jaime. Please."

"I'm serious."

"Maybe you are." He shrugs. "But just look at that girl. That's perfection. *Perfection* . . . and what I've come to find out in my many years on this great place is that perfection often makes people do things they normally wouldn't do."

I don't say anything.

"So many guys come after her, so many, Jaime."

Pause.

"And she's picky."

Another pause.

"Now you're here and she's floating."

"So what?"

"I'm just saying, young man. She can have anyone and you're the one who's here."

I look away.

"You," he goes.

"And that's exactly why I'm so skeptical," I mutter. "I still don't get it."

"Excuse me?"

"Nothing," I tell him.

"Okay," he goes.

Dominique rolls back out from the kitchen and around the counter and I race to the door and open it for her, and when she walks by me, my nostrils smell perfume, peaches and cream, and maybe even some strawberries.

So basically, they smell heaven as all those butterflies from the other day converge back in my stomach and start making some noise.

52

I IMMEDIATELY TELL DOMINIQUE ABOUT THE DEVIL Feeder show or spectacle or whatever it's gonna end up being, and she's super down and we start walking toward the Mission.

"So tell me about Vicious Lips," I say, as we stop at a crosswalk and wait for the light to change.

"We're vicious," she says. "So fucking vicious."

"I bet."

"You tell me about us," she goes. "Come on now, man. I know you Googled the fuck out of us once you heard the name."

The light changes and we cross this wide, foresty street called Dolores.

"You're good," I tell her. "And I did do exactly that."

"So indulge me then. And when you're finished, I'll tell you a little bit about Tiger Stitches."

"You found that?"

"It wasn't hard at all, man. And it's really, really damn good."

"Thanks."

"So Vicious Lips," she goes.

"Right. That fucking band."

Vicious Lips:

I smoked an Oxy last night around two in the morning, then started digging.

They're a three-piece band with Dominique on keyboards, percussion, and main vocals. This other black chick, Keisha California, plays guitar, and then this skinny white hipster, Mark Hopless, drums.

The girls are sixteen and Mark is eighteen, and they're pretty goddamn productive and ambitious. Kristen was right, too, they've got some decent cred.

Their EP, their only release so far, called *Songs About Kissing*, has three four-star reviews from some pretty dope music blogs that I respect, like the *MOJO* magazine website, which had this to say about the record.

Pulling inspiration from nearly every genre imaginable, Vicious Lips paints a gorgeous, dreamlike world on the surface, all the while creating an incredibly dark, edgy, and dare I say dangerous landscape just beneath the soft gleam. The combination is as sexy as it is unnerving, which almost feels like the same thing when you're listening to this wonderful debut. Obviously, the name of the EP pays homage to the great and seminal Big Black, which I personally found to be endearing and provoking, since I came up in Chicago during the rise of Touch and Go Records. Plain and simple, this music is stunning, original, and profound. Vicious Lips does an incredible job of controlling the chaos it openly invites into every song. These fucking kids—yes, kids—are creating complex, thoughtful music most decent bands don't achieve until their fourth or fifth record, if they ever achieve it at all. That's fucking crazy to me. And it's so damn endearing. There is hope for this generation after all. Songs About Kissing *is one of the best debuts in recent years, and easily one of the best records of the year. Like, all I want is some goddamn more right now. No pressure at all, kiddos.*

The tracks are listed on their Bandcamp page like this:

1. Furry Forests
2. The Chocolate Balloon
3. Crushes
4. Wet Kisses
5. The Fury & the Night

Besides the awesome reviews, they've also got some great write-ups in the *SF Bay Guardian* and the *SF Weekly*. They've played over forty shows in the less than a year they've existed as a band, and they even went on a mini West Coast tour with this band from San Francisco that I fucking love called Social Studies.

"So pretty much," I tell Dominique while we stand in front of this huge brick building on Fourteenth and Mission known as the Armory. "Pretty much you guys fucking rule. I personally loved all the songs, with 'Crushes' probably being my favorite, I guess."

Dominique is glowing, which she should be. She deserves the praise. The music is *that* good.

"And lastly, ya know, Vicious Lips is kinda who I wanna be when I grow up."

Dominique bursts into laughter. "Yes," she says, while catching her breath. "Just yes!"

"So there ya go."

"That was really nice, Jaime," she tells me after a deep breath.

"Good. I'm glad you liked it."

She leans into me, nudging me with her arm and saying, "I liked it a lot. You're really thoughtful and sweet."

My jaw clenches tight. "Good," I say. "I'm glad you think that."

"Really?" she goes. "It doesn't look like you do."

I look away and say, "It's just that you don't know me."

"So what?"

"That means everything."

"No," she says. "It doesn't." She grabs my hand. "This right here, right now, this is what matters. I know you right now and it's wonderful."

I don't say anything.

"And that's what's important. This here, right now."

53

MOTHERFUCKING DEVIL FEEDER. YES! ALMOST TWO
blocks away from the Twenty-Fourth Street BART station,
I can see the Live 105 banner hanging high over a plastic
table. It's sorta busy too, although I have no idea how many
people are around to see these two dudes shred.

"Awesome," I say.

"They're crazy," says Dominique. "They've got a genera-
tor and everything."

"Yeah. They sounded so serious about it last night. Like
this is a show for them right now. A real show."

"How long have they been around?"

"Eddie said something like six or seven months."

"What's it sound like?"

"I don't know," I tell her. "They wanted me to hear it for
the first time today. I think Brandon said they've put out
four EPs online."

"Damn. And I thought my band was ambitious."

"They do it differently than you guys," I say.

"Obviously," she says. "Look at them. And this . . . it's
impressive and a great fucking idea about stealing that banner. Like, look at all the people who have stopped just to

watch. Not only does the banner give them some extra time, these people probably think that Devil Feeder is some sorta new, big deal. One of the next big things."

"Maybe they are," I say.

"Could be," she goes. "I love it."

We cross the street at Twenty-Third and turn right on the sidewalk toward them.

"Eddie says that every week or two weeks tops, they record five new songs on some shitty mic and just load the tracks right up."

"Interesting," she says. "I dig that concept if it's right for your band. Like us kids right now, this generation, the amazing tools we have to push our art onto other people, it's so incredible and immense. You have to be really lazy not to have a presence for your art right now. Everything's at your fingertips, you just gotta push yourself. The kids who don't, they're just not serious, or they're entitled, or again, pure fucking lazy."

"I was saying the same sorta thing to my father when we were on the plane flying here. He was shocked at how good my music collection was for my age and my knowledge about all these amazing bands and their history. And I told him pretty much exactly what you just said. All the fucking information about these bands and records can be pulled up in a second online. All that great music is there after typing in a couple of keywords. It's so easy if you really fucking love this stuff. I mean, I knew more about Black Flag's first four years when I was nine than I've known about Britney Spears, even though I like a couple of her tracks."

"So do I," says Dominique.

"'Everytime,'" I say. "That one especially just because of that—"

"Scene in *Spring Breakers*," the two of us say together.

"That's one of the best scenes I've ever seen in my life," Dominique shouts. "It was so good."

"Totally," I go. "That movie is definitely in my top ten of all time."

"Easily," she says back. "Without a doubt."

While we wait at the last intersection before Twenty-Fourth for the light to turn red, Dominique, she swings her arm gently into me and then slides her fingers down my skin and wraps them around mine.

I swing my eyes over to her and she's looking at me already.

This is the fucking dream, right? This is what boys are supposed to live for. This is how we're supposed to gain our entry into manhood. By satisfying those curious, painful needs. By taking something sweet like this and claiming it and making it ours. By waiting for the night her parents finally go out, then ordering her to take off all her clothes and lie on her bed. By pushing her legs wider and putting your mouth on her wet, tight pussy. By making sure her eyes never leave yours after you've stuck yourself inside of her. And by placing your hands around her gentle neck and squeezing it a tiny bit when you come as you try to fend off the shame and guilt that immediately arrive because you weren't supposed to do that, even if you were. Even if it's the only way to not be called a "pussy" and a "faggot" and a "loser."

I turn my head the other way quickly and pull my hand away from hers.

"What's wrong?" she asks.

Shaking my head, I say, "Nothing."

"Hey," she says, putting an arm over my shoulders. "It's okay, ya know."

"What is?"

"Letting yourself be happy," she says.

"That's not what this is."

"What is it then?"

I start to say something but stop.

What am I doing right now?

Why am I so fucked up in the head?

Dominique hugs me, then slides her face into the side of my neck. It's so warm and calm. Every hair on my body stands straight up.

"Jaime Miles," she says, after lifting her head back up.

"That's me."

"You fucking rock, dude. And so do I. Like that's that, plain and simple."

"Plain and simple, huh?"

"Sure."

I shrug and then grab her hand.

I say, "The next time something is plain and simple will be the first time for me."

"Perfect," she says. "I'm hoping this trip is all about some fantastic first times for you, ya know."

My dick gets hard as we cross the street.

54

I'D SAY DEVIL FEEDER GOT MAYBE SIX MINUTES OF shredding in before two cop cars and four pigs shut the shitshow down. They sounded tough, though. Eddie played a fucking Rickenbacker bass through a Rivera guitar amp. He's left-handed too, which is cool to watch.

It was so huge, the sound I'm talking about. Big and massive. It was fierce too, and I really mean that.

Just so fierce and aggressive.

Like if I had to build a family of bands that could take them in and adopt them, it'd be like 400 Blows, Daughters, Federation X, and Coachwhips, cos of all the dirty reverb Eddie has feeding back to him from the microphone.

Anyway, they mowed down their first song, "Narc Dies Hard," to a crowd of at least forty people, who prolly had no idea why two kids dressed in all white denim with huge sunglasses covering their faces were center stage at a BART station in front of a radio station banner singing about snitches getting killed.

The first cop car rolled up right before they smashed into the second song, "Blubber Waves." Right before that, Brandon spotted me and yelled, "Booger Pussy!"

"Those pussies are always the best," said Eddie into the microphone. "Especially if they got hairy backs."

He looked up at me and flipped me off.

Then he said some shit to this girl in a red dress and cowgirl boots with long blond hair. She was carrying two bags of Taco Bell in her hand and Eddie was like, "What's up, you pretty thang? You got an extra Triple Steak Stack for me and my son."

The girl's face turned bright red, and she looked down at the ground.

"Oh come on, baby red. Red dream. Red teeth. How about a chalupa?"

The girl started walking really fast.

"Half a chalupa?"

She turned her head the other way.

"Gordita," he said.

I started laughing.

"No," he went. "Nothing."

Dominique laughed too.

"How about a packet of hot sauce?" Eddie said. "How about two packets of hot sauce and a quarter for looking at us for a split second while we were playing?"

The girl finally faded away.

"There's prolly seven taquerías within two blocks from here and that whore gets Taco Bell."

"Jesus," said Dominique.

"Bet she eats it all by herself, too. Bet she locks her

bedroom door and gobbles it down and uses every packet of hot sauce she took, and you know she took three handfuls, too. Everyone does that shit. They take way more packets than they need, and you usually lose a couple of them in your car or on your floor and then one day someone sits on one of them or something and it squirts all over their clothes and it really ruins that person for a couple of hours. How do you apologize for that? It's impossible. No one wants to hear that shit after they sit on a packet of hot sauce you thought you lost somewhere else six weeks ago." Eddie shook his head. "Disgusting." He cleared his throat. "Anyway," he continued. "That miss red, red moon, red nipples, red tongue perhaps, well she's also gonna eat ice cream in her sweatpants tonight and watch *Friends* and go to bed at ten."

"What the fuck," I whispered.

"Eddie!" Brandon shouted, pointing at the first cop car that had just arrived.

Eddie smiled, then went, "Thanks, guys, for coming out today! This next song is called 'Blubber Waves.' And don't forget to listen to us live on the air tonight. Live 105. Call them and tell them to keep playing Devil Feeder!"

He said the band's name in a super-high-pitched voice, and then Brandon counted off and they ripped for at least a minute, minute and a half before the second cop car rolled in.

Four fucking police officers converging quickly onto two fucking kids playing instruments to curious onlookers. I get it, I guess. Like, I get the point of stopping live bands just posting up and plugging in and playing outside people's homes. My father told me last night that a good friend of his from Findlay, Ohio, where he grew up, moved into a place right on the corner of Haight and Ashbury three years ago with his wife and newborn baby.

"They moved out two months later," he said.

"Why?"

"Cos of those street d-bags rolling thirty deep and taking over the sidewalk right in front of their apartment for hours and hours, harassing people as they walked by, breaking bottles, and playing those stupid bongo drums and singing Sublime songs and Goo Goo Dolls songs."

"Really?"

"Shit yeah," he went. "The fucking Goo Goo Dolls. Nobody wants to hear that bullshit anymore. No one I know wanted to hear it the first time around, so they especially don't want it being played by smelly fucking kids getting hammered on malt liquor and begging for money. And the weed, too. They'd smoke the worst-smelling weed and just get wasted and act like a bunch of dicks to everyone."

My father was really emotional as he was saying all of this.

"Or if it's not the trustafarian mobs, you got these other kind of retarded people who actually drive to Haight and Ashbury and post up on the corners and play whatever shitty original music they write after work or on the week-ends. They've got this grand idea in their head and think those corners are so relevant and magical. They still think it's some kind of mecca, even though they won't move there. Man, those people are assholes. At least the street goblins aren't delusional."

"Then why do they come to Haight and Ashbury?"

"The park, son. Golden Gate Park is just a few blocks away. One of the biggest urban parks in the world. Sleep for free at night under the stars and ruin the neighborhood for everyone who pays taxes to live there during the day."

"Shitty."

"Yup. So my friend moved because they couldn't lay their little boy, a child, down for a damn nap without the noise on the street waking him up two or three times. It's so stupid."

"People who cover Sublime should get jail time," I said.

My father smiled. "Absolutely. And the ones who cover the Goo Goo Dolls should get life."

Both of us started laughing until we realized we were laughing together. It hadn't happened before. And I hated myself for letting it happen.

My mother is in a fucking mental hospital and I'm cracking jokes with the man who ran her over.

I stomped out of the room immediately after noticing this and made sure I was all alone for a few minutes and punched myself as hard as I could in the chest.

Punching until I felt way worse than I felt good during the conversation with my father.

Anyway, point is, I get it. I understand the police squashing this shit. But four fucking officers showing up.

Like, come on. It ain't that big of a deal. Plus, Brandon and Eddie are supercool about it.

Eddie tells the cops exactly what they were doing and how many songs they thought they'd get away with, and the cops think it's funny.

And one of them, he even asks Eddie if he can get a CD, and Eddie grabs one off the table and hands it to him.

Fifteen minutes later, the cops are gone.

Eddie rolls right over to us, a huge grin smeared on his mug, and he goes, "You're Dominique from Vicious Lips, right?"

"I am," she goes. "You know my band?"

"I love your band," he says. "*Songs About Kissing* is one of my favorite records right now."

"Damn," I say. "Fucking famous and shit."

Dominique blushes. "Stop that," she says.

"I saw you guys open for the Saint James Society at Bottom of the Hill a few months ago."

"No shit," she says. "That was such a fun show."

"It was a great fucking show."

"I love the Saint James Society," I say. "That's so dope that you played with them."

Dominique almost seems awkward now, with all this attention. "It was a dream come true," she says. "That song of theirs off the first EP, 'Of Silver and Gold,' like, that song made me fall in love with them."

"It's so good," I say.

"Makes my pussy wet," she goes, laughing after saying it.

"Oh hey," says Eddie. "Damn."

He winks at her and like that, this surge of jealousy washes through me. It's weird even though it feels so damn natural. So violent. So angry. I actually feel anger toward Eddie for saying that.

This is when Dominique does the coolest thing yet. She hooks an arm around mine and then slides her hand into the back pocket of my jeans.

Total *Wonder Years* style.

And Eddie, he looks shocked that he's seeing this. That this is happening between me and her.

"So what about Devil Feeder?" Eddie asks.

"Shredded," I say. "It was fierce, too. I gotta hear more, though."

"But you liked it? What you heard at least."

Both me and Dominique say yes, and Eddie gets stoked. I can see the excitement on his face.

Brandon comes over now, holding the folded table and the rolled-up banner.

"Vicious Lips," he goes. "I love your band."

"Cool," she goes.

"You guys live was so perfect. You guys brought it that night. When I was having a cigarette outside after the show, I heard at least six or seven people saying that they thought y'all were the best to play that night."

"What about you?" she asks.

"What about me?"

"Did you think we were the best?"

"Shit," he goes. "I don't know. It was close between you and the Saint James."

"I thought they were better," she goes. "Hands down. They were the best band that night, and they're the best band we've played with."

"Not Social Studies?" I go.

"No," she says. "Although it's really close for me. Like, super-duper close, but I gotta go with my boys and girls from Austin in the end."

"That's nice of you," says Brandon. "How do you two know each other?"

Me, I go ahead and tell those dudes how me and her met, and then I slide my backpack off and open it.

"I got beers and champagne," I say.

"That's right," says Eddie. "For last night. Rad."

"Let's pop over to Dolores Park and have a few there," Brandon goes.

I look at Dominique, and she says she's cool with that.

"Perfect," says Eddie.

"I'm pumped to see that place," I go. "I read about it in this book, *Dickpig Sux*, and I've always wanted to just fucking lie in the grass and become cool or something."

"I remember reading that book too," Eddie says. "That dude really fucking romanticized it. He made it seem like the Garden of Eden or some shit."

"I remember hearing that some of those kids who came to SF because of that book, like, filled Ziploc bags with Dolores Park grass and were making smoothies with it," Dominique tells us.

"That's not real," says Eddie.

She shrugs. "That's what I heard. More than once and by different people."

"Fucking turds," Eddie rips.

"That pool still there?" I ask.

"Nah," says Eddie. "This boy and girl, super young and shit, maybe like eleven or twelve years old, they read that book too and got wasted on the roof."

"Oh shit," says Dominique. "I remember that. Fuck."

"What happened?" I ask.

"They started fooling around up there, and somehow they lost their balance and they rolled off and landed headfirst on the concrete around the pool and they both died."

"Jesus," I say.

"City closed that place after that."

"Fuck," I go, feeling like I just got punched in the stomach. "That's horrible."

"Yeah," Eddie says. "What a shitty way to go. Like dying as a virgin right as you're about to lose your virginity."

"Cos you knew they were gonna fuck in the pool."

"Right."

"I'm just hoping the boy maybe got his dick sucked a

little bit before they fucking popped against that ground,"
Eddie goes.

"Damn, dude," Brandon snorts.

"What?"

"That's fucking morbid," he goes.

"We have a song called 'Narc Dies Hard,' you faggot. A
song that's on an EP that we just gave to a fucking cop."

Me and Dominique are laughing.

"So please, dude. Fuck that morbid bullshit."

Brandon pulls a pack of cigarettes from his tight white
jeans and goes, "I guess you're right."

He hands a smoke to Eddie, then lights his own, and
then the four of us bounce to the park after packing Eddie's
white pickup truck with the gear.

55

"WAIT," BRANDON SAYS, TURNING THE BOTTLE OF champagne in his hands. "This is, like, a hundred-dollar bottle, man. You steal this shit?"

"Sure," I say. "You can say that."

"From where?"

"My father's wine cellar," I say. "Took the beers from the fridge, though."

"He's so loaded, huh," Eddie goes. "Like really fucking rich."

"I guess so. I mean, it seems that way." Holding my hand up and squeezing my thumb and index finger nearly all the way together, I say, "I know this much about the guy. Like, I prolly know more about you all than him. It's kinda weird."

This, like, collective sigh followed by a collective "Bullshit" immediately follows what I said.

"I've been living with my seventy-eight-year-old grandma who's been in a wheelchair for most of the last seven years," Eddie goes. "I haven't seen or talked to my dad since I was five, and my mom took off six years ago and I don't know where she is."

"I was adopted when I was four," says Brandon. "Don't

know who my biological parents are and don't fucking care."

We all look at Dominique now. She turns her eyes away from us, though, and doesn't say anything.

"You okay?" I ask.

"What?" she whispers.

"You okay?"

She nods and her lips squeeze tightly together.

"Hey," I say.

"I'm fine," she says. "Totally, Jaime. I am. I'm good."

"Fuck talking about this shit," Eddie snaps. "I hate wasting time and oxygen talking about people who are dead to me. Who never fucking cared about me for a second."

I reach into my backpack and hand Eddie and Brandon beers, but when I try to give Dominique one, she shakes her head.

"Really?" I say.

"Really, man. I don't drink anymore. I don't get high either. Not anymore. But thank you."

"Sure," I say, popping the cap off my beer with a lighter. "I'm glad we're hanging out."

Her body language changes like that and she's smiling again. She reaches over and puts her hand on my knee.

"Me too," she says. "It's really nice."

We're all somewhat sprawled out in a semicircle on the grass near the bathroom at Dolores Park.

Prolly like a hundred other people are there too.

Dominique's iPhone is lying in an empty plastic cup on top of my backpack. We're listening to *Live Execution* by Babyland. It's one of my favorites right now, and I'm stoked all these guys know about it too.

It's a live album from their last show ever at the Smell in Los Angeles in 2009. Man, I wish I woulda got a chance to see these guys live. The music is filled with so much rawness and emotion and edge.

James Morgan flew down to L.A. with his girl, Caralie, just to see the last show.

I know this because there's this rad video on YouTube of him being interviewed on the rooftop of the Standard Hotel during the trip.

Watching the less-than-five-minute clip is really a pretty amazing experience. You can tell he hasn't slept in days. He looks out of his mind.

And he's mumbling about some band he used to be in when he was nineteen called the Loiterers and this song called "Sleeping with Other Women" he wrote the night before with Devendra and how after he sang it to Caralie, she packed her shit and flew back to San Francisco, and how now he's gonna stay in L.A. for two extra days to try and bang M.I.A. or a minor Miley Cyrus ("make Billy Ray watch and give that creep a real achy breaky heart, that cunt") or Karen O ("but there's always gonna be Karen O left to slay, I guess"), and how he's definitely gonna beat the shit out of one of "those douchebag Good Charlotte brothers again," even though he can't recall which one he destroyed in Nicky Hilton's hotel room a couple years earlier (it really happened), and how he'll probably end up just living in L.A. now since he's got enough cocaine "to stay awake for a year."

Then he does two shots of tequila before singing "Sleeping with Other Women."

It's a pretty good song, too. I think the first verse goes . . .

"Well, I've decided to sleep with other women, didn't mean it to come to this, but this is my only real choice, things ain't working out, the way we talked about, not gonna sit here at night and hold my dick, gonna hit the town, drink that Kentucky Brown and fuck another chick, it's not that I'm not into you no more, it's just the way things are now, I think that I should score with another girl, think that I've given this a pretty good twirl . . ."

It's all so good.

One of the greatest interviews ever, I'm sure of it.

Eddie pops a joint from a pack of cigarettes, and Brandon opens the champagne.

"That Rickenbacker you were playing," I tell Eddie.

"Look at you, knowing about my gear. What about it?"

"The sound was nice, man. Thing hummed and pierced at the same time."

He lights the joint and goes, "I thought so too."

"I've always wanted to play a Rickenbacker."

Taking the joint from Eddie, Brandon says, "You play or something, homie?"

"I do."

"Really?" says Eddie.

"You didn't tell them?" Dominique goes.

I take a drink of beer and say, "Nah. I don't really talk about my music that much."

"Wait," snaps Eddie. "Your music? What do you play, dude?"

"Keyboard, piano, and guitar. Pretty much I can play anything, but the piano and the guitar are my main things."

"And you're good?" Brandon asks.

"He's awesome," Dominique says. "He's got a bunch of music up online under the name Tiger Stitches."

"What?" both Brandon and Eddie say at the same time.

I make a face. "Yeah. Why?"

"Dude," says Brandon. "That's the *Peril Alley* EP shit, right?"

"It is."

"Those songs are dope," says Eddie.

This is really bizarre. I don't understand how these kids know about my music. I know they didn't Google me after they split last night or at all anytime today.

So I ask them, and Eddie tells me that somebody posted a link to my Bandcamp page in some Growlers chat room and he checked it out.

It all makes so much sense now. This ain't like Joliet. These fucking kids are different. These kids fucking love music and love art. They're not just listeners or lookers, they're devourers and indulgers, and there's a huge fucking difference there, ya know.

They live for this shit. It's their passion.

And they can't get enough of it, which is why they seek it out instead of waiting around for it.

They're like me.

It's so fucking cool to see it with my own eyes instead of daydreaming about it and hoping it eventually exists and becomes a part of my life.

"Thanks, man," I go. "That means a lot."

"We've been dying to get a rad guitar player in Devil Feeder," says Brandon.

"Really?"

"Shit yeah," Eddie goes. "But everyone we've tried out so far has been a bunch of pilgrim dicks and mouth breathers."

"But I'm leaving in a week. What's the point?"

"Fuck you for thinking like that," Eddie snaps. "What's the point?"

"Yeah."

"Making some killer songs and puking them up to the world. This whole thing that happens every day," Eddie says.

I don't say anything.

"Life," he snaps. "This. All this opening your eyes and breathing and doing shit."

"What about it?"

"Come on," Eddie moans. He takes a monster pull from

the champagne, then cashes the rest of his beer and grabs another one. Popping the cap off, he says, "It only happens once, man. This is it. There's not another shot. So who the fuck cares if you're leaving in a week? What we might end up making is the only thing that's ever gonna outlive us. It's art, Jaime. It's timeless. Nobody can hear your excuses when you're dead. But they sure as hell can listen to your music."

I look at Dominique, and she says, "He's right."

"I know."

"Great," says Eddie. "Tomorrow night at seven."

"What's that?"

"Band practice at my house," Brandon goes.

"I'll be there."

"Now that's more like it, brah," Eddie snorts while Babyland performs their final song as a band, "Search and Rescue."

I'm grinning ear to ear.

Five years later and they're never playing again, but here we are, four fucking kids who were born years after that band was formed, getting off to their music at a beautiful park in San Francisco.

Like, what's not to love about that?

This is the only taste of immortality you can ever fucking get.

56

DOMINIQUE WRAPS HER HAND AROUND MINE AS we're walking out of Dolores Park. It's dark now. The sun bailed, like, thirty minutes ago and she asked me to walk her to the Church Street train station. She lives in West Portal, which means nothing to me.

"It's three stops from Church," she says.

"Great."

She giggles and goes, "I forget that you don't live here."

"You forget?"

"Yes. Because you fit in so well here. It's like this is nothing for you. Like you showed up in San Francisco two days ago, and all's you've done is have dinner with James Morgan, spend the day with my hot face, and join a fucking band."

"It's really nice," I tell her. "Incredible, actually. But it's hard for me to be all that stoked sometimes because it's so sick that I'm even here."

"It's not sick, man. Like, have you stopped to think that this is where you belong?"

"No."

"That's so sad," she says.

"But I don't belong here, Dominique. I don't belong with my father in his mansion with his maids. No way. That asshole violently took himself out of my life and stayed out of it. I belong with the lady who left with nothing. Not even a hundred bucks. The lady who walked out on everything she'd worked for since she was a little kid in order to save me from him."

"Dude," she goes. "I'm not gonna pretend like I know anything about your life and what that was like. But you're being really hard on your father."

"I know I am, and he deserves it."

"Maybe," she says. "Who am I to say he doesn't? But you've been in San Francisco now for two nights with him."

"So what?"

"How big of a monster is he? Like, you got to buy records yesterday and go to some crazy party at RVCA and see Toast. Then look at today, man. This has been such a rad, amazing day."

Letting go of Dominique's hand now, I say, "What's your point?"

"Don't get angry with me."

"What's your point, Dominique?"

We stop walking now and face each other on the sidewalk.

"Go on," I say. "Tell me."

"It's just that he seems to be treating you pretty okay, Jaime. He's been nothing like a monster to you."

I get worked up and start to say something, but she cuts me off.

She says, "I'm not done. You wanted me to tell you, so let me tell you."

"Yeah?" I snap.

"I'm not saying he didn't do any terrible things. Clearly he did something. But he's being really nice to you and letting you have your space."

"Great," I say. "Way to be a father."

"Would you want it the other way, Jaime? Would you really want him breathing down your neck and trying to spend every second with you?"

I roll my eyes and look away from her.

"Like, he's not being mean to you. He's not been the same person to you that he was to your mother."

"So what?"

"All's I'm saying is that you can totally hate someone for something they did to someone you love the most and care so much about. That's pretty natural to me, man. I get *that*."

"Exactly."

"But that doesn't mean you have to toe the same line as your mother. You can still hate him for what he did to her while forging out a relationship with him on some level. This is a little bit deeper than some person fucking over your friend at school. This is blood, Jaime. And your father helped make you, and your father is the only person you have if something happens to your mother. He flew to Illinois the night he found out to bring you back to his house and into his life. Isn't there anything in that you can appreciate?"

Swinging my eyes back on Dominique, I say, "No."

"That's bullshit."

"And what would you know about any of this, Dominique? Huh? How could you possibly think you know anything about my situation?"

"I'm not saying I do, Jaime."

"Really?" I say sarcastically. "Really?"

"Yeah. At least you have a fucking chance to see if the horrible man who fucked your mother over is the same horrible man who might fuck you over. At least you have a chance to find that out, man. Not everyone gets that."

"Why are you sticking up for my father?" I ask her.

Dominique throws her arms into the air and goes, "I'm not, Jaime. I'm sticking up for you and the opportunity you fucking have to at least get to know the man you hate so much and find out for yourself if he's really a monster or someone who made some terrible choices years ago. You have a real chance to see for yourself if he's still that same person or if he's changed because of that and become something better."

"Why is this all on me?" I snap. "Why can't he be the one who clears some way for a middle ground?"

"Jaime," she says.

"What?"

"He has."

"Bullshit."

"He came to you and brought you into his home."

"Because he had to."

"He still did it, dude. There isn't even a path anymore. He brought you right into his life. This is the middle ground, man. And it's all on you to decide if you can work in it."

57

ME AND DOMINIQUE, WE'RE STANDING NEXT TO THE escalators of the Muni station. She's got one earphone in her ear and I've got one in mine and she plays that Youth Lagoon song "July."

We're done arguing now. It wasn't even a real fucking argument, but it got personal, which invited, like, a thousand pounds of anxiety to show up, and then it got quiet for a block—a block that consisted of me trying to convince myself that I should bail. Jump into a cab and leave. Forget her forever. Wipe this random blip from my brain, then talk shit about her every chance I get for the rest of my life. Refuse to acknowledge all of her commentary on my life, which I openly invited and really hate—until Dominique reached over and grabbed me and said, "You don't have to make this a pissing contest, Jaime. It's not as personal as you think."

"I'm not doing that," I said.

"Sure you are. But you're hypersensitive to that kind of shit. It's fine. Just don't shut me out."

It was the first time in my life that somebody decided to make me feel better by telling the truth about how they felt instead of doubling down and blowing that anxiety up a million times over.

She was frowning, but it didn't feel like it to me. Her frown was so much better than anyone else in the world's smile.

Like five seconds later, I finally cracked and went, "I won't."

"Promise?"

"On all the mothers' graves in the world."

"Killer."

Dominique leans into me now, and she lays her head against my shoulder.

"Five minutes," she says.

"Till what?"

"The next train home."

"That sucks."

"Why?"

I don't answer her.

"Why does it suck, Jaime?"

"You know why."

She squeezes me now.

"Told you," I say.

"I wanna see you tomorrow."

"When?"

"Before you go to Brandon's."

"Okay."

"Come to my house," she says. "I wanna show you my synth and keyboard."

"We should make some music, too."

"Definitely."

"I like this."

"So do I, Jaime."

She lifts her head up. I can feel the glare from her eyes on me.

"Stop thinking about why this is happening between me and you," she says.

"It's hard not to."

"What I've come to realize is that nothing I can say will ever make you stop thinking."

"Probably not."

"So all I can do is show you why."

"You think that'll work?"

She giggles and then kisses the side of my neck.

"It already is," she says. Then, "I have to go now."

"All right."

Stepping in front of me, looking me straight in the eyes, Dominique says, "It's not that you don't know how to trust, Jaime."

"You're wrong."

"No," she goes. "I'm not." She grabs both my hands now. "I'm not wrong."

"Then what is it?" I ask.

"It's that you don't know how not to not trust."

Pause.

"So no more bullshit pseudo emotional armor."

Another pause.

"Quit looking for reasons to stay all alone."

"It's safe, though."

"No, it's not. This is safe."

I look away from her.

"This is real, man," she says.

She kisses my neck again.

"So don't try and stop it," she says.

"Why?"

"Cos you can't, Jaime. It's too late. It's already happening."

Dominique wraps her arms around me and squeezes me for, like, ten seconds. When she lets go, she says, "This part, right here."

"It's the best."

"It most certainly is," she says, as Youth Lagoon sings . . .

"Five years ago, in my backyard, I sang love away, little did I know that real love had not quite yet found me . . ."

After she kisses my neck again, she pulls the earphone from my ear and then disappears down the stairs.

58

THE FIRST TIME I EVER SMOKED THE BLUE, I KNEW there was no turning back the second I released the dragon from my lungs. Inhaling that smoke, it was like I'd just pumped my body full with the very happiest point I'd get to naturally during the day, except it was like I'd hit that point twenty times all at once.

This is the kind of happiness you only get by paying for it.

Or by stealing it from your mother.

My mother, she's the reason I smoke two instead of one this morning. I'm nervous and I'm anxious. Today is the day I finally get to talk to her. This should be so easy, ya know, it should be. It's a fucking phone call. But that's just not possible.

Easy isn't possible with this particular group of turd burglars.

Basically, this hospital administrator has told my father that he needs to be in the same room with me during the phone call.

"Not happening," I tell my father.

"Then you're not talking to her," he says. "Those are the rules that they set."

"Fuck that. Fuck you!"

I hold the phone to my ear and go, "Listen. My father will not be in the room with me."

The administrator guy starts to say something, but I cut him off.

I say, "This is the deal, man. These are the rules that I'm setting."

My father is standing there, just watching me talk. He looks angry. So what?

I go, "This is my mother. She's all I have, and she won't talk to me if she knows my father's in the room. He's a fuck and he treated her like shit and there's no way he gets to be a part of this. No way. He's not our family. He's a fucking monster."

"Jaime," the man says. "You don't get to dictate the rules."

"Really?"

"Yes."

"Okay," I say. "Then I won't talk to her."

"Then that would be your choice. Or you can simply allow your father to be in the room with you while you speak to her, and everyone wins."

"Oh, man," I say, laughing as I do. "You have no idea what you've stepped into."

"Excuse me?"

"What do you think is gonna happen when you tell my mother that she doesn't get to talk to me?"

He doesn't say anything.

"You think it's just gonna be okay with her, huh?"

"I'll explain what happened to her and that's that."

"She'll fucking lose it on you, man. She will come after you right away and try to hurt you very badly. And even if you stop her, it'll only get worse. She'll self-destruct right in front of you. She'll tune you out and become more violent. She'll start hurting herself once she's done hurting other patients. And she'll never listen to you again. You understand that? If you do this, if you enforce this petty, bullshit rule and allow the man who ruined her life to sit in on the phone call with the only person she loves, she's gone, man. She'll never come back. And instead of helping this woman and treating her problems and making sure she gets better, you'll be the one responsible for her demise and you'll be guilty of anything that happens to anyone else when she acts out. Because she's going to if she doesn't get to talk to me. And when she does, it'll be so violent and shocking. It'll be so ugly and you're gonna have to live with yourself knowing that none of it would've happened if you'd just let me talk to her without that awful man in the room."

"Jaime," he says.

"I'm hanging up in five seconds."

"Jaime."

"One, two, three . . . come on, dude. Four."

"All right," he says. "Fine."

"Thank you." I pull the phone away from my ear and look at my father. "So you're cool," I tell him. "You're excused. Go do whatever it is you'd normally do. Your presence ain't needed."

Pause.

"Dude," I finish, then leave the kitchen and walk to my room.

59

"I FEEL OKAY. I DO. IT'S A LITTLE BIT BETTER NOW than it was, but I'm not there yet. It's like when you're going to clean a window but you don't want to be cleaning anything. When you spray the cleaner on it and it starts to trickle down the pane. There's always that first, tiny bit of dirt that peels right off, ya know, and it looks a little bit better, nicer, but it's still dirty. And this is the last thing you want to be doing, but you know you have to get it done. You wish that more dirt would come off just by spraying it more. You wish you could just spray it a couple of times and walk away and it would be so clear and clean by the time you came back to it."

My mother pauses while I watch my hands shake violently.

"I want to leave so bad, Jaime. I want to walk to you. But I can't do that. I have to make sure I wipe all the dirt away."

"I know."

"I'm so sorry," she says.

Hearing the sound of her voice again is awesome. I've missed it. There hasn't been a single day in my life that I've never heard it. It's really comforting. It's also maddening.

Like, you did this. You. There'd be no need to walk to me if you'd never let the demons rip you away to begin with.

"I miss you so much, Jaime. My boy. My beautiful boy."

Not even the numb of the two blues is enough to deflect the sharp edges of each word she says.

"I miss you, too," I say. "But it's getting better now for sure, right? You're gonna be fine soon?"

I stand, then walk to the desk and drop an Oxy on it, covering it with a sheet of paper.

"I will," she says. "I have to. It's the only way I get you back. There's no choice in this for me, Jaime. I'd die if I couldn't have you back."

Crushing the pill down into powder with my lighter now, I say, "How does it feel to be sober?"

"Clear," she says. "The fog is gone and I feel everything so much more. That's why this is even tougher. I feel your absence and I feel all the shame and the guilt. All the remorse, it hurts so bad. There are no more shields or walls. When it comes at me, I know it's going to hit. And I know it's going to hit hard. No more ducking from it, Jaime. No more trying to hide from life."

I cut the pile of blue into two lines and roll a twenty-dollar bill.

"I feel myself living in my body again. It's been years. And it hurts. My body hurts."

I stare at the lines. I wonder if she was here, and she'd just said everything she just did, and then I handed her a mirror with these lines of Oxy on it, I wonder if she'd do them. It's hard for me to think she wouldn't. People have to want to quit something to actually quit it for good. Quitting usually doesn't work when that person is forced to for whatever reason.

"It's terrifying. Losing everything you've been leaning on for as long as I have, all these things you've counted on to keep you standing up, it's horrendous and frightening, but every time I've been ready to lose it and break down, I think about how you're supposed to feel fear when you're alive. You're supposed to be scared of some things and uneasy about some things. It's life. You're supposed to feel life. And I'll get to this breaking point and then think how nice it is to actually remember the day I just had. How nice it is to feel something about the day. It's gorgeous. It's so much prettier than the fog."

Pause.

"I'm glad I don't remember what happened last week, though," she says. "I'm so glad I don't remember breaking my finger."

This is when I lean down and snort both lines of blue.

"Jaime," she says.

Rubbing my nose, I say, "Yeah."

"I'm so thankful that you're different than me. That's the one silver lining, ya know. That as awful as I was, my son, my beautiful boy hasn't gone down the same road as me. You've been a saint. You're not out there hating me or getting wasted and doing horrible things and getting in trouble."

I snap my head all the way back and suck the rest of the Oxy out of my nostrils and down my throat.

Images of me slicing a switchblade through a strange man's hair, vandalizing cars and slashing tires, smash through my head.

"You've turned your back on all of that bullshit. I'm so proud of you. Life gets you high enough. I'm grateful for that. So thrilled and grateful my Jaime doesn't have any issues, no stupid addictions. You're too smart for that. And now I'm going to get back to being as smart as you."

Stepping back from the desk, this nausea hits me.

Sweat begins pouring down my face.

I sit back down on the edge of the bed and breathe slowly.

"This will all be over in a blink of an eye," she says. "We'll be back together soon, just me and my boy, and our life will be better than it's ever been."

"I hope so," I barely manage to say.

"I know so. Just a blink of an eye," she says again. "And it'll be like none of this ever happened. I can't wait for that. I can't wait to feel like tomorrow really is the first day of my life."

"Awesome," I say, after wiping the sweat off with my shirt.

"I love you."

"I love you, too."

Click.

The phone falls out of my hand and I run out of the room, sprint down the hallway and into the bathroom.

Two seconds later, there I am, on my knees, and my face is in the toilet and vomit is shooting out of my mouth.

All those drugs I've never done, and here I am throwing them up and everything else my body wants to push out because I did too many of them.

60

LESLIE IS GRADING PAPERS IN THE LIVING ROOM when I finally come back downstairs.

When she looks up at me, her face is angry and her eyes are like ice.

"What's going on with you?" she asks.

I shrug. "Nothing."

"Are you sick?"

"Why?"

"I heard you throw up. I was in the office."

"I'm fine."

Leslie's face hasn't changed. Neither has her glare.

"Are you okay?" I ask.

"No," she says. "Not at all."

"I'm sorry to hear that . . . I guess. Is there anything I can do to help?" I start looking around the room. "Where is my father?"

"He's long gone," she says.

"Should I call him?"

Leslie drops the stack of papers in her hand on the coffee table and stands up. She shakes her head. "No," she snaps.

"Well, what do you want me to do then? What's wrong?"

"I want you to stop being a fucking bitch to your father," she barks.

Just the tone of her voice startles me. Hearing those particular words come out of her mouth, this fucking blond hippie art teacher, it's fucking weird, and it really rubs me the wrong way.

"Say that again," I snort.

"You heard me the first time," she says. "Don't play stupid, Jaime."

I toss my arms into the air and go, "Who do you think you are, Leslie? My mother?"

"You listen to me," she says. "That man has been nothing but great to you since he picked you up. He's treated you with respect, kindness, and understanding, and I'll be damned if I'm going to stand in my own house—our house, not yours—and listen to you say those things about him to a complete stranger. Do you know how hurtful that was to watch? Do you know how bad that made him feel? Standing in his own house and having to watch his own son, his abandoned flesh and blood, tear him down like that and call him those names and say those things about him after he flew to Illinois on a few hours' notice just to bring you into his home so you weren't all alone. You ungrateful brat. If there's anyone being a monster, it's you."

The skin on my face is burning. My heart is racing.

"If it was so goddamn awful," I rip, "where is he? If he's

so hurt by what I said, then why the fuck isn't he here talking to me?"

"Because he actually has some respect and dignity," she hisses.

"Yeah, right. You don't know anything, Leslie. Nothing. You have no idea what you're talking about, so stay the fuck out of my business. This is between me and him."

"This is my house!" she yells. "You're in my fucking house and you will not disrespect my husband like that in front of me or him again."

I roll my eyes and even though I don't want to do this at all, I start laughing. I can't stop myself. I just laugh and run a hand over my face.

"What the hell is so funny?"

"This," I say, spreading my arms out. "This! Like, here we go again."

"What are you talking about?"

"Once again, my father is fucking gone, and the woman he's in love with is trying to define him to me. That's awesome."

A sudden hush comes over Leslie, and her face dries up and turns white.

"The only difference between you and my mother right now is that you're telling me how great he is instead of how awful he is, and I still don't even know who he is. Bravo!" I snap, smacking my hands together. "The woman he was in love with before you is the one who shaped my impression of him. She's had fourteen years to do this, though, so if you think you're going to make me feel bad about what I said and shed a different light on him with some passionate five-minute rant in the living room after I just finished talking to that other woman, you're about as crazy as she is too."

Leslie says nothing. She's fucking shell-shocked.

"I appreciate him for making sure his fourteen-year-old son wasn't totally alone and by himself after his mother almost died, but if he wants me to think he's anything other than what I know him to be based on what happened between him and my mother, he's gonna have to do a lot more than house his own fucking son. Dude's never given a shit about me until he legally had to. Never even pretended to maybe give a shit. Fuck that."

Leslie's head drops and her eyes close and I put my earphones in and walk out of the house.

61

DOMINIQUE MEETS ME AT THE WEST PORTAL STATION.
It's really windy and cold. When I look around, it almost seems like I'm in a different city. It was sorta sunny in the Haight and not very cold, and instead of mostly apartments and stoops, I see houses and driveways.

She gives me a hug. It's really fucking nice. Just to see her again and see someone smile and at least look fucking happy.

"You smell nice," I tell her.

"It's the least I could do. Are you hungry?"

"I could eat. Sure."

"Pizza okay?"

"Pizza's great. I'd eat it for every meal and snack if I could."

"You'd get so fat, though."

"But I'd never have a bad meal."

She grabs my hand and we walk away from the train station.

"Ya know, I really, really love your septum ring," I tell her. "I keep thinking about it. It looks so good on you. It just fits. It makes a pretty face just a little bit more pretty."

"Do you spend a lot of time thinking about me, Jaime?"

"I mean, not a lot. Not really all that much. Here and there, ya know. Like right after I'm done thinking about how amazing my father is and how rad my mother is too."

"Shut up," she says, pushing me gently, jokingly. "I'd rather you didn't think about me at all then."

"Not even the nose ring?"

"Nope." She's grinning. "Nothing about me at all."

"Never," I say. I reach up and touch the end of it. "I could never not think of this."

"You should get one while you're here."

"You think it would look good?"

"Yeah," she says. "Duh. Anything is gonna look good on someone who already looks so damn good."

"Maybe I will then," I say. "Maybe tomorrow."

"Not tomorrow," she says. "I've gotta be there with you if you get it, and tomorrow I can't."

"Why not?"

"Cos," she says, glowing now.

"Cos why?"

"Cos we got offered a show tomorrow night, opening for King Krule at Slim's," she says. "We got the e-mail this morning. The original opener dropped off the bill and that main dude, Archy, stepped in and wanted us to play. He's a fan, I guess. I mean, we were all blown away. He wanted an even younger band on the bill than his. I'm still a little shocked."

"That's so fucking cool, Dominique. I'm stoked for you. I like that band a lot."

"The show's sold out, too," she says. "And it's all ages, mister. So you can totally get in and be there. I'll put you on the list."

"Fuck that," I say. "I'll pay. Guest lists should only exist for family, cos they've supported you enough, ya know. They're probably a huge reason why you have a guest list."

Dominique grabs my hand again and says, "I've never thought about it like that. There's people who haven't come to some of our shows cos they couldn't get on the list."

"Fuck those people," I say. "Save a spot on your list."

"No," she goes. "As much as I love you saying that, you're getting a spot. The show is sold out. The only way you get in is to be on the list."

"Right," I say. "Great point."

"I'm so excited," she says. "I'm seeing my fucking dream playing out, and it's way better than I ever thought it would be."

"Good," I say. "I'm excited for you."

"Thanks, babe."

"So what's up with the pizza?"

"It's right around the corner," she says, and then pulls me into her and puts her head on my shoulder.

62

DOMINIQUE'S HOUSE IS SMALL AND CUTE. IT'S ONE
story and white with a garage and a tiny front lawn. It's so
quiet here too. Again, it feels like I'm in an entirely different
city, and I like it. The quiet and the grass and the trees and
the families.

We walk through the front door and right into the living
room. She tells me to take my shoes off. The floor is wood
with a dull shine. It's really clean inside.

"Is anyone else here?" I ask Dominique.

"No," she says. "My mom's at work. She's probably at the
Transmission Gallery."

"How long has she worked for my father?"

"Almost a year. It's been so great, too. Having inside
access to all this art and meeting the artists. Your father
really saved us," she says.

"How's that?"

"My mom was laid off from her old job. She'd been with
them for over ten years and made decent money, but we were
still barely getting by. It's just been her, ya know. She's raised
me and my older brothers all by herself, so when she lost her
job, it was so sad to watch her struggle. We all got jobs to help

out, but we weren't even making ends meet. She was really depressed but tried to hide it as much as she could, but we could tell. It was different. She was quiet and distant and she cried a lot alone in her room. We were all set to move into this tiny two-bedroom apartment in Oakland when she met your dad. Her background is in media relations, and he was about to open the second gallery in SoMa. A couple of days later he called her and offered her a job with salary and benefits. I've never seen someone as relieved and grateful as my mom was, because it meant we could stay in the house. We've lived here for eleven years. This is our home and when your dad hired her, it meant we could stay here. It was huge."

We walk into the kitchen, and she pulls two cans of Coca-Cola from the fridge.

"Where are your brothers?" I ask her.

Handing me one of the sodas, she says, "My oldest brother, Malcolm, just moved to Santa Clara. He got a scholarship to play college ball there."

"That's cool," I say.

"It is. He worked his ass off, ya know. He was getting looked at by Duke and UCLA and Kentucky until he tore his knee up really, really bad his sophomore year and didn't play his junior year. But he rehabbed and came back and when he got the Santa Clara offer, he jumped at it. He deserves it too. He's so good and he's so nice and sweet. I miss him a lot."

"What about Jamal?" I ask.

Dominique sighs, still smiling, and she goes, "Jamal's working out all day. He gets up at, like, six every morning in the summer and goes and works out until, like, three and then he goes to work till eleven washing dishes at the restaurant in Hayes Valley. But he'll be at the show tomorrow night. Malcolm might even be able to drive back and be there. I'd love it if you met them. They're so sweet, ya know. They were my protectors growing up. They really helped my mom raise me."

I take a sip from the Coke. Like, it's still just really fucking hard for me to hear how awesome my father is again, from all these people. So what if he's changed? So what if he's gotten his act together finally and done some rad shit for people out here? Does that excuse what he did to my mother? Does that make it okay that it took my mother's lame suicide attempt for him to finally claim a small part of his son? His only child?

I take a sip of my Coca-Cola. And I say, "You guys are really fucking ambitious. You're so driven."

"We are," she says. "Driven by the ghost of our daddy."

"Where is he?" I ask.

She looks away from me. "You don't have to tell me anything," I say. "You can tell me to shut the fuck up if you'd like. It's really not my business."

"He's dead," she says. "I never even knew him. He died from an overdose when I was seven, but my mother had cut all ties with him before I was born."

It all makes sense now. Last night when we were walking from Dolores Park and she snapped at me about my father.

"Jesus," I say. "I'm sorry, Dominique."

"No," she says. "No. Don't be. He was a fucking asshole, I guess. Just a piece of shit at the end."

"Did he ever try to reach out to you?"

"No," she says. "He never even wanted us. He was too busy being a rapper and a hustler in Oakland. It's so pathetic. Like, why the fuck do you keep making babies with your wife if you despise everything that comes with it?"

"Is that why you don't drink or get high anymore? Cos of him?"

Shaking her head, she says, "Not because of him. He's one of the reasons I stay sober now, but I decided not to drink or drug anymore because of Ricky."

"Your ex."

"That's him," she says.

She drops her face in her hand and squeezes her forehead. She looks so stressed out right now. Upset. Worn out just from her ex being mentioned.

"It's okay," I tell her. "Like, I don't need to know shit. I'm leaving in less than a week now."

"Don't say that," she says, looking up.

"Huh."

"Just don't say it like that. You're just leaving."

"But I am. And then I'm gone, and if talking about some

dark shit in your life makes you sick or uncomfortable, then don't do it."

Dominique rolls her eyes. She says, "Have you considered for a second that I do wanna tell you this stuff? I want to talk about it. I think it's fucking clear how much I like you, Jaime. And I wanna share myself with you. Think about that instead of jumping on me and telling me I don't have to and that you're leaving."

"I'm sorry," I say.

"Don't be. Just relax."

"Okay."

It's about time for some blue, I'm thinking. Like, I'm getting short with my patience. It's clear. Instead of listening, I'm telling her not to talk. It's awful and she's right. She's so fucking right.

And she says, "Ya know what, man? Fuck this conversation right now, actually. You wanna see my room?"

"Sure."

She takes my hand and goes, "Come on then. We're going this way."

Dominique's room is like a teenage girl's room, I guess. Except she has a keyboard synth set up against the wall on the right side of the room, there's a sampler on a small table next to the synth, and she's got, like, two microphones and an acoustic guitar and a bass set up next to the table.

This is the dream right here. I'm drooling just looking at the gear and thinking about how I'm gonna shred on all of it.

Her floor is covered with clothes. I mean, I don't even see more than a few inches of the actual hardwood floor when I look it over.

Her walls are painted bright pink. There's a walk-in closet to the left of the door. A desk and a computer is next to another closet on that right wall with all the cool gear. And her bed is straight ahead. It's huge and there's, like, six pillows on it and it looks so soft and comfy.

Ghostface Killah, the Knife, Kendrick Lamar, Thee Oh Sees, the Growlers, Beach House, Purity Ring, and Big Black posters are pinned all over the wall along with posters from all these Vicious Lips shows.

It almost feels like validation. All this time and energy I've spent seeking out amazing music and learning how to play instruments. Giving my fucking life to this stuff and not settling on being young as an excuse to not get into good shit or make amazing stuff.

This is the payoff.

Kicking it with Dominique and meeting someone who's been doing the same thing as me.

"I love this," I tell her.

"Sorry about the mess."

"Why? Just gives this place some more character, I guess."

She goes over to her computer and plays some music. That M83 song "Midnight City" comes on.

"One of my favorites," I say, and start dancing around a little bit.

"Of course it is," she says, then starts dancing too.

The smile on her face is priceless. She looks so happy, and I feel so happy as we dance to this song. It's like one of those moments that you wish could be looped so it never ends. These four minutes on repeat for the rest of your life. Cos part of you knows this might be the happiest you'll ever feel or even be capable of feeling. Part of you is scared that you'll hold this moment to such a high standard that everything going forward will suck and you'll find yourself living in the past all the time, letting the nostalgia dictate you and manipulate the way you feel about everything else.

"Midnight City" fades into "Gila" by Beach House, and Dominique pushes me onto the bed now.

My dick gets hard right away.

And then she crawls on top of me and stops when her face is directly over mine.

"What do you think?" she says.

"I think I really like you and that this is fucking perfect right now."

"Me too," she says, and then I lean up and we start making out.

Putting my hands around her neck, I gently push her onto her back, then run a hand down her body. It's so tight and nice and when my hand touches her jeans, I unbutton them.

"Oh yeah," she goes.

I pull back. "Is that cool?" I say.

"Duh," she says. "Keep doing what you're doing."

I pull her jeans down past her ass and then slide my fingers beneath her underwear. Her pussy is wet. I slide two fingers in and she moans and bites down hard on my bottom lip.

Just back and forth I go, finger-banging her as Beach House sings . . .

"Give a little more than you like, pick apart the past, you're not going back . . ."

Putting her hands on my shoulders, Dominique pushes me on my back now and crawls on top of me again.

"Your turn," she says, and then unbuttons my jeans and pulls them all the way off, laughing as she does it.

"Damn," she goes. "Look at you so hard."

She slides my underwear down but right when she touches my dick, I just explode all over.

"Fuck," I say, while shaking from the orgasm. "Fuck."

I turn away from her and sit up and pull my underwear back up.

"Fuck."

"What's wrong?" she says.

"I'm sorry," I go.

"Why?"

"You know why," I say. "Fuck. This is embarrassing."

Dominique looks hurt and sad.

"I'm sorry," I say one more time.

She doesn't say anything. She just lies back down as "Gila" fades into "Helicopter" by Deerhunter.

Me, I stand up and put my jeans back on and tell her I'm going to the bathroom.

"Jaime," she says.

I stop walking but don't turn around. "Yeah."

"Nothing," she says.

"I'll be right back," I say, and leave the room.

63.

"WHY ARE YOU SO MAD AT ME?" SHE ASKED. "YOU only get mad at me anymore when I see you."

"Are you serious?" I shot back.

"I'm curious," she said.

"You've blown me off twice in the last three days. I text you and you don't text back. What gives?"

"I've been busy," she said.

"Is it about what happened the other night? Me coming like that when you touched my dick?"

She paused.

I already knew the answer.

I already knew she was going to lie.

"No," she went. "You know me, Jaime. I'm not that shallow. I've been busy."

"Right."

"Hey," she went, and put her hand on my leg. "We moved really fast at first. It was a lot."

"That's what you wanted to do. Not me."

"I know," she said. "But I was wrong."

"So what are you saying?"

"It's been too much too soon."

"What?"

"But I still wanna see you and do this."

I felt sick and dizzy.

Numb.

"Is there another dude?"

"No," she said, after hesitating for a second. "No, no, no, no."

I didn't believe her. How can you believe someone who just admitted lying to you about how serious they wanted to be with you in the first place?

"I just need some time in between the days we kick it."

"Okay," I said.

"Yeah?"

"Sure."

We kissed and then I played her the new Death Grips record that she'd been begging to hear, but she made me turn it off, like, two songs in.

That's when I began to really understand what was happening.

We kissed again before I left her house and walked home.

I felt like shit.

I just wanted to be happy again.

Happy.

My mother.

What made her always smile.

Blues.

Oxy.

And that's the night I tried that shit for the first time.

And it worked.

I'd just manufactured happiness.

I found out there was a way to be happy whenever I wanted.

64

I LIE NEXT TO DOMINIQUE NOW. IN THE BATHROOM, I swallowed a blue, and I'm back in the castle. We don't talk about what happened. I never wanna talk about that ever.

That Beach House song "Better Times" is playing.

Dominique rolls over and drapes her arm over my body, her face against my neck, and goes, "I was with Ricky for about eight months. He knew Malcolm and I'd see him hanging out sometimes and I thought I was in love right away. He's a rapper, he's from Oakland, ya know. He was handsome, he had a nice car, always had weed and beers. It's so dumb thinking about that now."

"Why?"

"Just the way we all think we're so fucking different sometimes. You listen to different kinds of music than everyone else, you get piercings, tattoos, wear clothes that—"

"That make you stand out," I say.

"No," she goes. "That make you different. Standing out terrifies me, but being the same as other people terrifies me too."

"That makes sense."

"It has to. It's the truth," she goes. "And the truth

always makes sense no matter how fucking gnarly or amazing it is."

"Sure."

She kisses my neck and goes, "Anyway, when it comes down to feelings and relationships and boys and what attracts you to them a lot of times, it ain't no different than anyone else. It's not. All these people you're trying not to be like, they go through exactly the same things too when it comes to that bullshit."

The way her breath feels on my neck right now is comforting and safe and intimate.

And she says, "Things were really good at first. He'd always smoke me out and get me drunk and take me for rides in his car. He showed me how to record music, how to produce it. Everything was so fucking great."

"What happened?" I ask.

Her body tenses up now, and her breathing gets heavier.

She says, "We'd been together for a while and we still hadn't fucked yet. I was scared to. Ricky had always had so many girls around before we started dating. His raps are all about how he fucked all these girls and shit and there I was, his girlfriend, and he couldn't fuck that. So he cheated on me and when I found out, I was devastated. It crushed me bad, man. So fucking bad. And I blamed myself cos I wasn't fucking him cos I was scared. It was brutal. So one night I was at this party in the city and I got so drunk and out of control. . . ."

Her voice trails off. Her heart is pounding through her chest. I can feel it. Reaching over, I put my hand on her face and tell her it's okay.

And she says, "I ended up fucking this skinny hipster kid. I can remember thinking how fucking disgusting it was while he was on top of me, sweating all over me, how awful his breath smelled, and him saying all this shit to me. I couldn't wait for it to be over, but he was on cocaine and took a Viagra and it just lasted for so long."

She stops for a moment.

And Beach House sings . . .

"I don't want to know, we don't need a sign to know better times . . ."

"He left me in the room after he came. I was naked and dizzy, and I threw up on the floor. That was the last time I drank, man. The last time I got high. I'm an emotional person. I feel things so much and I'm so hypersensitive. I was acting out and thinking I was hurting Ricky when really, I was just hurting myself by doing that. What he'd done had already happened. It was so foolish to think I could make myself whole again by sleeping with a stranger. I was so ashamed of what happened that I never even told him."

"Damn," I whisper. "Just damn . . ."

"But he broke my heart so bad. He used me and then broke me and I hate him, Jaime. I hate him so fucking much."

"Better Times" fades into "Little Dreamer" by Future Islands and I say, "I'm so sorry that happened."

"No," she goes. "You never feel sorry for me. That's not cool. This isn't a pity party, I'm just telling you what happened."

Sliding my fingers from her face to her neck and down her arms very slowly, I ask, "So why are you doing this with me?"

"Because I thought it was going to be easy. I thought we'd just kick it and fool around and it would be nice because I think you're so cute and so talented and so smart and I'm so attracted to you."

"And I'm attracted to you."

"But I wasn't planning on feeling like this, Jaime."

"Like what?"

"So connected to you," she says. "It's crazy but it's true. I feel emotionally attached to you in every way, and it sucks now because you are leaving and I've gone too far deep. It's like there's no way I'm not going to get dismantled if I keep digging deeper, but there's no way I'm not getting shredded if I turn back now. So I'd rather keep digging. I'd rather have this short time with you and go all in and get destroyed instead of bailing and being miserable and wondering if maybe something would've happened differently in the end."

"Differently?" I say. "Differently how?"

"Like maybe you stay in San Francisco and live with your father."

I turn my face from her and pull my hand away.

"I know it's stupid and I know it won't happen, but that's how I feel."

"I could never do that to my mother."

"I know. And that's one of the reasons you're such a fucking rad person. That kind of loyalty is amazing. It's incredible, Jaime. I just wish you'd stay."

"Thank you," I tell her.

"This is so nice."

"It is."

I look back at Dominique, and she lifts her head and we kiss.

"I just want you here. San Francisco and Dominique forever," she whispers as Future Islands sings . . .

"And as we say good night, I hold you close and tight, no more raging suns, only waning ones . . ."

65.

I RIDE THE TRAIN TO BRANDON'S HOUSE. IT'S NOT FAR from Dominique's. I wanted to cry when I was leaving her. She had tears in her eyes and didn't want me to go but understood that I had to.

This is our relationship right now.

Defined by her understanding that I'm always gonna be leaving.

Awesome.

The train climbs this small hill on Taraval and when it pops over the peak of it, the Pacific Ocean opens up right in front of my eyes.

It's fucking killer, too. I've never seen anything like it before. I can see the waves violently crashing and birds in the sky and it never ends. That's the best fucking part about this right now. How everything beautiful in front of me never ends.

I get off at the stop Eddie texted me and walk to the house.

I can hear them playing from the street and walk to the garage door and knock.

Nothing.

I knock again.

Still nothing.

So I text and then knock again and the garage door finally opens up.

I walk in.

"What up, homie," says Eddie. He hands me a beer from a cooler.

"This is pretty sick," I say. "Thanks."

"You ready to get down, dude? Bring some of that Tiger Stitches shit to this mix?"

"Of course." I open the beer and take a drink.

There's a Gretsch guitar on a stand plugged into an Orange amp.

"That's so fucking pretty," I tell them, as I pick the Gretsch up and really feel it in my hands.

"Glad you appreciate it," says Eddie. "And this. All of it. Everything."

"I'm fucking stoked, dudes."

"Awesome," Brandon rips. "Welcome to the shitshow."

I laugh.

And Eddie says, "This is the world done proper, homie. And never let anyone tell you differently."

I put the strap over my shoulder and run my thumb down the strings.

"Fuck all those boring kids out there," he says. "Fuck them and their math tests and their science projects and their school dances, man. This is the only world worth existing in."

"Let's do this," I say.

Brandon punches a button and the garage door begins to close.

Before it does, though, I turn around and look outside. Right across the street, I see this boy with reddish hair wearing a tank top and shorts even though it's pretty cold out.

He looks seven, maybe eight, and he's standing in the front yard of his house all by himself.

He's holding a ukulele in his hands and trying to play it, trying to figure it out, and he's all alone and he doesn't care. He's just trying to make some noise that sounds right and good.

"Let's fucking rock," Eddie yells.

"Stop, drop, and rock 'n' roll!" rips Brandon.

And the boy looks over at us now and waves, right as the garage door closes all the way.

66.

EDDIE DROPS ME OFF BACK AT MY FATHER'S HOUSE
around midnight. I'm super fucked up too and surprised
he could even drive, cos I thought he was more fucked up
than me.

That Black Books song "The Big Idea" is playing in his
truck.

"So stoked we covered this song tonight," he says.

"One of the best songs ever made."

Eddie laughs and goes, "You're probably right, man. It's
good. See you at five tomorrow. Let's shred a little bit and
then head to the show."

"Word, homie."

"Tell Kristen I say hi too."

"Really?"

"Yeah, dude. She's such a fox, and her boyfriend's a twat."

"That's for sure."

"So you'll say something then?"

"Yeah, man. I definitely will."

We fist bump and I go inside. All the lights are off.

I grab two Coronas from the fridge and go upstairs.
When I flip the hallway lights on, I see this box sitting in
front of my door.

I pick it up and go inside my room, locking the door behind me, then sit down on the bed and open one of the beers.

I take a huge drink.

The box is unmarked and taped shut. I take one of my keys and stab it into the tape and rip it open.

Inside are two manila envelopes packed so full they can't even close all the way. There's a Post-it note stuck to one of them.

I take it off and read it.

My heart slides into the pit of my stomach now. Face turns white. I can feel it. Feel the fucking color leaving it once again.

The note is from my father and it says . . .

Since you have no interest in listening to anything I have to say or spending any time with me, I thought you could read about what I've wanted and tried to tell you all these years.

I pick up the envelope and reach into it, pulling out at least thirty smaller envelopes. All of them are addressed to me in Joliet, and all of them have been opened at least once and then sealed back shut and marked *return to sender*.

There have to be at least sixty or seventy enve-lopes here. I take three from different years and open them. Inside each one is a letter or a card or both. And the letters are long, too. Like five, six pages hand-written front and back by my father. The dates on the letters range from me being five years old to last year. I read the postscript on one of them, and it says to make sure I use the money wisely but to enjoy it a little bit too.

P.S. There are no checks in any of these.

P.S. There's no way I can deal with this right now.

I'm not reading another word.

Stuffing the letters back into the box, I stand up and dig the tinfoil out of my bag and rip a piece off.

I drop a blue on it and go.

Then open my notebook and start cribbing. And it just flows and it flows and it flows right out of me. Two pages, done in ten minutes, and after I read it three times and make two small changes, I turn my webcam on and hit record . . .

"For months we played nothing but the silent treatment game, long, cruel winter days spent justifying all of our wrongs and glorifying everything we thought we'd done right even if all of those things were just simple choices that anyone with a lick of common sense would do . . . Some nights she'd snore in her sleep and wake me up and I'd lean back against the cool wooden headboard and stare at her, knowing that there was nothing she was capable of doing that would ever stop me from loving her . . . For weeks I worked on a love letter for her in private, and for weeks I couldn't come up with good enough words and sentences that conveyed the way I really felt . . . It was maddening, it made me sick and furious, until I stepped back one day and stared out of the cabin window and watched the sick orange

and brown leaves of autumn fall off the tree branches and float so
passively and mercifully to their death . . . it was then that I realized
not every emotion can be captured with words, not every scene can be
described to perfection, and not every feeling is meant to be manipul-
ated and used for your own selfish purposes . . . she was sixteen once
and she worked at the town's swimming pool as a lifeguard, and she
looked better in a bathing suit than any of the other girls that summer, or the summers before, or the summers after . . . little did anyone
know that when she was ten, she nearly drowned in a lake and for two
years she wouldn't go near water, not even the familiarity and comfort of the shower in the only house she'd ever lived in could give her
the peace of mind to get wet again . . . it wasn't until Joey Harrison
pushed her into the swimming pool during gym class and she didn't
die, when she realized how silly fear can be and how our minds
are capable of taking away the simple pleasure and fun of even the
most innocent things . . . Not long ago I was at a show and this band
refused to play any of the songs they were known for because they
hated the idea of repeating the past, being stuck in a moment that
was created five years earlier, and the crowd booed and the guitar
player walked off the stage, and I appreciated the place they were
coming from even though the only reason they were still able to play
shows was because of everything they'd done before that . . . it's a
funny thing when life works that way . . . holding you hostage to
history while demanding you evolve and remake yourself in order
to survive . . . In Lexington I met this group of teenage cowboys who
talked about raiding their town on horseback someday, then riding
off into the mountains with their bounty and starting their own

civilization ... what's not to love about the imagination, what's not to love about dreamers, what is there to love about cynics, what is there to love about the dull, the shallow, and the defeated ... not long ago I sat on a stoop in the middle of a rainstorm and wrote furiously in a notebook, cribbing my whole life story in the hopes that all the water that hit the pages would wash my life away ... this is where we are, I guess ... twisting in the wind ... digging for our purpose, searching for a meaning, desperately reaching for anything, anyone, who can prescribe us definition and narrow our existence down to whatever two lines best describe the way they feel about us ... You have to try really hard to be bored in life ... and I wonder sometimes why a person who tries that hard to be bored can't put that much effort into anything else ... I don't believe in the notions of fate or chance ... I don't believe in people who say they don't know what they wanna do or don't know what they're good at ... I judge people based on their own opinions of their own self-worth, and I also judge the people who base their self-worth from the opinions of other people ... and I judge them cruelly ... hopefully one day, we'll all make good on the promises we made to ourselves ... and hopefully one day, we'll all understand that every moment has the potential to be the catalyst to the future we daydream for hours about each day and wish for ... two days ago I finished her love letter ... it was on the third anniversary of the day we broke up ... nothing I wrote could've changed our history ... I only finished it to see all the things I never appreciated about her and took for granted ... none of this will ever be easy ... This life will never, ever be easy, and that's what I love the most about it ..."

When I'm done, I hit the foil again and log onto all my social media sites and post the fucking video. By the time I've finished posting on the last one, the first three have over seventy likes already.

Fuck all these adults who can't keep their stories straight or the lies hidden.

The kids are doing all right, ya know.

All of us kids, we're doing pretty fucking good for ourselves, and you ancient people are dying.

You suck too.

67.

"HERE'S WHAT WE'RE GONNA DO, HOMIE. YOU WITH me? Cos this is important. This is the future we're talking about right now. The future and it's gonna be fierce and lovely and wonderful. Like so fucking wonderful. You ready?" Kristen asks.

Me and her are in the basement now. I heard her, like, thirty minutes after I was done posting that new poem online, and I couldn't be in that room with those letters anymore, so I dropped down and found her snorting lines the size of my middle finger on a mirror.

She hasn't slept since Saturday either.

She volunteered that golden nugget about three seconds after I said, "What's up?"

Nodding, I say, "Totally ready," and take a drink of beer.

"We're gonna start an artist collective somewhere. Buy a building outright with cash and fucking tune it up and move in just the sickest, dopest, coolest fucking kids and make our lives art just the way we're making art our lives. And money isn't an issue, man."

"It ain't?"

"No sir," she says. "I'll fucking straight-up rob Tyler and

steal all his drugs and cash and watches and car. Fuck him," she goes. "I hate him so much and that's how we'll pay for our art, live space. With all the shit I steal from him plus maybe a loan or two from your father."

"I love it," I tell her, because that's what you have to do to anyone in this state. I know from having to deal with my mother and some of her friends. Appease them, agree with them, and tell them whatever they're saying sounds great and is an awesome idea. And in this particular case, I actually think Kristen's idea is pretty okay. Not the artist collective as much as robbing Tyler or fucking him over somehow.

"Like Tyler is only cool cos he dates me and sells coke. That's all he's got. Without me or the booger sugar, dude would be a no one. Over seventy percent of his customers are my friends and acquaintances." She pauses and points up at the ceiling. "And family too," she finishes, laughing.

I take another drink of beer and go, "What'd he do?"

She throws her arms up and says, "He's a joke. That's what he did. And he's a slut. Ya know what?"

Kristen leans right into me now, and our faces are only inches apart.

"What?"

"I'm pretty sure he's sleeping with this chick Katie."

"Who's that?"

"One of my best friends," she says.

"Jesus," I say, pulling back. "Kristen. If you think that about both of them, it's prolly true."

"Right," she says, winking. "Anyway, whatever. Screw him."

She pulls, like, five grams of coke from her purse now and throws them in the air.

"He gave these to me before he took off for, like, five hours without answering his phone or texts. Like, really? You're gonna pay me with coke to look the other way? Fuck that."

She grabs one of the grams she threw and pops it open and dumps it on the ground.

"I like cocaine, but I'm not a whore."

Her eyes start to water.

"You're not," I tell her.

"I'm not. He's the whore."

"You're right."

Pause.

She looks so worn out and tired.

"Did Dominique text you?" I ask her.

She nods. "Yeah. They've got a show and she wants an outfit."

"That's what she told me, too."

"I love that girl, man. So much. She's like you, dude."

"What do you mean?"

"You're just good people," she says. "You're honest and you work hard and you don't fuck your friends over."

"I don't have any friends to fuck over," I say. "None."

"Bullshit. You've got me."

"For five more days."

"For life, motherfucker."

She throws her arms around my neck and kisses my cheek.

"I really hope he's not fucking that girl," she says into my ear. "That would bum me out so bad."

"It'll be okay," I say.

Letting go of me, Kristen makes a face and says, "What'd I just tell you?"

"What?"

"I just said how honest you were."

"Yeah."

"Don't start lying now to me," she says. "It's not gonna be okay. It hasn't been okay for a while."

"Then leave that pilgrim dick," I say. "Walk away from him and go be happy."

"I love him so much," she says.

"But does he love you?"

"I think so."

"Then why isn't he here?"

"I don't know," she says.

Grabbing the mirror again, Kristen mows down another line and then her phone rings.

"It's him," she says, glowing.

She jumps to her feet and walks to her bedroom and closes the door behind her.

I can hear her laughing as I'm walking up the stairs.

68

MY FATHER'S STANDING IN THE KITCHEN WHEN I walk down there in the morning.

Awkward isn't the right word to describe how this feels at the moment, but it's the first word that comes to mind.

He's wearing a superexpensive-looking suit and his hair is all parted and he's finally shaved all the scruff.

I flip my head at him and open the fridge and grab the orange juice.

"How's it going?" he says.

"Wonderful," I say. "Talked with my mother earlier, and she's doing really well and it looks like they're releasing her on Saturday morning, that's what she says anyway, and I can go back home on Sunday. I'm stoked. It's awesome."

"I'm glad she's doing better," he says.

I pour the juice in a glass and say, "Are you?"

"Of course I am."

"Good."

"So what's going on, Jaime? How are you liking the city so far?"

"I like it," I tell him. "It's nice. But I can't wait to get home. Be back with the lady who made me who I am."

I can see the irritation coming to a boil. I can see his body language shifting and getting a little bit more excited than it just was.

Like, you wanna stick some fucking letters that you wrote and were sent back to you in front of my door instead of coming at me like an adult, a fucking parent, and really talking to me and telling me those things that are probably in the letters.

Like, fuck that shit too.

This place is devoid of adults.

"Great," he says.

I chug the glass of juice and pour another one and stare at him.

"I think so."

"Okay," he says, then starts to walk away but stops.

I got him now.

Flipping back around to me, he goes, "Did you look inside that box I left in front of your door at all?"

"Box?" I go. "There was a box in front of my door?"

Blood fills the whites of his eyes immediately. I can actually see the pulse in his throat. He's an angry dude just like I am. I know this violence. It's the same violence that runs through me. And I've gone too far with it. What I just said was a real asshole thing to say.

"Leslie told me what she called you yesterday," he says. "She was crying to me, apologizing, begging me to forgive her for saying those nasty things to you."

"Listen," I say.

But he jumps back in, cutting me off. "She was right, though."

"About what?"

"Who's really being a monster," he says.

Now I'm all pissed again, and I say, "Screw that, man," as I fling my arms over my head. "I saw the damn box. I read the note you left and saw what was inside those envelopes."

"Did you read any of the letters?" he snaps.

"No."

He gets all worked up and actually loosens his tie.

And I say, "Why does that piss you off?" Then, "And who loosens their tie unless they're about to fight someone or beat the shit out of their kid?"

"Shut up," he snaps. "Just shut up!"

"Screw you," I go. "Tell me why that pisses you off."

"Because that's my story when it comes to you. Those letters were meant for you, and Morgan never gave them to you. She cashed the checks and sent the letters back to me without you even knowing they existed. That's why I put them there."

"Bullshit," I go. "You put them there to prove some petty point about how my mother had really lied to me about you ever trying to reach out to me. Me reading those letters isn't as important to you as making sure I knew that you'd sent me all that money and my mother took it for herself and kept me from knowing that you wrote to me a couple of times a year. Yippee fucking yay, dude. So you wrote me some letters here and there. Pat yourself on the back. I know now. Thanks for thinking about me . . ."

Another pause.

"Dude."

My father looks away from me now, shaking his head, and straightens his jacket.

"Those letters," he says. "Everything I've always wanted to tell you and for you to know how I feel about you is in them."

"They're letters!" I snap. "Letters. I'm right here, man. If you wanna tell me something, go for it. I'm five fucking feet away from you. Talk."

Wiping a hand over his face, then turning back to me, my father goes, "Why? You've already made up your mind about me. I'm the evil prick who ruined your mother's life. Nothing I can say is gonna change that."

"You gave me a box of letters."

"Cos I thought they'd warm you up to me and then we could talk about some of this stuff. But I was wrong to do that. You're not interested in any of it."

Images of me punching my father repeatedly in the face, then kicking him in the ribs smash through my head.

"You're fucking wrong, man."

He smirks. "No I'm not, Jaime."

"Yes, you are," I snap. "Start talking, dude. Right now. I wanna know why you turned on me and her. I deserve to know. Deserve to hear it from you and not read it in a letter you wrote some night cos you felt bad that I was about to turn eight and you didn't know what I looked like. So tell me. Why the fuck did you turn on her like that and beat her up? All she wanted to do was get back into the ballet. That's it. And you squashed that. You went back on the agreement you two made and when she acted out because of that, you went after her. You took yourself out of my life, man, and I wanna know why you did that."

My father charges at me now, stopping just inches from my face, waving his finger wildly.

"Read the letters," he says.

"Talk to me. I'm right here. Just tell me what happened. I deserve to hear it from you. I deserve to hear both sides, damn it."

But he steps back and says nothing.

"Really?" I go. "You can't even talk to me?"

"I'm not going to go there," he says.

"Cos you don't wanna say those things about yourself."

"That's not it at all," he says. "That's not it, Jaime. I'm not going to do that. It's too painful for me. I've worked so hard to close those wounds, and telling you won't do any bit of good."

My father starts walking to the back door.

"Really?" I go. "You're walking out on me again?"

"I'm sorry," he says. "I can't tell you why all of that happened."

"Fuck!" I scream after he leaves the house. "Just fuck you! I hate you!"

This is when I ball my right hand into a fist.

After a few deep breaths, I punch myself in the chest as hard as I can until I literally beat the tears out of my eyes.

That fucking prick.

69.

I SORTA FEEL LIKE A DICKHEAD TO BE DOING THIS, but Dominique has band practice right now and can't kick it, Kristen is still sleeping, Brandon's out surfing with some friends, and Eddie's flipping two bikes he fixed up to some kids in Oakland, and there's no place to go except here.

I knock three times on the door of the Whip Pad and wait while I listen to the XX album XX.

It's gray in San Francisco today. Really windy, too. And I'm wearing a black hoodie and tight blue jeans and my white slip-ons. A black bandanna is tied around my neck.

The door finally opens and this black dude, who I'm pretty sure is Omar Getty and is wearing just a pair of cutoff jean shorts, answers.

"Can I help you, little dude?"

"Is James here?"

"James Morgan?"

"Yeah."

"Who are you?" he says.

But before I can answer, James emerges in the hallway and says, "Gerry, man. It's cool. Let him in."

"Thank you," I tell him as I walk inside.

James is standing near his door, wearing a black V-neck tee, a pair of tight black jeans, and a navy-blue beanie rolled up tight around his forehead.

As I move toward James, I say, "I'm sorry, man. This isn't what I wanted to do, but nobody else is around."

"You okay?"

"I don't know." I stop walking. "Like, I should leave, actually."

"It's cool, Jaime Miles. You're fine. Come on into the room."

"Thanks, man," I say, and he closes the door behind us.

"I listened to your music," James says. "Me and Savannah did when we came back here after dinner."

"Yikes."

"No yikes," he says. "It was good, man. I really dug it a lot. You're fourteen, right?"

"Yeah."

"I wish I'd had just a drop of your ambition when I was that age."

"Were you writing then?"

"Nah," he says. "I was all into sports and shit when I was your age."

"Well, thanks for listening, man. That's really cool. I don't even know what to say without feeling like some little fanboy gushing over his hero."

"Well, I ain't no hero," he says. "And if you gush, you're gone."

I laugh.

Me and him are sitting at the table in the middle of his room, drinking cans of PBR and listening to Kendrick Lamar blast from his stereo speakers.

There's also a small mirror with tiny lines of cocaine.

"So what brought you down here, man? Something wrong or did you just wanna say what's up?"

"Both," I say.

"Your dad still acting like a troll digger?"

"More like a blubber cheek," I say. "It's just all weird."

"Families, man. Shit is so tough. Like, I always wanted chicks or shitty friends to be the roughest parts of my life to navigate through, but it was always family. Isn't that bizarre? That the people you share blood with, who know more about you than anyone else will ever know, who brought you into this world, are usually the people who make your life insanely difficult and complicated."

"It is," I say. "But what do you do about it?"

James lights a cigarette and says, "The first thing you do is make sure you're never like them. We can't do anything about looking sorta like them, but we can do something about acting like them."

"Right."

"Then after that it's different, man. A lot of people make amends and brush all that bad shit under a big, bloody rug and it works for them. Wouldn't work for me but did for a lot of people I love and respect."

"What'd you do?"

"I took all that anger and bitterness and resentment and I channeled it into my art. Like, I was never gonna be unhappy like them. So discontent even though from the outside, it looked like they had a wonderful life and all their shit was so together. But it wasn't. So I bailed, man. Being an artist wasn't a way to pay any bills or make a living to them, so I was dead fucking set on proving them wrong. And in that process, I found a better family out here, man. And sure, there's problems still and there's fights but in the end, none of these people look down on each other, none of them will refuse to support what you're doing, and none of them will ever hold bloodlines over your head and think you owe them something because they brought you into this place. You owe them nothing, man. And you owe everything to yourself and the people who believed in what you were doing."

Just being able to sit at this table again and hear James Morgan talk about life a little bit is unbelievable. I'm sure he's been a fuckhead and a drag to some people, but then again, those people who feel that way have probably been the same things to someone else.

Snorting another line of coke, James slides the mirror in front of me. "Just one," he goes.

"I prolly shouldn't, man."

"Just get rad once with me in the Whip Pad, dude. One line. I mean, my favorite fucking Kendrick Lamar song is playing, dude. Hi fucking power. Kill that rail, Tiger Stitches. Do it for me, man."

Taking the straw from James's hand, I slide it up my right nostril and plug my left one with my finger and bang it right up there as Kendrick Lamar (and James Morgan) sings . . .

"I'm standing on a field full of land mines, doing the moonwalk, hoping I blow up in time . . ."

Immediate fucking charge to my brain and my body. Like, damn. I'm really fucking high and it happened so fast.

"Whoo," I snort, sliding back in the chair. "Jesus Christ, man."

"Right," says James.

"Right," I say back, giving him a high five. "Damn."

"What are you doing tonight?" he asks me.

"This chick I've been hanging out with a little bit since I got here, her band is opening for King Krule at Slim's."

"Nice," he says. "What's her band?"

"Vicious Lips."

"And she's your age and opening a show that big?"

"She's sixteen," I say.

"Same fucking thing when it comes to that. You kids," James says. "You ambitious little brats. You're figuring it all out now. Using the media culture perfectly to your advantage. Good job on that."

"There's no need to wait for people to come to us anymore. We're coming for them, for you, and we can post as many songs as we want, as many pictures of our paintings as we want, as many videos as we want, and if it's good, people are gonna grab onto it and devour it and pass it along to the rest of their world without some label or PR company or manager taking twenty percent just to do what we can do, what I can fucking do while drinking a Corona in my underwear and listening to the Fresh and Onlys or Mazzy Star."

James laughs and smacks his hands together. "I love it, homie. Fucking Tiger Stitches."

We fist bump and he goes, "There's a show on Thursday night at the Great American Music Hall."

"Who?" I ask.

"Youth Lagoon is playing, man."

"For real?" I ask. "Like, they're playing on Thursday? I love that band to death."

"Me too," says James. "But it's a twenty-one-and-up show, man."

"Fuck," I groan. "Why'd you tell me that?"

"Really," says James. "That's all you got? Like at the very least, you can stand outside and listen to the show from there. You can hear it clear as the night. Come on, man. That's better than nothing."

"You're right."

"I was in Seattle with this girl Caralie I used to love for a long time. While we were there, we found out the Black Angels were playing a free show, so of course, we're like, we gotta do this, ya know. They'd just released *Directions to See a Ghost*, so we showed up early to get in line cos it was first come, first serve. But while we were waiting, they fucking sound checked their entire set and we could hear it like we were in the front row, man. And both of us had seen them at least three times before, so we rocked gnar in line and when they were done, we bailed. We'd just heard the set and to this day, that remains one of my favorite shows or sets or afternoons ever. Just standing outside with all the real fans and listening to a band you love play their set. It's fucking awesome. And that's why I told you."

He does another line and then passes the mirror back to me.

"Well, thanks for the heads-up, man."

"You gotta show up for something like that while you're here, man. While you have that kind of access you will never get back in Joliet."

"I know."

"Good," he says.

I pound another line right as Gerry walks into the room.

"Damn, man," he goes. "You really do have a habit of getting teenagers high on coke."

"Kid's fucking dope, man," James snaps. "He can handle this shit."

"Absolutely, I can," I say.

"It's time," says Gerry. "We gotta bounce and check out that space for the party next month."

"Cool," says James. Looking back at me, he goes, "Do you think your dad has fucked Savannah?"

I shake my head. "No. Not at all. I think he wants to and he would, but I don't think that's happened. Why?"

"Cos she hasn't fucked me yet."

"So what?"

"I like that girl."

"Maybe she just wants to be your friend."

"Maybe," says James. "But I think it's something else with her. It's almost like there's someone she doesn't wanna let down or make them think less of her by fucking me, and I thought it might be your dad, since he flew her out here and was pretty hands-on the other night."

"I'm sure they haven't, dude. That dude's been in bed with his wife every night since I've been here."

"All right," he says. "I was just wondering."

"Word."

Both me and James stand up, and he gives me a hug.

"Have fun at the show tonight," he says.

"Thanks, man. Thanks for everything. This is awesome."

As I'm about to leave the room, James goes, "Only you can make the right choices for you, Jaime. The ones you can live with. Don't let anyone else dictate your happiness, man."

"It's not that easy, though," I say.

"Oh, I know. It's probably the hardest fucking thing in the world. But it's your life, dude. Those other people ain't gonna be around when you're fifty and miserable and wishing you'd done what you knew what was best for you thirty years earlier. If you haven't made the right fucking choices for your life, it'll be just you and a lot of misery, and that's no way to live. Misery is something you destroy, not dwell in, dude. Tiger fucking Stitches."

70

BRANDON'S PARENTS LET US SHRED FOR AN HOUR tonight. The three of us, me, Eddie, and Brandon, we decide to call our project Skullburns. It's a lot more melodic and poppy than the Devil Feeder stuff, but it's still tough as nails.

We work on the four songs from last night three times each and then decide that tomorrow night in Eddie's neighbor's garage (it's soundproofed), we'll record them live and throw 'em straight up on the Internet with a logo that Brandon drew and some pictures we'll take with our phones.

It's that easy. It really is. And if the music is any good, people are gonna listen and share it and talk about it.

Kids in Florida and Idaho and Texas. Kids in Japan and Australia.

Kids everywhere.

They're gonna be so stoked. Another piece of the blueprint presented to them. Another reason to stop making excuses and start doing shit and start taking their lives and their art seriously.

Before we bounce to the show, we skate the two blocks to the beach (Brandon has an extra board for me).

The sun is setting. This is why we're here. Because when we opened the garage door after destroying, for the first time in a day and a half the sun finally broke through the threshold of gray to say hi.

"This is the best part of living way out here," said Brandon. "Getting to see this over two hundred days of the year."

"It's so epic," I said, my eyes huge and excited. "It's just massive and perfect."

Eddie put his arm around me and went, "Come on then, homie. Let's grab the best fucking seats in the world then."

We take off our shoes, and I roll my jeans past my ankles and we run through the soft sand to the edge of the beach.

Everything is so much clearer right now, right here. The wind is crisp and clean and the sound of the waves crashing touches my fucking soul. It really does.

I could stay here forever. There's no bitterness, no hurt feelings, and no ulterior motives.

Everything right here is real. There's nothing phony or fake about the ocean, the beach, and the sun and the birds and the huge cliffs that poke up through the fog a mile away.

There are no lies here. No fucking lies. And nobody is angry.

People should be more like the ocean. More people should try to be as beautiful and kind and nice as the setting sun is to them.

After the three of us share a tall can and a joint, Eddie

walks over to the huge brick wall separating sand from street.

"This is perfect," he says. "Right here, dudes. Perfect."

I look at Brandon and he shrugs and then Eddie takes a can of black spray paint out of his backpack.

He shakes it up and then starts spraying in this pretty killer script.

"He's good," I say.

"He's been doing graffiti since he was eight, man. That's kinda how me and him met. We both got popped on the same night three years ago for tagging in totally different parts of the city, and we both got brought into a juvie holding facility. We met in a holding cell."

"That's pretty sick, man."

"Devil Feeder was born that fucking night."

"Righteous."

When Eddie finishes, the word "Skullburns" tattoos the wall now.

"Come on!" he yells, waving us over. "Hurry up before the pigs show up."

Me and Brandon run over, and then Eddie yells at some random stranger to come over too.

After we all converge on the wall, Eddie hands the stranger his digital camera.

"Let's do this," he says.

"Do what?" I ask.

"First band photo," he says. "It's fucking dope."

So the three of us get situated. Brandon sits down with his back against the wall. Eddie stands next to him with his arms folded across his chest. And me, I stand a little farther away from the wall and, like, five feet from those dudes with my hands shoved into the back pockets of my jeans.

The guy takes the photo, and the three of us run over to him to see it.

It's so perfect.

"This is really happening now," I say.

"Of course, homie," says Eddie. "This is fucking life. Life happens. And when it does, you better have something happening too or it'll swallow you right up and destroy you."

"Fun days, fun days," Brandon goes.

"Rad days," I say back.

And Eddie says, "Rad days are fucking here, my man. Skullburn '77."

71

DOMINIQUE CALLS ME WHILE WE'RE RIDING THE train back toward downtown and SoMa, where Slim's is.

"Do Eddie and Brandon need to get listed?" she asks.

"No," I say. "They got tickets awhile ago. But thanks. We just nailed those four songs down too. We're calling our project Skullburns. Recording tomorrow night at Eddie's neighbors."

"You sound so happy, Jaime. The excitement in your voice, oh my gosh, it's thrilling," Dominique says.

"I am happy," I tell her. "I've never been this happy."

"See," she says. "All the more reason to stay."

"Nice try," I go.

"Think about it," she says. Then, "So what's up with Kristen?"

"What do you mean?"

"She hasn't returned any of my texts or calls. Is she okay?"

"I don't know," I tell her. "She'd been up for a couple of days when I saw her last night."

"She's prolly crashed out then. Bummer."

"I'm sorry," I say.

"Don't be. Trust me, I had a backup wardrobe plan, and I think you're gonna love it."

"Can't wait," I say. "Can't wait to see you and watch your band."

"It's so exciting. This is the dream, ya know, the reason we fucking kill it every day and work so hard," she goes. "Anyway, we're about to sound check, so I'll see you soon. And also, after the show, if you're not busy, there's something I have to show you. Just me and you. That I need to show you and you *need* to see."

"I'm totally in. So stoked."

Click.

I text Kristen and write . . .

Hey, just hoping you're okay, doll. On my way to the show with Eddie and Brandon. Eddie thinks you're a babe too! Anyway, hopefully I run into you at Slim's! :)

Putting my phone away, I say, "Dominique is, like, the nicest person in the world."

Eddie, who's brown-bagging a tall can, he nudges Brandon and goes, "Look at our boy . . . he's glowing."

Brandon's laughing.

"Just fucking glowing."

"I am," I say. "It's just been so different here, ya know. You guys, Dominique, Kristen . . . you guys have been really nice to me and genuine. It means a lot. Not a whole lot of people have ever been kind to me, ya know. So when someone or some people finally do, it means a lot. It's been really cool to actually enjoy meeting new people for once and to enjoy fucking talking to kids. I've always hated it since I started school. Nobody's ever been nice to me at all, and I don't know what I did but it's just the way it's been, so I'm grateful for you guys."

"Then stay here," rips Brandon. "Stay in San Francisco."

"I can't do that. I will never do that to my mother."

"Sure you can," says Eddie. "And she'd understand, I'm sure."

"No, she wouldn't," I snap. "It would kill her if I told her I was living with my father. It would actually kill her, or she'd kill herself."

"Shouldn't be that way," Eddie goes. "Parents are the worst sometimes. So fucking selfish, and they don't listen even though they say they want to."

"If something happened to her, I'd never forgive myself."

"You're gonna have to leave her sometime," Brandon goes.

"Probably. But it's me living with my father that would slam the nail into her coffin. Me telling her I'm living with him and not her."

"But you hate him too," Eddie goes. "You'd be in San Francisco because of us, your bandmates, and Dominique. She'll get that."

"No," I say, shaking my head wildly. "No, she won't, and that's all that matters. Me staying here is me picking him over her and if that happens, she's done."

"That's so fucking stupid and selfish," Brandon says. "Parents, adults making kids pick between them. Like, fuck you guys for falling out of love like that and squashing your romance. That's what it is, ya know. They've lost the romance and the passion between them. Once you lose the passion with anything, your life gets darker and darker and darker. It's like a freefall or something, and these people just drown themselves in their misery and want everyone to live in their pity parties. Fucking assholes."

"It is what it is," I say. "And she's my best friend and she's the reason I'm even playing music and making sick art."

"She's also the reason you can't be happy," Eddie says. "And if she really fucking loved you the way she says she does and is supposed to, then she'd support anything you do in order to be happy."

"I know, man," I snap. "I know. But I can't break her heart. It's that simple. If it breaks again, it'll be for good and she's over. I can't do that to her. Not after everything she's done for me and saved me from. I can't do it. I won't fucking do it."

72

WE SKATE FROM VAN NESS AND MARKET TO SLIM'S.
About a block before we get there, though, we stop and hide
in an alley and share another tall can and a joint and I pop
an entire blue.

Side note: When I was grabbing my take for the day from
the bottle, I noticed I only had eleven left, and it's made me
very nervous and edgy and I haven't stopped thinking about
it since the second I did the count.

Anyway, Slim's. There's a huge line out front, and the
scene is totally alive. Tons of kids since it's all ages. Pretty
kids and smiling kids and dancing kids and kids with great
hair and nice eyes and stoked lips and lovely clothes.

Dominique is standing with a grip of people on the
sidewalk out front. I recognize Mark and Keisha from the
pictures on the band's Tumblr page. I see Dominique's
mother too—wonder if she knows me and her daughter have
been kicking it so tough and would be angry if she found
out, since my father "saved" her and is responsible for them
not having to move out of their house.

The three of us, Skullburns now, head straight for
them. Dominique looks up and sees us coming at them and

she yells, "Yes! My boy and his band are here!" Then cuts straight through the small circle and jumps at me.

I catch her, but barely, and I'm thinking if her mother didn't know before about us, well, she definitely knows now.

She kisses the side of my face over and over and over again as I set her down.

"Yay," she says. "Hi!"

"Hey." I look at what she's wearing now and I go, "Wow."

I go, "Nice, Dom. You really did have a wonderful backup wardrobe plan."

"See," she says. "I knew you'd love it."

"Obviously."

"You look really cute too." She grabs my waist and leans into my ear. "Hot," she says.

What I'm wearing is a pair of skinny tight black jeans with a black bandanna dangling from the right back pocket. Plus a navy-blue T-shirt of one of my favorite bands ever, A Place to Bury Strangers, which says *Kill* on the front of it with a stencil of a pig. I've got my Members Only jacket on and a pair of black slip-ons, and I've tied an American flag bandanna around the ankle of my jeans.

Now here's what she's wearing. This pair of see-through and shredded black stockings that run all the way up to the top of her thighs, all-black Chuck Taylors, this black cardigan, this dope gold chain that hangs to the bottom of her stomach with a pair of mini golden binoculars attached to it, and then this huge white T-shirt under the cardigan that runs past the top of her stockings. On this T-shirt, though, is a black-and-gray stencil of a tiger face with stitches all over it, and under the face, spray painted on in black, are the words *Tiger Stitches*.

Like, this is getting ridiculous, ya know. How amazing and thoughtful and wonderful this girl is.

It's just too fucking good.

I almost wish she'd do something that sucked, so I could at least have one shitty point of reference to dwell on so I can feel a little bit better when I finally leave San Francisco.

"Dominique," I say. "That's so fucking sweet of you."

"I did it myself at band practice. Mark helped me with the stencil. You like it?"

"I love it."

"Good," she says. "I made you one too."

I grab her and pull her into me. "Every time I see you, it's better than the last time," I say. "And the first time we kicked it, I thought it was the perfect time. Like a hundred out of a hundred, and here we are again and it's just so much fucking better. I never thought I'd have a girlfriend as good as you."

Fuck! I think immediately after I've said this.

My hearts starts racing and my mouth gets dry.

Stepping back from me, Dominique says, "What'd you say?"

I stutter.

I'm thinking, *You idiot, Jaime. You goddamn fool. You and your stupid mouth. You and your stupid fucking mouth and tongue and teeth. Idiot!*

Wiping the sweat off my face, I go, "I . . ." I stop. Then, "I, um . . ." I stop again. "Like, nothing," I finally say.

"Stop it," she says. She's still smiling too. "Just stop it. You know what you said, Jaime."

I nod. "I do."

"Oh my god," she goes, and puts her hands over her face.

"I'm sorry," I tell her. "I didn't—"

But before I can finish, she throws her arms back around me and goes, "You just made me happy, boo. I've been wanting to say something like that all day to you. Jaime." She kisses my neck. "My Jaime, my boyfriend."

"Yeah," I say. "I am." Even though I think it's a horrible place to go there like this. With me leaving in a few days. It's stupid and I wasn't thinking right. I do feel that way, but I'm not going to be in San Francisco after Saturday. I'm leaving, and it's the worst idea ever to push me and her even closer together given the reality of the actual situation.

She kisses me again and then takes my hand and introduces me to the rest of Vicious Lips, who both look really nice and sharp and pretty as well.

Mark is a little bit taller than me. He's got thick, shaggy brown hair, and his bangs are pushed across his forehead from the right to left. He's super skinny and scrawny, and he's got a giraffe tattooed on the inside of his left forearm.

Mark's wearing a pair of supertight black cutoff jean shorts, a pair of orange-and-white Keds with no socks on underneath, and a gray-and-maroon-striped tank top.

Keisha is a fucking babe. Like, she's actually up there with Dominique now that I'm seeing her in person.

Her hair is dyed purple and hangs down her back. She's super skinny and taller than me and has a nice rack.

What she's wearing is this: A short, tight white dress, a pair of white, shredded stockings, a pair of all-black Chucks, and a huge gold chain with a golden gun attached to it.

After them, Dominique introduces me to her brother Jamal. He's fucking ripped and has a tiny Afro with a Z in his 'fro, and when he shakes my hand, he stares me dead in the eyes and his face stays straight.

Dominique's mother gives me a hug and says it's nice to see me again and that she's so happy that Dominique has been so excited and happy all week.

"That's cool," I say. "I have been too."

When I say this, I look back at Jamal. He's still grilling me with his eyes and it doesn't bother me, but I don't fucking like it either.

Before me and Brandon and Eddie jump in line to get inside, Dominique takes me to their van so I can store my backpack in it. I jacked my father for another bottle of red wine, and since they're checking bags at the door, I'll lose it if I try to get it past them.

When she's done locking the van back up, she runs her

fingers up and down the side of my face slowly. I'm leaning against the van, looking up at her, just in awe of her beauty and her smile.

"This is the most excited I've ever been about anything," she says.

"It's gonna be great," I say. "This is so huge for you guys. And you're gonna kill. I mean, you signed two fucking copies of your EP when we walked over here. Kids know who you are, they love you."

"I'm not talking about the show," she says. "I'm talking about this. Here. Me and you."

"Oh," I say. Then, "Dominique, I'm excited too, but—"

"You're leaving," she snaps. "I know. You don't need to keep saying it. I know you're not gonna be in San Francisco when next week starts, but I don't want to think about that until you're gone. Until I text you to hang out and you can't because you're three thousand miles away. I'll think about it then, but right now, I want to enjoy you being here. Cos that's what's real right now."

"All right," I whisper. "You look so pretty tonight."

"So do you."

"Where are we going after the show?"

"I ain't telling you that, dude. It's a surprise. But we're gonna take my acoustic guitar with us, and it's gonna blow you away."

"I can't wait."

"Me neither," she says, then leans into me and we kiss

and we keep kissing and keep kissing, and I even put my hand over her pussy and press on it a couple of times and she bites my bottom lip and moans.

She says, "Nothing makes me happier than seeing you at my show."

"You should get in there."

"Kay . . . ," she says. "See you inside, Jaime Miles."

We kiss again, and this time she puts my hand over her pussy and I rub on it until she bites my bottom lip so hard it bleeds.

"Vicious teeth," I say, as I wipe the blood off with my hand.

"Vicious pussy, too," she says, then turns around and runs inside the venue.

73

BY THE TIME WE FINALLY GET INSIDE, IT'S NEARLY filled to capacity, which Eddie says is at least six or seven hundred. Place is huge. Two levels even. It's fucking electric in here too. That MGMT song "Kids" is blasting from the house speakers, and Brandon is singing to it as the three of us make our way to the backstage area. I've never been in anything like this. Not even close. It seems even more intense than that last LCD Soundsystem looked in *Shut Up and Play the Hits*.

Since I have an all-access wristband, I can escort these guys with me. It's pretty fucking cool. Even though I always thought that people who make such a big deal about having this kinda access were jerks and booger pussies, it's totally cool to see pretty much everyone out in the crowd staring at us while we head back there, wondering who the fuck we are and why the fuck do we get to hang tough backstage and what they'd probably do to trade places with us.

Right when we get inside the area, Eddie turns back to the crowd and yells, "Devil Feeder!" and flashes the rock horns.

"Skullburns!" Brandon yells, and when he turns back

around, he bumps into this super-skinny guy who's, like, flamboyantly gay but dressed supersharp, and he's really handsome, too.

"Well, hey there," he says, grabbing Brandon's arm.

"Hey," Brandon says, then stops walking and starts talking to him.

Eddie throws his arm over my shoulder and says, "I snuck in three one-shooters of Jack Daniel's in my underwear. I'm pretty excited about that."

"Let's mow them scuds down," I say.

"Atta boy."

Right before we descend these stairs that lead to the greenrooms, I look back at Brandon again and he's really chatting up that dude now. He's laughing and keeps bumping into him and he's blushing.

I don't say anything, though. It's weird. But I don't wanna assume anything, so I just follow Eddie down the stairs.

Me and Eddie, we do our shots of whiskey real quick and then pop into the Vicious Lips room. The band's all in there with Jamal and Dominique's mother and Mark's girlfriend, this babe with long black hair and bangs cut crooked across her forehead, who looks like she wants to look like Karen O and that's totally fine by me.

There's one girl in there just snapping a ton of photos of the band, and this other guy is holding a video camera.

"Okay," he says. "You guys ready?"

And everyone in the band says they are.

Me and Eddie, we look at each other and shrug. They don't go on for another ten minutes. Even all the way down here, the anticipation and the noise and the house music ("Such Great Heights" by the Postal Service) just vibrate through the walls and through the floor.

King Krule is a huge band right now. There's a ton of industry people hanging around the hallway and in their room. Eddie's the one who tells me they're industry people.

"All those press passes and sleazy, asshole-looking dudes in suits smelling like they bathed in a tub of shitty cologne," he says. "That's how I know."

I'm, like, nervous for Dominique. For Mark and Keisha. For all of us who know them. This is a way bigger deal than I ever imagined it would be. It's a massive thing. Every last hair on my body is standing straight up because of the energy and anticipation swarming through my gut like a million bees.

Keisha and Dominique sit down alongside Mark now on this leather sofa. Dominique's in the middle. Mark's girlfriend hands Dominique an acoustic guitar. Keisha's already holding one, and Mark has a tambourine in his hands.

"Whenever you guys are good," Mr. Cameraman says, "just start playing."

Dominique looks up at me and winks. This small grin cuts to the left of her face. Then she looks at Keisha and then Mark and she nods and counts off. . . .

"One, two, one, two, three, four . . ."

Vicious Lips starts playing. It takes me about ten seconds to finally recognize the song they're performing. Eddie, too. Cos he turns to me right as I'm about to turn to him and he goes, "Mazzy Star."

"'Look on Down from the Bridge,'" I say. "Fuck. My mother used to listen to this song late at night all the time. She'd just play it over and over and over, looking out the window of our living room. It's beautiful. My mother always looked so beautiful when she listened to it."

When Dominique starts singing, fucking chills slam down my spine and I get dizzy from it. I just watch her sing and play guitar. Her eyes are closed. She's singing from the bottom of her heart. Her mother is crying as she watches her, and Jamal, finally that dude smiles. How can you not? This is mesmerizing. Stunning. This . . .

"Everybody seems so far away from me, everybody just wants to be free . . ."

Immediately after those words leave her mouth, Dominique finally opens her eyes and looks right at me and smiles. Eddie nudges me and my heart is fucking melting.

Like, holy shit!

Holy shit!

I think I'm in fucking love with this girl.

Holy fucking shit, man!

74

ME AND EDDIE ARE STANDING OFF TO THE SIDE OF the stage and to the back of it in the all-access area. We can see the entire space from here. See all the happy fucking kids just packed in and laughing and waiting.

I don't see Brandon anywhere and when I ask Eddie, he says, "I don't know where he went, man. Dude does that at shows. He wanders. Meets a ton of people. Dances. Laughs. That's his thing, homie. He's out there somewhere with ten new friends and a smile."

I really like what Eddie just said. You can tell him and Brandon are true friends. That they care for each other and understand each other and let one another be who they are.

Scanning the first couple of rows in the crowd, I see so many babes and they're all sorta looking in our direction, and it's nice to know that the hottest girl here is the one that likes me and isn't lying about it and won't play any mean jokes on me or make me feel like a loser for wanting to be with her so badly.

The house lights dim suddenly. Then the whole room goes black, and everyone starts screaming and whistling and clapping while that Cage song "I Found My Mind in Connecticut" from his album *Depart from Me* starts bumping.

"Sick!" Eddie yells. "So dope!"

Me, I'm clapping and right when the chorus starts . . .

"Every morning I just lay in bed cause I don't wanna wake up, pick my stupid face up, give my shit away . . ."

This flashlight cuts across the floor and out walks Vicious Lips, and they take the fucking stage to an applause and an appreciation that I've never come close to witnessing before.

It's so special.

And they deserve it all and probably so much more.

When the lights are brought back up a tiny bit, there's my girl standing front and center on the stage behind her keyboard synth, next to a blue-and-white Gretsch guitar lying in a stand, a tambourine hanging from a hook on the side of the synth.

Keisha is to her right and Mark is set up on his sick drum kit to her left, but he's facing both of them.

After a few seconds of her checking her gear, the applause begins to die and she leans forward into the microphone and says, "Thank you so much . . . wow." She looks like the happiest person in the history of the world. They all do. And then she says, "Thank you all so much for coming out tonight."

Some girl in the crowd yells, "We love you!" and people

cheer again and Dominique laughs and says thank you one more time, then "We're Vicious Lips from right here in San Francisco. This first song's called 'The Fury and the Night.'"

Dominique rips her cardigan off now, and then it begins. And, like, a minute later this entire place is fucking jumping and ten times more alive than it was when we walked in.

About halfway through their third song, "Wet Kisses," I look to my left and see Jamal walking toward me.

I ain't nervous, though. Like, her mother gave me another hug after the first song was over and told me how impressed she was with me from all the things Dominique has told her so far.

"What's up, man," I say.

He stands right next to me and crosses his arms.

"It's so good," I say next.

"Yeah it is, man. My sister is special. She's the most talented and caring person I've ever met, and that includes my momma."

"She's great," I say. "She really is."

"I'm glad to hear that from you," he snorts. "Cos that girl on stage, dancing and slamming on that keyboard and ripping the crowd to pieces with that angel-like voice, that girl is too good for anyone."

I look up at him. "Excuse me?"

"You heard me, man. You know exactly what I said, and it's the truth and you know it too."

I don't say anything.

"If she was as smart as we know she is, she wouldn't be messing around with no dudes ever. She'd just focus on her music and get big and then deal with all the dicks later."

"Hey, man," I snap.

"What?" he snaps.

Eddie hears that and steps towards us. "Yo, Jaime, what's up?"

"This don't concern you, homie. Stay the fuck back."

"Fuck you."

I put my hands on Eddie's shoulders and say, "Relax, man. It's fine."

"Asshole," I hear Eddie mumble.

Turning back to Jamal, I go, "Listen, man. Dominique is amazing, and that's how I'm treating her."

"Good," he says. "And it better stay that way, because if you fucking hurt her in any way, if you ever lie to her or talk shit about her or doing something funny behind her back and make her sad or make her cry, I promise you I will track you down and take you out. She's the most important person in my life, and I will protect her and defend her with force."

"Okay, dude. I got it."

"Do you?"

"Yeah."

"I will ruin you if you make her cry."

"Dude," I say, throwing my arms in the air. "I got it. She ain't gonna cry from anything I do."

"Jamal!"

Dominique's mother yells this at him.

"Get over here," she says. "Leave that boy alone. I work for his daddy."

"You should go," I tell him, smirking.

"That attitude gonna get you hurt," he says.

"Jamal! Now!" his mother goes.

But before he walks away, he says, "Hurt her or dishonor her in any way and you're a dead man. She's better than you. She's better than all of us."

Jamal walks away and Eddie puts his arm around my shoulders again and I whisper, "I know, dude."

I whisper, "She's way better than I'll ever be."

The fourth song of the set is a cover of Nada Surf's "Blonde on Blonde," and me and Eddie freak out. I love this song. It was the fourth song I learned to play on the guitar. So cool they're covering it. This set is insanely fucking good. Me and Eddie, we run to the front of the stage and start singing along with everyone else around us. . . .

"I've got blonde on blonde, on my portable stereo . . ."

Hearing half a crowd this big, so maybe four hundred people, singing along with you has gotta be such a monster fucking thrill. And when the song is over, I look over my shoulder and see Brandon making out with that guy he bumped into earlier.

I'm shocked to see this. Stunned, I guess.

I grab Eddie by the shoulder and say, "You see that, man?"

"What?"

"That," I say, pointing.

"Oh yeah. What about it?"

"I mean nothing, I guess. I just didn't know he was gay."

"He ain't. Dude flips both ways, but he's been into boys a lot more recently. It's all good. That dude loves to suck some cock," Eddie says, then walks over to this girl who's been making eyes at him all night long and starts talking to her.

The last song of the set is this new one they wrote a couple weeks ago called "In the Time of the Horned Lions," and it rips better than any other of their songs in my opinion and flows better too. The tone is perfect, and it's got some edge. Dominique played it for me at her crib yesterday right before I left.

I'd say it'd find a nice home anywhere on Beach House's *Bloom* record.

Or on any Blouse record, for that matter.

"So we just wanna thank you all so much again for coming here and supporting us tonight. It means everything to us. Vicious Lips loves you all. This is our last song and it's a new one. King Krule is up next . . ."

The song starts and about thirty seconds later, she sings, *"Kingdom come, then kingdom go, these city lights, this neon glow,* reaching far and running fast, these lions eat what they can catch, the days they move, the nights they fly, perfume, makeup, pretty skies, lions sleep and lions grin, steal the air, and you will win..."

Chorus: "Wilderness, and beasts, the makings of a feast, horned and angry lurking by, these lions hurt, these lions die... In the time of them... In the time of them... In the time of them, this whole time we've been... alive...

"Trees full of peaches, a young girl rips them off, somewhere in Los Angeles, these junkies rob a loft, people come and people go, you forget all their names, it ain't important, it's really nothing, you're just living for the day, so twirl baby twirl, your smile fills the sky, these lions they're a-coming, don't forget to kiss me bye...

"Wilderness, and beasts, the makings of a feast, horned and angry lurking by, these lions hurt, these lions die ... In the time of them ... In the time of them ... In the time of them, this whole time we've been... alive...

"Love won't save the world, love won't save these lions, you make your feasts and drink your wine, and stop your fucking crying, please baby please, she begged, just come back to me, she gets down on her knees but he still fucking leaves, these lions eat, these lions sleep, this world it never stops, and it's cool and it's fun, our lives they're worth a lot...

"Wilderness, and beasts, the makings of a feast, horned and angry lurking by, these lions hurt, these lions die ... In the time of them ... In the time of them ... In the time of them, this whole time we've been... alive... alive... alive... through thick and thin and ugly shit we're all still alive... alive..."

The lyrics are great. Some of the best lyrics I've heard by any band in a while. But the best part of the song is right after the last chorus ends, when Dominique finally grabs that Gretsch, throws it over her shoulder, and slams her foot on the pedal and starts shredding with Keisha for about two minutes. This killer riff that rips through the crowd. It reminds me of the "Outro" on the M83 record *Hurry Up, We're Dreaming*, when that guitar just cuts in like a knife does to skin and bleeds all over anyone listening.

When the song finally ends, the band walks offstage to thunderous applause and Dominique, she runs over to me and hugs me and kisses me and before I follow her down the stairs, I take a nice, long look around at all the people staring at me, jealous of me, wishing they were me because my fucking girlfriend just owned seven hundred people for forty-five minutes and did whatever she wanted to them. Made them drink blood out of her hands and got them all turned on.

75

"WHERE ARE WE?" I ASK DOMINIQUE. "ARE WE EVEN
in the city anymore?"

"Oh yeah," she says. "It ain't much farther. We're so
close, and you're gonna thank me for the rest of your life for
bringing you here. Trust me."

Dominique and me, we're climbing this hill and it's
pretty cold right now and I just told her about how I saw
Brandon kissing that gay dude.

"I kinda thought that about him," she says.

"Really?"

"Yeah. Some of his mannerisms, how clean and shaped
his fingernails were, the eyes he was making at you at
Dolores Park."

"What are you talking about?"

"Oh, you didn't notice that," she says.

"No," I say.

"Yes, he was," she says back, laughing. "It was clear to
me and Eddie."

I've got her guitar in one hand and that bottle of
wine in the other, and I was able to smoke half a blue in
the backstage bathroom before we took off from Slim's

and jumped on the BART and got off in what's known as Bernal Heights.

"I'm pretty sure tomorrow when you wake up, Vicious Lips is gonna be the biggest thing in San Francisco."

"No way," she goes.

"Yes way," I say back. "That crowd ate everything y'all cooked and plated for them."

She laughs.

"Then all those suits backstage who wouldn't shut up."

"So annoying," she says.

"I really do mean it, Dominique. Your band is absolutely going to the next level soon and then another level after that."

"I hope so," she says. "I want it to happen so bad. We all do. That's why we work so hard all the time. Nobody works harder than my band, Jaime. We say we're gonna get something done and then we go get it done."

"That's the way it should be."

"We're young, but we've played a lot of shows in this city with a lot of older people who've been doing this here for years and they're not doing shit. Just treading water and still opening at the same bars on the same shitty weekday nights. A lot of them are just assholes who roll their eyes at us until they see us play and how we own the house every time. But seriously, some of those shows, all I hear backstage is a bunch of fucking coked-out hipsters who don't think they're hipsters talking and talking and talking and never doing. No way it should take you four months to put out an EP and book a handful of shows. No fucking way. You should put out two EPs in four months. And a lot of them don't even tour. Like, how the fuck are you gonna make a living off your music if you don't tour? Like, that's the next step for us. I'm graduating a year early from school and we're hitting the road right away for the whole summer. Starting in August, each of us is putting fifty bucks a week into a band bank account so we can be on the road for three months straight. If you really want this, you have to go places with it, literally. We ain't ever gonna be the coked-out band talking about the rad shit we wanna do till sunrise, we're gonna be the band who talks about the shows we just did on the West Coast and East Coast and about the two albums we put out last year."

"I think you are already that band."

"Not yet," she says. "But we're getting there."

"Are we?" I ask. "Are we getting there?"

"Oh yes," she says. "Just another minute or two, baby."

As we near the top of the hill, Dominique wanders over to me and hooks her arm through mine.

"You ready?" she says.

"Absolutely," I tell her.

"Okay then," she goes. "Close your eyes and take my hand and wait till I tell you to open them."

"Sure."

I've never felt more comfortable in my life. More excited and comfortable and cared for too.

There's no one else I'd ever trust to do this with. Not even my mother. And this is the thing about Dominique, I trust her. That's why I love her now. I finally began to believe the things she told me. I finally realized she meant everything. When I saw her actually doing all the things she told me she was going to do, that was when I believed she meant everything she was telling me.

That's so beautiful too. This is how you know if someone really likes you or loves you. Once I got that, she got my heart.

And now she has all of it.

We stop walking. Wherever we are, there's a strong calm and quiet about it.

"Okay," she says. "Open them."

"Holy shit," I say, covering my mouth and even staggering a couple steps backward. "It's so beautiful, Dominique."

She starts clapping, and I grab her and throw my arms around her and kiss her.

What I just looked at is the city of San Francisco lit up and sprawled out in front of me. We're at the very top of Bernal Heights and from here, you can see past the city and into the ocean.

It's the most gorgeous thing I've ever seen besides her face.

"Oh shit," I say, kissing her again. "I will definitely be thanking you for the rest of my life."

"But that's not it," she says. "We've gotta walk about fifteen more feet to see the cherry on top, Jaime."

"There's something sweeter than this still?" I say. "Jesus, I'm getting spoiled tonight."

"Oh you have no idea," she goes, squeezing my hand as my dick plants into my zipper and my jeans push out a few inches.

She opens her backpack and takes out this huge flashlight and after moving a few feet closer, she turns it on and yeah, fucking yes, it just got a whole lot sweeter.

There's a piano up here. It's just sitting about five feet from the edge of the hill.

I cover my mouth again and go, "No way," and then I kiss her and run to it.

"Has this always been here?" I go.

Shaking her head, she says, "No. Just since last week. Mark—"

"From your band?"

"Yes," she says. Then, "Mark and two of his friends found the piano in this old, abandoned church near Hayes Valley. They broke in to tag the place and saw the piano. After they tuned it up, they went back the next day with a truck and loaded it up and brought it up here that afternoon. We got a bunch of people together then and had a picnic and jam session that night. One of the most fun nights of my life, actually. Isn't it so great?"

"It's the best, Dominique. You and your friends are amazing. All of you, you're so sincere and creative and nice. This is probably the coolest thing I'll ever see in my life and

I'm seeing it with you . . . this beautiful girl, this girl that I, ya know . . ."

My voice fades a bit and my throat gets dry. I've never done this before. It's tougher than I ever imagined.

Dominique grabs my hands and goes, "The girl that you what?"

"Ya know . . ."

"What?" she goes, giggling.

"The girl that I love," I say.

Dominique lets go of my hands and throws them against the side of my face now and we start making out.

When we stop for a second, I go, "I'm sorry if I—"

"Shhhhh," she says, then kisses me again. "Just don't. Don't say anything else right now, Jaime."

She kisses me again and then slides her lips down my chin and then down my neck. She sucks on my neck and licks it and then sticks her tongue in my ear.

I'm moaning as she undoes my belt and jeans. She pulls them down past my knees and puts her hand on my dick.

"Hey," she says.

"Hey."

"You happy?"

"I'm the happiest."

She giggles. "Good." Then she kisses me again and says, "I love you, too, Jaime."

When she drops to her knees, she pulls my underwear down too and immediately swallows my dick.

How I always imagined and fantasized how good this

would feel when it happened, times that by a thousand and you're still not close.

Dominique works my dick and I put my hand on the back of her head. She takes all of it to the back of her throat. She sucks and she sucks and sucks it while I stare at all the big, bright, shiny lights of San Francisco, the whole city in front me, laid out like a big map of awesome, and about a minute after she started blowing me, my body jumps and it jolts and her head stops bobbing and I come in her mouth.

This is the closest I'll ever get to being a king.

A fucking god.

When she gets back on her feet, she takes a drink of water from the bottle in her bag.

"They do anything like this back in Joliet?" she goes.

"I see what you're doing."

"Do they?"

"No."

"They have anything like this there?"

I shake my head no.

We kiss again and she holds her arms out toward the city and goes, "Just something to think about."

"Dom," I say.

And she goes, "You should really know what you're leaving before you actually decide to leave it. And that's the last thing I'm going to say to you about it."

She grabs my hands again and we turn toward the cityscape together. "This," she says. "This says more than enough anyway."

76

WE STAY UP THERE FOR TWO HOURS. WE PLAY THE
piano together and sometimes I play the guitar while she
plays the piano and sometimes it's the other way around.
I'm pretty buzzed on the wine and her. She's fucking perfect. And me, I don't deserve any of this, but it's nice to get it.

Images of me and her making music together in a studio, of me and her riding bikes around the city, of us lying
on a blanket in Dolores Park laughing and holding hands,
the two of us huddled together on the beach watching the
sun set for the seventh night in a row, of me opening for her
band at some huge venue, her and I moving into our first
apartment together, of us driving down the coast in a van
singing along to that Shins song "Phantom Limb," me making dinner for her every night, the two of us reading to each
other and getting those words tattooed on us together, of me
and her running around a loft in Paris laughing and screaming and fucking and quoting Rimbaud and Burroughs and
Bukowski, smash through my head.

At one point, she stops playing and goes, "What are you
thinking about?"

"Nothing," I tell her.

"Sure about that?"

"I'm sure, love."

"All right," she says, grinning from ear to ear. "Let's play a song we both know together now."

"Which one?"

"You pick."

It takes me all of five seconds before I go, "What about that Postal Service song, 'Such Great Heights'?"

"I can't play it on guitar," she says. "But I can do the piano."

"Perfect."

She hands me the guitar and then she sits down on the bench while I jump on top of the piano.

After I'm done tuning, I take a swig of wine and go, "Ready?"

"Freddy."

I laugh and then bang my foot against the piano three times and we begin the song.

It's so radical. This song with her, here. Her voice and her fingers on those keys and San Francisco as the backdrop.

Best. Night. Ever. And that's what scares me too. As epic and huge as this night was, what if we just peaked? There's no pressure on either of us when we know it's already gonna end and how it's gonna end. Maybe that's the reason this is working so well and why it's so easy. We've gone fucking deep together, but we did so knowing that the other person would only have to live with each other's scars and histories and demons for a week.

It's pretty easy to look past something for a week.

Most people spend years together before they finally fucking break and let the scars ruin them.

The way we play this song is slow. It's the same speed as Iron and Wine's version of it. It's such a beautiful song too. And the lyrics. These goddamn gorgeous words.

Dominique finally joins me when we come to the chorus. I look at her and smile and then I look over my shoulder and back at the city as we sing . . .

"But everything looks perfect from far away. 'Come down now,' but we'll stay . . ."

77

IN THE MORNING, MY FATHER CALLS ME INTO HIS office and says, "I want you to go somewhere with me."

"Why?"

"Cos I think it's something you need to see while you're here."

"I've got plans," I tell him. "How about a rain check?"

"I'm not really asking you, son. I'm telling you. And we're leaving in five minutes."

I use those five minutes to smoke half a blue and stress hard about how many I don't have left.

"About a month after we found out your mother was pregnant, the two of us came to San Francisco for a week."

"Why?"

"She'd never been before. I already loved it here, and I'd talk about it a lot because I wanted us to move out here someday, so we decided to go before she got really big with you inside her and it became harder for her to travel. It was one of the best weeks she and I had together. I want you to understand that we were very happy once."

"I know you were."

"I want you to understand, Jaime. Not just know, and there's a huge difference. She was the love of my life. I adored her. I worshipped the ground she walked on, son."

I see pain in my father's face while he's saying this. Him saying this also makes me wanna vomit and push him into the water we're standing over.

The two of us are at Fort Point. It's right under the Golden Gate Bridge. We're leaning against this red railing on a lookout point about twenty feet from the water. Even though the sun is shining and there isn't a cloud in the sky, it's freezing and I'm miserable.

"There was a time between us where there was nothing I wouldn't have done for her. Nothing, Jaime."

"Why are we here?" I finally ask. "What's the point of this?"

"Horrible, devastating things happen in relationships and in marriages sometimes, and no matter how goddamn deeply those two people might love each other, it can be impossible to come back from it. But you try, ya know. You put on your happy face and you try to remember how you fell in love, not why. Remember that, son. Always remember to dream about how it happened. If you try to remember why, it'll get ugly real fast because it won't make any sense. Love doesn't make any sense, and it's not supposed to. But if you try to go back and remember how it happened, it's almost like you can relive it. Certain days the two of you shared, days when it felt like you'd found perfection in an imperfect world, an imperfect life. Days that tattoo themselves to your goddamn soul and swallow your heart. Days when you firmly believed without a doubt that the life you were living and the person you were living it with were too beautiful for either of you to deface or smear shit on. Because that's what you were telling each other and you meant it and you believed it and you knew the other person did too and that's all you need when it comes to love. Two people who believe that the other one loves this life as much as them, because when someone tells you they do and they tell you they love you and talk about buying a house and starting a family and all the pets they'll have, what other choice do you have than to believe them? If you don't, how do you even believe yourself when you say those things?"

My father stops. He looks awful right now. The wind is blowing right through his hair, and he's rubbing his face over and over with his hand. He looks sick and worn out.

"Are you okay?" I ask.

"Huh?"

"Is everything all right?"

"Yeah," he says. "I'm sorry. Your mother's favorite movie—"

"Is *Vertigo*," I say.

"Exactly."

"What about it?"

"This is the first place your mother and I came to after we checked into the hotel."

"Why?"

"Because this is the place where they filmed that famous scene of Scottie saving Madeleine from her suicide attempt."

"Oh, man. It is. Now I see it. Wow. But wasn't most of the movie filmed in San Francisco?"

My father nods.

"So why did you come here first?" I ask. "It's kind of morbid, right?"

"It's not," he says. "Scottie thinks he saves her from killing herself. It was beautiful to him. When someone saves someone else, especially someone they're falling in love with, it means so much more than the literal of what actually happened. It's so much deeper than anything else there is. That bond that forms in the aftermath. The immense trust that blossoms up overnight. That understanding that the two of you survived that, the worst moment of your lives together, and nothing can destroy you now and neither of you will ever let anything bad happen to the other."

"What are you talking about right now?"

"Nothing," he goes. "I just wanted to tell about the trip."

"The trip?"

"Yes, son. The trip your mother and I took to San Francisco before you were born. It really was a happy trip. It was the last trip we would ever take together too. I'm not sure I've ever seen her smile as much as she did when she was in San Francisco. My father, who was my hero, you never met him because he died before you were born, he was out here too when we were."

"Did he live here?"

"No," my father says. "But he had a lot of friends here, and he flew out a week earlier so we were able to spend some time with him. He got diagnosed with lung cancer about a month after the trip and passed away three weeks before you were born. Your mother adored him, so it was nice he was out here. And he really adored your mother, too. They were very close. It was good for them, I thought. He could make her laugh like no one else could, not even me. It was something else. He really cared for her and she really cared for him. I wish you'd gotten the chance to meet him."

"Okay," I say. "What is this all about, Dad?"

"Thank you," he says.

"For what?"

"For addressing me as Dad twice in a row."

"Did I?"

He nods. "You did."

"I didn't even notice it."

"Still," he says. "Thank you."

He turns away from me now and slides his hands into his pockets and shakes his head.

I haven't seen him like this yet. Broken. Sad. Remorseful about something, even though I'm not sure what.

I have no clue, actually.

"Hey," I tell him. "Dad."

He turns around. "Yeah."

"We should go. I'm meeting Dominique for lunch in an hour."

"Okay. Just give me another minute or two."

"What is going on with you?" I ask.

He doesn't say anything.

"Hey," I say. "Justin."

"Jaime," he says. "I just want you to know that your mother loves you and she's done everything for you since she left our apartment that morning."

"I know."

"And we were very happy together once. And we were so excited that you were coming into our lives. I loved her so much. There was a time when the two of us were happy with the life we were making."

"I got it."

"Remember it," he says. "Remember it and understand that your mother is a wonderful woman who loves you very much. Remember it," he says one more time before turning back to the water and leaning against the rail.

78

"DO YOU THINK YOU'LL ACTUALLY EVER GET A TATTOO?"
I ask Dominique. Me and her, we're eating sandwiches from
the Haight Street Market and drinking coconut water in the
Panhandle, which is this park that stretches about six blocks
just two blocks off Haight.

Both of us are lying down, wearing sunglasses, and barefoot. She's got an hour before she has to be at work, and she's
really excited to go stand outside the Great American Music
Hall with me tomorrow and listen to Youth Lagoon's set.

"Just to hear him live is totally enough for me," she said
while we were waiting for our sandwiches at the market,
holding hands, one earphone in her ear, one in mine, listening to this song "Black Hills" by this band Gardens & Villa.
"I love this idea," she continued. "When *Year of Hibernation*
came out, I'm pretty sure I spent the next three months listening to only that and getting really angry that what I was
writing was nothing close to anything he was doing on that
album."

Back to the park now and the tattoos.

"Yeah," she says. "I'm sure I'll have at least one. This is
tattoo city, ya know. But I'll prolly end up with a lot of them,

actually. Malcolm's got, like, six already. I went with him when he got his last one and it didn't seem all that bad. What about you?"

"I don't know," I say.

"Why did you ask me that?" she goes.

"I saw this picture today in my father's office of him and my grandfather. See, my grandfather had all these tattoos from the war. He was totally sleeved. Beautiful, stunning, elaborate ink. My mother's told me about them so many times, it was like she was obsessed with them or something. She's shown me pictures too. Just amazing. So anyway, in the picture, my father is young, like seven or eight probably, and he's wearing this white T-shirt and jean shorts, and one of his arms is covered in tattoos drawn with some colored markers. It's like a whole sleeve of tattoos just like my grandfather's but in marker, and my grandfather's holding the marker in one hand and a Budweiser in the other."

Dominique laughs.

And I say, "They're both smiling and look so happy and it looks really fun, like they were having the best time ever."

"That's really cool," Dominique says.

I don't say anything.

"You okay?" she asks.

After a few more seconds of nothing, I finally sigh and then go, "I just wonder what happened is all. My father adored that man. My grandfather was his hero, but my mother told me that my father cut my grandfather off a couple of weeks before he died. He didn't attend the funeral, wouldn't talk about him to anyone, and that was his hero up until what, a few weeks before the man dies from lung cancer."

"Death freaks some people out. They can't handle it, and sometimes they get angry at the person who's dying."

"Maybe," I say. "Maybe something else, though."

"Like what?"

"I don't know, and I actually don't care. My father seems to be on some almost, like, God-ordained mission to open up as little as possible while I'm here and that's fine. He's a dick."

"Hey," she goes.

"Sorry," I say. "I'm sorry."

"It's okay."

"I just wonder sometimes."

"About what?"

"I wonder how you can be that happy during one moment in your life with one person, throughout an entire day with them, like they obviously were in that picture, and end up having nothing to do with them in the end. Nothing at all. Like, where did that one moment go? Where did that one day go? How did it all slip away? The happiness, the smiles, the fucking joy of it all. What happens to people?"

Dominique shakes her head and whispers, "I don't know. But it does go away with so many people. Quickly," she says. "And then it's just gone for good."

"I know. And it's just so damn sad. Like, do people just forget how happy they once were? Do they forget that they once made each other so fucking happy and that things were gorgeous and beautiful and every day it was a fucking privilege to have each other and to know each other and love each other and how awesome it must have felt at one point to have that?"

"They do forget. Obviously. They do."

"But why?"

"I can't answer that."

Pause.

"I know," I whisper.

And then Dominique, she goes, "I have an idea."

"What's that?"

She pulls out a Sharpie from her backpack and says, "Draw on me."

I smirk. "You're crazy. You have to go to work soon."

"So what? I'll go all marker-tatted up. Come on, it'll be fun. You say you're good at drawing, prove it."

"You sure?"

"One hundred percent in."

I sit up now and take the Sharpie.

We kiss first, and then I ask her what she wants.

"Surprise me."

"Sure."

I grab her hand and think for a minute before putting the tip of the Sharpie against her skin and move it slowly.

It's easier than I thought it would be.

I draw for the next fifteen minutes at a pretty furious-like pace. I draw a dragon and an eagle and two snakes and connect them with ropes and hands and wings and crosses.

Like, twenty minutes after I started, Dominique looks at it and then looks at me and then looks at her arm again.

She kisses me and tells me it's really good and then takes her phone and holds it up over us.

"Smile, babe."

I do.

"Lovely," she says, then lays her head on my shoulder and takes the picture.

"There," she says, holding it so we can both see it. "It's real history now. Pictures are forever. So let's not lose this moment. Let's never lose what we have and what we mean to each other. Let's always stay happy, let's never end up like them," she finishes, before kissing my neck and telling me she loves me.

"I love you, too."

"Forever," she goes.

"Right, love. Forever," I go back, hardly able to stomach the words now.

79

ME AND MY FATHER AND LESLIE ARE EATING CHINESE food in the kitchen, and New Order is playing on the record player.

Since we went to the Cigar Bar & Grill on Saturday night, this is the first time I've eaten with both of them. It happens, I guess. Lots of fucking things happen, I'm finding out.

"I can't believe you two saw the final LCD Soundsystem show," I say. "I'm so jealous."

"Oh, that was so much fun," Leslie goes. "Great show, crazy trip."

"How did you guys end up hanging out with James Murphy?" I ask.

"You don't know?" my father says.

"What would I know?"

"I guess you don't. I thought your mother would've told you."

"Told me what?"

"We knew James when we lived in New York before LCD. And your mother and Nancy, their keyboard player, were close when she first moved there."

"No," I say. "No way."

"It's true. Nancy even asked about her a couple of times after the show backstage and at the after-show party."

I'm so floored right now. So fucking floored. Who are these people? It's insane to me who they know and who they're friends with and who they hang with.

"Maybe she didn't want to talk about that time," my father says.

"Oh no," I say. "She talks about it."

My father rolls his eyes and Leslie laughs.

"Why are you laughing?"

"Just the way he said that," she goes. "It was funny."

"No, it wasn't," my father snorts right as the back door opens so hard that it slams against the wall, shattering the window in it.

"What the fuck?" my father yells.

The three of us jump out of our seats and run over there only to see Kristen stumble in and fall onto the floor crying— no, bawling her eyes out, and curling up in a fetal position.

My heart is breaking right now.

It's so sad. She's so sad.

"Kristen," Leslie says, dropping straight to her knees next to her. She throws her arms around her daughter. She's crying too, and goes, "Baby, what's wrong? Tell me. Please."

Kristen looks up at Leslie with a face full of tears and hate and says, "Fucking Tyler is what's wrong! That asshole! He's cheating on me!"

"Scumbag," I rip. "Government scumbag! Ahhhh!"

"What are you talking about?" my father asks as he stands there so very casual and cool with his hands in his pockets like a jerk. "I don't understand."

"He's cheating on me," she shrieks. "What don't you understand about that?"

"Do you know this for sure?" my father says.

"Really, dude?" I snap. "Really?"

And Kristen screams, "Yes! I'm sure! He hasn't been returning my calls for the last few days, so I followed him this afternoon and I caught him kissing Rachael by her car."

"That fucking creep!" I yell.

"What'd you do?" my father says. "Did you do something dumb?"

"No," Kristen goes. "What the hell do you think I did?"

"What?" my father snaps.

"I jumped out of my car and confronted them. I went nuts. I kicked him in the balls and fucking dumped his ass right there."

"Oh, baby," Leslie says, trying to squeeze her daughter now. "Come here."

Kristen pushes her away.

And my father goes, "So just like that, huh, you broke up with him? Did you even talk to him first?"

"What the hell was there to talk about?" she screams. "I saw them kissing."

"You should've karate-chopped him in the throat and stabbed his dick with a switchblade."

"Jaime, stop," my father snaps. "Be reasonable, guy. Be mature."

"What?" both me and Kristen say at the same time.

And I say, "Stabbing his balls and busting his neck woulda been the reasonable thing to do, man. And fucking up that bitch grill of his."

"I said stop it, Jaime. This isn't any of your business."

"Bullshit it ain't."

"You should've gotten his side of the story, Kristen."

"What fucking story?" Kristen goes. "I saw it."

And Leslie goes, "Thank god you didn't punch him."

"You don't think you rushed to judgment?" my father goes.

I can't take this anymore.

And I say, "Your daughter just got her heart ripped out by some sleazy, sweaty, phony and all you're worried about is your cocaine connection?"

"Thank you," Kristen says.

"That's not true," my father says. "It's just strange to me. He doesn't seem like the type."

"I saw him doing it! He is the type! Fuck!"

And I say, "The type. Dude is a drug dealer. He makes money off of other people's misery. And apparently he causes it too. Stop thinking about your nostrils, man, and start thinking about your fucking family, dude. Christ. For once in your life think about your family and not yourself. Just for once!"

The way my father's face changes right in front of me, how it goes from plain to demon in a split second, it scares me a little. A lot, actually. This must have been what my mother was afraid of. The change in this man and how quickly it comes.

Stepping toward me, he grabs my shoulders and yells, "You're way out of line! You're fucking heartless, Jaime!"

"Fuck you," I shout right back, ripping myself loose from him. "That's your kid. Even if there was another side, it's still your fucking kid. She needs your support, man. Not your questions."

"I said stay out of it!"

"Okay, okay, okay," Leslie shouts, standing back up. "Everyone just calm down."

"No," I say. "This is bullshit. She's fucking heartbroken. That is the story. Period. Put your family first!"

"Ahhhhhhhhhhhhhhhhhhh!" my father screams, and then punches the wall, putting a hole twice the size of his fist through it. "You stay out of this!" he screams so loud my ears start ringing. "Get out of my fucking house, you punk!"

"Justin," Leslie says, and grabs him. "Stop it."

"Get out of my face, Jaime," he yells again.

Stepping backward, startled, nervous, I look at Kristen, who's looking at me, and she's just broken and done right now.

"Out of my face!" he screams again. "Out!"

"Fine," I say. "Fuck this anyway, and fuck you. You

should start fucking Tyler," I tell him. "Lick that coke right off his dick."

"Jaime," Leslie snaps.

"Fuck you too, Leslie. I'm out," I rip, then flip around as fast as I can and bail from this stupid fucking house.

80

"YO, HOMIE. I NEED YOUR HELP WITH SOMETHING tonight after we're done laying down these tracks."

"Sure," says Eddie. He's wearing a white Growlers T-shirt, a pair of cutoff black jean shorts, and a black beanie, with a black bandanna tied around his neck. "What is it?"

"That Tyler fuck," I say, after taking a swing from the PBR he handed me when I got to his neighbor's garage.

"The worst dude ever."

"Yeah, him," I say. "He fucked Kristen over bad, so I'm hitting back hard since no one else is going to. My father certainly ain't. Fucking troll was trying to blame her."

"What a pie grinder," Eddie says.

"Right."

"Well, I'm totally down, man. You think it might help with her?"

"I don't know, dude. I really don't."

Eddie shrugs, then says, "It doesn't matter, actually. You need my help, I'm there. We gotta stick together, ya know. Can't count on anyone else if you can't count on your friends and your band."

"So true."

"How we gonna hurt him?"

"We're going straight for his balls, man. We're gonna cut 'em off."

Eddie makes a face. "Huh?"

"That blubber cheek's got a brand-new BMW. I did some Facebook stalking and found out where he lives. The car is done. Cars are my specialty."

Eddies grins. "Sure," he goes. Then, "You're a weird dude."

"I know."

"It's cool, though. Everyone's a weirdo."

"That's what they say, but I'm not so sure anymore. I'm not."

"No, man. You're wrong. Everyone's a fucking weirdo, everyone's a little bit crazy and a little insane. It's just that some people are better at hiding it than others. They're in denial. But it's true. We're all insane. And there's nothing wrong with it. This one's for the freaks, homie. Tonight is for the freaks."

81

WE RECORD FOR, LIKE, THREE HOURS. IT'S GOOD. THE songs are actually great, considering we've only played three times together. Eddie's neighbor had a couple of nice mics for us to use, he had some percussion shit that I laid down separately afterward, and he had a fridge full of beer and some weed for us.

It was perfect.

During the last take of "Swindle Big/Or Die Trying," the final song we record, that dude Brandon was making out with shows up in a brand-new red Lexus.

His name is Doug and he's twenty-two, and he tells us that if we want, on Saturday night, him and his friend Milo are doing their pop-up store at seven in this parking lot in Potrero Hill and we can play a quick set.

"Really?" I go. "That can happen?"

"Yeah, man. Toward the end around eight. You guys will be good for at least thirty minutes. We do it every time we bring out the store, and it's always been about thirty minutes before the fuzz gets there."

"Can you do it?" Eddie asks me.

"Yeah, I can. I don't leave till Sunday morning."

"We're in, dude."

"Awesome," says Doug. Then him and Brandon kiss and Doug goes, "Come on, Mr. Big, we've got some catching up to do. I missed you this morning."

"Let's go," says Brandon.

As they're walking out of the garage, Eddie goes, "You top or bottom, Mr. Big?"

Brandon shrugs and Doug goes, "Don't know. We'll find out soon, though."

They jump into Doug's Lexus and Eddie goes, "Good for Brandon."

"Sure."

"Let's go beat up that Beamer now, homie."

82

THE SHIT WE BRING WITH US: MY SWITCHBLADE,
three cans of spray paint, a pound of sugar, two bags of beef
jerky, and six PBRs.

Eddie gives me one of the bikes he just fixed up to ride.
We're heading to Tyler's loft in SoMa.

"What if he ain't there?" Eddie goes.

"We wait it out, dude. That's what the fucking snacks
are for."

"You're good," he says.

"Again, cars are my specialty."

M83's "Midnight City" blasts while we ride. It's a nice
ride too. Pedaling through the Mission on a fucking mission
with probably the coolest kid I've ever met.

It takes us prolly twenty minutes to get there. His crib
is in this alley called Sumner Street. It's really small and
narrow but sure enough, there's his Beamer parked on the
sidewalk against the building to leave room for other cars
to get by.

"Dude," says Eddie. "It's right in the open, man. Like,
everyone who lives in this alley can see us."

"That's why we gotta be quick, man."

"I don't know," Eddie goes.

"You don't have to do this," I say. "I'd understand if you didn't. Hell, I'm just stoked you came with me. But I'm making that car ugly. No ifs, ands, or buts about it. It's fucking getting what he deserves."

"Fuck," says Eddie. Then he slides out a pint of Jim Beam and takes a huge swig.

"Just stay back," I say. "Be the lookout."

"No, fuck that," Eddie rips. "I'm in. How we doing this?"

"Let's stash our bikes here, next to this fence. I figure we're gonna have about one minute. You tag the fucking car and I'll handle the rest."

"Sounds good."

"Even if anyone sees us, they won't do anything. We'll be long gone before the cops come. It's gonna be fine."

"It has to be, right? Cos cars are your specialty."

"Fuck you." I laugh.

"Let's get this booger pussy."

We fist bump and me and Eddie, we fucking do this shit.

And yeah, we fucking do it right. We do it really fucking well.

83

KRISTEN OPENS HER BEDROOM DOOR AFTER I KNOCK.
I'm holding two Coronas. She's wearing just tiny pink shorts and a black cashmere crewneck sweatshirt that says *Murder City Devils* on the front, and she's listening to the Beach House album *Bloom*.

"Here," I say, handing her a beer.

Her eyes are red and puffy. "Thanks. Come in," she says.

There's eight empty bottles of Corona next to her night-stand and a mirror with lines of blast lying across it.

"You wasted?"

"Beyond wasted," she says, lying down on her bed. "Come on, Jaime. Sit down here," she goes, patting the spot right next to her.

I sit down on the edge of the bed instead.

"Don't be such a baby," she says. "Come here."

I take a swig before swinging my legs up and scooting all the way back to the headboard.

"How's it going?"

"It sucks," she says. "Everything sucks. I'm such a fuck-head."

"That's not true," I say.

"Yes, it is," she says back. "I blew it last night. Not only did I miss the show, I didn't make anything for Dominique to wear."

"It was okay, though," I say.

"Not for me," she says. "Like, I fucked up and slept through the entire day. It would've been so huge for me to have my clothes on her for that show but no, I had to stay up for two and a half days and miss everything. I just suck so bad right now. I'm blowing it, and this has to stop."

"What's that?"

"This," she says. "Those lines of coke on that mirror are the last lines I'm ever doing. I'm done with this shit. All of it, for good. Tyler, the coke, maybe even the drinking, my stupid friends. Done with it, Jaime."

I take a drink and don't say anything.

"Where'd you go after you and Justin got into it?" she asks.

"I met up with Eddie and Brandon. We recorded in Eddie's neighbor's garage."

"Recorded what?"

"Four tracks. We started up a project this week called Skullburns."

"Damn," she says. "Really?"

"Yeah."

"You guys are a bunch of little go-getters. Good job."

"What else is there to do?"

She smiles finally. "Right," she says. "Besides date some

fake-ass hipster asshole and do all his drugs, then sleep through the good shit, what else is there to do?"

I start laughing, and her phone goes off. She picks it up and looks at it.

"Are you fucking serious?" she screams, sitting up.

"What's up?"

"Tyler!" she snaps. "That pig cheats on me and then has the audacity to fucking accuse me of fucking his car up."

"What?" I say, trying to act as shocked as I can.

"What a loser! I've been here all night. Fuck him!"

"What's the text say?"

"'You know anything about this, whore?' And then there's a picture of his car all fucked up." She starts laughing now and says, "Damn, it is fucked up. But I didn't do it. Ugh! Kudos to whoever did, though. Rad."

"Can I ask you a question?" I say.

"Sure."

"Would you ever go back with Tyler?"

"Fuck no. Never. I hate him. I will never talk to him again!"

"That's the truth?"

"Yes."

"Okay then."

"Why?"

"Cos I know who did that to his car."

"You do?" she says.

Pause.

This smile eclipses her entire face.

"Oh my god," she goes. "I love you!"

Kristen lunges at me and hugs me.

"You are so incredible. I wanna be like you when I grow up."

"Shut up," I say.

"But seriously," she goes. "That's amazing. You did that for me?"

"Of course."

"Damn," she says.

"I hated that guy from the second he walked into the restaurant that night."

"That's right. You have."

I take a drink. "Big-time."

When I look back at Kristen, I find her just staring at me and smiling.

"What's up?" I say.

"No one's ever done something that cool for me. No one's ever stuck up for me before."

"That's what I do for the people I love. I got your back. I always will."

"Thank you," she says.

I take another drink.

"Just thank you," she says again, and then she puts a hand on my face. "You're so cute," she says.

I don't say anything.

"So cute and sweet and perfect."

I don't know what to do.

"I should do something nice for you."

"You don't need—"

But before I can finish saying that thought, Kristen's mouth is on mine. Her tongue down my throat, wrestling with my tongue.

I throw my hands against the sides of her tight body and lean forward and push her on her back.

"Fuck me," she says. "Please. I've wanted you to fuck me all week."

I get on top of her now and she pulls off her sweater. Her tits are so nice and round and perfect.

"I want you," she says as we kiss some more. "Please," she goes. "Fuck me."

I can't, though. No way. I shouldn't have even done this. I'm with Dominique.

Pulling my mouth from hers, I say, "No, no, no."

"What are you doing?"

"I can't do this."

"No. You can. Just fuck me. I want you to. I've wanted you to."

"No," I say, as she tries to pull me back down to her. "We're not doing this. I'm with Dominique. I can't do that to her."

Covering her face with her hands now, Kristen goes, "That's right. You are."

I slide off the bed and stand up. "I'm sorry."

"No," she goes. "Don't be. You're right. We can't do this. Not to her. Never to her."

"Yeah."

Kristen pulls her sweater back over herself.

"It woulda been nice, though," I say.

She smiles. "It woulda been amazing."

"Totally."

Pause.

"I'm gonna go to bed."

"All right. But Jaime."

"What's up?"

"Thank you."

"For what?"

"For being one of the good ones."

"I'm not sure I am."

"Yes, you are," she says. "You are definitely one of the good ones, boo."

84

"ABOUT A MONTH BEFORE YOU WERE BORN, YOUR mother and I were doing really good. We were still living in that tiny apartment, but I'd just gotten this really nice promotion that I knew was going to lead to a lot more money for us over the next year. Still, though, we didn't have much and we needed to get your room ready, so I decided to make everything myself. Your crib, the shelves, the dresser and bookcase, the closet door. Just everything. I'd done a lot of carpentry to get by when I first moved to New York, and a good friend of mine had a studio that he let me borrow so I could build those things after I got off work."

My father is standing in my room. I'm sitting at my desk. I was writing the lyrics for this new song, "Sticking to My Guns," after finishing this new poem.

Last night, before I went to bed, I grabbed the box with all the letters in it and put it in front of his and Leslie's bedroom door with a note that said, *If you can't talk to me, then I can't read these.*

My father is wearing a pair of black dress pants and a white V-neck T-shirt with a pair of shades hanging from the V.

"It was hard on us," he continues. "I was putting in twelve hours a day at the office and then another three or four after that at the studio. Your mother didn't want to use what I was making. She wanted some store-bought stuff. She was angry that I was spending time at the studio, but I always begged her to come there with me and be with me, but she refused and she iced me out. We barely spoke for those two or three weeks. Everything I made was good, though. It was quality. Way better than anything we could've bought, Jaime. The day after I brought everything to the apartment and set your room up, I came home after work and she'd smashed the shelves with a hammer and kicked in the side of the crib. The day after that we went to the store and bought all new stuff, which she hated the second after we set it up."

"She was pregnant, man. Like, cut her some slack."

"I did," he says. "I never said anything about what she'd done. Not a word. I loved her with every ounce of my being. She was my dream, my angel. I loved that lady to death."

"Why are you telling me this? If this was in one of the letters, I guess I'd rather read it now."

"Man," he goes. "You can be just as cold as she was when you want to, ya know that. So damn cold and cruel."

"Listen," I say. "What I know of what happened, what you did, that's as fucking cold as it gets, man. What you did. So she complained about some furniture . . . who fucking cares? You hit her and pushed her to the ground. Don't even say it's the same. They're not even in the same universe."

My father takes a deep breath and squeezes his fore-head.

"What?" I snap.

"Remember, your mother loves you, Jaime, and deep down, she is a wonderful person."

"What are you talking about when you say that shit to me? What?"

"I went back to Ohio to visit my father the day after they admitted him to the hospital for the last time. Your mother was about to burst and didn't want me to go. She begged me not to go, but that man was my hero and he was going to die within weeks. I wanted to see him while he could still talk and carry on a conversation. I knew he'd be a vegetable soon before he finally passed, and I wanted to just talk to him and tell him how much I loved him."

"All right."

My father takes a deep, deep breath and wipes the tears from his eyes.

"Man," he says. "It's been awhile since I took myself back to that hospital room. Man . . ."

"What?"

"My father was a very handsome man, Jaime. Very handsome and very charming."

"Great. That's awesome."

"During my first visit to see him that last trip, probably twenty or thirty minutes after we started talking, he looks me dead in the eyes and goes, 'I can't die with this on my chest, son.' I told him he could tell me anything, anything at all. And that's when he told me about him and your mother, him and my wife."

My world, it flips upside down and the blood drains from me. Everything is fuzzy. My hands and fingers are numb. Heart is broken, it's gone.

"Jaime," he says.

"What'd he say?" I mutter.

"He told me about their affair. They'd been sleeping together for three years. They were in love. That's why he had been in San Francisco. He was there to try and convince her to leave me and marry him so he could leave everything he had to her and you, since I didn't have anything."

Falling forward, my head drops against my arms on the desk.

"I was devastated, Jaime. In one cruel swipe, I'd lost my hero and the love of my life. The two people I loved the most, who I trusted the most, trusted with my life, had been betraying me for years, plotting and planning, even having a conversation about running out on me and getting married."

Lifting my head back up, I snap, "Just shut up! Okay? Just shut the fuck up!"

"Jaime," my father starts.

But I say, "Stop it! Please!"

"It's the truth, Jaime. I'm not lying. I'm—"

"I don't think you're lying!" I yell. "I don't, but just stop it. Fuck, man. Just stop talking about it and leave me alone."

"I'm sorry, Jaime. But you deserve to know."

"Shut the fuck up!" I scream again. "Please . . . okay? Just please stop talking about it . . . Dad."

85

YOUTH LAGOON OPENS WITH "DROPLA" OFF THEIR *Wondrous Bughouse* album. Dominique, she seems pretty upset with me too. For a lot of reasons, I'm thinking, even though she tells me she's fine, which is bullshit cos she's not.

I was half an hour late meeting her at this taquería on Eighteenth and Valencia. I'm really wasted, too—at least four blues deep, like, six or seven beers, some dope I got a hit off of while I was walking through the Haight trying to wrap my head around what my father told me and if it was true or not (I declined my mother's phone call from the hospital today) and what it means and who the fuck do I know and really have in my life who isn't a monster, who isn't the most selfish person ever, who doesn't lie.

Also, she could easily be pissed about me not telling her I was sorry for making her wait. Or maybe it was the rant I went on about all women being cunts and whores at their core. All of them. No exceptions or anything. Cos they are. And it's evil and they think they can just get away with it. They think they can destroy you before they mow you down and that it's fine and that they can just walk away from the damage they've done and leave you to live in the ruins like it's no big deal.

Cunts.

And whores.

All of them.

We're standing outside Great American Music Hall, on the edge of the Tenderloin, like, twenty feet from the entrance of a strip club, and it's the worst day and night ever in my life, but then Youth Lagoon begins playing and everything changes. It really does.

For the first time since me and her rolled up, like, twenty minutes ago, she smiles and says something.

She goes, "Yay. My favorite on this album."

It's a start at least, and I say, "Mine too."

"I remember when Keisha texted me that he was going to be on NPR playing songs off this, I freaked out. I cleared my entire day. At first, when I heard it, I didn't know what to think."

"Me either."

"It was really good, but it wasn't what I expected. *Year of Hibernation* cut me so deep and left such a fucking mark on me that it's all I wanted. Like, I refused this album for a week even though it was great, because it wasn't *Year*."

I'm laughing because I did pretty much the same thing, except my denial of the record lasted a month.

"Then the band was driving to Santa Barbara to play this small festival and Mark put it on and it became an addiction. A different one, though, and it's all I listened to for the next month. Now I'm here. Listening to it live, and it's even better than I imagined."

Me looking at her right now, her leaning against the wall next to the box office, looking gorgeous and happy, it dissolves the hate I've been holding in me all day—poor girl doesn't even know about my father telling me that stuff—and all the ice melts away.

"It's so rad to just watch you talk about music you love," I tell her. "To see your physical reaction to go along with the thrill in your voice, there's nothing I'd rather watch. Nothing, Dominique. Like, what's that Frank O'Hara line?"

She shrugs.

"'I look at you and I would rather look at you than all the portraits in the world.'"

Her face lights up even more. "That's fucking beautiful," she says.

"I feel that way every time I look at you," I say, as that song "Raspberry Cane" ends and the song "Posters" begins.

"Jaime," she says, blushing. "Come here."

We kiss finally. It's great to feel those lips against mine again. Her tongue whipping against the walls of my mouth.

"What has been going on with you tonight?" she asks.

"I don't know what you're talking about," I tell her, as I start dancing around like a weirdo on the sidewalk. "No idea. Everything is perfect. I'm so good right now."

Dominique grins and shakes her head. She starts dancing around with me and here we are again, another magical fucking night, the two of us on a sidewalk somewhere in San

Francisco, listening to one of our favorite bands in the world play some of our favorite songs ever.

Thank god for Youth Lagoon.

Once again, arriving in my life and saving me, for a while at least.

James walks outside holding a record, signed by Trevor, and a T-shirt. He tries to hand them to me but I go, "It's for her. This is Dominique, man. Dominique, this is James Morgan."

"Whoa," she goes, looking stunned. "Nice to meet you. How do you two—"

"We're old-school homies," says James, winking at me. "Jaime's, like, my best friend now."

"Jesus," I go, laughing.

"You two kids have fun now. I'm gonna go back in. See you at Savannah's show tomorrow night, homie."

"Thanks again, dude."

"You're fucking incredible, ya know," Dominique says. "How in the hell . . ."

"I'll never tell," I say. "Never."

"I love you," she goes. "Even if you think I'm a cunt."

"The biggest one for sure."

She laughs as Youth Lagoon begins playing "July."

Both of us jump up and down and she grabs me and we twirl around in circles, singing together.

When the song is over, this younger-looking black kid walks past us and goes, "Roxys, bud, coke."

"What's that?" I ask. "You got blues?"

"Yeah. Follow me."

I look back at Dominique. "I'll be right back."

"Where are you going?"

"Nowhere. I'll be back in a second, though."

"Jaime," she goes. "No."

"You coming or not?" the dude says.

"Yeah."

We walk around the corner and cut into this alley.

"How many for eight?" I go.

"This many," he says, and whips out a knife.

"Whoa, man. Whoa. What are you doing?"

"Give me all your money."

"What are you doing?"

Dude grabs the back of my neck and pushes me into the wall.

"All your money, bitch. Now."

"Fine," I say. "Fine."

He lets go of me. Slowly, I turn around, see the knife again.

"It's cool," I say, then I push him and try to run, but he grabs onto me again and tackles me.

"Dude," I yell.

"Give me your fucking money."

I kick him and get to my feet, then—

POP!

Dude just drills me in the stomach.

BAM!

He hits me in the face, and I stumble back and fall down.

I'm totally helpless as he opens my wallet and pulls out all the money. All thousand dollars.

"Fucking faggot!" he yells next. "Just listen to me next time."

"Fuck you," I say. "Fucking worthless piece of shit. Fucking pussy."

"Oh yeah?"

"Fuck you."

BAM!

BAM!

BAM!

He kicks me three more times.

BAM!

He punishes me in the face with this last kick.

"Jaime," I hear. It's Dominique.

The guy who robbed me takes off like a punk, the pussy he is, and she drops down next to me.

"Are you okay?"

"I'm fine." I sit up.

"You're bleeding," she says. "Come here."

"Don't touch me!" I scream, knocking her hands away. "Don't fucking touch me right now."

She's crying. "Why are you yelling at me?"

"I told you to stay back there. What are you doing here?"

"What were you doing?"

"Stop it," I say. "Stop asking me shit. What the fuck are you doing?"

Pushing myself to my feet, I go, "You're pissing me off."

I can feel the blood running down my face. Taste it in my mouth. It's fine.

My mother hits harder than that dude.

But that guy stole my money, which is her money.

It's not some full-circle shit. But it's sorta close to some full-circle shit.

"I'm gonna call 911," she goes.

"No!" I scream. "What is your problem?"

"I'm just trying to help," she cries.

"I don't need your fucking help. I don't need anyone's fucking help."

"Jaime," she gasps, reaching out and grabbing my arm.

"Get the fuck off of me, Dominique. Get away from me right now."

"Fuck you!" she screams. "You're an asshole. Just like every dude's an asshole. So screw you."

She flips me off and rolls right out of the alley.

Using my shirt to wipe off the blood, it hurts. I can feel the pain setting in.

"Goddamn it!" I kick the wall. "Fuck."

I lean down and reach into the sock on my right foot. I've got a hundred bucks in there.

I take it out and then I call Dominique.

She doesn't answer.

But, like, five seconds later I get a text message from her that says, *You broke my fucking heart. You're a junkie and an asshole. I hate you. Go back to Illinois. Hate you!*

I start to text something back, but I stop. What's the point? She's right. Everything she said is the truth.

I'm no different than my mother and my father.

I'm selfish.

I'm a junkie.

I'm the bitch.

I'm the cunt.

And I'm the fucking whore.

86

"YOU POOR THING," SAVANNAH SAYS. "WHO WOULD ever want to hurt such a cute face?"

I'm sitting in the kitchen of the apartment above the Transmission Gallery with my shirt off.

Savannah, she's sitting in front of me, cleaning the blood off my face with a damp towel.

I wince every time she touches me. My face stings. My ribs are covered in pain. She picks up the lit joint from the ashtray on the table next to it and takes a hit and then puts it in my mouth so I can take a hit.

"What happened to you?" she goes.

"Just a misunderstanding," I tell her. "No biggie."

"It doesn't look like it's no biggie."

"It's over," I say. "Everything is."

"What do you mean?"

"This," I say. "It's all over."

Savannah's hair is hanging straight down her back. She's wearing a large red-and-black flannel that's unbuttoned down to the top of her chest and a pair of tiny black cutoff shorts.

The Growlers record *Are You In or Out?* is spinning on the player.

I took a cab straight here from the alley. She'd just gotten back from moving all of her paintings to the other gallery for the opening tomorrow night. My father was here twenty minutes before I arrived, and she said he was sick and worried because he hadn't been able to get ahold of me all day and night.

"I had a feeling I was going to see you tonight, though," Savannah says.

"Really?"

"Yeah. I don't know why, but when we started talking about you, I couldn't help but think you'd make your way over here sometime tonight."

Savannah gives me another hit and then picks up her bottle of Pacifico and takes a drink.

"Weird."

"Maybe," she says. "This has been an interesting week."

"That's an understatement."

She laughs.

And I go, "What do you think about my father?"

"I think he's a good guy, Jaime. I think he's genuine. He's got a really good heart, and everything he does comes from a really good place."

"That's what you truly, honestly think?"

"Yes, it is. I don't know anything about what's happened to him, but he was hurt badly at some point in his life. It's really obvious to me. I see it in him. And I can tell that it's where all of his sincerity is coming from. He cares about people. He cares about his life and he's passionate about it."

"That's bullshit. He was all over you in front of Leslie, in front of everyone at dinner on Saturday. It was embarrassing."

"It was what it was. But there was nothing malicious about it. He was a little drunk."

"How can you justify that?"

She stops wiping my face and goes, "I wanna show you something."

"What is it?"

She stands up. "I'll be right back."

I take a drink of her beer and text Dominique, apologizing for what happened and everything I said.

I was a monster back there. It was pathetic.

As I'm taking another hit off the joint, Savannah hands me a picture in a frame and my jaw drops.

"I found this two days ago in a drawer in the other bedroom."

"Oh my god," I say.

"I think that might have something to do with what happened on Saturday."

The picture is of my mother and father. In it, they're sitting on a rooftop in New York and my mother, she looks exactly like Savannah. It's shocking how similar they look.

"Jesus," I say. "Just wow. And look at them." I look up at Savannah with tears in my eyes. "They look so happy. So pretty and happy."

"It's an amazing photo."

I'm floored right now.

I wipe my eyes and Savannah sits back down.

"Your father is so deeply wounded, Jaime. He's scarred forever. Whatever happened is something I don't think he'll ever recover from. He's moved on in every other part of his life. That's obvious. But as far as his attachment to certain parts of his past, I think he'd do anything to get back to this rooftop."

"To re-create the day. Relive a certain day."

"What?"

"Did he take you on the roof with him at all?"

"Yeah," she says. "A couple days ago. We sat up there and drank a bottle of wine."

I take a deep breath.

"Your father loves you so much, Jaime. When he talks about you, the passion in his voice is unreal. It's contagious."

"What is wrong with these people?"

"Nothing and everything at the same time."

I laugh.

"You're right," I say.

Savannah slides the towel down my face one more time and says, "When someone is living with one foot in the present and one foot in the past, it can be really difficult to understand why they do some of the things they do. It can seem really off and hurtful, but if that person is real, if they're genuine about what they're doing, it tends to start making a lot more sense once you realize how big the void is and that all's they're doing is trying to dump a little bit of sand into it."

"That's fucking beautiful," I say. "So you're a poet, too."

"No," she goes. "That's your job, Jaime. I watched the new one you posted."

"Did you like it?"

"I loved it."

"I want to have sex with you," I tell her. "Right now. I want to be inside of you."

She blushes and smiles. Puts her hand under my chin. "I want that too."

I lean forward, but she turns away.

"We can't, though."

"I know."

I put my hand on her face.

"Thank you," I tell her.

"Thank you," she tells me back.

"I should get going now. I'll see you tomorrow night."

"I can't wait."

She puts a hand on the back of my neck and pulls me into her. We kiss twice on the lips and that's it.

And that's perfect.

She walks me to the door and before I leave, I say, "James really likes you, ya know."

"I know." She's grinning ear to ear. "He's on his way over."

"Nice."

"It'll be fun," she goes. "That's what he's there for. He's that guy."

"The fun guy."

Savannah cracks up laughing. "The fun guy. Absolutely."

87

IN MY ROOM, I PUT ON A PAIR OF JEAN SHORTS AND A tank top. I call Dominique. She doesn't answer, so I leave her a voice mail.

I say, "You have every right to never speak to me again. I'm so sorry for what I did and what I said. I was an asshole. I was everything I've always railed against and hated. I fucked up. I love you and I fucked up. I've got two days left and we're playing a show on Saturday night. If anything, I'd love to just see your face one more time . . . even if it's for a second. Just one second. If you can't do that, I'll understand it even though I'll hate it. My world was floored this morning. That's not an excuse for the way I treated you, but that's why I was in the mood I was. I'd do anything to take this night back, but I can't and it's over. Moving on from it because I'm seeing the brutality of what it's like when someone wants to go back but can't. Anyway, dancing with you to Youth Lagoon. Beautiful. You're beautiful and I love you and I'm sorry."

I set my phone down on the desk and then I spit on my hand and start jacking my piece. A minute later, I come into a paper towel. After that, I drop a blue on some foil and take a fucking run with it.

I smoke the entire thing over the next ten minutes, then I open my notebook up and turn my webcam on.

I'm good to go.

Hitting the record button, I start reading . . .

"In my head there's a perfect world and my mom isn't fucked up and my dad never hit her, I dream often of this perfect world because it's pretty there, and outside my window is a garden and a blue jay and a robin and an eagle . . . at night, the lights go off and ugliness begins to breathe, danger everywhere, the captain yells, jump off the ship if you wanna save yourself . . . me, I never listened cos I never trusted anyone but her, and so every night I sank, every night I drowned in the horror of the nightmare I was born into . . . it was the end of August and all the farmers were taking the crops out of the field, I'd watch the neighbor girl dance in her bathing suit, her skin shining from the suntan lotion, her face filled with life, water from the garden hose killing off the final ticks of heat from another brutal summer . . . when I was eight, I stole a pack of baseball cards from a store down the street . . . later that night I felt so guilty that I threw it away without ever opening it . . . one day I'll be like the moon and no one will hate me . . . one day this will all be over and we'll sail on the backs of hawks and butterflies and problems won't exist and funnel cakes will take care of any anger . . . next fall, when the next crop is due out, I'm gonna rig an old pickup and take my sweetheart for a joyride . . . California is where we'll head, either that or Charleston . . . fountains in the woods crumbling from age, no water can ever give a person their youth back . . . the key to youth is the heart . . . I refuse

*to get old and turn out like all these madmen ... youth forever, kids
or nothing, tomorrow night, I'm jumping from the ship ...*

There's only one thing left to do now. I dump the rest
of the Oxys into my hand and walk into the bathroom and
drop them into the toilet.

No more fog.

No more glass castles.

No more ice.

I flush the toilet and watch those blue dreams swirl
around until they're gone.

This is for me and no one else.

It's better this way.

When I'm through splashing water on my face, I walk
back into my room.

And this is what I'm thinking about as I lie in bed, reading James Morgan's book *Wicked Babes, Righteous Dudes*.

I'm thinking about staying in San Francisco until I fall
asleep.

88

"I'VE NEVER FELT BETTER ABOUT MYSELF OR MY LIFE, Jaime. It's nice to feel good naturally again. I'd forgotten all about it. It's nice to remember what I said to someone the day before, it's nice to remember what someone said to me the day before, it's nice to not lose time. I'm not losing time anymore. I'm happy, and when you get back home, it's going to be different."

"That's good," I say. "I'm happy."

"Why couldn't you talk to me yesterday? Was it your father? Was he behind that?"

"No. Something happened . . . I, ya know—"

"Don't stick up for him, Jaime. Don't you dare. If he was behind that, I need to know. That prick."

"Stop!" I yell. "Just stop it. It wasn't him."

"He's not telling you things, is he?"

As much as I want to tell her everything I know, I can't do that to her. Especially now that she's doing so well and she's clean. No way. Never.

So I say, "No. We've barely even talked since I got here. I've barely seen him."

"Some parent he is," she says.

"Would you just quit it, Mom? Please? It's been fine here. San Francisco is nice, but I can't wait to get home and see you."

"So you're liking it out there?"

"A little bit. Yes."

"We went there once," she says. "Me and your father." My grip on the phone tightens. "It was incredible. Your grandfather was there too, so it was really special."

I feel sick.

"Your father wasn't nearly as fun and full of life as his father, though, so sometimes me and him would just sneak off together and do things Justin didn't want to or wasn't up for."

I shouldn't have taken this call either.

"It's a beautiful city, but Joliet is pretty good too."

I'm shaking. "Right."

"Oh, I can't wait to see you on Sunday. I look ten years younger, Jaime. It's incredible. This is a fresh start for us. Me and my boy."

"Good."

"I love you, Jaime."

"I love you, too, Mom."

"And tomorrow I'm going to wake up and remember this conversation. It's exciting."

"Yes, it is."

"Me and my boy back together in two days and your father worlds apart from us again, where he can't hurt us or lie anymore."

"Yeah."

"Cos that's what he does best."

I don't say anything.

"He was nothing like his father, and that was a shame."

"Whatever you say, Mom."

Pause.

"Whatever you say . . ."

89

KRISTEN COMES RUNNING UP THE STREET IN SHORTS and a drenched-in-sweat T-shirt. I'm sitting on the grass in the front yard with the guitar, working on a new song called "Graveyard Loving" and that other song, "Sticking to My Guns." "Graveyard" would be perfect for Skullburns since it's got this nice surfey, psychedelic rhythm to it, but it ain't gonna happen. Maybe we can work on it later at practice after we're done going through the set for tomorrow night. Who knows, though? Most likely it'll stay with Tiger Stitches, like the other song.

Taking her headphones out, she goes, "What the hell happened to your face, dude? I'm gonna kick someone's ass."

"It's okay," I say. "It was my fault."

"Who did it?"

"I don't know. So it doesn't matter."

"Jesus, man. You're always scraping. Showed up here with some damage and just as it was almost gone, you got more."

"Damage," I say, grinning. "Consider it an accessory for me."

Kristen falls onto the ground now and stretches out.

"I forgot how nice it was to be up early and run. I feel great right now. I'm so excited to have Tyler out of my life and to be done with the partying. I've already put together a dress, and I've got a contract with this band Pops to do another one for a show in two weeks at the Independent."

"Dope," I say. "That's awesome."

"I'm also making something for you to wear tomorrow night, dude."

"Really?"

"Yup. And you gonna look good, baby doll."

She grabs my arm and squeezes it.

"About the other night," I start.

"Don't," she says. "It's fine. I don't feel weird about it or anything. I wanted to do it. I really did."

"Me too."

"That's the difference between you and a troll like Tyler. You consider other people. You've got real feelings, not just mood swings based on being high or coming down. That's what I'm excited about the most. Feeling everything again."

"Me too. I'm done with those blues."

"Really?"

"Yeah."

"I'm so proud of you. Is it weird?"

"A little bit, I guess. I'm a little shaky. I feel like I got a cold. Sweating a lot. But beyond that, I'm good. This is good. My mother's sober and clean now too. It'll be better when I get back. So much better."

"So you're definitely not staying," she goes.

"I can't."

"Yes, you can."

"No . . . I can't."

"I get it, Jaime. You're terrified of what your mother might do if you leave her. You don't want that on your conscience. Who would? That kinda guilt ruins lives. I've seen that play out in my family."

"So you know that I can't."

"Thing is," she says, "how did having you there with her all these years make a difference? She still almost died."

"She partied too hard."

"Really?"

"Yes, really," I snap. "What else do you think happened?"

Kristen shrugs. "I don't know . . . my father said that she had shattered her right pinkie somehow and had to do surgery on it when she was in the hospital. Then I'm on your Tumblr last night."

"Okay."

"Watching your videos, and I notice the date on one of them. It was recorded the day before she OD'd, and your face, it's fine. No bruises, no bumps, it's totally normal."

"What the fuck are you trying to say?"

Shrugging again, she says, "I don't know, Jaime. Cos I don't know what it all is or means. What I do know is that something seems a little off about it."

"It's none of your goddamn business."

"It is. You're family."

"Again," I snap, "this is none of your fucking business."

"The thing about the truth, Jaime, is that it's powerful. There's a reason for that old saying, 'The truth will set you free.' It's liberating, man. The lies I've been telling myself for months about Tyler were destroying me inside. I haven't felt this free and clear in so long. And it all started by getting to the truth, then acknowledging it."

"Stop it," I snort. "Just please stop this and let it go. Okay? This is my shit, nobody else's. It's mine."

"You've been alone for so long, Jaime. So fucking long, man. I know this is tough, but you need to realize now that you're not alone anymore. There's people here who love the fuck out of you and will do anything to help you."

"No," I say. "Just stop." Pushing myself off the ground, I go, "I'm really happy for you, by the way. And I'll see you tonight."

"Jaime," she says.

"I'm done," I go. "I'm leaving. It's over now. Okay?"

She doesn't say anything and I run into the house, lock myself in my room, and lie in bed and listen to Future Islands.

90

DOMINIQUE'S TEXT MESSAGE COMES TO ME WHILE I'm walking on the beach on my way to Brandon's house for our last practice before the show. It's long, too. It says . . .

Thank you for apologizing, Jaime. I know you mean it, and it's really nice to know someone who means what they say. That said, you really hurt me last night. I just wanted to help you. I knew you were taking Oxy but I didn't know you were that far gone, and I don't want that in my life. Even if you are leaving on Saturday, I can't have someone I love and adore putting themselves in those kinds of fucked-up situations and letting it bleed into my relationship with them. I just can't have it, and I'm not sure I want to see you before you leave. I won't be at Savannah's opening tonight because I can't see you right now. I have something for you, though. Maybe tomorrow. I don't know. Maybe I'll just send it to you or give it to my mother to give to your father. Sorry, love. What happened last night shook me to my core. I've come too far in my recovery to let someone else just fuck my world up. It's selfish, man. I didn't take you for a selfish person before last night. I love you. Have fun tonight.

By the time I'm done reading this for the third time, I've stopped walking and am throwing up in the sand. Here I've been, my whole fucking life, resenting my mother for her behavior and what she's put me through, yet the first time I'm allowed the freedom to have a life, the first time I find a girl who cares about me and loves me and thinks I'm great, who is so nice to me, I act exactly like my mother.

It's so sick. And this is why I have to go back, because we deserve each other. Misery loves company, and I don't deserve to have these amazing people in my life. They're better than me. Better than my mother. This is the truth. My decision is final.

91

THE DETAILS FOR TOMORROW NIGHT ARE THESE: AT seven forty-five our set starts in the parking lot right next to this bar called Thee Parkside, which is also a show venue, and they've okayed us to play for a half hour. We're meeting at Eddie's at six. We're playing four songs. They've got a cameraman all lined up to shoot the show. We plug in. We rip. Destroy. Shred. Smile. Then it's over and I go home and fly far, far away. But it's all on record. We've got the songs online. We'll have the show online too. This is the point. Making something dope, something you're stoked about, and pushing it on the world to give yourself a larger meaning and longer existence than your own life.

"Art is the only immortality we have," Eddie says. "To be able to positively affect people for generations after we're dead. This is what it's about. We're kids and we have everything we need to change someone's life. You need to have the dedication. That's it. Dedicate your life to making good shit and push it on the world. I get a fucking boner just thinking about it."

We skate to my father's gallery in SoMa. Doors opened just an hour ago, and there's already three hundred people there. That dude Joel from the Brian Jonestown Massacre and the movie *Dig!* is spinning records.

Savannah looks stunning. And she looks so happy and relieved. Anyone who's ever put their heart and soul into their art, that kind of dedication, the amount of work, the insane hours spent alone making things that can dramatically change some people's lives, stimulate some people's lives, the weight of it crushes you every time. It buries you and suffocates you and isolates you, and when you're finally done, you can't hide the relief. It's washed all over you, yet you're also sad because it's gone suddenly. You've given it life and given it wings and it's taken flight for the world to hopefully see.

She's wearing this dress that Kristen made this morning. It's black satin and strapless. It's got all these different white cloth shapes sewed onto the front and back of it. She's wearing these black leather boots that run up to her knees. Her hair is pulled up and back. Her lips are covered with bright, shiny red lipstick. And she's got a black bandanna tied tightly around her neck and pushed to the side.

Eddie, he goes straight for Kristen. Me, I go straight for Savannah. She's standing in a group that consists of James, Michael, and Renee from Lamborghini Dreams, some members of Thee Oh Sees, Terry Malts, the Fresh & Onlys, and the Richmond Sluts.

"Yes," says James. "My man."

He gives me a hug and introduces me to everyone. Just like I wished for, I'm able to shake John Dwyer's hand and tell him how much his music means to me and how rad his band shreds.

James tries to hand me a glass of white wine.

"I'm good," I say.

"No one here cares, dude."

"It's not that. I don't give a fuck about anyone here. It's some personal shit right now. That's all."

"I respect that," he says. "Heard you got a show tomorrow night outside of Thee Parkside."

"Who told you that?"

"Your lovely stepsister. She's been bragging about you all night. Maybe I was wrong the other day."

"About what?"

"Maybe these people really fucking care about you, man."

I look at Savannah and she winks at me.

"Maybe," I say, before James tells everyone how he found his skateboard in the back of a closet and took it out for the first time in seven years. He says how he went to the DMV parking lot all by himself and for an hour, he grinded the pavement and pulled off every trick he ever knew how to do one by one and when he was done, he took the board and threw it in the garbage.

"I just wanted to prove to myself that I still had it. That I'm still as young as ever. It was rad. A youth check every few years is necessary at my fucking age. I haven't felt that young in ten years. I still got it, baby. I'm still good. Spring break, spring break, spring break forever," he says.

And this right here is why the man's a fucking hero.

92

I'VE BEEN WATCHING MY FATHER FOR THE LAST fifteen minutes from across the room. Savannah's already sold three paintings at ten thousand dollars each. There's probably six hundred people here too. And that Yeah Yeah Yeahs song "Soft Shock" is playing from the invisible speakers.

My father's been on the phone. Texting furiously. Looking around to make sure nobody's near him. He even ducked into the bathroom to make a phone call.

It's strange. So when he sneaks out the back door of the gallery, I follow him.

Sure enough, just like I thought, there's my father and there's Tyler and there's my father about to buy cocaine from Tyler.

Anger shoots right up through me.

I burst outside, startling both of them, and I go, "Really, dude? Are you fucking kidding me?"

"Jaime, go back inside," my father snaps.

"Screw that."

"Scram, you faggot," Tyler says, smirking and laughing. "You fucking loser."

"Hey," my father snaps at Tyler. "Just watch it." Turning back to me, he goes, "Jaime, please. Go inside."

"Get lost," snorts Tyler.

Me, this is when I lose it. I snap. I run right at Tyler and deck him in the face, knocking him backward. Then I hit him again.

"Jaime," my father screams, then grabs me like a fool.

I push him away from me and when I spin back around, Tyler clocks me in the side of the head, then drills me in the ribs, right in the same spot I was kicked the night before.

"Ahhhh!" I scream.

When Tyler comes at me again, my father cuts him off and just starts jacking him so hard and so fast.

Just *BAM!*

POW!

CRACK!

POP!

Tyler's staggering around, bleeding now, and right as my father is about to land another blow, a fucking cop car blasts down the street right at us.

Tyler, he swallows, like, three bags of coke and then runs at my father, who's not paying attention, but I cut him off now and pop him one more time right as the cop car comes to a screeching halt and two cops storm out of it, guns drawn.

It all happens so fast too. Like a blur. I don't even really remember it. Just that in less than a minute, me and my father are on our butts on the sidewalk next to each other in handcuffs. And Tyler, he's in cuffs on the other side of the street.

It's so fucking perfect, actually. You couldn't write a more fitting fucking scene than this.

93

"THIS HAS GOTTEN SO OUT OF CONTROL. MY GOD. IT has to stop. I've got to stop this shit. I've got to change," my father says to me.

The two of us, we're still cuffed, still on the sidewalk, both our heads resting against the brick wall behind us.

"How could you do that, man?" I ask him. "How could you speak to that dude after what he did to Kristen?"

My father's eyes close. I see the shame and the guilt smearing themselves across his face.

"Hey," I bark. "I asked you a question."

My father's eyes open slowly now, and he goes, "The night your mother left with you, I was passed out drunk in bed."

"I know. She told me."

"I was so furious with her when I woke up and figured out what happened. So angry at her and myself for what I'd done. I knew I'd lost you for good. There was no way I was ever going to get you back. I was frantic and desperate. I called every one of our friends and her parents, and nobody had seen her, let alone talked to her. After a day with you two missing, I called the police. I was so scared for you, Jaime. I didn't know what she was going to do to herself or you. A couple of hours after the police originally made a report at the apartment, they called me and asked me to come into the station. For the next twenty hours, they held me and interrogated me. Your mother still hadn't been heard from, and they began thinking I'd killed both of you."

"Jesus," I say.

"I was sick. Morgan was capable of anything, Jaime. There were a few hours where I thought she might've killed you and then killed herself and made it look like I had. That's where our relationship was the night it happened."

"How did it happen? Like, how could you do that to her? If it was so awful, why couldn't you just leave and end it?"

"Because of you. I tried to gut it out because of you, Jaime."

"That's bullshit."

"It's not," he says. "Ya know, if I'd have found out about her and my father even two months before you were born instead of weeks before, I would've left and figured something out. But you have to understand, she could've gone into labor at any minute at the time my father told me. There was no way I was going to leave her. She had no money. She'd isolated herself from most of her friends. There was no support system for her in New York beyond me at that point. And her parents wanted nothing to do with me or you, which meant her as well. So I bit my tongue and went back and saw it through."

"Bit your tongue?" I ask.

"I didn't tell her I knew about her and my father until you were six months old, Jaime. It was crushing. Having to pretend that my wife, the love of my life, hadn't been in love with my father, hadn't been sleeping with him for years, and hadn't entertained the thought of leaving me for him so she could inherit everything that I should've. It was humiliating."

"Why did you finally tell her?"

"Because she had lost all the weight from the pregnancy and was starting to drink heavily again. She was doing lots of cocaine, staying out all night, taking lots of painkillers and antidepressants. Her mood swings were insane. Sometimes I wish I hadn't told her I knew. I wish I'd filed for a divorce and custody of you."

"Why didn't you?"

The pain on my father's face right now, it looks excruciating. His face is wet with tears and sweat.

He says, "Because I wasn't sure I wanted to have you."

He starts crying really hard.

"Because I thought you might not have been mine. I thought there was a good chance you were my father's. I used you to get back at Morgan."

"How?"

"She wanted to dance again, but we needed money badly, and I was starting to make that really good money that was promised with my promotion. So I used that and you. I used both situations to prevent her from being able to dance. It was the only thing I could think of to get back at her for what she'd done. The way she'd broken my heart, which has still never fully healed or been put back together. And it worked. And it also made her so fucking crazy, Jaime. And I'm so sorry I did that. That I used you like that, like a goddamn piece on a checkerboard, so I could get some sort of revenge on her and my father because he was obsessed with watching her dance. It moved him to the core of his soul, and I always thought it was really cool of him to take that much interest in my girl and what she did. I was blind to his infatuation with her. And I was blind to how much she adored the attention he gave her. I was so busy doing construction jobs during the day and going to business school at night. She loved attention, loved the spotlight more than anyone I've ever known, and I knew that but I never thought . . . ya know . . ."

He bites down on his bottom lip.

"With my own father. Fuck . . . it hurt so bad. And you, god, just a fucking baby and stuck in the middle of cruel, cold brutality. Emotional violence."

Me, I'm stunned right now. I'm so sick to my stomach. I go, "Am I your kid?"

"Yes," he goes. "Yes. You're my boy, and I'm so proud of that. I love you."

"What the fuck," I go. "What the hell is wrong with you two?"

"It was so long ago, Jaime. We were messes. Plain and

simple. We had been for so long. And after you were born, I began to see that. I saw I was a huge part of that problem. When I told your mother that I knew about her and my father, she fucking laughed. She shrugged. She told me I should be more like him and maybe I'd get the same kind of love and passion from her."

"Is that the truth?"

"Yeah."

"How do I know that?"

"There's three letters from your mother to me. I still have them in a safe box at the house. You can read them, but I wouldn't. I'd take my word on this, because I don't think you should read some of those things she wrote because you know her differently than I do. You are going back to her."

This right here, this is the worst I've ever felt in my life. It's also the happiest I've ever felt. To know my history. To know what I was really born into. To finally see the monster mask I've always painted on my father's face wash off in a shower of his own tears.

"The night I hit Morgan, I came home from work late. She was sitting in the kitchen, wearing her ballet dress. She'd been drinking and doing coke all day. We got into a fight. She kept coming at me. I would walk away and she would follow me and keep going and running her mouth. We were in the living room and she was laughing, and I asked her what was so funny and she told me how much of a better fuck my father was. She said, 'The things he would do to me in bed are things you can't imagine, little boy.' And I snapped, Jaime. I admit it. It was shameful what I did, and I wish I hadn't done it. I regret it so bad. She said that shit so I backhanded her. When her face swung back around, she was bleeding. She charged at me and that's when I pushed her to the ground. She lay there sobbing for ten, fifteen minutes, and I went to my office and drank a bottle of whiskey. When I woke up, you guys were gone. I was so torn up inside, Jaime. But I was also relieved. She was gone, out of my life, and that made me happy. When you two finally popped back up on the radar in Joliet, I agreed to give her full custody because I wanted her out of my life for good at that particular time. Over the years, though, I just missed you so much and began slowly talking to Morgan again. It was nice. I got to hear how you were doing. How talented you are and all the cool things you were doing. But every time I asked to talk to you, she said you didn't want to, and I understood. I gave you away to her and I deserved that from you. I did. And now, I'm so happy to have had you here with me and my family. I love you, son. I want you to stay here, with us, I do so badly."

"I can't, though."

"I know. But I thought you should hear me say that, because it's true. I know I've been kind of distant this week, but I thought giving you some space to deal with everything was the best thing to do."

"It was," I tell him. "Thank you. The kids I've met here, the things I've been able to do and see, that's what I needed after what happened with Mom. I needed to breathe, not keep suffocating. So yeah, thank you."

"You're welcome."

94

NO CHARGES ARE FILED. NO TICKETS ARE WRITTEN.
Thirty minutes after we got handcuffed, they're taken off,
but not before a nice little crowd of curious family and
friends has gathered around us.

Leslie's pissed.

Kristen's disgusted.

Savannah's laughing.

And James Morgan and Eddie are taking photos of us.
In handcuffs. Out of handcuffs.

I go up to Savannah and say, "I'm sorry if we ruined
your night."

"You didn't at all," she says, giggling. "I mean, now it's a
real party. Cops, fights, and handcuffs. That's legit. You two
boys are fucking crazy. Especially you. I love you to death,
man."

"Thank you. I love you, too."

"Awwwww," she goes, as she gives me a hug. "I'm gonna
miss you so much."

"You leave tomorrow?"

"Yeah. But I'll be back in a couple weeks to see James."

"Really? The fun guy?"

"Yeah. He got kinda serious last night. It was nice. I've always liked him a lot since I've known him but was scared to death of his life, his history, cos everyone knows it. He makes no secret about his private life or past. But there was something there besides sex last night, so I'm gonna go with it."

"That's great."

"Never, ever go against the urge to be happier, man. Never," she says, hugging me again, and when she lets go, I walk with Kristen, holding her hand, and explain to her what happened and by the end of the story, she's laughing and crying and telling me that she's gonna go out on a date with Eddie next week.

"Sweet," I say.

"God," she goes. "It's not gonna be the same here without you, man. It's gonna hurt to see you go."

"I'll be back."

"It still ain't the same," she says. "But I get it. Your mother needs you. You're loyal. I just hope she appreciates how great you are. Like, seriously. I really hope your mother stays the fuck clean and stops making your life harder than it needs to be."

"So do I."

"Cos you deserve that, Jaime. You deserve to be happy and to have good friends and to be treated nicely. You deserve people's kindness, not their bullshit. You've dealt with enough bullshit. It's time to be happy, dude. Happiness forevah!"

95

"HEY."

"Hey," Dominique says.

It's one in the morning and I'm still up, working on that "Graveyard" song and a new poem, trying not to acknowledge my weak, sick-feeling body, trying to keep my mind off of Joliet.

"Thanks for calling," I say.

"My mother told me what happened at the opening. I wanted to make sure you're doing all right."

"I'm doing okay. But what a shitshow."

"Sure sounded that way. You and your father in handcuffs."

"Yup. But it was actually the most perfect thing."

"Really?" she goes. She sounds shocked by me saying this. "How?"

"It was the first time this week we actually talked man-to-man, heart-to-heart. Like, really talked about things. My past. What really happened between him and my mother. It was pretty incredible. I don't even know if I've fully digested everything he told me."

"Is that good or bad?"

"I don't know. But it was the truth. I mean, the truth is always hard but it's clean, ya know? It's really fucking clean, and I feel lighter now. Like a ton of weight has been lifted from me."

"That's good," she says. "I'm happy for you."

"I miss you," I say.

"I miss you, too. But you do understand where I'm coming from, right?"

"I do. And I owe it to you to tell you where my head was all night."

She sighs. "Okay."

"Earlier that day, my father came into my room and told me some things about my mother and him. It really shook me. Now that's not an excuse at all for what I did and how I treated you, but I was really hurt by what I'd heard."

"How so?"

"To find out that you've been lied to your whole life, it sucks. But the even bigger thing was that for the first time, I started seeing my father as something other than this evil, horrible, awful man, and I wasn't ready for that. I wasn't ready to feel that about him, and I lost myself. I got lost in my own fucking skin and it did not go well. Obviously."

"Obviously," she says back.

"And I'm sorry. I can't take what happened back. I can't erase the things I said to you, so all's I can do is apologize and hope you can forgive me."

"Jaime," she says. "I know you're sorry and I accept your

apology. "For me, though, it's the Oxy and what you tried to do to get more. I think it's terrifying. My father died from a drug overdose. His addiction is the reason why he lost his family. And I was so sick when I saw you lying in that disgusting alley all bloody and beat the fuck up. That's how so many stories about my father started or ended. Fuck that and fuck you for pulling that shit. All I wanted to do was help you, and you pushed me away so easily. You pushed me away like my father did to my mother."

Dominique's crying now.

And I say, "I was selfish. That was so selfish of me. And I'm done with that shit. I flushed every single last pill I had down the toilet last night."

"Really?"

"Yeah. I've been a mess for a while on those things. But I felt happy on them. I didn't even know what happy was any-more before I swallowed that first one. The night I started doing Oxy, this girl I really liked a lot, she humiliated me on purpose. She fucking asked me to do these things for her and I did them because I thought she really liked me. But it wasn't true. I did what she wanted and she fucking laughed at me and then kicked me out of her house after I'd done them. I hated what happened. It was the worst feeling in the world. When I got back home, it was an easy choice. My mother was always happy after she did those blues no mat-ter how miserable things were in her personal life. And it worked. It was so fucking awesome. Just like that, I'd found a way to manufacture happiness. And that's what I've been addicted to, Dominique. Happiness. I was sick of being angry all of the time. I just wanted to be happy."

"Jaime, my god," she says. "That sounds awful."

"It gets worse."

"What do you mean?"

"That black eye I had when I got here?"

"What about it?"

Taking a deep breath, then slowly exhaling, I go, "My mother . . ."

Pause.

"Hey," she goes.

"My mother's the one who gave it to me."

"Oh my god."

"It wasn't her fault. She was so drunk. She doesn't even remember it. But the next day, after it happened, I think she started to remember a little bit about the night before, and she didn't accidentally overdose. . . ."

My voice fades.

And Dominique goes, "What happened?"

"She tried to kill herself. It crushed her. What she'd done to me, her boy. And she wrote a note and everything. When I got home from school and found her, I threw away the note before the paramedics came, because I knew they'd put her away for a lot longer and I was scared. She's all I've known my whole life. I didn't know I had a father who actually wanted me in his life. And I didn't know there were kids out there who would be nice to me and kind to me and want to talk to me. All's I knew was hurt, pain, ridicule, and my mother. My best friend. Who taught me how to stick up for myself and not give a shit about what anyone else thought of me. How to be tough as nails and how to keep my head. But she wasn't tough. She was just hiding her weakness with booze and pills. God . . . ," I say. "I'm so sorry I did that. Of all the things I know how not to be, it's that, and I was and I can't take it back and that hurts the most. How I hurt you and lied to you."

"Jesus, Jaime. I had no idea. God, you can't go back to that. You have to stay here."

"I can't do that, Dominique. She'll die if she doesn't have me."

"You don't know that. She's sober now. You've never known her sober. Maybe she'll be able to handle life by herself without leaning on you all the time."

"I don't know."

"Jaime, you can't."

"It wouldn't be fair to her, though. To just abandon her right after she's gotten better and clean."

"When has she been fair to you?"

"It's different."

"No. It isn't. You deserve to be happy. You deserve your father, your friends, and me. Stay here. Be with me. I'll help you stay clean. I love you. Please, think about it at least."

"Dominique," I whisper.

"What?"

"I can't do it. I love you, too, but I can't abandon the woman who took care of me for fourteen years and just leave her all alone. I know what it's like to be alone. It's miserable and it hurts. It makes you hate, and it makes you angry at everything, and I can't do that to her. She's never alone when she has me."

"But you're alone when you have her."

"She deserves to have someone there, and it needs to be me. I'm her world, Dominique. I owe it to her."

Dominique doesn't say anything.

"I'm sorry," I say.

"There's nothing to be sorry about. You're an amazing person, Jaime. How can anyone be mad at you when you're doing the right thing?"

"And that's what sucks."

"Because it's not the right thing for you."

96

SINCE IT'S MY LAST DAY IN SAN FRANCISCO AND I don't know when I'll be back or if I'll ever be back, my father makes reservations at the Cliff House, this massive and gorgeous restaurant that sits right above the Pacific Ocean.

It's the prettiest place I've ever eaten. We are seated in the Terrace Room. From the window next to our table, we can see the Sutro Bath ruins and Seal Rocks and the entry to Golden Gate Bridge. It's fucking incredible. God, I'm gonna miss this place so much.

I sit next to Kristen, and my father and Leslie sit across from us.

After my father orders crab cakes and calamari for appetizers, Kristen and him excuse themselves. Say they're going to the bathroom.

"Leslie," I say. "I wanna apologize for the other day. I was so rude to you."

"Jaime," she says. "No. You didn't know certain things. Of course you came at me like that after I came at you. I thought your father had said more to you than he had."

"Still," I go. "It was rude."

"Under any other circumstances, maybe. But where

you were coming from was a place of frustration. I get it. And you were right. All that needed to happen was for your father to talk to you."

"I'm so glad he did."

"He's going to miss you terribly. He loves you so much, and he's so proud of you. He admires you. Gloats about you. And he's crushed you're leaving, but he understands why you're going back and staying."

"I know he's going to miss me, Leslie. My mother, she's a train wreck. We all know that. But my father was trying to buy cocaine off of Kristen's ex just a night after that piece of shit almost destroyed her in a super serious way. That was fucked up, Leslie. My mother would've never done something like that. Never."

Leslie looks away from me and lowers her head.

"Don't try to pretend that things aren't messed up here, because they are. That was a terrible thing he was doing."

"It was, Jaime. And he knows that. He's promised me and Kristen that he's going to make changes."

"And you trust him when he says that?"

"Yes, Jaime. I do. I think Kristen does too. Your father has made some awful choices before, and he's always come through and learned from those mistakes. He's got a track record of keeping his word."

"I hope so, because that was as messed up as it gets."

"Kristen punched him later that night."

"Really?"

"Yes. And I made him sleep in the other guest room."

"Wow."

"Nobody's perfect. There has been a lot of dysfunction in our house over the years, but we stick together. Always. We stay strong, Jaime. What your father did is unforgiveable, but we're going to move on and Kristen and I trust that he'll not do anything like that again."

"That's cool," I say. "I respect that a lot."

Pause.

"What a wild, strange week."

"Right," she says. "Seeing you and your father in handcuffs crying, but not crying about being in handcuffs, was the most maddening, hilarious, odd thing I've ever seen."

"It was the perfect way to actually have a real conversation. No one was going anywhere. We both had to listen. Like, really listen, and people don't do that a whole lot anymore."

Leslie just stares at me, shaking her head. "You are so mature for your age. It's really impressive, Jaime."

"I've had to be. I've taken care of everything back home for so long. You learn so much about people and life when you actually have to face it and answer it. When there's real consequences to almost every action you take or everything you say."

"Yes, there is."

"I really hope I'm making the right decision."

"We all do," she says. "And we'll always be here for you. Okay? Always, Jaime."

"Thank you," I say, as my father and Kristen are coming back to the table with presents in their arms.

"What is this?"

"You won't be here for your birthday," my father says. "So we're doing your birthday today."

Burying my face in my hands because this is too nice, this is too good, I go, "Don't do this, guys."

"Why not?" asks Kristen.

"I want you to be mean to me or something. I can't have all of this."

"Come on, Jaime," my father says. "Just enjoy it. This is for us, too."

"How so?"

"This is the first time I get to see my son open presents. I've wanted to see this for fourteen years," my father says.

Nodding, I say, "Thank you. I'm just not used to this much attention."

"Open mine first," says Kristen.

She hands me a medium-size box. She looks really excited for me to unwrap it.

My father and Leslie bust their cameras out as I open the gift.

It's records. Five of them:

1. *Crystal Castles* by Crystal Castles
2. *A Child But in Life Yet a Doctor in Love* by Magic Bullets

3. *Yellow House* by Grizzly Bear
4. *Goodbye Bread* by Ty Segall
5. The Jay Reatard/Deerhunter split seven-inch single where Jay Reatard covers the brilliant Deerhunter song "Fluorescent Grey," which is also the title track of the EP they released in 2007 and I heard for the first time two years ago. And then Deerhunter covers the infamous Jay Reatard song "Oh, It's Such a Shame," which I first heard around the same time.

Looking back up at Kristen, I go, "This is amazing. I don't have any of these on vinyl, and this one"—I hold up the Deerhunter/Jay Reatard split—"I don't know where you got it, but I've had zero luck finding it."

"It's from my own personal stash," she says, winking. "I ordered it from Matador Records three, four years ago, and I know how much you love Deerhunter and I know it's rare."

"I can't take this," I go. "It's yours."

"It's not even up for discussion. You take it and you play the crap out of it. I love Deerhunter and Jay Reatard but you, you really love them. It's totally something you should own. Case closed."

"Thank you," I say.

"Take good care of it."

"You know I will. This is so cool."

"Open the rest," she goes.

The second gift is a pair of these ill white Van's slip-ons with black trim, from Leslie.

The third present is a brand-new Crush Pro Orange amp. It's from my father. I look over at him and go, "This is the only amp I've ever dreamed about having. How did you know?"

"I might've talked to your buddy Eddie last night. He might've said something about you saying how badly you've always wanted one."

"Man," I say. "I'd say I'm speechless, but that would be annoying cos you're not speechless if you say that out loud, and I've always hated it when people say that."

All of them laugh and I go, "I'm so grateful for what I've had here this week. It's amazing."

"And this is the last gift," my father goes, handing me an envelope.

I open it and there are five one-hundred-dollar bills in it. Under the last bill, this makes me kinda lose it. But in the best way ever.

Under that last bill are five tickets to a Rolling Stones concert in Chicago in August.

"No fucking way," I rip. "No way. The Stones? Really?"

"Yes," my father goes.

"Five tickets?"

And Kristen says, "The fifth ticket is for Dominique. I texted her this morning to see if things between you two were smoothed out and if she still wanted to go."

"Still . . . ?" I say.

"I had Kristen ask her on Wednesday," my father goes.

"You guys are amazing."

"So are you, son. We all hope this is the start of a real relationship with us now."

"I'm just so blown away by how great everything has been. I love it here."

"Good, Jaime," my father says. "That's really good to hear."

I'm about to start crying, so I excuse myself from the table to use the restroom.

While I splash cold water on my face, everything becomes so clear to me. So obvious. This is my fucking life.

My Life.

And I'm staying here.

I am.

I'm staying here, and I refuse to feel bad or guilty about it. Not anymore. No more guilt about being happy without my mother around.

My mother, she's an adult. She should be able to take care of herself. And she's clean now. And she's had a wake-up call, and she's the one who tried to kill herself and ended up forcing me onto my father anyway. Forcing me to be in San Francisco.

She did this.

Not me.

Her.

And my heart knows that it belongs here. In San

Francisco. Rushing back to the table after I dry my face off, I go, "I've got something to tell you all."

"What's up?" my father asks.

I look at Kristen.

I look at Leslie.

Then I look at my father.

"What is it?" Kristen asks.

"I'm gonna stay here. I want to live with you guys and be in San Francisco."

All three of them look fucking shocked.

"Are you for real?" Kristen says.

"I am. I'm staying with you guys. I'm happier here. I'm way better at life here. This is what's best for me. So let's go back to the house so I can call my mother and figure this out before the show."

"Yes!" Kristen goes.

And my father, his face bunches up and tears start rolling down it.

"You really mean it," he says.

"Yes."

He starts crying.

"Are you okay?" I ask him.

"I'm just so happy," he goes.

And Leslie, she reaches over and grabs his hands, tears forming in her eyes too.

"It's the best news," Kristen says. "Dominique is gonna be so happy too. She's gonna lose her shit."

"You think?"

"Come on, dude. Duh," says Kristen.

And then my father looks up at me and goes, "I know I really screwed up last night. God, it was terrible what I did. But we finally talked like men, Jaime. And this is the happiest day of my life."

97

"THE BEST PART ABOUT SEEING YOU TOMORROW, about going back home and getting you back, is how amazing it's going to feel. It won't be artificial. I'm going to feel all of it, Jaime."

I'm standing in my bedroom, shaking. Wishing I had the blue, but I don't because just like her, I need to feel this. I need to feel life again.

"I'm so happy you're doing well, Mom. I'm excited to see you, too."

"A fresh start," she says. "A new life. Tomorrow is really going to be the first and best day of my life. I love you."

"I love you, too. I really do. I mean that. I love you so much."

"What's wrong?" she asks.

"What?"

"What's wrong, Jaime?"

"Nothing. What do you mean?"

"You just told me three times in a row how much you mean that you love me. What's going on?"

I don't say anything.

"Jaime," she says. "Come on, my boy. Tell me. Go ahead."

"It's just I've been doing some thinking."

"Okay?"

"Ya know, a lot of things have happened. Good things for both of us."

"Jaime," my mother starts. Her voice is shaky, though. "I've taken care of you for fourteen years for better or for worse. Please, just tell me what's going on."

"Okay," I say. "I've decided I wanna stay in San Francisco. I wanna move here and live with Dad."

Silence on the other end of the phone.

It's killing me, too.

This conversation.

"Mom," I go.

She clears her throat. "Yes."

"That's what I've decided."

"Okay. I understand that. Can I just say something?"

"Of course."

"I deserve this."

"Hey—," I start.

But she cuts me off.

She says, "No heys or buts, please. I'm crushed right now, but I deserve this."

"No," I say. "It's not about you."

"Oh yes it is!" she snaps. "It's all about me."

"It's not, though," I snap back. "For once, it's about me. My happiness. I'm not staying out here because of Dad."

"What'd he tell you?"

"It's not about that," I press. "It's not about you or him. It's about me and having friends for the first time and being in a band and having a really cool girl who likes me a lot."

"You can have all that here. I've never stopped you from doing any of that."

"It's different here, though."

"So it's my fault that the kids in Joliet aren't as cool and nice as the kids in San Francisco? I don't get it, Jaime. If this isn't about me, then what is it about?"

"Me!"

"So you're choosing your father over me?"

"No."

"It sounds that way."

"Mom," I go.

"Just don't," she says. "Stop trying to explain yourself. I get it. I fucked up. I'm sorry. I put you in this position, and for the first time in your life, you've had a choice and you haven't chosen me. I always chose you, though. Don't forget that. I always chose you, Jaime."

"It's not like that."

"Oh yes it is," she says. "Please spare me your justifications. It's exactly what it is. So you're going to live with your father. Maybe I'll be able to visit sometime."

"Hey."

"Yeah."

"I love you."

"I love you, too, Jaime. And I wish I'd gotten the chance to show you me clean, me sober."

"I'll see that tomorrow when me and Dad fly out there to pack my things."

"Will you?"

"What do you mean?"

"Nothing," she says. "Just nothing. I'll see you tomorrow."

"Mom."

"Tomorrow, sweetheart. I love you."

"Yeah."

"Good-bye."

98

MY FATHER DROPS ME OFF AT EDDIE'S CRIB RIGHT AT
six. Everything's been finalized. We fly out tomorrow
morning into Chicago. Take a car to Joliet. Rent a U-Haul.
Drive it to my house and pack my stuff, and then me and
my father will drive across country, back to San Francisco,
together.

The drive will take us three days.

"Bummed about the Stones," I said in the car.

"We'll go see them in Oakland instead."

"I made the right decision."

"Okay. I trust that you did," he said. "Have a great show."

"Thank you."

Eddie and Brandon are in the driveway, loading gear.

"Damn, boy," says Brandon. "Looking sharp."

"Kristen put it together," I say. "Eddie's new girlfriend."

"I hope so," says Eddie. "Now get the fuck over here and
help us load."

What I'm wearing is this: a white V-neck tee under this
orange long-sleeve Hawaiian shirt, which is under this blue
jean jacket that has a black Growlers patch sewn onto it. I'm

also wearing tight black jeans and a pair of sick black leather cowboy boots with spurs on them.

It takes about twenty minutes to load our gear into the back of Eddie's truck.

When we're finished, we sit in his garage and the two of them share a blunt.

"Well," says Eddie. "Next time you visit, we'll have to play another show and puke up another EP."

"Yeah. That'll be rad," I say.

"When do you think you'll come back?" Brandon asks.

"Pretty soon, actually," I say.

"Cool," says Eddie. "Like some end-of-the-summer bullshit?"

Taking a hit, I go, "More like some next week bullshit."

"What?" they both ask.

"I'm moving here," I say. "Me and my father are going to pack a U-Haul tomorrow with all of my stuff and drive back to SF."

"Dude," says Eddie. "Congratulations. Welcome home."

"Best news ever," Brandon says. "You're gonna love living in the best city in the world."

"I think so too."

"This calls for a shot," says Eddie.

"Nah," I go. "I'm good."

"Really?"

"Yeah," I say. "But thanks."

"Well, fuck you then," he snorts, grinning. "The two good thirds of Skullburns deserve a shot."

I laugh and watch the two of them take not one, not two, but three shots.

"Skullburns," says Eddie.

"Skullburns forevah," I say back.

99

AT LEAST EIGHTY PEOPLE ARE IN THIS ALLEY-SLASH-parking lot when we are finally ready to play. It's gray out and windy and perfect. Kristen's there in the front row. So is James Morgan and so is Michael and so is Omar Getty.

Love these Whip Pad, Lamborghini Dreams dudes.

Into the microphone, Eddie says, "Thanks for sticking around, homies. We're Skullburns, and we thought this was going to be our first and last show but fuck that, it's just the first. To new beginnings. This first song is called 'I Saw Her First.'"

Brandon counts off and we go. I'm nervous for about three seconds and then it's like nothing. It's just like being back in Brandon's garage practicing.

It's really cool, and most of the kids seem to be really into it.

On this song, I'm doing backup vocals and keyboards too during the intro and the bridge.

Just having James Morgan there is like a fucking dream come true. And then this dream, it gets even better, just like that.

Toward the end of the song, I notice Dominique sneak into the crowd.

My fucking heart races.

She has no idea about the news either.

She's wearing these black tights, this really big white Purity Ring T-shirt, and this tight black leather jacket. She's also got an acoustic guitar on her back.

She winks at me and I wink back.

Her being here, it makes all the difference in the world.

Her being here, it means I made the right call earlier. If there was any doubt, Dominique's appearance just erased it like that.

The rest of the set goes awesome.

The third song we do, we cover Sonic Youth's "Making the Nature Scene," which I do lead vocals on. When we play it, everyone loses their minds. It's pretty epic to see. I love this city and I love my band and I love my girl at the back of the crowd looking pretty and singing along to one of my favorite songs of all time.

100

DOMINIQUE STILL HAS NO IDEA THAT I'M STAYING.
Me and her, we're walking down the street holding hands after
the band finishes loading the gear back into Eddie's truck.

"This is so crazy that I'm here," she says.

"Why?"

"Cos what's the point? I'm just gonna be sad for a week
and cry."

I smile. "Really? You'd cry over me for a week?"

"Shut up," she laughs. "Don't make fun of me."

"I'm not. I'm just asking a question."

"Ugh. Well, I think I'm gonna come see you."

"When?"

"Maybe in August. Before school starts back up. I don't
want this to end because you're going back. So I'll come
there. I'll save money from work and get a ticket before the
end of the summer."

"Awesome," I say. "Thing is, I won't be there."

"What?" she snaps. "Is your mother sending you somewhere else?"

"Nah. She's not."

"Well, where will you be? I'll fly anywhere to see you. I
promise. I will."

"You shouldn't plan on that," I say. "Spend your money on records and clothes and gear."

"What are you talking about, Jaime? Do you know how hard this is for me? I won't see you for so long."

"You'll see me sooner than you think."

"When? How?"

"How about in, like, four days when me and my father get back to San Francisco with all my stuff?"

The look on her face right now, priceless. I can't even describe it.

She gasps and holds her hand over her mouth and goes, "You're not fucking with me?"

"I'm not fucking with you."

"Baby," she goes. "Yes!"

She throws her arms around me and we make out and then she grabs my hand and starts fucking running.

"Where are we going?" I say.

"I don't know," she says. "I'm happy."

101

ME AND DOMINIQUE, WE CLIMB THIS RUSTED LADDER on the side of an old warehouse in the part of the city known as Dogpatch. She says she found out about this place from Keisha when they went out tagging their band's logo around the city, like, six months ago.

She says it's nice up there.

She says people don't climb up there because the ladder is actually broken.

She says this right as she pushes off the wall and glides to the side of the building where the beginning of the fire escape is and grabs it and pulls herself up.

"It's easy," she says. "Come on."

Doing what she did, I fail twice. But the third time is a charm, and she pulls me up with her, then we climb onto the roof.

Immediately, she starts running around and twirling and giggling. She looks so relieved. She seems so relaxed.

Up on this roof, where it feels like we can lick the moon and sleep in the clouds, up here Dominique tells me she wants to go to Paris one day and live in a loft and go out dancing every night.

She says, "I wanna listen to Francoise Hardy records while it rains outside, and while I furiously crib pages in a notebook, then read them to you as you chase me around the loft in my underwear, and I throw the pages I just read to you into the air and then we'll laugh and spin around in circles on the hardwood floors, and I'll also become an expert on Sartre by reading him for three hours every morning."

She says, "I wanna walk through the jungles of Asia and jump off the sides of secret cliffs into the gorgeous water and lie in the sun all day and trace notes in the sand with my fingers. I wanna build a tree house in Prague and listen to teenage death songs all day and study Ginsberg and Rimbaud and Wilde and learn everything there is to know about the Decadent movement and memorize every word of every Wes Anderson movie and read every Denis Johnson short story and learn every single note and lyric of every 13th Floor Elevators song. I wanna recite Nietzsche, I wanna scream his words out loud while I dance in the heavy London rain. Have you ever seen that movie *The Beach*?" she asks me.

"One time. A few years ago," I answer.

"It's one of my favorites. You should read the book, too," she says.

"I'll buy it right away," I tell her.

And she goes, "We should read it together."

She goes, "We should buy a couple of books every month,

really awesome books like James Morgan ones and everything by Poe and Hemingway and Hunter S. and Zachary German and Burroughs and we should buy a binder in New Orleans and we should keep notes in it as we ride the train around the country, just the two of us, chronicling our lives, and then we'll bury it one day in some garden in San Francisco with a copy of *Vertigo* and a copy of *On the Road*. And after that, we'll rent a motel room in Lawrence, Kansas, and we'll spend a week straight reading every word Bukowski ever wrote out loud to each other while Mazzy Star and Wendy Rene records spin all day. His poems especially," she gasps. "That's what I want my first tattoo to be, actually."

"What's that?" I ask.

"I wanna get his poem 'Bluebird' tattooed on my ribs. It's the greatest piece of writing in the whole history of the world."

Me, I say, "I love that poem."

And then she kisses the side of my face and keeps twirling under the light of the moon, laughing like the soft, mad child she is, before falling into my arms and after I catch her, she does the same thing except this time she's not reciting Bukowski. This time she's singing that song "Leader of the Pack" by the Shangri-Las.

Finally, me and Dominique, we sit on the edge of the roof with our legs dangling over the side of it and we split a bottle of Coca-Cola I took from the show, and we split a cupcake that someone made and brought there, and she asks me if I'm scared to see my mom.

"I'm not scared," I tell her. "I'm happy to see her. I miss her so much."

"You're doing the right thing, though," she goes.

"I know I am," I tell her. "I'm just so nervous about what's going to happen to her when I leave. It's going to be really sad to leave her."

"I feel so bad for you," she goes. "We're kids, ya know, we shouldn't even be put in these situations. We shouldn't have to make these kind of choices just because two people couldn't hold on to the special feelings they had once, which brought you into the world in the first place."

"But I had to make the choice. So it is what it is now."

"And you made the best choice ever. You made me the happiest person. Seriously. Nobody right now is as happy as I am. Here," she goes.

"What's up?"

She leans into me after taking a bite of the cupcake, and we start making out.

A couple of dogs bark and I even think I hear an owl in a tree, maybe not. But maybe so.

Anything is possible on a night like this.

And then Dominique, she takes out her phone and goes, "Have you ever heard that song 'Lottie Mae' by the Riverboat Gamblers?"

"I haven't," I say.

"The band is from Denton, Texas. They're pretty good. Like, some devastatingly tough Texas punk rock. And they made this one absolutely perfect record, *Something to Crow About*. Anyway," she goes, "the last song on that record is the song I'm talking about. Listen to it," she says. "It's so sexy."

She plays it, and she's right. The song starts out real slow and real dark, like some old, real, country tough song from the fifties or something. It's so good. It's mesmerizing. The entire aesthetic of it is haunting. Devastating.

She squeezes my hand.

She leans into me and she goes, "I can't wait to dance with you in Paris one day."

Turning to her, I go, "We'll have a mailbox in Berlin, too."

"Good."

"Great."

We kiss with this passion that's unlike anything we've done before.

It's really intense, and my body even shakes as I gently push her on her back and slide her shirt up and pull her tights down. I stick my fingers into her pussy and she sucks on them when I pull them out.

With my dick hard as a rock now, she goes, "I'm ready for you."

"Are you sure?"

"Yes," she says. "I've never been more ready for anything."

Getting on my knees, I unbutton my pants and push them down. Man, I don't know how long I'll even last. Like, I could blow my load now.

Seriously, it takes everything inside of me to not come this second.

My skin sucks back into my ribs. My back tightens. My shoulders tense. A line of sweat runs down my forehead.

And I don't.

Phew.

Like that, the entire sensation levels off and I sigh.

Sliding her white lace underwear down to her ankles, I lean over her and place my hands just above her shoulders on the cool gravel of the roof, and she goes, "Fuck me."

Scooting right in between her legs, right up against her bare pussy, not a trace of hair that I can feel, I grab my dick with my right hand and guide it inside of her.

She moans and grabs the back of my neck, pulling me down to her, and she spits in my mouth.

I swallow it right down and then she does it again as I pound her really hard a couple of times.

I really start fucking this beautiful girl now. It's so crazy. It feels so amazing. The two of us. Together. The two of us, fucking each other for the first time ever, me losing my virginity to this queen on the roof of some graffiti-covered, abandoned warehouse in San Francisco.

It's the boss.

Dominique moans.

She bites my neck and she bites my chest and, like, three seconds later, I can't hold it any longer.

"You can come," she goes.

"Okay."

"Pull out, though."

"Right," I say.

I pull it out and shoot onto the roof.

Pulling up my undies and jeans now, we kiss and then I lie down next to her and we stare out into the sky, her head resting on my chest, the two of us passing the bottle of Coca-Cola back and forth again while the Saint James Society song "My Dearest Friend" hisses out of the speaker of her phone.

102

"SO WHAT'D YOU WANT TO GIVE ME?" I ASK HER.

We're back, sitting on the ledge of the roof again, and she goes, "This." Then she takes her septum piercing out and hands it to me.

"You don't have to give me anything now," I tell her. "I'm coming back."

"Just in case," she says. "I know how much you love it."

"But I'm coming back."

"Not for four days. Please," she says. "Keep it. Just this reminder of me and everything you love about me."

"Okay," I say, then slide it into the tiny pocket I used to keep my Oxy in.

Dominique grabs her guitar now and starts tuning it.

"I just took your virginity," she says.

"I know you did. I'm still in shock."

She grins. "You took mine, too," she says.

"What?"

"Not literally," she says. "Figuratively."

"I see."

"I love you," she says. "Do you understand how much music we're going to make?"

"A ton."

"Yes, we are." She begins tuning her guitar.

"This is the first song I learned on guitar," she goes.

"What song?"

"'Maps,'" she says. "Those Yeah Yeah Yeahs dolls." Then she begins playing it.

"Oh, man. You are the fucking best," I say.

"You ain't so bad yourself," she says back, and we start to sing.

Once again, the two of us, singing together with a view to die for, except this time there's no end in sight. It's me and her. It's me and this city. It's me and the rest of my life.

Leaning over, she kisses my neck.

After that, it's time for us to belt that chorus out . . .

"*Wait, they don't love you like I love you, wait, they don't love you like I love you . . .*"

103.

IT'S TWO P.M. WHEN ME AND MY FATHER PULL INTO
the driveway of my house with the U-Haul.

Both of us are nervous.

My father, he pulls out this one-hitter from his pocket and smokes it.

"Really?" I say.

"What? For the nerves."

"Come on, man," I say. "Keep it together."

"It's weed."

"It's the perception, man. The idea that I'm going to a more stable place than this."

"Right," he goes. "You're too smart for your own good."

"I'm not smart. I've just seen way too much."

As we're hopping out of the truck, the front door opens and my mother steps outside.

She wasn't lying, either. She does look much younger now, and much healthier.

"There he is," she says. "My boy."

I run up to her and give her a hug. But I can smell booze on her breath, although I don't think she's wasted.

"You look great," I tell her.

"I told you," she says.

She looks away from me now and down at my father.

"Justin."

"Morgan."

Pause.

"It's good to see you," my father says.

"I bet it is," snaps my mother. "Why aren't you gloating? Huh? Now you've got everything."

"Oh, come on," he goes.

"My career, my life, and my boy."

"That's not fair at all," he rips.

"Stop it," I go. "None of this shit. This isn't about you anymore. It's about me. You two had your time. Now it's my time."

"He's right," my father says.

"You'll say anything to win him over."

This clearly irks my father, but he doesn't rip back at her.

He goes, "Jaime, I'll see you tomorrow at eight." Then he turns around and starts walking back to the truck.

"Justin," my mother goes.

He stops but doesn't turn back around. "What?"

"Will you join us for dinner tonight, please?"

"Really?" both of us say to her.

"Yeah," she goes. "It'll be nice. I promise. No fighting."

My father finally spins back around and looks at me. I shake my head, trying to tell him to say no, but he goes, "Sure. That sounds nice. Are we eating here?"

"No," she says. "I'm thinking pizza at Michael's. It's Jaime's favorite."

"Perfect," he says. "What time?"

"I'll make reservations for seven."

"All right," he says. "I'll see you both at seven."

I follow my mother into the house. It feels surreal. This whole thing right now, it just feels off. It's like, I know her, I know my mother. There's no way she's this calm right now and this stable. Not with what's happening. It seems so odd to me. Like an act. But I'm not gonna say anything. I just wanna go with it and make this as easy as possible.

The house is spotless too. Even though I ain't staying, she cleaned the hell out of it.

She asks me if I want something to drink and I tell her no, and then she walks into the kitchen and says she's gonna get more water even though her glass is nearly full.

While she's in there, I hear a drawer open and I hear what sounds like pills shaking in a bottle. I walk in there to see what she's really doing and I watch her quickly shove a prescription bottle filled with something baby blue and white back into a drawer.

She gulps down what I'm sure is either Oxy or Percocet with the glass that she has not filled back up.

"What are you doing?" I ask her.

"Taking some Aleve. I've got a headache, dear. It's about the only downside to being clean again. Even though I love feeling things again, I feel pain too sometimes. I used to never feel pain. That part was so great. Never feeling the hurt."

"You also didn't feel a lot of happiness, either," I go.

"Yes, I did."

"It didn't seem like you did."

"Fuck!" she snaps at me. "Eight days with your father is gonna make you an asshole to me too?"

"Hey," I say. "I'm not being mean. I'm just finishing your thought."

She rubs her face and goes, "I'm sorry, Jaime. That was horrible of me to say. I just . . . this isn't what I was expecting to happen, ya know. I'm not sure what I'm supposed to do now."

"Be happy for me. Be okay with that."

"I can't," she goes. "I'm not gonna just be okay with any of this. I'm losing my whole life, my boy. I don't know if I can do this without you."

"What was really in that prescription bottle?"

She glares at me and hisses, "Aleve. It's none of your business anyway. You're leaving. Stop asking questions, damn it!"

Just like that, I'm absolutely terrified now about what's gonna happen to her.

It's just like her too.

I shouldn't have expected anything less.

How she just turns the attention back on her and

her struggles. It's all my fault. I'm the last thing standing between this and her life falling apart, even though that's the furthest thing from the truth.

This beautiful woman has been crumbling apart for years. I've never been able to stop her from doing anything she's wanted to do. She's only ever needed me to patch her up again and again and again.

Still, as much as it pisses me off, I would die if something happened to her. I would never forgive myself.

"Fine," I say. "Aleve."

"Thank you."

"But never tell me it's none of my business again. I saved your life. I've saved it so many damn times. Never say that to me."

"You should feel relieved then," she says.

"This is the furthest from relief I could possibly ever feel, Mom. The absolute furthest. This is the hardest thing I've ever done. You just don't appreciate anyone else's struggles."

"That's not true."

"Bullshit."

"Stop attacking me, Jaime."

"Stop taking drugs."

She shakes her head and whispers, "You'll never understand."

"That's such a cop-out, Mom. But hey, I'm gonna stop this before it goes any further."

"Thank you," she goes.

"I need to pack up."

"Yup," she sighs. Then, "You look so great, my boy. I mean, you look like you're really happy. Happier than I've ever seen you. It's cos you're leaving me."

I ignore her comment and head up the stairs, listening to the drawer open again and pills shake in a plastic bottle.

104.

IT'S 6:40 AND I'M READY TO ROLL. I GO DOWNSTAIRS and find my mother sitting on the couch in the living room, looking at photos of her and my father in New York before I was born.

Photos I've never seen before.

Photos she must have been hiding from me all these years so she could keep up the lies about my father and make it seem like there were less amazing moments than she's ever let on.

My mother, she actually asks me if I want to look at the photos with her and I tell her I don't. That if she's had them all these years, she should've showed them to me before today, anytime really, and my mother, she doesn't say anything.

"I'm done packing too," I tell her. "We should get going."

She looks so nervous and horrified now. "Well," she goes. "So now what?"

"I don't know."

"Our last dinner together."

"No, it won't be."

She gives me the coldest look ever and says, "Our last dinner together, my boy."

It's devastating. I can't deal with this. My mind is already made up.

Leaning down, I give her a hug and say, "I love you."

"I love you, too, Jaime. I love you so much. And I'm gonna miss you."

It's all feels really, really off. I nod and go, "Yeah. I know you will."

"When will I get to see you again?" she asks, totally discounting what she just fucking said about this being our last dinner.

It's the drugs and the booze taking over again. Now this is the same woman I remember.

Shrugging, I go, "I guess once I get settled in we can figure it out."

She presses her lips tightly together and forces a smile. "Sure. Okay."

"Mom," I blurt out. "Are you going to be okay?"

She lets out the fakest laugh I've ever heard and says, "I will be totally fine, Jaime. I've got a great doctor now that I get to see tomorrow. He's gonna make sure everything's okay, and then I'm gonna focus on the dance school I'm gonna start. I can see it all right now. Opening night," she says. "And you'll be there, your girlfriend, and maybe even your father and his family. Everything will be so perfect. Everything will be in bright lights again. Especially my name. Everything I ever wanted. Life will finally be perfect again."

She looks so dazed right now. It makes me sick. God, she's not well. She's still living in this fantasy world, and it's so sad and so disheartening and I wanna help her but what am I gonna do? It's been years of us all alone and I've never been able to figure that part out.

And maybe someday I will.

Maybe someday I'll be able to really help her instead of cleaning up all of her messes.

"We need to go. Did you make the reservations?"

"No." She smiles. "We'll be able to find a table, though."

"Sure."

She stands up and walks over and grabs her purse. "Why don't you drive?"

"Why?" I go.

"Cos I like it when you do. Please drive us there. One last thing for your mommy."

I take the keys from her. Once again, I can't say no. She's obviously trashed.

105

DINNER AT MICHAEL'S PIZZA. I RELUCTANTLY TELL MY mother details about the band and the show, and she takes credit, of course, for getting me into the guitar.

I also tell her about making music with Dominique, and she takes credit for that too because of all the time she had me spend practicing the piano and buying me a keyboard, then buying me the software to make my own music.

Basically, she takes credit for everything. "I always knew to give you a rounded view. To get you interested in other things besides sports or just trying to get into a good college."

"Whatever happened to kids just being kids?" my father says. "Letting them choose what they want to do."

"Well," my mother says. "He wouldn't have this band, he wouldn't have this girl and the music he makes with this girl if I hadn't pushed those things on him. So all the stuff he fell in love with in San Francisco, which just happen to be the reasons he wants to live there now, he wouldn't have these things if it wasn't for me."

"Wow," my father goes. "You'll not give him any credit, huh."

"I wasn't saying that at all."

"Sure you were."

Her face gets red and she drops her fist against the table. "You think you know everything. You always have. You've been with him for what, eight days, and you think you've got the last thirteen years figured out and that you know him."

"I think I'm getting a pretty good idea of who he is, yeah."

"Bastard," she says.

"Here we go," my father snaps. "Here comes the psycho I remember from all those years ago."

"Just stop, you two!" I snap. "Please. Stop."

My mother, she rips, "You think you can just take my boy. Just take what I've made, the only thing I've loved for the last fourteen years."

"He wants to go, Morgan. I'm not taking him from you at all. It was his choice."

"How many lies did you have to tell him about me to make him turn on me?"

"Oh, this is rich," my father says.

"You're a monster."

"Just stop!" I snap again, only this time I scream it. "Jesus Christ. Just stop and shut up. Both of you."

"Hey," my mother snorts.

But my father, he goes, "Just let the boy talk, Morgan."

"Fuck," I go. "You two are ruthless. Jesus. Making all of this about yourselves. Why is it that I've always had to act like an adult my whole life?"

"And what's wrong with that?" my mother snaps.

"I'm fourteen," I go. "I shouldn't have to be picking you up from bars. I shouldn't have to be driving you to the store cos you're too drunk to drive. I shouldn't have to pick you up off the couch and carry you to bed at night. I should've never had to feel guilty when I asked to go do something with the kids in the neighborhood. Jesus. You've been the kid, Mom. Not me. You've been the child, and I don't want to be the adult anymore. It sucks. I hate seeing you lose it. I hate seeing you sick. But I can't be your caretaker anymore. I'm happy in San Francisco. I love you. But I was more happy in the last eight days than I have been in the last fourteen years."

Even though that felt so good to say, I still feel like shit. Sometimes, though, that's the way it has to be. Sometimes, you just have to put somebody else's feelings aside and do what's right for you.

My mother, she starts crying. She covers her mouth and bawls. Nodding slowly, she goes, "Okay. At least I know now. I never knew you felt this way. You've never told me."

"Cos I didn't want to hurt you."

"But it's okay to now since you don't have to deal with me anymore?"

"You tried to kill yourself, Mom."

"What?" my father goes.

"You started this whole thing by hurting yourself."

She stands up. "I'm going to leave."

"Morgan," my father says. "Just sit down."

"Fuck you," she snaps. "Just fuck you! You finally got what you wanted. You finally have your son."

"This isn't fair to him," my father goes.

But I turn to him and tell him to stop. Cos he needs to. This isn't his battle. It's mine.

"Mom, I'm coming with you," I say. "I don't trust—"

"Trust what, Jaime?" she snaps. "That I won't have another accident?"

"Yeah, Mom. I don't trust that."

"Then come with me. I'm just going home."

"Okay," I go. "I'm coming too."

Glaring back at my father, she goes, "It was nice to see you, Justin. If you weren't such a prick, you'd be the greatest person I've ever met."

"Good night, Morgan," my father says. "I'll be over at eight to pick up Jaime."

"Bastard," she grumbles as I follow her outside.

106

BACK AT THE HOUSE NOW, I'M IN MY ROOM, DOING one last look around to see if I forgot to pack anything. I haven't. I'm all set to go.

As I'm walking downstairs, I hear a cork popping out of a bottle of wine in the kitchen.

I walk into the practice room and sit down at the piano. Sitting upright, I put my hands on the keys.

From the kitchen, I hear my mom snort something and then giggle. Closing my eyes, taking a deep breath, I go for it. I start playing.

Schumann's op .9. The last piece I was working on earlier that night when she hit me.

I haven't forgotten a note. Furiously slamming the keys, I make magic with my fingers. The rust doesn't exist. This right here, it's as good as I've ever played it. Less than a minute into it, my mother is in the room dancing on her toes, twirling around with the biggest smile in the world on her face.

It makes me so happy to see her dance, even though she's wasted and high. She looks like my pretty angel, just so happy and so great. Just me and her. And when I'm done, she leans against the piano and goes, "That was perfect."

I almost fall off the bench.

"That was so perfect, my perfect little man. I'm so proud of you. How did I dance?"

"Like you always do, Mom. Like the best ballet dancer in the world."

"My boy," she says. "I just hope that girl knows that she's getting the best boy in the world."

"I know she does. Here," I go. "Wanna see a picture of us?"

My mother blushes. "Really?" she goes. "You want me to see her?"

"Of course, Mom. I love this girl so much."

I bring up the picture of me and Dominique in her room.

"Oh my," she goes. "She's beautiful, Jaime. How old is she?"

"Sixteen."

"And older," my mother says. "Look at you. I always knew you were going to be a little heartbreaker, a little charmer."

"I won't break this girl's heart, Mom. There's something between us. I don't know exactly how to put it into words. It's so unique and special. We're perfect together. I know that doesn't mean much cos I'm fourteen, but she's made me love life in a way that I didn't think a fourteen-year-old kid could."

Sitting down next to me, tears rolling down her face, my mother, she goes, "I'm sure gonna miss you."

"I will miss you, too, Mom."

She puts an arm around my shoulder now, and she goes, "Listen to me."

"Okay," I whisper.

"I know I've never said this to you before or if I have, I know it's been awhile."

"Okay."

And she says, "I'm proud of you, son."

Water fills my eyes.

"I'm so proud of the boy you've become. And I'm happy for you. I can tell you're happy. And I'm sorry I put you through all of this."

"Then why are you drinking again?"

"Because I'm gonna be completely lost without you. Absolutely just lost, and I don't know how to handle it."

She begins bawling and buries her face in her hands.

Me, I hug this fucking beautiful person, this amazing angel I have the honor to call my mother, and go, "It's all right."

"No, it's not," she says. "I've caused a lot of damage. So much of it. And I'm sorry. I'm so sorry, but now I look at you, I see you smiling and so full of life again. My boy, my sweet guy is happy, and you've been the best son. I don't know where I'd be without you. That's why I'm terrified. I don't know how to live without you."

"You'll have the dance school, ya know."

"Bullshit," she snaps. "Bullshit. I'll have nothing."

"Yes, you will. Just get off this shit. Quit using the drugs and booze to escape. Face the world."

"What are you talking about? I'm not using."

"Bullshit," I snap. "You've been using all day."

"No," she cries.

"I saw the pills."

"Why are you doing this to me?"

"Cos you need to stop it. Just stop and be sane again. Please. It's killing you."

"You're killing me," she snaps back. "You're the one leaving, not me. You're gonna be the one who kills me."

"Don't say that," I plead. "Don't do this to me."

"So you want me to lie then," she says.

"You just did when you said you haven't been using."

"Screw you," she goes.

"Mom," I say, grabbing her. "I just want you to feel life again."

"I can't," she sobs. "I don't want to. I won't be able to if you're gone. Don't you understand?" she says. "After all these years."

"What?" I go.

"You are my life. Without you, there is no life."

I have nothing to say to that. Never, ever, ever will I be able to fix her.

After a few more minutes of her crying, I say, "Let me play you something."

"What?" she goes.

"How about the *Black Swan* intro?"

She looks at me and smiles. "Really?"

"Yeah."

"Oh wow," she goes. "Thank you. I'd really love that."

"Okay."

Right before I start, she stands up and goes, "Play it perfect."

"I will."

And right as I begin, she starts to dance around the room. It's an insane scene. But the crying has stopped and she's smiling and she looks so happy.

It's the only thing I can do for her now.

And when it's over, she walks over to me and kisses my forehead and goes, "Thank you."

"You're welcome."

"I'm going to bed now."

"Mom," I say.

She turns around.

"Wanna watch a movie with me? Maybe an Audrey Hepburn one?"

She shakes her head. "Not tonight, sweetie."

"Are you sure?"

Pause.

"Mom."

"Yes."

"I'll play anything you request right now. Anything."

"Thank you," she goes. "But it's okay. I need to go to bed. We've got an early morning coming."

"Fine."

She leaves the room and then a few seconds later, I hear the drawer open again. I hear pills shaking around and then I hear her walking up the stairs slowly and then I hear a door shut.

107

WHEN I OPEN MY EYES IN THE MORNING, MY MOTHER is standing over me. It's hazy in my room. Like everything is kind of fuzzy and gray and yellow. It's like a strange twilight. It's like a dream, but it's not.

My mother's face is all done up, like big-time, like she's about ready to take the stage in New York or something. My heart, it slides slowly down my chest.

Her hair is done up too, into these two pigtails, and she's wearing this long brown trench coat and pink pajama pants.

"Hey there, sleepyhead. Come on . . . let's go."

For real, I think for a moment that I might still be dreaming, but I'm not. I can touch her and she's cold. She's so cold.

Yawning, stretching my arms, I go, "Where are we going, Mom? Where's Dad?"

"He's not here yet. We still have time. Our time."

"What are you talking about, Mom?"

"Remember those drives we used to take through the country?" she goes.

"Yeah."

"How about another one with your mom, sweetheart? Just one more. One last drive."

"But I'm so tired," I say. "I want to go back to sleep."

"Please," she begs. "You're leaving so soon. This is the last time I get to be with you here. Just come with me. One last drive through the country like the old days. And we can listen to whatever you want to. Don't you remember those really nice times when me and you were gonna never leave each other and just be mom and son forever, together?"

The way she's looking at me is weirding me out. I'm breathless for a moment. I feel really anxious.

"Please," she begs again.

I know I shouldn't. I got a long day in front of me, but it's her. It's my mother and I'm leaving and all she wants is this one last drive. Drives that I always loved to take with her too. And I go, "Okay, Mom."

She nods and goes, "The last drive. Doesn't that have the most beautiful ring to it too?"

"Just let me get dressed, okay?"

"Sure," she says. "I'll be downstairs waiting."

And we leave the city. That Youth Lagoon song "Montana" plays on my phone, since she said I could play whatever.

The sky right now, it looks so different to me. It looks like it's daytime, but the stars and the moon are still kind of hovering a little bit and the roads are empty for the most part.

The fields and the houses we fly by look so dreamy.

My mother, she's holding that same thermos she always does, and I know it's filled with red wine because I can smell it on her and I can see the red lines it's left on her lips and I wonder if she's even slept.

I wonder how many bottles she's drunk already.

As we climb over this hill, she accelerates the car really fast. We're probably doing, like, eighty miles an hour as she begins to talk about the very best ballet performance she gave in New York once.... Her best one ever, she's saying.

She goes, "There were two thousand people there. It was *A Midsummer Night's Dream.* I was the lead, of course. Your father was in the front row. He'd sent me the most beautiful bouquet of flowers before the performance, and all the other girls were so interested and jealous. We were so much in love. He was my man. My beautiful man. And boy, I nailed it that night. I've never felt more alive in my life. Before that night or any time after. The standing ovation was deafening. My ears were ringing, and I had tears in my eyes as I took my final bow. Everyone loved me back then, and everyone knew I was about to become the best ballet dancer in New York City."

Tears begin to fall down her face. Slowly, the car veers into the other lane.

"Mom," I go. "What are you doing?"

"Huh?" she whispers, looking at me with a pair of the most haunting eyes I've ever seen from her, and I've seen so many.

"Look at the road, Mom," I say. "Please just pay attention."

She giggles and then slides back into the proper lane.

"Maybe I should drive now, Mom. How about that?"

"No!" she snaps. "No! You don't want to drive anymore, remember? You're leaving. There's no driving left for you to do."

"Oh, come on," I say. "Let's just go back home."

"In a little bit, my boy. In a little bit we'll be home."

I sigh and try to remain calm, even though my stomach is in knots.

And she goes, "When you were born, you were my everything. Deep down I knew that my old life was never going to come back to me. I knew, Jaime, and you were my savior."

I bite my bottom lip.

"I love the ballet."

"I know," I whisper.

"And it was taken from me for good. Taken!"

"Mom."

"And I love you, my sweet boy, just like I love the ballet."

"What are you doing?" I ask.

"And I can't let you be taken away from me for good. I'll just die. I know this."

Prolly like two miles in front of us, coming at us in the other lane, is a semi truck.

"You are my last link to the happiest time of my life," she says. "The last link."

"I love you, Mom. We will still be a family. Still be together."

"Oh, I know," she goes. "Me and you will be. We'll always be together now. Forever."

She takes another drink and unties her coat.

I turn white.

She's wearing her ballet dress.

Holy shit.

She looks at me now and says, "We are always going to be together, Jaime. Just me and my beautiful boy."

Then she veers the car back into the other lane.

I start yelling for her to quit it. I scream for her to stop, just please stop, just please let me drive and take us back home.

But she shakes her head and her smile grows and she grabs my phone and turns up the volume all the way.

This is what she wanted anyway. This was her plan.

And in front of us, the semi keeps coming hard. I'm sure it's honking and I'm sure the driver is wondering what the fuck is going on. And I'm sure he's getting really nervous.

Then all of a sudden, my mother cranks the volume down and she looks at me. Her eyes say it all. This is her peace. This is what she needs to happen and this is how she gets to have me no matter what, all to herself again.

And she says, "Just me and my boy and my favorite dress. I love my ballet dress. I love my sweet boy."

And the strangest thing happens next. With the semi less than a hundred feet from us, this beautiful calm just washes over me. This light shines into the car. I'm going with her. I have no choice now and it's fine. I'll let her have what she wants. For the last eight days, I had the best life a boy can ever have. I loved a girl. I got to hold her hand and listen to my favorite bands with her. I got to look at her and sing her a song. It was perfect. I had my taste of perfect and I'm okay with this now.

When she holds her hand out to me, I take a deep breath and look into her eyes. They look so angelic and then everything gets blurry cos it's time. The fog swarms in and the haze blows everywhere and I take her hand and I squeeze it and I nod and she goes, "Are you ready?"

I whisper, "I am, Mom."

The semi is twenty feet from us now, and I close my eyes one last time as I brace myself for impact. Brace myself for the end.

Images of me and Kristen laughing and dancing in the basement to that Naked and Famous song "Punching in a Dream," of me and my father standing near the ocean talking about *Vertigo* and my mother, of me and Eddie and Brandon writing songs and skateboarding together, of me and Savannah getting stoned and listening to Portugal. The Man, of me and James fucking Morgan talking about what it means to actually live life, smash through my head.

And finally, an image of Dominique and me standing at the top of the train station holding hands, listening to Youth Lagoon, pounds through my head and that's the one I want. The last memory I see is the happiest moment

I've ever had, and I won't lose it now. I'll have that moment for eternity.

And none of this is fair. Nothing was ever fair in my life. Squeezing my hand so hard I think it's going to break, I open my eyes for the last time and look at my mother, and she looks so peaceful. This woman who's done nothing but battle her whole life is finally at peace, and this is good enough for me.

I just hope the papers get it right and I hope that Dominique will never find anyone better than me. And I hope . . .

BANG!

CRASH!

SMASH!

This is all over now.

This is the end.

108

I SHOOT UP STRAIGHT IN BED AND CAN BARELY breathe. I'm covered in sweat. I'm panicked. Looking around my room, I'm still here, though. Still in my room, and my mother, she's sitting next to the door, crying, wearing a brown trench coat and pink sweatpants.

I feel so sick seeing her in the coat and sweatpants.

"How long have you been in here?" I ask.

"Long enough," she says.

"I'm not taking that drive with you. No way."

"What drive?" she asks.

"The one," I start to say.

Pause.

Looking around the room again, this here, this is real life. Not a dream.

And I say, "Sorry, never mind." Then, "Have you slept yet?"

"Why do you care?"

"Come on, Mom. Just cos I'm leaving doesn't mean I don't care."

"Sure it does. But I'll answer. No, I haven't."

"How long have you been watching me sleep?"

"A couple hours, I guess."

"Why?"

"Cos this is all I get now. These last few hours with you."

"That's not true," I snap.

She stands up. She's as shaky as I've ever seen her. That Lewee Regal song, "Broken Ever Thus," quickly smashes through my head as she says, "Sure it is. Once you leave, my life is over."

"Don't say that," I go.

Sitting on the edge of the bed, she stares at me and says, "There's nothing left to say besides that."

"Mom," I go, reaching out for her.

But the doorbell rings and she says, "That's your father. It's time to go, my boy."

She stands up and walks out of the room.

Hold it together, I tell myself. Just hold it together and everything will be okay.

Oh, those lies we try and fool ourselves with. The responsibility that will never stop even for a lie.

I get dressed and go downstairs. My father, he has half the truck loaded already.

My mother, she's in the kitchen and I watch her swallow an Oxy.

When my father comes back to the front door to grab more boxes, he goes, "You look exhausted, son. Did you sleep last night?"

Looking over at my mother, I go, "I did. I had to. She's still here."

"Huh?" he goes.

"Nothing," I say, as my mother looks over at me and smiles.

It's the same creepy smile from my dream.

It shakes me.

And when my father turns around with that last load, my mother goes, "I hope you do so well there."

"Me too."

"I'm gonna be sorry that I miss all of that."

"What do you mean?" I ask.

"Nothing," she says.

I go to the door and help load the rest of my shit into the truck.

When we're finished, my father locks the back of the truck. My mother is standing in the doorway. We both watch her swallow something and wash it down with water, and my father says, "Go do what you need to do. I'll be waiting in the truck."

"Yeah," I go.

I walk up to my mother.

"I didn't do anything wrong," she sniffs. "I saved you when you were a baby boy, and I made sure you had a great life."

"Okay," I say. "But I can also have a great life there."

"What am I supposed to do?" she goes. "I'm so lost now. I don't know what to do."

"The dance school," I go, spitting out the first thing I can think of, even though I know it won't do shit.

"Whatever," she says, crying again. "I have nothing without you. Life won't matter without you."

"You'll be just fine," I say. "This will all be fine."

"But it won't," she goes. "So just go. Stop worrying about me. I'll do what I need to do."

"What does that mean?" I ask.

"I'll never be a problem for anyone again," she says.

"Jaime," my father goes.

I turn around.

"We should get going now."

"All right."

I look back at my mother and say, "I'll call you when we stop for the night."

"Don't," she goes.

"Why not?"

"I won't be able to answer."

"Mom," I go.

And she says, "I didn't do anything that wrong. I helped you become who you are. I'm a great mom."

"You are," I say.

"Were," she says.

"What?"

She stares at me and goes, "Nothing."

She goes, "Have the best life ever, my boy. I didn't do anything wrong."

"Jaime," my father goes again.

"Coming," I say.

Before I turn back around, I look at my mother again, her face in her hands, sobbing, her with no sleep, her, the most gorgeous person in the world even though she's completely lost.

I try to hug her again, but she pushes me away and says, "Just go, please. If you aren't gonna live here, just leave and let me be."

Nodding, I say, "Okay."

Turning around, I walk to the passenger side of the truck and get in.

We pull away.

As we turn out of the driveway, I look in the passenger-side mirror and watch my mother crying.

It really might be the last time I see her.

It's the worst I've ever fucking felt.

Two blocks later we hit a red light and it just floors me. I can't go. I just cannot go with my father and live in San Francisco. I can't leave my mother like this. She never abandoned me.

Fuck the suicide attempt.

She took me in the middle of the night and saved me.

I can't leave.

Never.

Until it's on her terms, not mine.

I just can't.

My mother, she said to me one time a few months ago, while she was totally blacked and I know she doesn't remember, but she said to me, she went, "You should get the hell away from me someday soon. I'll only destroy you after I'm done destroying myself. So just go. Leave me. It'll be the best thing for you."

I never said anything about it to her.

You don't ruffle that kinda feather, especially when you're aware that the person who said that has no recollection of it.

So I let it pass.

I never thought I'd ever have the chance to leave her either.

But now, knowing what I'm doing, I can't leave. I just can't.

What I wanted to say to my mother that night was, "If I leave, you will die. That's the truth. You will really kill yourself. And there's no way I can live with myself knowing that you only did it because I left."

This is the truth.

The only one that matters.

I can't let her die.

Life anywhere else won't ever be any good knowing that I left this amazing woman alone with her demons, and it was those demons that killed her.

Right as the light turns green, I look over at my father and say, "Turn around."

"Did you forget something?" he asks.

"Yeah," I go. "My priorities."

"Jaime," he starts.

I cut him off and say, "Turn around now. I can't leave her. I'll never be able to live with myself if something happens to her again."

He groans and says, "She tried to kill herself when you were there, son."

"But she didn't die. I stopped it. Cos I was there. I have to go back."

"What about San Francisco and your girlfriend and your band?"

"What about it?" I say. "I'd rather know my mother is alive than play another song with my band. Turn around now."

"You're for real?"

"I've never been this for real about anything before."

"Fine," he goes. "Okay. But if you change your mind—"

"I won't," I say, cutting him off as he flips a U-turn in the intersection.

"But if you do."

"I won't," I snap. Then, "Thank you."

And my father, he drives back the two blocks and pulls into the driveway.

My mother is still sitting on the front steps, crying. She looks up as I hop out of the truck.

"What's going on?" she asks.

"I'm staying here with you," I go.

"Really?" she gasps.

"Yeah. Really. I'll never leave like you tried to leave me."

"And I'll never do that again."

Standing up, she gives me the biggest hug while my father unlocks the truck and says, "I'll call the rental place and have them pick this up tomorrow."

Walking back over to him, I say, "Thank you so much."

"You're welcome, Jaime. But how are you going to explain this to Eddie and Dominique and Kristen?"

Shrugging, I go, "I ain't sure yet. But I'll see you in Chicago for the Rolling Stones."

He grins. He says, "This is what you want?"

"This is what has to happen right now."

"And you're okay with it?"

"No. But I'm doing the right thing, and sometimes the right thing ain't what you wanna do."

He hugs me and kisses me on the forehead and goes, "You're a good person."

"Thanks, man. So are you. I had an incredible run in in San Francisco."

"Yeah, you did."

Pause.

"The Stones," he goes.

"Yeah, the Stones."

This is when he says he's going to walk up the street and call a cab to take him to the airport.

This is when I watch him walk away, down the driveway, and disappear around the corner.

"I'm gonna unload all your stuff now," my mother says.

"I'll be down in a second to help."

"Where you going?"

"My room for a minute."

"Okay," she goes. "Well, I'll be out here."

Walking inside the house, I go straight to the kitchen and open the drawer where all her pills are at.

I take four Oxys, then rip off a sheet of foil and jog up to my room.

This is the only way to get through this now.

I want back inside the glass castle again.

I want in so bad.

Just like my mother, feeling nothing in Joliet is better than feeling anything in Joliet.

109

SITTING DOWN AT MY COMPUTER, I DROP AN ENTIRE blue on the foil.

I'm so excited too.

Something about this, it leaves me thrilled and in love.

Cutting a pen in half, I grab a lighter and I chase this fucking dragon. Its tail is so big and hazy and my eyes blur for a moment before I'm back.

The corridors are as beautiful as ever.

So perfect.

The fogman is back in his palace.

After three more hits, I set the foil down and then turn off my phone.

I thought about texting Dominique and texting Kristen and Eddie, but I can't right now.

I don't feel like letting anyone else down again until I have to.

Turning on my webcam, I hit the record button and go for it.

Another poem.

Another lullaby.

"Blonde on Blonde" by Nada Surf rolls in and then out of my head.

It was so beautiful to hear Dominique sing that on
Tuesday night.

I'm gonna miss her so much.

Staring straight into the camera now, I go, "There are
reasons we do everything in life. Some of them are harder to
explain than others. Some of them are impossible to explain
unless you're in that person's shoes. This is one of those
moments. I loved every fucking second in San Francisco."

Taking a deep breath, I lean out of the camera lens and
take another hit.

Now I'm ready.

Squaring up straight again, I go, "Here it is."

I say, *"In the shadows is where I found the most comfort, away from
all the noise and the distractions, away from the excuses, face-to-face
with the isolation and the vast silence, never a part of anything or
anyone, but a reminder that yes, you're still fucking alive . . . when
the car broke down in the desert, the only thing I grabbed for the endless stroll was my notebook and my pencil . . . there was no way I was
going to stop this recording, no way this story was not going to be told,
I've always understood the importance of stories, just think about
that . . . we are nothing without our stories . . . It rained once for six days
straight and when the rain finally ended, it was immediately replaced
by a fog so thick that some people swore it was smoke . . . this was the
first time I saw her eyes . . . in the fog . . . these golden wandering eyes
that faded into this dark brown hair, which hung just perfectly down
her back. . . . For the next two days I followed her through the fog and
watched her from afar . . . every time she laughed, I felt alive, but it was
her singing that kept the journey moving, her voice that gave comfort*

to my soul and justified the worth of my curiosity . . . I often dream of these sunny afternoons where I'm swinging so high I can taste the sky . . . those dreams usually end with me jumping from the swing into the ocean and laughing all the way to the bottom of the ocean floor where the only thing I see are more shadows . . . two days after we started walking through the desert, my notebook was full . . . we'd eaten cactus and tamed snakes and started a cult after meeting twenty beautiful girls and boys who were listening to the Growlers and Beach Fossils and racing dirt bikes through the sand. . . . One day I really will get to Paris and I'll teach my girl all about Sartre . . . and I'll pour absinthe all over her body while she quotes Rimbaud . . . In Mexico me and her danced all night and drank tequila and she finally forgave me for that one choice I made even though that choice kept us apart for so many years. . . . the notebooks were the key to everything . . . she was able to read about what had happened since the day I'd left her that first time, and it was because of those stories that we were able to find each other once again and get right back to the place we'd left each other all those years ago . . . these are our days, this is our time . . . the only things we'll ever truly own are our days, and our time, and our stories . . . this is our life and this is our only fucking chance in this special place where the sun triggers a million possibilities and the moon gives us the quiet we need to try and understand what we did with those possibilities . . . and hopefully we did a lot . . . there's nothing sadder than a person with no stories of their own . . . there are no excuses for a dull life . . . there's no time for regrets . . . everyone is given a choice to own their world, everyone is given a blank notebook . . . your memories are only as good as the life you fucking lived . . . so live a good life . . . make history . . . burn through page after page and drink

the fucking air ... In Vietnam we rode motorcycles and talked about
a park in San Francisco ... In Cambodia we took turns telling each
other the story of how we got here ... how we got to this place ... We told
our stories ... our stories ... and we laughed ... and we drank ... and
we flipped another page as the stories moved on ... the only real cur-
rency in this fucked-up world are the stories we tell each other in the
downtime of our lives ..."

I pause.

Rub my face.

I feel so sick and sad. I miss her so much. I just wanna
touch her again, feel her skin, hold her, and taste her.

This is when I remember what she gave me. Her septum
ring. I still have it. Digging into that tiny pocket, I slide it out
and squeeze it tight.

"Such Great Heights" begins playing on my computer.

Opening my hand up, I stare at the ring. It's all I have
left of her.

I love her.

Goddamn, I love that girl so much.

Looking back up into the camera, I say, "These are our
stories. And our stories will never leave us, and they'll never
let us down."

Pause.

"The end."

I take a deep breath now and smile. Then I open my
mouth, put Dominique's septum ring on my tongue, and close
my lips, knowing I may never taste anything so good again.

Blazed Playlist

Side A: Electric Clouds, Fierce Waves, Sand Lightning

1. "Lupine Dominus" by Thee Oh Sees (Turn this up as loud as you can and fucking smile all day cos you deserve to and it's also really good for you and your friends.)
2. "Distracted" by Terry Malts
3. "Waterfall" by the Fresh & Onlys
4. "Acid Rain" by the Growlers
5. "Helicopter" by Deerhunter (Every version is amazing, but especially check out the video of them performing this song live at the Pitchfork Music Festival. It'll change your life!)
6. "Fuck You" by Get Dead (This is your anthem song, kiddos.)
7. "HiiiPoWeR" by Kendrick Lamar
8. "Dancin' Shoes" by Murder City Devils
9. "Black Hills" by Gardens & Villa
10. "Age of Consent" by New Order (Just dance and dance and dance y'rself clean!)

Side B: Blue Dreams, Blue Mountains, Blue Dawns

1. "The Big Idea" by Black Books
2. "Little Dreamer" by Future Islands
3. "Gila" by Beach House
4. "Lottie Mae" by the Riverboat Gamblers
5. "You Weren't There" by Lewee Regal

6. "I Found My Mind in Connecticut" by Cage
7. "Dive" by Tycho
8. "July" by Youth Lagoon
9. "Paid (Shotgun in the Limo)" by Jon Gunton
10. "Spent Nights" by Magic Bullets

Side C: Kickin' It Tough (Kids Forever)
1. "End of the Summer" by Fifteen
2. "They Will Kill Us All (Without Mercy)" by the Bronx
3. "Ice Water" by the Riverboat Gamblers
4. "I Was Denied" by Thee Oh Sees
5. "Young Blood" by the Naked and Famous (Crank this and go fucking dance in the streets and on the tops of roofs until the sun comes up.)
6. "Come On Now" by Gringo Star
7. "How Ya Livin'" by AZ featuring Nas
8. "Cabin Fever" by the Brian Jonestown Massacre
9. "Ballad of the White Horse" by the Saint James Society
10. "Five Fingers" by Aesop Rock

Side D: Our Beautiful Nostalgia (These Stories and Memories Are Ours)
1. "Sweetest Kill" by Broken Social Scene
2. "Drift Dive" by the Antlers (Let this song swallow you and carry you away.)

3. "By Your Side" by Beachwood Sparks (their version; watch video on YouTube as well)
4. "Sixteen Blue" by the Replacements
5. "Heavy Breathing" by Vows
6. "Sleepwalk" by Santo & Johnny
7. "Streets Were Raining" by Pyramid
8. "Knot Comes Loose" by My Morning Jacket
9. "Balance" by Future Islands
10. "White Dove" by Sleepy Sun